PASTEL ORPHANS

PASTEL ORPHANS

GEMMA LIVIERO

LAKE UNION
PUBLISHING

Text copyright © 2013 Gemma Liviero
All rights reserved.

Published by Lake Union Publishing, Seattle

www.apub.com

Amazon, the Amazon logo, and Lake Union Publishing are trademarks of Amazon.com, Inc., or its affiliates.

ISBN-13: 9781477830147
ISBN-10: 1477830146

Cover design by Patrick Barry

Library of Congress Control Number: 2014922225

Printed in the United States of America

*To the many who were lost, and the many
who were left to continue without them.*

PART ONE

HENRIK

CHAPTER 1

Mama tells me that Opa has died. I am not sure if I should cry, because death has never been discussed before, and Mama has to explain that Opa is now in the earth. The discovery of death is shocking, and I picture my grandfather lying alone in the ground, his ears full of soil. Death is too close—as close as the thinking chair for bad behavior. I can't see it from where I'm standing, but it waits for me quietly in the next room. It knows I will come eventually.

I don't know Opa. I don't remember meeting him, though Mama says I did. Mama never talks about him, only to tell me that he is on top of the piano. In the photo he has a mustache and baggy trousers. I do not like looking at the photo before today because the face with the angry mouth and one long eyebrow tells me that I am not welcome to look at him.

But death has made him kind. I cry immediately when I see that Mama's eyes are filled with tears and when she tells me that I will not meet him again until I am in heaven.

• • •

Today I am still crying so my mother tells me a secret. She says that when you die, all the angels make two straight lines on either side of the stairs of gold that lead to the gates of heaven. Such perfect creatures, with bow lips and costumes of white, stroke your shoulders with hands as smooth as petals. Trumpets sound majestically as you approach the top step, and the tall gates open magically to reveal a lace-covered table topped high with cakes filled with chocolate, apple, and cream. To receive your reward, it is important to say three Hail Marys just before entering, in honor of all those you have left behind.

I stop crying because suddenly I have a picture of death in my head and it is not as bad as I thought, not like the one of Opa lying in soil.

Emmett, my father, is so tall that I have to tilt my head right back to get a good look at him. He is leaning against the sink in the kitchen in our first-floor apartment. He has dark blue eyes that shine black at night.

"Karolin," he says softly, shaking his head, "enough of that." He tells Mama that she is filling my head with nonsense, though he does not sound annoyed, and his eyes have wrinkled as he watches us over his round glasses.

When I go to bed that night, I think about the stairs and trumpets and golden gates, but I have added to Mama's secret: I walk through the door and eat all the creamy desserts. My stomach aches with emptiness until I fall asleep.

It is Christmas morning and I have woken early to go sit by the tree. Mama was up late in the kitchen with Frieda, our housekeeper. Frieda has the day off because she has her own family to celebrate with. I have never met her family. They are not our friends, says Mama, they are people we know.

Mama has put onto the shelves little painted statues of the baby Jesus and Joseph and Mary and lambs and a cow, and gold stars hang from the ceiling. Under the tree there are lots of presents wrapped in red-and-silver paper. I pick one up to shake because it has my name on it.

Mama and Papa come out of their room. Papa has his arm around Mama. Mama picks me up and says, "Merry Christmas, Henrik."

Soon every one of our friends arrives, including Reuben and Marian and my friend Zus. Our apartment is full of people, and songs play on the gramophone. Mama drinks a lot of the wine that Reuben has brought with him. She is laughing through her shiny red lips and her small teeth, which have gaps like fences.

I open my presents: a wooden dog with wheels, books, and a toy gun.

The table is covered with plates of food that everyone brings. There is baked lamb and chicken and stuffed peppers and pickles and fried-onion tarts and potato and pumpkin pies and sticky potato pancakes and sauerkraut. For dessert there are sweet pancakes, jam baked in dough, tarts, and biscuits in the shape of stars with icing, and there is sticky fruit pudding and cheese. I eat so much until I feel sick.

Everyone is happy today, especially when Mama and Papa dance in the living room. By the afternoon I am so tired, I fall asleep on the couch while everyone is talking around me.

Sometimes I crawl into the space between Mama and Papa in their bed and Papa wraps his arms around me and squeezes my stomach; then I roll over and snuggle into Mama's back.

Sometimes we walk to the markets and my father whistles a tune.

Sometimes Mama plays on the piano and Papa hums along and makes me do it too.

Mama reads to me at nighttime. I like stories about puppies and soldiers.

1931

Mama says that inside her belly is my little brother or sister. I am wondering how a small person has been able to get in there and ask her this.

Papa laughs so hard he cries and Mama says that they prayed so hard to God that he sent one of his angels.

"Will my brother have wings?" I have already decided that it will be a boy.

"Hopefully," says my father.

"Stop it, Em," says Mama, with the smile she uses when we are playing a game. "You are playing with his head." She turns to me with her serious face. "Not really an angel. It is just an expression. A baby is a gift."

"Will he like the same things as me?"

I am already starting to worry what my brother will be like, and if he will like me.

Since the day my sister came home from the hospital, things have changed. Everything outside has gone quiet, as if all the noises have been trapped inside. I wonder if it has something to do with my sister's arrival. I do not like her. My parents spend much time with her, as if she is the older one, as if she deserves more attention. There is no point to her, lying there in her crib with nothing to say. She does not look at me when I speak to her; she does not even open her eyes. And she is always crying, always wanting, always greedy.

Mama and Papa rush to her whenever she makes a noise like a lamb. Sometimes I take a book to where my parents are sitting—since they no longer come to me—and I read my practice words in front of them. Though some words are hard and I use another word to fill in for the ones I don't know. I am trying to distract them, to turn their attention onto me, but they look like they are thinking of something or *someone* else. Mama tells me to lower my voice and her eyes dart towards the hallway as if she is waiting to hear my sister breathe. I want to scream at them that Greta is a tiny nobody, that she does not need so much attention, and she does not deserve it.

Papa is spending more time at work and does not always join us for dinner. Mama still checks on Greta, but now I notice that she frowns if she is disturbed during her afternoon rest.

It is then I make a plan. If Greta cries more, she might not be so loved. One day I break off a thorn from the roses that Papa brings home for Mama, and I put it in Greta's nappy while she is sleeping. This wakes her up. Mama drags herself out of her resting chair. She picks up Greta to feed her but still she cries. It is some time before she finds the barb. Mama thinks it has somehow got into the washing. Another time, I sneak into Greta's room to shake her crib, to wake her up, and then I sneak out. I have to do it again because Mama is very sleepy.

Mama does not smile when she comes to nurse Greta this time. It seems my plan to take back some of my mother's love has worked.

Later, I enter Greta's room and see that her eyes are open and she is not crying this time, which is something new. She is just lying there without noise, staring at a picture on the wall; it is a picture of a teddy bear kneeling at his bed, saying his prayers. When I put my head over the crib, she turns her head. Her eyes are big and blue and round. Then she smiles, despite what I did. This makes me feel guilty, and I touch her little fingers and tell her that I am sorry about the thorn.

CHAPTER 2

1933

I have found a use for Greta. The other day I spilled milk on Mama's very expensive red-and-gold rug in the living room. I say that Greta did it and I do not get in trouble, and Greta is too young to get in trouble. Another time, I am sliding up and down the hall in my socks and I hit the small table at the end. A glass vase smashes on the floor. I say that Greta did it. Greta hears me tell this lie and she doesn't say otherwise. She doesn't understand what I am doing.

It is Greta's birthday and she is two, but I am seven and therefore I am wiser. She follows me around the apartment, copying everything I do. I march up and down the hallway and she does the same behind me, but her steps are out of time with mine, and when she turns too quickly at the end, she stumbles. I tell her that she is not very good, that her legs are too short and that she will not be a soldier like me.

. . .

My sister has stolen my secret. After we have eaten Greta's birthday cake and Mama sits down to drink her coffee, Mama talks about the gates of heaven and the angels, and how more cakes are there. My sister is too young to understand this. I am burning with so much anger I want to explode, and I quote my father: "Nonsense!" I am shocked when my father taps me sharply on the back of the head.

"Be quiet, Henrik," he says in his low, even tone. "Never speak to your mother like that again."

This confuses me. Why is it that my father can say what he wants and I cannot? When I am a soldier, he will not be able to tell me what to do. I stop myself from saying this out loud. I have said it before and the result will only be the same. His neck will go red and then I will be sent to the thinking chair without dinner.

My father asks me why the sullen face and I tell him that things are different and I do not like my sister. He looks across the table at my mother but no words are spoken. They do not tell me that I am bad for saying these things. After that, my father brings home small gifts wrapped in brown paper.

One day, he brings me a book called *Robin Hood*: a large colorful picture book. Robin is handsome and has many followers. He rides horses and stops carts filled with strange-looking people dressed in bright clothes and wigs, to take their money to give to the poor. For days I pretend that I am Robin, and Greta sits in a box—she is playing the victim I steal from. I take her bangle as part of the act and she cries—not tiny cries but screaming, screechy cries, which send our housekeeper out of the kitchen to see what is happening.

"Bangle," says Greta. Mama comes out of her room and tells me to give it back. I tell her it is just a game but Frieda is "fed up." She doesn't like me, I can tell. She has mean eyes that narrow every time she looks at me, as if I am bad. Frieda says that I must be punished but Mama defends me and says that I am just energetic and excitable, that I am just having fun and need more things to occupy myself.

Another day, I open more brown wrapping to find pieces of wood, glue, paints, and a picture of an aeroplane. My father shows me what to do and I have to complete the rest on my own. There are many pieces to put together and at night Mama has to tell me to put it away and get some sleep.

When all the pieces are glued, I paint the plane red and black and white. I watch it dry, willing it to do so quickly. While it is still sticky—I cannot wait another second—I take it out to show my parents. I cannot wait to see the surprise on their faces. It is magnificent.

I walk into the sitting room where the sun comes in like yellow sheets across the dark brown furniture. My parents have their heads bent, talking fast and low, and my mother is shaking her head in disbelief.

I stand at the door, waiting for them to see me. When they don't hear me, I kick the floor with the tip of my shoe. They both turn with a kind of shock, and Mama's eyes are red from crying, but this can't be true because she smiles at me as if there is nothing wrong.

I show them my creation and Papa examines it, frowning slightly. "It is quite good," he says. "But the wings are a little crooked. Next time, you need to take more time . . . not so rushed to get it finished."

My mother says differently: "It is beautiful, Riki." Though her words are in whispers and sound only half-true, as if she can only give half the joy, or half the love. Perhaps the other half she has to save for Greta.

. . .

Greta draws on my chessboard: pink dots on the white squares, which looks like a disease. She does not get in trouble because my parents say she is too young to understand what she has done wrong. She sometimes takes my toys and other things, and I often have to find new hiding places for them.

When I tell my parents what is happening, they tell me not to be so selfish, that she can enjoy those things too. But they are my things! They were given to me! How can that be selfish? I wonder this bitterly, in secret, seething. I put my red, black, and white plane on the floor and crush it with my foot. Afterwards I cry, wishing that I hadn't done that, and put the cracked and smashed pieces in a small box to hide under my bed.

It is late when Papa comes home from work, and he calls me into the sitting room. He holds his arm firmly across the front of his coat. I think he has another present and I feel excitement about to burst from my chest.

"I found something as I was walking home today."

Though the excitement is still there, there is now a sinking feeling in my chest also. It is perhaps not a present at all.

"Now, before I show it to you, you have to promise me something."

"Yes," I say, and he is telling me something about responsibility, but I'm not really listening. I am too busy staring at the small bulge beneath his jacket. I shift from one foot to another. The wait is almost unbearable.

"You have to promise me that you will always look after Greta. You will grow to love her one day and then you will appreciate her. You must also learn to be patient—you must not be so quick to act. Sometimes you need to be more thoughtful. Do you understand?"

I am not sure what he means but I remember that Mama has called me energetic and I nod, my eyes still burning a hole through Papa's coat.

"But before you take care of Greta, I have someone else who needs your care."

He lifts back his coat and I see a bundle of gray-and-white fur. It is a kitten. I go to take it but Papa puts up his hand.

"Be patient. This little kitty has very sharp claws. If it scratches you, you have to wash your hands straight away."

He hands me the kitten so gently, as if it might break, and I stroke its soft fur and rub it against my cheek. It has bright blue eyes, like Greta.

"You have to think of a name," says my father.

"Robin," I say, "after Robin Hood."

"But it is a girl, I think," says Papa.

I think about this and decide that Robin is still a good name and it would be a waste not to use it, even if it is just a girl.

I take the kitten and show Greta, who squeals with delight.

"Give me!" she says.

"No," I say. "I am responsible for its life and it might die if I don't care for it. It also has weapons on the ends of its legs and if they scratch you, you could get a disease and die." The seriousness of my words has much effect on Greta. She frowns and draws her hands back out of danger.

After a while, Greta cannot contain her desire anymore and she goes to touch Robin again. I let her stroke the soft fur and tell her that she must be patient.

Today, Mama and Papa do not talk to Greta or me. Greta is no longer the favorite one. We have been cast out of the kitchen because my parents want to continue their conversation in private. My father has been telling Mama it is a sad day, yet outside there are people celebrating in the streets. They blow whistles and run past our window. Children sit on the shoulders of their parents and clap. From the window, I watch my father leave the building and disappear into the crowd.

Later, when Papa returns, he slams the front door as he enters. He is not happy like the people I have seen passing below our windows. He carries a newspaper, which he throws down onto the table.

"Have you heard?"

"Yes," says my mother. Because of that one spoken word, the air in the apartment has grown cold.

Papa sighs loudly as he slides angrily into a chair, making the legs squeak against the floor.

"Do you want something to eat?"

My father shakes his head and picks up the paper. "Listen to this," he says, but he suddenly notices that my sister and I are standing near the table. His eyes are wide and wild, as if we have frightened him, as if we have appeared like ghosts.

"Children, you must leave. Your mother will call you to dinner soon."

My sister and I leave, but I pull on my sister's hand to sit back down outside the doorway to listen. Greta is obedient to me as always and sits down beside me. But she is prone to make noise, like shuffling her feet. She cannot sit still. If she makes any noise, I will have to send her to her room.

I hold my finger to my lips and she nods, agreeing to be quiet. It is at that moment that my feelings change. I feel like we are the same, not only joined in our plot to listen, but that we are one person: that we share the same spirit, which God has put inside us.

Also in that moment I notice many things about her: like the fact that she is patient, not like me, and that she is quiet and brave, and that she adores me. She has a small upturned nose and her hair is very blonde, much lighter than mine, and soft, like feathers. This all comes to me in a rush, and I wonder how I did not see these things before. I give her a smile of encouragement to show that she is doing the right thing and I will not fail her.

I turn back towards the doorway to the kitchen, where my parents are having a serious discussion. My mother is telling my father that it is only temporary, that people will see him for who he really is.

Who, I am wondering, are they talking about? Whoever it is has upset my father.

"He will make things bad for all of us. He will change things. Look at the people! They would see the end to us."

"Things won't change," says Mama. "You have done nothing wrong. It is your blood only. You and the children are more German than those fools in the street."

I can hear the clinking of pots as my mother washes them in the sink. I hear the clicking sound as she lights the gas for the stove, and the shuffling sound as my father turns the pages of the newspaper.

"Listen to this," says my father, agitated still: "*. . . he who dares to injure or insult honest German work with the spirit of a Jewish-Marxist worldview that brought Germany to its grave will be judged by the people.*"

"It is propaganda. The intelligent ones will take no notice. It won't be tolerated."

My father reads some more from the paper but they are words that make no sense. I do not understand why such words are bad enough to upset my father, or anyone. They sound very dull. I grab Greta's hand and we creep down the hallway. One of the floorboards creaks under my step and we run the rest of the way to my room. She sits on my bed, waiting for my instructions, but I am suddenly bored with her company, and with the talk of my parents, and decide to read. I send her away.

Later, as my father tucks me into bed, I ask him why Germany is dying.

He looks confused as he thinks about my question. "I do not understand you, Henrik."

"You told Mama today that Germany was brought to its grave."

His eyes widen then, and he smiles and nods that he understands. "You have been eavesdropping. What have I told you before, hmm?"

"Why are people happy in the streets? What are they celebrating? Who were they?"

"Fools. Just fools who have very small brains." I picture their brains like I have seen in a medical book, and feel almost sorry for the people. My father continues: "It is not something that you need to worry about, and by the time you are grown, you will never see the things that I am seeing. Enjoy your childhood, little Riki. There will be time enough to be serious later."

He kisses me on the head and tells me that life is a good thing and we will celebrate it in our own way.

"Tateh, why can't I go to school yet? Zus goes to school."

"Henrik, do not call him Tateh. You must call him Papa."

But Zus calls his papa Tateh and lately, because of Zus, I have been calling my papa Tateh. Zus's tateh and my tateh have been friends since before I was born. They met at university. Reuben wears a strange little hat and has the kindest eyes I have ever seen. His hand is so gentle on my shoulder, and he is always very happy to see me. He and my father hug when they see each other, but sometimes they argue too, and one time I heard him ask my father why he no longer comes to their meetings.

"I am Catholic now."

"Like hell," says Reuben.

And the two of them laughed hard, and my mother and Reuben's wife, Marian, laughed too. It wasn't funny. Parents' humor is rarely funny, except when Reuben does a little dance while Mama plays one of her tunes on the piano. Greta finds this more funny than I do but she finds me funny too. I copy Reuben's dances and Frieda's strict high voice: "You must do this for you are a naughty boy, Henrik." This has my sister rolling on the floor laughing.

Sometimes I pretend that Teddy is talking to her in this voice too. Teddy also dances, plays the piano, and sings. Sometimes he has the voice of Papa. One night, Greta is laughing so loudly that Mama has to come in and tell us to keep it down, that Greta needs to sleep.

"No," says Greta, "Riki is so funny."

"Yes," says Mama, "he is funny but he is also keeping you up and making you as excitable as he is."

Today I saw the strangest thing. As Mama and I were walking to the markets, with Greta in the stroller, I saw a giant yellow star painted on the window of a dress shop.

As we walked along we saw another one on the front of a café. A woman and a man were scrubbing at it with brushes.

Today is Saturday and it is quiet outside. When I say this to Papa, he raises his head and stares out the window, as if he has seen something that I can't. This quiet, my father says, is like the gray silence before the storm.

Chapter 3

1935

We are going to Reuben and Marian's for dinner. I look forward to seeing them again because their apartment is very big, and Zus and I run around and hide in all the bedrooms and no one gets angry.

But they have a new place, which is nothing like their old apartment. It is farther out of the city in a large building, where there are lots of buildings, and they have to share a kitchen with the other people who live on their floor.

Zus tells me that some men came to the door and gave his father a note. They were told that their old apartment was needed by some important people and that an expulsion to other accommodation was necessary.

"What is *expulsion*?"

"Vacation."

"You mean a holiday?"

"No, not a holiday. Like a temporary placement."

Reuben is a lawyer and said this thing they are doing, this expulsion, is not legal but they were told that the instructions came from the Führer himself, that it is for Reuben's protection that they do this. Zus tells me that the Führer is making lots of new rules and they must do what he says.

But Zus tells me that he likes it at his new temporary placement because there are many others just like him there, and they get to run around the building together. He also tells me that his parents don't seem to mind who he spends time with. Here he can play with whomever he wants. I am feeling very envious.

At dinner, our parents toast each other and Reuben says a prayer to thank God for the families they are blessed with. Then we gorge ourselves on soup with dumplings, salted fish, pancakes, and pastries that are sticky on top with seeds and mushy fruit inside. They are delicious and Marian says we can have two.

After dinner, our parents instruct us to play outside the apartment for a while. We run down the corridors, chasing each other, and Greta can't keep up, and Mama comes out to say that I must look after Greta, that I must not let her out of my sight. I promise, because Greta is my obedient servant now and I am her master. We run up and down the stairwell. Some people sit at the bottom of the stairs smoking cigarettes and they tell us to be quiet. We do this and then we forget and make noise again, and then Greta falls over and cuts her knee and wails and Zus and I carry her between our arms, like a swing, up three floors to the apartment.

Mama applies a damp cloth to Greta's knee and Marian gives her some sugar lollies, which stop her crying almost instantly. Marian says that sugar is the best medicine. Mama carries Greta to the couch and Greta falls asleep on her shoulder while Zus and I go to his room to talk. It is small and his big bed fits between the walls, as if the space was made for it.

He shows me his collection of stamps that he has been saving for two years. His father brings home many envelopes from work. He has clients from all over the world who send him these for Zus. There are colorful stamps from France, Poland, America, and even one from Australia that has a picture of a bird on it. Zus tells me this strange fat bird with a big head is called a kookaburra. I say the name and Zus laughs. And we both keep saying the name and laughing until we run out of laughter. I say that one day I will go to Australia but I have no idea where it is. Zus shows me a map and tells me that it takes months to get there by boat. We decide that we will go there together. He says that the sun always shines there and the beaches are softer than his mattress. We bounce on his mattress to see how soft it is, and I find it hard to believe that anything could be softer.

Mama comes to tell me that it is time to leave. I ask if I can stay the night with Zus, and Mama looks at Papa, who says nothing. He is staring at his shoe. Then Papa and Mama look at me wearily and neither responds. I don't know why but I do not ask again. It is as if they are both asleep when they look at me.

Greta is asleep and Papa carries her down the stairs to our car.

Mama and Papa hug Reuben and Marian and tell them to take care and that they shall see them soon, but they are not joking and smiling like they usually do when we part. I do not want to leave and tell them this, and for some reason, when I get in the car, I start to cry—silently so that Mama and Papa don't hear. They say that I have to be strong. They are not looking and so do not see that I am already crying, that I am not strong.

Greta lies across me on the seat. She is sucking her thumb and looks like a doll. One of my tears falls on her cheek.

My parents take us for a picnic to the park by the lake, which is outside the city. It is warm and beautiful and we take lots of food. Frieda has baked shortbread and we also take a loaf of bread and slices of beef and some lemon soda water. Greta runs with me in the park and we find other children there to play with. Papa hires a boat to row and we put our hands over the sides and splash.

We are walking towards the tram that will take us to the train station when suddenly there is a lot of noise ahead. People in the streets are yelling and several bottles are smashed on the road. A man is lying in the gutter while another one kicks him in the stomach. His groceries are scattered across the street—broken bottles of sauce and pickles. There are several people around him stomping on his purchases, busting open the brown packets. Food squirts out the sides.

A policeman comes and yells at the angry group. My father starts to go and help but my mother holds his arm. Someone else helps the man up.

"It's all right now. It's over. Don't get involved," says Mama.

We turn down a side street, taking a different route to the station. Papa says we will walk and catch the tram from a different stop. This way is longer and I complain that my legs will give up if we have to walk any farther, but Mama and Papa ignore me. They have gone very silent.

Mama walks me to school, which is only two blocks from our apartment.

I have friends. Their names are Rudolf and Fritz. I do not like the lessons as I do not understand what the teachers write on the board, and I am too afraid to tell Papa, who, Mama says, is a very intelligent man. Mama had my eyes tested to see if I am having trouble seeing, because I don't understand many things, but my eyes are fine. She thinks that I am too easily distracted.

At lunchtime, Rudolf and Fritz and I play pirates but soon the game turns sour. They gang up and say that because I am a Jew, I have to be the one who dies first.

I say I am not a Jew, that they are making this up. Though I don't understand why, if I was a Jew like my friend Zus, it should make any difference.

Rudolf announces: "My father says that Jews are not allowed to learn things anymore, that they must stay stupid for the good of the German race."

I punch him in the chest, knocking him over, and then I punch him again. A teacher sees this and tells my mother, who comes to collect me. Mama does not wear any kind of look in her face. It is blank, as if there is no one living inside of her.

She holds my hand but I pull away from her. I am very angry with Rudolf but I don't want to go home yet. I want us to stay friends.

The next day, when I get dressed to go to school, Mama is still in bed and Greta is in the kitchen eating bread on her own. She says that Mama won't get out of bed.

I creep into Mama's room, which is in darkness because she has not pulled open the curtains.

"Mama, I have to go to school now," I whisper.

"You will not be going anymore."

"But I have to go. I have to learn mathematics and history." Not that I think you need those to become a solider, but I want to see my friends. I want to apologize for punching Rudolf.

"You cannot go to that school anymore. It is too dangerous. We will find you a new school."

"But I can fight, Mama." I am shaking with anger and frustration. They cannot just send me away like that. "What about my friends, Rudolf and Fritz?"

I kick the wall and there is now an indentation.

"They are not your friends," she shouts. She is sitting up now and I notice that she has not taken her makeup off from the night before, and her hair is sticking out like straw. There are black smudges around her eyes.

I start to cry and she reaches towards me but I shrink back from her touch and run down the hallway to my room and slam the door behind me. I pull closed my curtains, climb under the covers, and slide Robin underneath with me. She is curious at first, sniffing my bed, and then lies sideways to sleep.

I do not understand why everything has to be so complicated.

I must have fallen asleep because when I open my eyes, my mother has entered the room. Her hair sits neatly around her face, which has been cleaned. She is wearing a dress I have never seen before. She is holding a plate of food: sausages and cabbage and onions. She says I can eat in bed if I like.

"Riki," she says, "I am sorry for shouting and I am sorry for school. The truth is, the teachers are not being fair and a lot of children are not going there now. We will find you another one where the teachers are better."

I do not mention my friends again.

When Papa gets home, he comes in and touches the top of my head.

"It will be all right," he says. "There are other schools."

"But Papa," I say, "it was only one fight. They are my friends. We will make up."

"Henrik," he says solemnly, taking off his glasses and rubbing his eyes. I notice that he is thin in the face and his eyes are circled in gray, as if he has been wearing Mama's makeup, which has smudged. "It is not the number of fights . . . it is the cause of the fight which is too great this time. And this is just the start. That school does not discourage the violence by some children or the views they bring with them from home."

"Why did they call me a Jew?"

"Because they are ignorant and their parents are ignorant. Because they don't know any better."

"Why are Jews different?"

"They aren't. All people are all the same."

• • •

It has been a week since I last went to school and it is very boring at home. Greta is constantly coming to my room looking for company but I send her away. It has been months since I have seen Zus.

In the kitchen Mama is shelling peas for dinner.

"Where is Frieda?" I ask. It has been days since she has come.

"Frieda is finished here now," she says.

"Who will do the work?"

"Me," she says.

"Why can't Frieda come?" I ask.

"Because new laws have been made and she is not allowed to work here."

"What new laws?"

"Laws which tell people where they can work and where they can't."

CHAPTER 4

1938

I sit at the window. It is raining outside and the sky is pale gray, the color of my coat. The organ grinder is playing his music across the road today. Sweet and lively music that makes me want to dance. Each day he is somewhere different. Sometimes he plays several blocks away from here.

Mama puts a coin in a cup at the front of his machine whenever we see him, and he smiles at Mama and winks at me out of his dark brown face. Papa says that he is a beggar, but his coat is nice and he wears a nice hat. Sometimes he has his little daughter with him. She sits beside him with her chin in her hands and watches everyone pass, with her dark eyes below black brows. The daughter is not there today.

The sound of an engine drowns out his music, and I look down and see that a shiny black car with a long bonnet has parked across the road from us. On the bonnet of the car is our country's new flag. It reminds me of two bent or broken walking sticks lying on top of each other.

Two officers get out of the car. One is short and the other is tall. They wear black, buckled jackets; long, shiny black boots; and hats. They look very smart and I think that it would be good to be a policeman and wear clothes like that with badges on the front. The short one has many badges. I think that it is a shame that their nice clothes are getting wet.

I watch them instruct the music man to get into the backseat of the car. The man shakes his head and raises his arms. The officers speak to him for several minutes. They are saying things that I can't hear because their voices are too low. The organ grinder shakes his head again, looks back along the street, then climbs into the back of the car.

The tall man climbs into the driver's seat. Just before the short man gets in on the passenger side, he looks up at me and waves. I wave back. I am thinking that it is an important job to be a policeman. I would very much like to be one when I grow up.

They drive away and leave the man's machine on the sidewalk. Every now and again I go to the window to see if it is still there. I set up a chair to face the window and read a book so that I can see who comes and collects the organ. Maybe it will be his daughter and I will invite her in for bread and tea. She needs to know that her papa is with the police. Someone needs to tell her.

It grows dark and I am tired and Mama tells me that it is time for bed. I tell her about the music machine, which is covered in rainwater now. She looks down at the street below and shrugs.

"Two men came and took him."

She looks back at me with fierce eyes, as if I have just said something bad, before she turns back to the window to pull the curtains together. She walks away.

In the morning, I wake up and remember the organ grinder. When I look outside the window, the music machine is gone.

I am woken by the sounds of smashing glass outside and yelling, and I see people run down the street with fire torches. I am scared and run to Mama and Papa, but they are already up and watching from the window. Greta does not wake. She can sleep through noises.

"What is happening?" I ask.

Mama takes me in her arms and pulls me into the armchair.

"It is a riot," says Mama in a weak voice, like she is talking from far away.

The yelling is louder now and there is more smashing. I peek over the windowsill. Several people throw bricks through the glass window of the bookshop, which had been painted with a yellow star.

Papa is pacing up and down, running his fingers through his hair and fiddling with his glasses, taking them off and putting them back on.

"What is a riot?" I ask.

"People who complain in a violent way."

"What do they complain about?"

"They are jealous and don't like that some people have shops."

It sounds a very silly reason to complain. I tell Mama this but she is not listening. She is stretching her long neck even longer to look over the window ledge.

"I can't stand by and watch this. Where are the police?" Papa says.

"They are there," says Mama. "But they are pretending they can't see."

I have decided that I will not be like those policemen, who stand idle at such events. If I were a policeman, I would hit those vandals with a baton.

"I am going out," says Papa. "I have to help."

"No," says Mama. "There is nothing you can do. One man against a dozen."

Though it is clear there are more than a dozen. I can hear more destruction and yelling happening farther up the street.

Papa ignores Mama and grabs his coat to go outside. Mama pushes me to one side and rushes towards him.

"Emmett, no!"

But Papa has gone and slammed the door behind him. I am suddenly very scared for Papa and wishing that he had listened to Mama. I feel tears welling in my eyes and attempt to wipe them away before Mama sees.

Mama comes back to me, and she has seen.

"It is all right, Riki. Papa will return."

Suddenly whistles are blown. Cars come screeching down the street and the people with torches vanish down alleyways and around corners.

Mama takes me to the kitchen to make me milk with chocolate. I keep staring at the doorway, waiting for Papa to enter. Mama says I can stay up till Papa gets back.

It is some time later when there is commotion outside the door and lots of talking. I hear the key in the door and Papa enters. Behind him are several people. There is an old couple: a man who looks like Reuben, but older, with a long beard; and his wife, who is trembling and looks very ill, her scarf wrapped tightly around her yellow face.

After them, a younger woman enters, and she is carrying a baby. The baby is sleeping in her arms.

"Karolin," says Papa. "Get some blankets and warm some milk."

Mama doesn't move straight away. Papa takes her arm, and I follow them into the kitchen.

"We don't have that much milk," she says quietly, so the visitors can't hear. "Why are they here? Who are they?"

"It is not safe for them. Their shop is completely smashed, and their apartment behind it. They have nowhere to sleep tonight."

"All right," says Mama. "But no more. We don't have the room."

Mama puts a blanket around the old lady known as Mina. She and her husband, Isaac, will sleep in my room.

I want to complain about this but remember about the people in the street who were complaining by riot and know that this is not the right thing to do. That sometimes complaining can hurt people.

The younger woman will sleep on the lounge, and Mama pulls out the crib, which used to be mine—and then Greta's—for the baby to sleep in. The baby's mother is so grateful that she holds my mama's hands, and Mama's face is no longer hard. She smiles and drops her shoulders, then hugs the woman.

I yawn because I am so tired now. It is after midnight. When I wake up, I am on a mattress in Greta's room and don't remember how I got there. I can hear talking down the hallway.

When I enter the kitchen, everyone is sitting around the table. Greta is sitting on the old man's knee and he is singing a song very quietly in her ear in a language I don't understand. I wish I could sit on his knee also, but I am too old for that now.

"This must be Hansel," says Isaac.

I am confused and he sees this.

"Don't you know who Hansel is?"

"No," I say.

"Why, he is the brother of Gretel," he says, pointing at Greta. I frown and nod because I am frightened of looking stupid, like I sometimes did in class.

"No matter," he says. "You will know eventually."

Mama pulls up another chair at the table and I have some porridge made with water, not milk, and some tea. I like that there are so many people here. It makes the place warmer. It reminds me of Christmas as it was before.

• • •

Papa has to go out and see about some building materials to fix the man's shop. The man is too frail to walk so Papa must go alone. While he is gone, Isaac asks me if I play chess. Of course I do. Papa has taught me but it has been a while since we played. Papa has been very busy "in thought" lately, says Mama. He has much to think about.

I take Isaac's pawn with my knight and then his knight with my castle. It is going well but the game suddenly turns and Isaac has taken both my bishop and my castle and then he takes my queen and checkmates with his other castle. I am shocked that I have not foreseen this move. This game is far more difficult than when I played with Papa. I am suspecting that Papa has not been playing at his best.

Isaac claps his hands. He says that he enjoyed the game and congratulates me on my moves. He says that I am a very good player for someone so young, that I am a "strategist" in the making.

I cannot find the word in my spelling dictionary so I ask Mama what it means. It seems that I will make a good policeman or soldier after all, and someone who can plan ways to protect shops from being broken into.

Mama spends most of the day with the two women and the baby. Greta won't leave the baby alone. She shows off some of her toys and shakes things in front of the baby's face to get him to look at her.

Papa comes back in the afternoon. He says he has boarded up the front of the shop and arranged for a glass repairer to come the next day.

I am happy that our visitors will be spending another night. Mama goes to the market for more supplies. Papa and Isaac drink some brandy that night. Papa used to drink this only on special occasions, but these days he seems to be drinking more of the Christmas drinks. And Mama is not afraid to use the good cutlery.

The next day I am sad to say good-bye to our visitors, and Papa says they are welcome to come again.

Late afternoon, a package arrives addressed to me. Inside is a picture book and the title is *Hansel and Gretel*. It is the most beautiful book. It has a golden spine and the pictures are shining with color.

I read the whole book over and over again and then I read it to Greta, who clings to me afterwards.

"It is all right," I say to her. "It is just a story. Things like that don't really happen."

Today we pass Isaac and Mina's bookshop and there is another yellow star painted on it. Papa knocks on the door but there is no answer.

Mama says that they have probably left to live with their relatives outside the city, where it is safer.

The organ grinder is not anywhere anymore.

CHAPTER 5

I ask Mama if we can go and see Reuben, Marian, and Zus.

She shakes her head and keeps cooking, and Papa is ignoring me, as if I don't exist.

"Can't you hear me?" I say louder. "I want to go!"

Mama starts to cry and runs from the room. Papa sits at the table, staring at an empty plate which awaits his food.

"Papa," I say. "I want to go. Why does that upset Mama?"

He pulls me to him and squeezes me, and his body is shaking and his face is burrowed in my neck. Then he makes a strange howling sound and I realize that he is crying and I start crying too.

I pull away from him and watch his face, which is a new face he has not worn before. "Papa, I'm sorry if I upset you."

"Henrik, you have done nothing wrong. It is just that Zus is no longer living there. They have moved far away, where we can't visit them."

"Why?" I feel my throat get tight as I choke back tears.

"Because they are Jews and the Führer is afraid of people like Reuben who speak freely."

"Is it another expulsion?"

Papa's face is wet with tears and he nods to his lap.

"Where is their new place?"

"Somewhere else, where the Führer cannot look at people who are smarter than he is."

"Why can't we visit them there?"

"Riki," he says wearily. "No more questions."

I walk away and Mama returns to Papa, her eyes dabbed dry, and I hear her say under her breath, "For God's sake, Emmett. He has to be told."

"No," he says firmly. "For his own sake we cannot tell him anything."

"And just keep him here in the apartment?"

"If we have to."

I go to bed and have nightmares that there are monsters outside our apartment. They are crawling through our windows and underneath the doors. They are carrying Mama and Papa away and I am screaming for them to come back.

I wake, my face wet with tears, and I run into my parents' room and find the safe space between them on the bed, not caring that I am too old now for such behavior. There I stay and sleep in the crook of Mama's arm.

Mama is teaching piano today. Hilda is her last pupil. All the other ones no longer come because they have moved away or their parents have decided that it is best they no longer bring their children here for lessons. I miss the children. I miss the sounds of music being played—sometimes well, sometimes not—and I miss the conversations with other children now that I am schooled at home by Mama and Papa. I am to start another school next year, far away, and I can't wait to make new friends.

I ask Mama where her music students will be taught now. Will they be in the same place as Zus? She says, yes, many of them. I think how lucky they must be to get to play with Zus.

When Hilda is leaving, I ask her if she will ever come back, because I like her, though I don't tell her this ever.

"I have a new teacher," she says brightly, her pale red curls in two tails on either side of her head.

"Why do you have to go?" I am so disappointed. After Hilda there is no one else to come.

"Because Mama is taking me to another music teacher whose whole family is Aryan. But if you like I can write to you."

"That would be splendid," I say, though it is not. I want to see her, not write to her. I do not ask her what an Aryan is because it sounds like something I should know, perhaps something that is taught in school, and I ask Mama later when Hilda is gone.

"It is another kind of German."

"Do Aryans have their own teachers?"

"Yes."

"Why?"

She does not answer but closes her eyes.

"I'm sorry, Riki," she says. "But I am tired after the lesson. I need to lie down."

She lowers her eyelids over her wide gray eyes, and I watch her walk away. She has a straight back and her hair is pulled up into a pale bun at the base of her neck. I have never noticed this before but my mother is very pretty.

Mama is at the sewing machine stitching the hem of one of Greta's dresses. Greta is playing with an empty cotton reel at Mama's feet, rolling it across the floor for Robin to chase. Robin chases after it, her paws making the softest of thuds on the shiny wooden floor as she bounds after it. She runs too fast for her own legs, sometimes sliding for several feet and then hitting the wall.

I go to the sitting room, where the curtains are always closed now. I open them up to let in the dusty light. I look through the bookshelves, trying to find something to read. Mama has given me some tasks to do today: some word writing and some chapters to read. Papa makes up mathematics task sheets and when he comes home from work, he asks me questions like: What is twelve times twelve? What is one fifth of one hundred?

Today, though, when Papa comes home, he doesn't ask me any questions. His forehead is covered in sweat and he tells Mama he is not hungry.

The next day he doesn't go to work at all, or the next day after that.

Papa tells me that he is no longer going to work, that he has lost his job. Papa is an architect. He designs buildings. He has designed a synagogue and a museum.

"Will you find another job?" I ask.

"I do not think so," says Papa. "Not in this city anyway."

It is very cold and Mama and Papa only put the heating on in the afternoons and turn it off before bed. They say that they have to be careful with money now that Papa is not working and Mama has no more pupils.

I notice that Greta has a button missing off the top of her dress and wonder why Mama does not fix it. She is spending more time lying down now, when she is not making meals. The rest of her time she spends with Papa, listening to announcements on the radio, which sound very dull. When I ask if we can go to the park, they say it is too cold. I look out the window and see that other children walk along the street wearing heavy coats and hats.

I promise Mama that I will keep my hat and coat on and I won't complain about the walk, but she still says no.

I walk to Greta's room. She has begun reading my books now and I help her with the words. Mama doesn't read to Greta anymore so it is up to me to teach her. Greta loves words. She finds so many new words and comes to me for explanations. That is what I must be. I think I will make a fine teacher, though I haven't given up on being a soldier either. I wonder if I can do both—if I can soldier on the weekends and teach during the week.

"All right, children," says Papa. "We are going out today to see a film."

We both scream and laugh and run around in circles. Greta asks if Robin can come too but this request is refused.

Mama takes time to dress Greta and braid her hair. Mama has ironed my best shirt and Papa has shined my shoes. Mama does not wear a new dress but one of her "old favorites."

She puts a scarf around Greta's neck and ties up her ankle boots. Greta is pink in the face from smiling, as if she might burst.

On the bus, we pass large Nazi flags hanging on the front of buildings, and we cross a large square and there are hundreds of people dressed red or gray or black, with laced black shoes and boots, and scarves and hats.

We get off the bus and walk into a café where we can order food from our table. The ceiling is high and there is a large mirror at the back of the room. There is a counter where people order from too, and I can smell coffee, burning sugar, and dough. We take a table in the corner. It is round and there are wooden chairs around it. Greta rushes to take the chair closest to the window. We make funny faces at the people who walk past the window. Greta pulls out her ears.

"Stop it," says Mama. "Don't encourage her to do bad things."

Papa orders soup and bread for him and Mama, and cakes for Greta and me.

When we are finished, we walk another block to the cinema. It is a beautiful building with a large stone archway. On top of the archway, there is a big poster of the actors from the film. We enter the cinema and then walk down some stairs into a large room with golden columns. At the front there are red curtains. After we sit down, the curtains open and people burst onto the screen. It is the most exciting moment of my life.

The film is called *Captains Courageous*. It is the best story ever told about Harvey, a boy who becomes a seaman, and the friends he makes. It is terrifying in parts and Greta squeezes my hand when Harvey falls overboard, and then she screams when Harvey's close friend is caught in ropes and swallowed up by the sea. Mama takes her on her lap and Greta puts her head on Mama's chest. Several people have turned around to look at us. When Harvey is finally reunited with his father, I have to hold back my own tears and pretend that my forehead is itchy to wipe them away.

At the end of the film the screen goes black and no one is leaving. A loudspeaker in the cinema says that there is an important announcement: there is another film about to start.

It shows the Führer, the leader of Germany, speaking to a group of people. He is shouting at them as if they have done something wrong, as if they can't hear properly.

Papa whispers to Mama that they have to go but Mama shakes her head and whispers back, "It won't look good. We must stay."

The film continues for many minutes.

When it is over, Mama and Papa take our hands and drag us from the cinema, and Greta and I nearly trip over our own feet, we are walking so fast.

"It is a disgrace," says Papa.

"Hush," says Mama. Several people walk past us and stop to look at Papa.

We get on another bus which will take us home. When we sit down, Mama says, "I can't do this anymore."

Papa says nothing.

"I liked the film," I say. "Can we see it again?"

"I did too," says Greta.

"No you didn't! You started crying," I say.

"No I didn't!"

"You're a liar."

"Stop it, children!" says Mama.

I look around and there is hardly anyone on the bus, but then I notice someone in the corner who is looking at us. It is a woman. She was in the cinema also. She wears a dark coat and is staring straight at me. I wonder why she looks angry, what it is that she doesn't like. Papa looks at her too and then taps me gently on the head with his hat.

"Don't stare," he says.

I look away but still feel her eyes boring into us. When we get off the bus, she is watching us from the window.

That night, I cannot stop thinking about the film. I stand on the bed and I am Harvey, and my bed is the ship, in danger of sinking in the stormy sea.

Suddenly the light goes on and Mama is standing there.

"Go to sleep, *Harvey*," she says with half a smile. "Tomorrow you can sail the sea." She is not angry, just sad and tired looking.

I pull the blankets up over myself and dream of the sea.

CHAPTER 6

Papa doesn't leave the apartment anymore, only Mama. She goes to the market on Tuesdays and Fridays. She does not cook as well as Frieda and when I tell Papa this he says: "She is doing her best under the circumstances."

"What circumstances?"

"When I was a younger man, before you came along, I promised your mother that I would take care of her always. That she would have new dresses made by a dressmaker and she would have a cook. I have not honored my promises. Your mother does all that now."

I go to the kitchen to see Mama. There are saucepans steaming on the stove and she is concentrating on her tasks. Her apron is covered with flour. I tell her that she is a wonderful cook—better than Frieda.

Mama smiles and kisses me on the head. "You are a good boy, Riki. I think you will be a fine man like your father one day."

Dinner is awful that night. Mama has burnt the bread and the sauerkraut is missing any flavor. Papa once said that it is impossible to make sauerkraut without flavor. I do not say anything but Greta blurts out the truth.

"Yukky," says Greta.

I look from Mama to Papa. They are silent and don't even look up from their meals. I frown and shake my head at Greta, who has put down her fork and is pouting now with arms crossed.

Papa is fixing a broken heating radiator. He has pulled it apart and is scratching his head. I lie on the floor on my stomach to watch him. Greta copies me to do the same. Her elbows are on the floor and she balances her chin in her tiny hands on her tiny arms, but they are not strong enough to hold her head steady, and it wobbles instead. Mama has not brushed Greta's hair today. Some of the strands are knotted and bunched at the back like a nest.

Sometimes Papa curses but he no longer worries that we will hear this.

Papa suddenly grabs his chest and stops working.

"Are you all right, Papa?" I ask, and Greta asks the same.

He pauses. "I'm just catching my breath." Then he commences work again.

I look at Greta, who is squeezing her lips together, trying to understand what he just said. I don't know why but her expression makes me laugh.

I get up and run down the hallway and then we are galloping like wild horses.

"Not too much noise," my father calls. "You will wake your mother."

Papa is spending more and more time inside his bedroom. The radiator is still in pieces—pipes, nuts, and screws—though it has been moved to a corner of the room so that no one trips over it.

Often Papa will come out still in his nightshirt. I notice that he is very skinny, that his collarbones protrude above his shirt. When Greta comes to see him, he does not pick her up and swing her around like he used to. Sometimes he does not even notice that she has entered the room.

Mama and Papa continue to sit by the radio, listening to speeches. Sometimes they say things: "How dare they?" "Other nations will be watching." "They can't get away with this for much longer. Social injustice is not acceptable in the Western world."

Sometimes they just listen—still, like statues—when they can't find anything to say.

One night Papa leaves and does not come back until morning. Mama says he is out looking for a job at the factories, but I can tell now when Mama is lying, because she talks slower, more carefully, as if she is thinking harder.

A week later, a man comes to our door. He wears a big coat and fake hair. I know that it is fake because on one side I can see his real hair underneath, which is a different color, and the false hair does not sit correctly at the front, almost like his scalp has lifted.

He brings with him an envelope and pulls out some papers which he gives to Papa. The man is not young. His face is heavily lined. When he pulls off his gloves, his fingers are covered in black-and-purple ink.

He notices Mama, who has entered the room.

"I can see where your daughter gets her good looks."

Mama doesn't smile at him but leaves the room again. The man turns to me, smiles, and pats me on the head.

"But this one is a lot like you," he says to Papa. I cannot tell if this is a good thing or not.

I am sent to bed because Papa, Mama, and the man have to talk business.

It is the day after the visit from the man with the wig. Papa does not come out of his bedroom. Mama is at the market. I sneak around Papa's office. I have seen where he hides the key to his desk drawer and I open it to investigate the envelope.

Inside are three cards and some other papers. I open one of the cards and see that it has a picture of Mama—not one of her better ones, because she is not smiling. The next card has a picture of Greta and the third photo is of me. I remember this photo being taken by Papa several weeks ago. There is no card for my papa. I am about to put them back in the envelope again when I notice the mistake.

They have got my name wrong. Instead of Henrik Hansel Solomon, it is Henrik Hansel Klaus. Of course I cannot say anything because I am not supposed to know where Papa hides his key or what is inside the envelope.

Papa does not come out of his bedroom at all for two days, and a doctor arrives to check on him. He places several bottles of medicine on the table.

"It is a shame," he says to Mama, "that such things happen to good people."

Mama thanks him and he leaves.

"Is Papa getting better?" I ask.

"Not yet."

"Why isn't he in the hospital?"

"He is not allowed," she says. I can tell that she is only partially listening, that she is thinking of something else.

"Is it because Papa's mother and father are Jews?" Mama twists her head sharply.

"Who told you that?" I have Mama's full attention now.

"Zus." It is something I remembered only recently. When Zus mentioned this about my grandparents the last time I saw him, it had not meant anything. Now I am wondering if there is a connection.

"Your grandparents have nothing to do with us. Don't talk about things you don't understand. The hospital is too full, that is all. There is no room for Papa."

"Are *you* allowed in the hospital?"

"Yes," she says.

"And me and Greta?"

She pauses and bites her bottom lip. "Yes, of course."

"Because we're not Jews."

"That's right. Because we're not Jews."

Mama gives Papa his medicine and takes some soup to feed him in bed. We are allowed to visit him in the evenings for several minutes, but that is all. Mama says it makes him too tired to talk.

We stand in front of his bed and he talks softly.

"How are you, Henrik?"

"I am fine, Papa."

"And you, Greta?"

"Splendid," she says. She has copied this word from me. "Can we go to the lake tomorrow?"

"Not tomorrow," says my father.

Mama comes back in.

"Time to leave, children," she says, the corners of her mouth flickering and her voice rising slightly to sound bright. But I know she isn't bright and cheery. I have seen her crying at night. She sleeps in another room now and has some wine before she goes to bed.

• • •

The weather is getting colder and I am so cold. Only the heater in Papa's room is allowed on all day. The doctor comes back and also says that it is cold in our apartment.

He and my mama are in the room with Papa for hours. When they come out, Mama and the doctor have a drink and she feeds him some leftover wurst. He thanks her very much and she rustles in her handbag and brings out some marks.

The doctor shakes his head. He is not old and not young and when he wears his glasses, he reminds me a bit of Papa.

"You should think about what I said."

Mama looks away. She is thinking hard about something.

Mama says that she has to go into the city and see a lawyer and then she will come back. She says that the meeting is about getting her property in order. The lawyer needs to contact Papa's family. She says she has to leave us alone in the apartment and we are not to leave for any reason; she says that I am in charge.

"What if there is a fire?" I ask.

"Well, then you leave, silly."

"Where will we go?"

"You go see our neighbors."

"But Papa said he dislikes them. He says they don't like children."

"It is all right to go there if the apartment is on fire."

"What if they don't have time to help Papa?"

"Henrik!" yells my mama, who is frustrated. "It will be fine. It is only for a couple of hours."

When Mama is gone, I tell Greta that I am in charge and that she must be very good; otherwise, I have to send her next door to the neighbors.

She nods gravely and returns to her room and shuts the door, and that is where she stays the whole time Mama is away.

PASTEL ORPHANS

Several days later a woman arrives. Mama introduces her as Papa's cousin, Hannah. She looks quite severe and angry, though I don't know why she is angry at Mama, who is being so nice and offering food. I have not met her before because Mama says that Hannah and my father had a falling-out after he married Mama and turned his back on the family.

She is staying for a few days.

I lie in bed and find that I can't sleep, so I crawl down the hallway to take up my listening position outside the kitchen.

"You should stay till the end," Hannah says.

"He doesn't want that. There is nothing more I can do and we do not have enough money to look after all of us here. The identification documents cost most of our savings."

"How do you know it is any better where you are heading?"

"You know why," says Mama angrily. "Are you deaf and blind?"

"Of course not," Hannah says, a little more softly and a little more sadly. "Every day we live in fear." There is silence.

"We have a house and my sister will be there to help with the children. Emmett wants this. There is no other option. I have to think of the children now. I will die before anything happens to them . . . before they are taken away."

I am worried. Who will take me and Greta away?

Christmas is small, as if our apartment no longer has the space for it. Mama does not spend much time in the kitchen but she and Greta make some biscuits in the shape of Christmas trees. They ice them in pink, then sprinkle them with more icing sugar, which looks like snow.

Mama says that our presents will come soon, that they have not had time to organize Christmas. Two of Mama's friends come also. They are elderly.

"Poor little lambs," says one of the ladies, eyeing us constantly, as if there is something wrong with us, as if we have a condition that can't be named.

I wonder then if the reason we do not go out is that we have the same sickness as my father.

For dinner, we have sauerkraut and baked fruit, and the pink biscuits, which taste quite bland.

CHAPTER 7

1939

Mama announces that we are going on a holiday to see her sister and we are taking a train. She has pulled out the suitcases from the hallway cupboard and wipes the dust from them.

Greta says she doesn't want to go, that she doesn't like trains. I tell Greta that she is making that up just to be difficult.

Mama helps each of us pack. We are leaving tomorrow, and it sounds exciting that we are travelling at night.

It is the afternoon that we are leaving, and our suitcases are by the door. Mama is wearing her best suit and a smart hat.

I am wearing my trousers, braces, a white shirt, a buttoned cardigan, and a coat, which is too short in the arms now, and my shoes are scuffed. Papa isn't well enough to polish them.

Mama calls us into the living room to tell us about the trip. She says we will travel through the night so we can sleep, and that we must not talk to anyone. She is looking mostly at Greta when she says this.

"Riki, from now on, when we are out, or if someone asks you, you must introduce yourself as Henrik Klaus, not Riki Solomon, and you, Greta, are Greta Klaus. I want you to pretend you are actors in a moving picture."

I remember the identification cards and it makes sense now. Mama has been planning this trip. I don't like this plan because I am remembering that I did not see Papa's cards.

"And what about Robin?"

"Papa's cousin and my friends will take turns looking after Papa and Robin. And on other days, Papa will look after Robin."

I know that Mama is lying, because Papa can't get out of bed.

"Why can't Robin come?"

"I doubt she would be happy to travel . . . and besides, Papa likes the company. It will be good for him."

"How long are we staying there?"

"For a few months, possibly longer."

"But I thought it was just a holiday."

"It will be a long holiday."

"And Papa . . . when is he coming?" It has taken me a bit longer to ask this question because I fear the answer.

"Your papa might join us later . . . I'm not sure when."

"No!" I say. "We can't leave without Papa!"

I run into the room to see him. Inside his room it is dark and I can hear his heavy breathing. Hannah is there also. I did not see her go in. She must have crept in during the night. Mama has followed me in.

"Papa," I say, "you have to get better quickly." He lifts one eyelid but he doesn't say anything. It is as if he doesn't know me.

"Come out, Henrik," Mama says gently. "I want to explain."

Mama closes the door carefully so that it doesn't make a sound.

"Is it because someone will take us away? Is that why we are going?"

Mama blinks and looks at me.

"It is because the place we are going to is better," she says. "Hannah is looking after your father and after he is better, he will come and join us."

"What about our things here?"

"Well, Papa and Hannah will try to sell the place and put money in our bank."

"But why can't we just stay here until it is sold?"

"The place is too big and our savings are gone, dear Riki."

"But I don't want to go."

I see there are tears in her eyes, and she turns to put the back of her hand against her mouth. I rush forward to hug her and Greta does the same. The three of us cry but I do not understand why it has to be so sad. Soon Papa will join us and we will have lots of money in the bank and we will be living in a new apartment.

"But why do we have to go so far away from Papa?" I ask.

"Because Berlin is not safe at the moment. There is a lot going on here. There are a lot of changes that are not for good."

I remember that Reuben, Marian, and Zus were sent far away because Reuben said something that someone didn't like.

"Has Papa said something bad?"

"No," says Mama, "of course not."

"Mama, is it the Führer who wants to change things?"

"Yes."

"What things?"

"He wants to take nice places from good people and give them to only those people he likes."

"Why?"

"Because as the leader he can do what he likes."

If I were the leader, I wouldn't change things. I would make sure that everyone was happy.

"Now, children, you have to say good-bye to your father, but one at a time. You first, Greta."

Hannah has gone to the kitchen so that we can speak to Papa in private. Greta disappears into his room. She is in there for five minutes and Mama keeps looking at her watch. She is walking around in circles, looking nervous. Occasionally she walks to the window. I start to get nervous and stand and walk too, but she tells me to stop moving and sit down.

Greta comes out. She is smiling. Smiling! After she has said good-bye to Papa! "He says he might be able to come soon. He said that one day we will all be together."

Mama purses her lips. "Go on, Henrik. Go and say good-bye to your father."

I enter the blackened room, which smells like disinfectant and sweat and old wood and cod-liver oil and chemicals. I think how horrible it is for my father to be trapped like this.

I sit near Papa. I am scared at first to go too close because his eyes are closed and his breathing is loud and scratchy. But then his arm stretches out and he grabs my wrist gently with long bony fingers that remind me of the skeleton in *Treasure Island*.

"Hello, Son," he whispers through cracked lips that barely open.

"Do you need some water, Papa?"

"No."

"When will you be better? Will you be coming soon?"

"I don't know, Riki. Nothing is ever certain. Time means very little."

I do not ask him what he means because I can tell that it hurts him to speak.

"You are older and more responsible now. Take care of yourself, and take care of your mother and sister too. I know you can do it."

"I will, Tateh."

He opens his eyes into slits and I can see that his eyes are the color of the deep ocean, which again reminds me of *Captains*

Courageous, and this thought makes me cry. I lie down beside him on the bed and he moves slightly to let me in.

"There, there," he says, stroking my head. "Everything will be better soon. As long as there is a sun and a moon, there is another day to love and fight."

"Tateh, I love . . ." I don't finish because my words have turned into a whine, and I begin to sob so hard that my chest hurts.

Mama enters. "Henrik, go to your sister," she says in an urgent voice.

"Good-bye, Riki," says Papa.

"Good-bye . . ." And I run out of Papa's bedroom and down the hallway to my room, where I throw myself on the bed. I hold Robin tightly to my chest and she purrs loudly in my ear.

A short while later Mama knocks on the door to say that we are leaving. Her voice is weak and her sentence cracks in the middle. When I come out, she is cleaning her face in the kitchen. I see that her makeup is smudged and her eyes are red and puffy. In front of the entrance mirror, she layers her makeup thickly to cover the red blotches on her cheeks, then paints her lips brightly once more. She is wearing the lovely coat that Papa bought her several years ago. It is light blue, lighter than her eyes, and the scarf around her head is patterned in the same color.

At the door she looks at Greta and nods her head, and then turns to me and frowns, just slightly, as if she should alter something but can't. She checks that our papers are in her handbag. She has done that four times in the last few minutes, forgetting that she has already checked. Her hands are shaking.

"All right, children," she says. "It is time to leave. I want bright, happy faces all the way to the train station. If anyone asks, we are going on a holiday. Now, remember about your last names. We are actors in a play. Do you both understand?"

I nod. Once Greta sees me nod, she nods also.

We catch the bus and Mama smiles at everyone. She sits near some people and remarks on the lovely coats of the other children and how pretty they are. It is a different Mama than I have seen, but then I remember she is now an actress, so when the people turn to me, I smile, wider than normal. We get off the bus and walk to the train. My bag is very heavy and I have to carry Greta's as well. Mama also carries two suitcases.

The pavement is slippery with snow and we step carefully, except for Greta, who slips and falls and starts to cry. A policeman rushes to help. He is very handsome and asks if Greta is well enough to walk.

Mama answers for her sweetly, and the officer can't help but smile back and asks if we are going on a holiday. Mama says yes, that she is visiting her sister but that she is looking forward to returning to Berlin, which is the best city in the world.

The officer carries one of Mama's suitcases and Greta's. Mama buys some tickets. We have to talk to the officer some more while we wait for the train, and Mama lies that she is a widow.

Greta whispers to me, "What is a widow?"

I whisper back, "None of your business. Be quiet."

"What is your name?" the man asks.

"Karolin Klaus."

"Well, Karolin Klaus," he says, "I hope we meet again."

The officer continues to smile. Greta is staring at Mama curiously. I grab my sister's arm and squeeze it, just in case she is thinking of saying anything that might give away our disguise.

We climb aboard the train when it arrives; it has a picture of an eagle on the front carriage. It is filled with people, and we find some seats at the end that are not taken. Mama collapses in the compartment. She has taken off her smile and it is the old Mama again.

The officer waves to us as the train takes off.

"Snake!" Mama says, her teeth together. I don't know why she doesn't like him but this makes me laugh, and then Mama smiles and laughs, but only briefly. But any laughing is good because she does not do that as much as she used to when I was small like Greta.

"Mama, why is he a snake?"

"He just is," she says dreamily, looking out the window. We watch the lights of the city disappear behind us. We watch the buildings get smaller and then there are less buildings and more trees and smaller houses. The train ride is bumpy and the door rattles and air creeps in, making a whistling sound. I breathe on the windows and this leaves a white mark.

Mama wraps scarves around our necks. I take mine off again. Greta doesn't. She puts her head in Mama's lap and I watch her eyes start to droop with sleep.

A ticket man comes and asks for our tickets and our papers. He looks at our pictures and at us. Mama has put her bright smile on again but this officer doesn't notice. He does not smile back. He takes his job very seriously.

It is almost completely dark. Mama pulls out a tin and opens it. Inside are pastries filled with cheese and sausages. I take two of each. I go to take another one but she says it is for Greta when she wakes.

The train makes a nice sound. It is like music. It goes *che mm che mm che mm* and makes me sleepy. I lean on Mama's shoulder.

Mama wakes us very early in the morning and tells us that we have to change to another train. We step across the railway line and wait an hour. I breathe out for as long as I can, and watch the steam rise from my mouth. Greta does the same.

This platform does not have many people. They are old here. We get on another train and it rattles across countryside. The sun has just come up, and its orange light shines so brilliantly across the tips of pointed roofs and through our window that I have to squint to see. We pass lots of fields with cows and horses and sheep and geese, and then we come to another train station.

"Where are we, Mama?" I say.

"Zamosc."

This station is much smaller than the one in Berlin. There are only a few people waiting. The platform buildings have tiny windows. We cross the tracks and walk to the park where we are to meet my aunt Femke. We pass a fountain where the surface of the water has frozen.

"Is this where we are going to live?" asks Greta.

"No, not here," says Mama. "Our house is in a little village. It is still a distance yet."

Mama tells us to wait in the park while she buys two sodas. Then she returns and we drink these and have the bread and cheese that she has also brought. We wait and wait, and Greta and I lie on the snow until Mama tells us to get up again. People pass us by and wave from carts and cars, and we wave back.

Mama looks at her watch and frowns. Then a small truck pulls up beside us. It has a high front bonnet and a tray on the back. Femke gets out of the truck. She looks like Mama, sort of, but she is smaller, wiry, and her face is hard and lined. She wears a gray skirt down to her ankles and boots, and a shirt buttoned all the way to her neck. Over this she wears a drab gray coat which looks like a man's. Femke has more lines around her eyes, and the veins are protruding on the back of her hands, which are also wrinkled. She is like a dried-out version of Mama.

Mama rushes to Femke and they hug, though Mama is more affectionate than Femke, whose arms do not stretch all the way around Mama, but rather bend at the elbow. Mama calls us to stand to attention beside her.

"This is Henrik and Greta."

"Hello," we say.

Femke says something that I do not understand.

"In German, please," says Mama to Femke.

"Tsk," says Femke, but she does not hug us. She turns away, disinterested, so we say nothing more.

I cannot fit in the front of the truck and have to sit in the back. Greta asks if she can sit with me. While Mama is thinking about her response, Femke says that it is all right.

"Is it safe?" asks Mama. "It will be very cold."

"Of course it is safe," says Femke. "It is nearly spring. It's not that cold." She turns to us. "Just hold on to the sides in case of the bumps." Mama frowns.

Our bags are put in the back also. We drive along a track which is bumpy and not smooth like the roads in Berlin. There are no pavements to walk along. There is nothing here—just areas of land with houses, the same as we have seen from the train.

There are blankets in the back, and Greta and I huddle underneath them because the wind is nipping at our cheeks. The blankets smell like grass. My nose feels frozen and Greta's looks red.

We pass a factory with large open doors. Inside I can see that people are making furniture. There are big trucks parked in front. Then we pass another building with smoke coming from the top, and there is a strange smell. We pull in here. Femke climbs out of the vehicle, takes a tin from the back, and walks to the open doors. Mama gets out of the truck to ask if we are both all right, if we are not too cold. She tucks the blankets tighter around us.

When Femke comes out, the tin is gone and she carries two bottles. On the front of the bottles are colored labels. The letters on the first one spell "Wódka" and the other spells "Rum."

"I am worried about the children in the cold," says Mama.

"They're fine. We are nearly home."

We drive and I have had enough of driving. We pass many more fields and houses and finally the truck pulls into a lane. Greta and I stand up on the tray and hold on to the roof of the cab to stop from falling. We can see over the front of the vehicle towards our new home. It is a brick house with a chimney on top, like the ones I have seen in stories. I am slightly shocked because I thought that we would have moved to another apartment, in a building where there are other boys my age.

Femke unlocks the front door, which opens straight into a tiny kitchen. It is dark inside despite the daylight. The windows are cloudy and small. The floor is not polished and there is one main room with a couch, piano, side cabinet, a small table with chairs, and an oven and stove near a chimney. Femke turns on a lamp and I notice that most of the walls are brick, the same as outside, without plaster. The furniture is worn and old. There is only one photo on the top of a piano, which has a layer of black dust.

"Is this where you lived with Oma and Opa?" I try to disguise my disappointment by raising my voice high at the end.

"Yes," says Mama. She points to two people in the photo in plain clothes, like Femke's. The woman is not thin and the man is tall and grumpy. I recognize the man from the photo in Berlin. Oma died very young, Mama tells me, and Opa died nine years ago.

"Do you remember?" she asks. "You were very upset."

I nod so as not to offend her by not remembering. It is hard to believe that Mama is related to these people.

Femke looks at me and I think about the witch in *Hansel and Gretel*. She frightens me a little, in the way she looks at me intensely, like a vulture. I have never seen a real vulture, but I have seen pictures of their faces before they eat their prey.

"It is a blessing that the girl has your blue eyes and light hair," she says. "But the boy . . ."

". . . Is a blessing also," says Mama, whose look is fixed.

"I was just going to say that the boy is darker, that's all . . . an unusual mixture." Though I have a feeling that she is holding back from saying more.

We are led to rooms at the back. There is a toilet and bath in a room just outside the back door. Before that there are two more rooms. One has a large bed and the other has two smaller beds.

"This used to be my room," says Mama. "I shared this room with Femke. This is where we will be sleeping now."

"Where is my room?"

"In here with me and Greta. Greta and you will share a bed and you can pick which one."

I look into the room at the two narrow beds.

"But I can't sleep here . . . not with you."

"Henrik!" says Mama. "There is nowhere else."

I am thinking that Femke has a large bed and wonder if she and Mama can't sleep together in that. I am a boy and not long until a man. I make my suggestion but no one responds. Greta is not listening. She is looking at the small chipped statue of Mary above Mama's old bed.

"You have spoiled him," says Femke.

I do not like what she says and I walk away from them to sit at the table in the kitchen, where Femke has already lit the wood in the stove. At our old apartment we had a gas stove that didn't smell like smoke. I cough and make it sound slightly worse than it needs to be.

Mama comes back and kneels in front of me and places her hands on her knees.

"It won't be bad at all," says Mama. "This is a beautiful place for children. There are boys here you can play with, and a school, and you will like it in time. Sleeping is such a short time, and once you are asleep, you don't know anything. It is the rest of the day that you have."

"You pander to him," says Femke. Her voice is high and sharp, not at all like Mama's, which is soft and low.

"Femke," she says. "Please . . ."

Femke disappears out the back door and returns with some wood.

I go to my new room and bounce on both the beds, and Greta does the same.

"This one," I say. And Greta bounces too and agrees.

"This one," she parrots.

Then I bounce on the other one. "No, it is this one. It is better," I say.

Greta crosses the tiny distance between the beds and bounces. "Yes, this one."

"Greta," I say fondly. "You don't ever have an original thought."

"Yes I do," she says.

"What does *original* mean?" I say, thinking that I will trick her.

"Unique."

I am surprised that Greta is so clever.

I go to the toilet outside, for I am bursting. The hole in the toilet is large and I can't see the bottom. It smells like vinegar and wet soil and there are gaps between the roof and walls. I imagine at night that the seat will be too cold to sit on. There is no bathroom indoors but there is a washstand for our hands.

Greta is bursting also but she is scared of the hole. She thinks there could be animals at the bottom that might try and climb out, or more sinister creatures hiding there, waiting to bite her. When it is her turn, I have to stand outside the door.

I tell Mama that it is dumb having a toilet outside. Mama says that Femke never bothered fixing the place up. She says we will all get used to it.

I tell her that Berlin is nicer.

"How do you know? You just got here."

CHAPTER 8

Femke cooks "pork stew" in a large saucepan. Mama says that she has a headache and lies down with a wet cloth on her head. When I ask her if she is all right, she says she will be. She just needs some time to adjust to everything. I understand this because she must share her room also, and there are no mirrors here, only a tiny one in the bathroom.

Later, Mama apologizes to Femke for not helping with dinner. She says that things will be different when she is feeling better. Femke ignores her and puts a steaming bowl in front of me. I have never tasted this food before. The meat is salty and wonderful and the vegetables are so full of flavor and covered in sauce. It is like thick soup. Greta puts some on a spoon and sniffs it and dips her tongue in it before she puts the whole spoon in her mouth. She likes it too.

My mother picks up her fork and stirs it around but she doesn't eat.

Greta makes a slurping sound and Mama is suddenly distracted from her bowl to remind Greta of her manners. Then Mama stirs her food again. Femke is watching her, waiting.

"Don't do that," says Femke.

"Do what?"

"Think like that. You have changed."

"How can you understand?"

"I understand a lot," she says, raising her hands in angry disbelief. "You are not a Jew, so eat it."

Mama rushes from the room. I do not understand why Mama is not hungry, but the food is so good I can't stop eating. Greta is doing the same and the sauce dribbles down her chin. Femke dabs at it roughly. She does not have gentle hands like Mama.

Femke turns to me like a bird about to take a worm.

"Good, huh?"

I nod.

"Good Polish food. It was good for your mother once, you know."

Grown-ups are so confusing. Sometimes I don't want to understand what they are talking about, but I have a suspicion that this has something to do with Papa. Mama once said that Papa doesn't like pork because he didn't grow up with it. We have never eaten it before tonight.

After dinner, Femke fills up a sink and says that I must wash the dirty plates and Greta must dry while she goes outside to get more wood. She says she is looking forward to spring, which will be here shortly, that she is sick of the cold weather and long winter. She says this to the window in front of her, and I am not sure if she is talking to us.

She brings the wood inside, checks the fire and windows, then goes to her room. She does not come back out again.

Greta looks at Femke's doorway curiously, then looks at me. I pinch my lips tightly together like Femke, cross my eyes, and put my hands on my hips. Greta giggles. I have to tell her to be quiet. I do not want Femke to come back out.

When I go to our room, Mama is not moving. She is in the bed that I chose but I decide not to wake her. Greta and I open our suitcases and find our pajamas.

The floor is cold on our feet and we climb into bed, and suddenly I am glad that Greta is next to me because she is warm. I lie facing the wall and she snuggles into my back.

Mama takes us to the paddocks at the rear of the property, where there is a barn. Mama says that we have acres of land and six cows and that Femke milks the cows and sells the milk in vats to the villages, factory owners, and to other places in the city, like restaurants and shops.

In the barn there are lots of chickens too and three pigs and several piglets making snorting noises, like Greta does when she sleeps. Greta chases after one of the piglets but it is too wiggly and fast to catch, and I laugh and so does Mama. She is happier today and says that she has had the best sleep she's had in a long time. She says that she is glad to be home.

Today Femke shows Greta and me how to milk a cow. Mama has taken the truck to the markets to buy food and supplies for the farm. The milk makes a tinny sound when it hits the bucket. Greta's hands work the udder well and much milk comes out. I squeeze at each of the teats but only drops come out.

"You don't pinch the poor cow," says Femke. "Look at your sister, who is working out the milk gently. The cow doesn't even know that Greta's taking any."

It is the first time that Greta has done something better than me.

• • •

Femke asks me to load a vat of milk onto the back of the truck, which she has parked near the barn. The vat is so heavy that I can hardly lift it, but I pretend it is no trouble. Femke picks one up and she doesn't struggle or groan at all.

Today it is Christmas. Well, it isn't really Christmas. Mama has decided that since we didn't have a "proper" Christmas last year in Berlin, that we will celebrate it today.

Femke doesn't like the idea. She says that Mama was always the crazy one, with all the fanciful ideas.

I can't imagine Mama crazy. She is always so calm.

"It isn't right," says Femke. "It will give the children strange ideas."

Femke takes me outside and says that she is going to show me how to chop the head off a chicken. Mama and Greta are inside cleaning and dusting. Mama says that the place has been let go, that the curtains haven't changed in thirty years. She wants to paint the walls in our room, the only ones that are plastered, and to sew new curtains for the kitchen and sitting room. She has wheeled out the old sewing machine and has bought some fabric.

Femke picks up a chicken, which is squawking and flapping its wings angrily at her. The noise is so bad it makes me feel restless.

Femke lays the chicken on a table in the barn and chops it at the neck. Blood pours from the hole at the top of its body. The headless body then flutters itself upright and leaps off the table, falls sideways, and rights itself again before running around in circles. I put my hands over my face, and Femke laughs at my reaction. She tells me to catch it but I refuse to move.

"Stop being so childish," she says. But I *am* a child, I want to say.

She chases the chicken and puts it into a sack. I can still see it fluttering inside the bag, and take a step backwards, fearful that this dead creature will escape.

I have eaten chicken plenty of times but I am shocked that the food Mama serves begins like this.

"How do you think chicken got to your fancy plate in Berlin?"

When the headless chicken is no longer moving, Femke removes it from the bag and shows me how to pluck the feathers. I take the chicken outside so that Femke can't see my look of disgust as I finish the job. After the last feather has been removed, I go and tell Femke and she carries the carcass back towards the house.

When we return, we see that Mama has brought in a baby pine tree and is placing glass and paper decorations of gold, pink, and green on its branches. She has a box full of shiny decorations, some made by Femke and her when they were children. The box is old and splitting at the base. Femke says it has not been opened since Mama left. Tonight, we are having baked chicken, zucchini and onion fried in lard, and preserved fruit with creamed cheese. I am a little disappointed by this menu, especially in view of my mother's idea of making this a special Christmas occasion.

Mama is more talkative at this meal and she speaks in Polish to Femke so that we cannot understand. I hear my father's name mentioned, and Femke looks over her spoon at me as she puts it in her mouth.

After dinner, Mama pulls out two parcels wrapped in brown paper with silver ribbon for Greta and me.

"Merry Christmas!" she says excitedly.

Mine is a notebook with a leather cover. Inside, the pages are blank. I am disappointed that there is only one present, though I don't show this. Greta opens hers and she has a silver locket on a chain. Mama helps her put it on.

"Riki," she says. "You have to write about your experiences."

I don't tell her that I don't want to write.

"And I have something for you too," says Mama, passing another present to Femke.

Femke looks surprised and embarrassed. "What is this for?"

"It is a thank-you for having us here with you. I am very grateful."

"It's your house too," Femke says, not so spitefully this time. She touches her neck and turns away. "Well, I've got nothing to give you."

Mama doesn't mind. She has always said that she prefers to give presents rather than receive them.

Femke opens her wrapping and there is a box of lavender-scented soaps.

"Thank you," says Femke.

Mama plays some Christmas tunes on the piano and we all sing along, even my aunt. Then Femke and Mama sip vodka. Femke is more talkative as well tonight, and they talk about when they were children and how hard their father made them work, and about how Femke was the brightest of the two but it was Mama who went away to study music at the Warsaw Conservatory.

"Where are all the photos of us?" I say. At our apartment, Mama had many photos displayed of me and Greta and Papa but, apart from the one of Oma and Opa on top of the piano, there are none here at all.

"Yes, where are the photos that I sent you?" says Mama. She gets up and searches through the drawers in the side cabinet until she finds what she is looking for.

"Tsk," she says to Femke. "You could have put them out."

There is one photo of me standing, wearing breeches that go down to my knees, the waistband high above my waist. My expression is fierce. I remember that I didn't want the photo taken. There is also a close-up photo of Greta; she is looking upwards, towards heaven, her face glowing like an angel's.

There are photos of Mama and Papa on their wedding day. Papa has smooth black hair combed over to one side, and a pointed chin. He has a long nose that reaches the top of his lips, which are wide and narrow. His skin looks very dark against Mama's, and his eyes look black—but I know they are blue. They are the darkest blue I have ever seen.

I miss Papa and tell Mama so. She hugs me and says that she does too.

"When is he coming?"

"I'm not sure."

After that, Mama does not want to talk anymore and tells us that it is time for bed. She is the first to climb into bed and turns to face the wall. She has gone silent.

Greta climbs into our bed. She leans over and kisses me. "Happy Christmas, Riki," she says, and passes me a piece of paper. It is a drawing of the two of us milking a cow. The cow is smiling. I kiss her on the forehead like I have seen Papa do.

"Happy Christmas, Greta," I say and turn off the lamp beside our bed.

Mama has spent much of the day at the sewing machine while Greta and I explore the farm. We have done our milking and are allowed to run around the fields. I have seen other children walk and cycle by our house and look forward to meeting them. Mama tells us that we will be going to school soon.

When we come inside, Mama pins up the lilac-colored curtains and ties them back with yellow cord.

Femke pulls down the sides of her mouth. I have grown used to the meaning of this look. It means that something is not completely distasteful.

"You still have skill with the sewing machine. You have that, at least."

In between our chores, Greta and I run in the fields and when there is nothing to do, I find other things to do.

One time, I leave a chicken head on the kitchen table for Femke to find, with a note under it that says, "Has anyone seen the rest of me?" Then I pull Greta's arm so she will come and hide with me, and we watch from behind the door when Mama and Femke enter.

Femke looks at the note and shakes her head and mutters something in Polish.

Mama laughs so hard there are tears in her eyes.

Another time I take some of the white paint that Mama has been using to paint the walls in our bedroom and draw a square in the fields.

I tell Greta that it is the "safety square," that when you walk inside it, nothing can harm you. Then, as luck would have it, thunder comes from the sky.

Greta looks at me fearfully because she hates the sound of thunder.

"Oh no!" I say. "The thunder gods are angry that I have revealed such a secret."

"What secret?"

"The one I just told you, stupid. About the safety square."

Greta nods as if she understands.

I tell her a story that comes into my head right at that moment, about how once, everyone was trying to leave a giant safety square that went around a fortress and had been put there by the king and queen of England. But when the people stepped out of the square, the king and queen could no longer protect and control their people nor stop them from going mad. Then the thunder gods got so angry they shot bursts of lightning at the people as they tried to step out.

"Now the thunder gods are angry that I have revealed the secret," I say.

Greta is standing just inside the square and I am outside. She goes to walk towards me and I tell her to stay or she will be zapped to dust by lightning. The urgency of my tone convinces her to stay, since I am right about most things. But it may not be that she believes me. It may be that she *wants* to believe me.

I tell her that she must stay there until the thunder passes. It starts to rain and I run inside where it is dry, to watch her from the window.

"What are you doing?" asks Mama, who has walked up behind me. "And why is Greta sitting out there in the rain?" The rain is getting heavier. She doesn't wait for my response, but rushes outside and I follow.

"Greta!" calls Mama. "Inside now!"

"No," Greta says stoically. "The thunder gods will strike me if I leave."

"Oh, Henrik, you naughty boy!" Then Mama turns to Greta angrily, though her anger is directed at me. "In the house now, Greta! You are more likely to be killed from the rain and cold than from the thunder gods. Your brother makes up silly stories." Mama smacks me on the arm and tells us both to go inside before we catch our deaths.

Femke says that my practical jokes will lead to trouble one day. Another time, I put a milk pail on Greta's head and tell her that she has to twirl around three times and then count to twenty. Then she has to follow my voice and walk towards me. I tell her that if she can catch me, she can have one of my books.

The game starts off well but after a while, when she is tired from wandering around the large paddock, she trips and falls face-first, her teeth hitting the metal pail as she lands hard on the ground. This knocks out both her front teeth. There is lots of blood but she only starts to cry when she sees that there is blood on her hand. I carry her into the house.

"She fell over," I say. "She wasn't looking where she was going." But I do not give the exact circumstances and neither does Greta, as if she thinks she will be in trouble too.

Mama gets a cup of water and rinses Greta's mouth out until the water runs clear.

"You have to be more careful," says Mama to both of us. "Henrik, you have to keep a better eye on her."

I don't say anything but Greta smiles at me. When she smiles, there is a gap now and I feel guilt rise from my neck to my cheeks. She tells Mama that her mouth is feeling better, and she will be more careful when she runs, and she won't do anything too silly. She has trouble saying words that end in *t* and *s* and I start to laugh, close to hysterically. Then Greta does too. It is not so bad; it is her baby teeth that she has lost.

CHAPTER 9

Mama has begun to teach Polish to Greta and me. She says that if we want to go to school, we have to learn Polish.

The words are more complicated than German words and we practice them over and over again. Now, at dinner we are to ask for things in Polish and if we don't, then Mama and Femke won't respond.

I do not like the language. It sounds angry and looks messy.

We pull out Mama's old bike from the back of the barn. Mama helps me oil the chain and then we paint the bike so that it looks new again. Greta wants the bike too but she can't ride. I show her how, but the handlebars wobble a lot and she can't steady the front wheel. It turns too sharply and she falls onto rocky cow dung. I think she will cry because she has grazed her elbow, but instead she gets up and tries again. I think that it is all right; nothing too bad can happen to her now, with her front teeth already lost.

After several goes, she is still riding unsteadily but she can stay on for ten seconds.

Mama and I clap.

Greta and I find a tree. It is wide and large and sits at the entrance to the forest behind our farm. I tell her that it is a magical tree, that only good things can happen if you believe in its magic. I tell her that it is also where we can store our memories, that the tree will remember and tell future generations about us. I tell her that if she tells the tree her hopes and dreams, they will come true.

Every day for a week she goes to the tree and whispers things to it. I watch her and don't know whether to laugh. It is fascinating to me that she does this, that she continues to do what I say.

One time I am watching her from the window and Mama comes to stand beside me.

"What is she doing? Is she talking to the tree?"

"Yes," I say.

Mama puts her hands on her hips. "Riki, this is not another one of your tricks, is it?"

But I don't have to answer her. She already knows it is.

I wander across the field to where Greta is talking, and she appears irritated that I have disturbed her.

"What are you saying?"

"You said I must keep it secret."

"Oh, but it is all right to share it with family, those of the same blood. The dreams and secrets are still sacred amongst family."

She tells me then, blushing slightly but also pleased.

"I have asked the tree to watch over us, to keep us together. I have asked the tree to keep a special eye on you because you are important, because you make people happy."

I get a lump in my throat and feel suddenly undeserving.

"That is very good," I say in a formal-sounding voice. "But you know what we should do? I think that we should put new wishes in a tin beneath the tree and leave them there, and then we don't have to keep coming back and reminding it."

I take one of Femke's storage tins from the kitchen and hope she doesn't miss it. Then both Greta and I write our notes on pieces of paper, secretly, and place them in the tin. We bury it in the earth.

"This can also be a place in the future to leave messages," she says excitedly.

I think then how intelligent she is—much more so than me. And I think that this will be the last time for tricks, that she is worthy of much better.

It is the first day at our new school. I am thirteen and Greta will be turning eight later in the year. Mama is driving us there and picking us up afterwards for the first week. It is a long walk because our farm is on the outskirts of the town, past the brewery. Mama, with the help of a neighbor, is building an extra seat on the back of the bike so that I can take Greta to school and back.

The school is a big square brick building with two floors and classrooms off to the side of a long hallway.

Mama greets the teachers. We take Greta to her class first.

It is a school that has both Catholics and Jews. Mama says that we are Catholic and the teacher looks at me longer than she does at Greta, as if she is waiting for me to agree or give a sign of the cross to confirm this. I do not understand adults sometimes.

Mama tells the woman in charge, in Polish, that the children only speak German. And the teacher nods. The teacher says to us in German that we will be speaking Polish soon enough.

Greta perhaps thinks she is only here to look at the school and then go home again. The other children look at Greta as if she is a new jewel. They are excited but Greta isn't. She doesn't like being looked at and turns her face into Mama's arm. There are paintings around the classroom and toys on the benches to the side. Without the pictures, the room would be very dull, with scuffed, pale walls.

The teacher shows Greta her desk, but when Mama tries to walk away, Greta starts crying. Mama turns back to her but the teacher draws Mama from the room. I go to Greta and crouch beside her.

"My classroom is next to yours, all right? And whenever I can, I will come and see you." From my pocket I take my handkerchief, which Mama has spent many unnecessary minutes ironing, and wipe Greta's face.

Then I go to my classroom. Mama puts her arm around my shoulders. I am still a head shorter than Mama. I wish I could grow faster and be tall like Papa. Mama says it will happen soon, that I need patience. I am embarrassed when Mama kisses me on the cheek in front of everyone.

There are more boys than girls in the class, and the teacher is a man with shiny hair like my father. I am given a spot at the end of a long bench seat at the front of class. Everyone has writing books and a pencil, except me. The teacher talks in Polish and I struggle to understand his directions. The children lift the lids of their desks, the bases of which are all joined together. Other students pull out their books. I lift my lid but there is nothing inside. The teacher passes me his book. The first lesson of the day is German. The next lesson is mathematics, then Polish, and then it is art class.

The teacher comes to my side and says that it is all right for me to just observe for the first few days, but he hands me some paper and pencils to draw with.

The children break off into groups at lunchtime. Some talk to me but they don't speak German. Some know a little bit of German but are not really interested in talking to me. Then there are some Jews who speak another language to one another. It is awkward and not like in Berlin, where I could make friends straight away. I find Greta and we sit on a bench together to eat our bread with cheese and bacon.

We have to draw the teacher, and the class becomes talkative and enthusiastic.

I concentrate on the shading around his small, unusual face, with the large cheeks and beard, and tiny round eyes. Because he reminds me of a cat, I draw some whiskers below his nose. Then the teacher says something in Polish that I don't understand. He walks around the class examining the pictures, and I am suddenly embarrassed that I have drawn whiskers. He switches to German as he approaches me. I have covered my drawing with my arms. "Let me see," he says firmly, his dark brown eyes fixed on mine like they will burn a hole in them.

I take away my arms. His eyes roam over my drawing.

"Hmm," he says, nodding to himself. "Interesting . . ."

He takes it to the front of the class and holds up the drawing for the rest of the class to see. The other children snigger, and when the teacher smiles, their sniggers erupt into laughter.

"The winner," he says, first in Polish and then in German, "is Henrik Klaus."

I am surprised. I was sure that I would be punished for drawing whiskers.

Mama picks us up in Femke's truck and I tell her that I need a work pad and pencils. I tell her about the day and about the drawing. Mama says that she always thought my wicked sense of humor would be my undoing.

"But I won a prize," I say, and present the bar of chocolate.

When we arrive home, I ask Mama to help me with my Polish. I am determined that I must learn it quickly so that I can talk to the other children.

• • •

I have been at school for several months. I have two friends, Jonas and Rani, who are Jewish, and one friend, Jasper, who is Catholic. We race each other at lunchtime.

Greta doesn't like the school very much. She has not learned the language as well as me, and sometimes the others mimic her accent. I tell her that they are not being mean; they are only wanting her attention because she is very pretty. But she wants to follow me. Jonas, Rani, and Jasper don't seem to mind her there since she doesn't say anything, just listens.

Greta and I used to ride all the way to school but since my friend Jonas doesn't have a bike, we walk part of the way after we reach his place. One day, on the way home from school, Jonas says, "Let's have a running race across the field." I tell Greta to stay on the side of the road and watch the bike.

We race across the fields and down another track, and I am way out in front. He catches up when we come to another field, but I will not give up until I can outrun him, until I have won. Finally, we stop, once Jonas is out of breath and declares that I am the winner. We have been gone for a while and I suddenly remember Greta. We run all the way back, but we are slower now because we are tired, and it is getting dark. When we reach the spot where we left Greta, neither she nor the bicycle is there.

We call her name and knock on the doors of houses close by to ask if they have seen her. We go to the brewery as the workers are leaving and they have not seen her either. I am so worried and so is Jonas, and we despair together. We walk back to the school and find a teacher still working. I am too afraid to go home and tell Mama that we have lost Greta.

It is dark now and the teacher offers to drive us home. "The first thing we need to do is tell your mother."

My legs are trembling and there is a pain in my chest such as I have never felt before, even worse than when we left Berlin.

When we enter the front door, Greta is inside, eating a piece of bread with jam. Her eyes are red and puffy. I have never felt so happy, and I rush to hug her. She turns away from me, more interested in licking the jam.

"What do you have to say?" says Mama

"I'm sorry," I say to Greta.

We learn from Greta that she had tried to follow us on the bike, thinking she would meet us halfway. She had begun to go roughly the same way we had, but then the fields and tracks confused her, and with the sun quickly fading, she had panicked, heading in a different direction. By nightfall, she was distraught and began wheeling the bike when her legs became weary from riding across the thick grass. Someone drove by and saw her, and was kind enough to bring her and the bike home in his truck.

Mama thanks the teacher for bringing me home, and then for the next ten minutes Mama lectures me on responsibility.

Later that night, Greta whispers in my ear just before she falls asleep.

"I can ride now. I rode for thirty minutes."

I kiss her on her soft cheek, which smells like sweetened dough.

CHAPTER 10

Several times, we have been to the markets in the city. There are many shops there, in the square. Mama takes me and Greta to the shoemaker—an old Jew. Mama says that we each need a new pair of shoes for school, that the ones we have are too worn.

Then we stop at the market stalls and Mama buys some flour and cheese and ginger, and later that night she makes cheesecake and gingerbread.

She looks better now—not so thin. She seems a lot happier, though I know she misses Papa, and every day she is hopeful that the postman will deliver a letter.

At school we have an athletics competition: Jews against Catholics. We cut out *J*s and *C*s and pin them on our shirts. The sports teacher thinks this is funny and adjudicates the trials. The next day of our competition, several parents come to the school to see what is happening. They don't like what we are doing, segregating by religion in school—there is enough of that happening elsewhere. But the teachers assure them that it is harmless fun.

So far, the Catholics are winning. I am on the Catholic side, even though we have never been to church.

I look forward to art classes. We get to draw objects and sometimes there are free periods when we can choose who we want to draw. I draw Greta but I make her eyes bigger and her cheeks plumper.

"You like to caricature," says my teacher. I have not heard of this before. "You perhaps have seen it somewhere in Berlin newspapers?"

"Maybe," I say. "But I can't remember," which is true. Perhaps I have seen it done before.

"It is very good."

I draw Femke and my friends and cows, and soon I draw scenes as well, and other portraits that are not in caricature. Soon my drawing book with its leather cover is bursting with pictures.

Mama says that I am very talented, that I am like my grandmother on my papa's side.

We are playing soccer after school when someone points towards a group of people walking along the road towards us. As they get closer, I see that they are Jews. Some of them have long beards and skullcaps. There are women and children too. There are around sixty people.

One man comes to the fence and asks us where the mayor resides. We direct him towards the city. When they walk away, we feel sorry that they still have so far to walk with their heavy suitcases. The women do not smile at us and the children look at us wearily.

That night, I tell Mama and Femke what I saw and they do not look surprised. Mama tells me that the Jews have been expelled from Germany, that many are coming our way and some will go as far as Russia. I ask them why they all have to leave; surely there is room in Germany for some.

Femke says it is because Adolf Hitler hates Jews. "He wants everyone in Germany to look like your mama and Greta." I am hurt that she doesn't say my name also, and think that she did this purposely because I look more like Papa, and she doesn't like him.

Mama and Femke have decided that we must go to Lublin by train from Zamosc. They have business there and Mama has to pick up a package from a lawyer's office, which has been sent from Germany. She also needs to sign for some money.

Mama and Femke instruct us to sit in front of them on the train but we don't want to travel backwards, so we sit across the aisle facing forward. Two men in robes, with long beards, board the train and sit opposite us. The older one, who is frail and thin, wears an enormous circular fur hat that reminds me of a lampshade.

Greta whispers in my ear, one hand covering her mouth so the sound does not escape to other ears: "Why is he wearing the hat?"

"To keep the lights on inside his head," I whisper back, mock-serious.

She looks at me to see if I am telling the truth.

"Is that true?"

"I don't know. You will have to ask him."

Greta stands up and crosses the aisle to whisper something in Mama's ear, and Mama says something quickly, then tells her to sit down again.

Greta whispers in my ear to tell me that Mama says that some Jewish men must wear the hat as part of their custom.

"What do you think the animal on his head would think of this custom?"

"I don't think he would like it," says Greta, frowning.

Greta stares at the hat, her mouth open. I nudge her to stop, but she doesn't. Whether it is her curious look or the seriousness of her words, I suddenly find the whole thing funny and fight back laughter, so much so it hurts, and my eyes start to water.

And then a tiny giggle escapes me, like a squeak, and I have to cover my face with my hands to stifle the sounds. My amusement, now in the form of snorting, spreads like a sickness to Greta, who can't hide it at all, and she collapses against me in loud fits of laughter.

Femke is so angry there is red fire leaping from her eyes when she looks at me. Mama looks horrified and puts her finger to her lips for silence. Femke says, "Be quiet." She thinks she whispers this but it comes out like a loud hissing sound, and several people turn to look our way.

The older man with the hat purses his lips and stares at Mama as if she is the cause of all this. Mama apologizes for our outburst. He doesn't respond but the younger man smiles. He presses his hand on the leg of his older travelling companion and says, "They're only children." Then he turns and looks directly at me, smiling with his black eyes as if he can also see the humor.

My laughter stops and I tell Greta to stop also, which she does instantly.

I don't know why but I feel guilty that he is not angry. For the rest of the journey, I stare outside the window at the dull countryside. I am too ashamed to face them.

In the city we stop and have tea and cake at a bakery, and then Mama and Femke go inside a lawyer's office while Greta and I wait outside on the pavement.

I notice that there are many Jews walking with suitcases. Some are led into various buildings. Greta asks what they are doing, and I tell her that they are looking for new places to live.

"Why?" asks Greta.

"Because they are Jews and they have been sent from Germany."

"Will Papa be sent soon?"

"No, silly. Papa is not a Jew."

Mama and Femke come out of the lawyer's office, and Mama is wiping away tears. Femke tells us to hurry along or we will miss the train, and we walk at a fast pace to the station.

"I told you that the Jew would screw you for every cent."

"Shut up," says Mama, suddenly angry. "It is not their fault. It is not Hannah's fault that she can't sell the place. The jewelry that they sold is enough for now. We are lucky to have that."

"Mama, what has happened?" I say, but do not look at Femke because she will give me dagger looks for asking about grown-up business.

"Oh, Henrik, your father's cousin was supposed to sell the house but she has been told that she can't."

"Because she is a Jew?"

"Yes," says Femke, curtly.

"Well, that is hardly her fault," I say, repeating Mama's words. "And what about Papa? Will he still come if the place isn't sold?"

Mama turns to Femke as I say this, but Femke turns her head away. She does not look pleased about something.

"Yes," says Mama. "Hopefully."

We board the train and this time Greta and I face Mama and Femke.

"What is fornication?" asks Greta.

"This is what I don't like about church," says Mama to Femke, after we have returned home from church. "It leads to too many questions."

Mama decided that we should attend church to say some prayers for Papa, for Jews, and for Germany. She said that the church is a safe place, and that with all the unrest we must practice our faith. I tried to tell her that we can pray for Papa without going to church, but this did not work, and we were forced to go.

Mama ironed my best shirt and Greta's pale pink dress with the lace collar, which had become too small for her, and Mama had to quickly lower the hem.

Femke said that she is far too old to start practicing now.

At church, the priest talked about fornication as part of his sermon, saying that sex is a sin before marriage, just as murder and stealing are sins. Greta repeats these words.

Femke laughs. "See, it is a waste of time. It did not work on you."

"Silence," says Mama, but she is smiling slightly.

They think I am too young to understand what they have said, but I know that at some time Mama and Papa might have sinned.

Mama responds to Greta's question: "It is young girls and boys who spend too much time together under the same roof before they are married."

Femke laughs again. I have not seen her so humorous before and I start to laugh also. Mama asks Greta to go and fetch some eggs from the barn.

"Just tell her the truth," says Femke after Greta is gone. "She will hear it from one of the boys at school sooner rather than later. They all talk about it."

Femke is right. We have already discussed it at school, Jasper, Rani, Jonas, and I. It is when a man's penis enters a woman's vagina. Sometimes it leads to a baby, and sometimes it doesn't. When I first heard of it, I tried hard not to imagine Mama and Papa. It sounds too disgusting.

"Not yet," says Mama. "When she is a little older."

The following weekend we do not go to church, or anytime after that.

• • •

One afternoon, I arrive home from school and Femke and Mama are sitting around a new radio that Mama has bought in the city. Greta goes out to feed the chickens.

Mama and Femke turn the dial and there is a strange station that is being broadcast in Yiddish. Then they turn to another one and a man is speaking in German, and he is reciting an article written by another German. He says: "If the Jew wants to fight, it is fine with us. We have wanted that fight for a long time. There is no room in the world for the Jews anymore. The Jew or us, one of us will have to go."

I say: "I do not understand why Germans hate them so much. They are my good friends. In school they do not make trouble, and look at my shoes." I hold up my shiny brown shoes that the old Jew made. "They are clever."

Femke is sitting in the corner, stitching up a hole in some linen. She squints at me over the top of her glasses.

"You are a Jew, you silly boy. Did your father never tell you?"

I stand up. "What did you say?"

"Femke is being ridiculous," says Mama, avoiding my eyes.

"I am not a Jew. My father's parents were Jews."

"What do you think that makes you and your father and Greta?"

"Quiet, Femke! That is enough!" warns Mama.

"I am not a Jew. My grandparents were Jewish but I am not a Jew."

"He should know for his own sake," Femke says to Mama.

"We are not Jews!" I shout.

"It doesn't matter what you think, Henrik. Right now it is up to the Germans to make the decision. It is your blood that counts. That is the misfortune."

"Misfortune!" says my mama. "What do you mean by that?" But Mama does not wait for Femke to answer. She turns to me.

"Calm down, Henrik. Emmett stopped practicing the faith after we met so that we could get married."

"It is not what he does. It is his blood. You are in denial. Your children are Jews, whether you like it or not. If it wasn't for Jews trying to run Germany, then this country would be better off. Then the Führer would not be sending them here and making them our problem."

"You can't believe that," says Mama, raising her voice. "It isn't true. The Jews did not make trouble and they did not want control of the country. It is power and control that Hitler seeks. He is mad. He wants Germany in his own absurd vision." She turns towards me with her arms outstretched. "Don't listen to your aunt."

"No, don't listen to your aunt," mimics Femke. "Your mother chased your father. Did she tell you? They met in Warsaw while she was studying music, and when he got a job in Berlin, she chased him there too."

But I do not want to listen to Femke.

"I am not a Jew!" I shout. "If we were Jews, it would say so on our identity cards." But as I say this, I am remembering the false name. I run from the house and across the paddocks until I find a lonely field on someone else's property and sit beside a cow, and I tell myself and the cow that I am not a Jew. I am thinking of all the things that have been said in the past, of the way my father looks with his smooth, dark olive skin and dark brows, and of how I look the same.

It is very late when I return. The house is quiet. Femke and Greta have gone to bed. Mama sits on the couch under the yellow glow of a kerosene lamp.

"Sit down," she says.

I do, but I am careful not to look at her. I feel not just deceived, but foolish also, for not seeing what was right in front of me.

"Part of what Femke says is true," she says. "But much of her talk is because she is a bitter old Pole who does not concern herself with children's matters.

"As far as the Germans are concerned, yes, you are a Jew. Your father was born a Jew but renounced the faith to marry me. Your grandparents weren't happy. They were Zionists. Do you know what they are?"

I have heard only pieces of information. Mama explains that they are people who stick to the old practices and want to return to Palestine, rather than assimilate into the countries where they are living. She says that my father's parents returned to Palestine and had no contact with their son after he married Mama. They have had no contact with Papa because they are unhappy with his choice of a wife.

I start to sob and hope that Femke doesn't walk out from her bedroom and call me a sissy.

"Riki, I am sorry I have not discussed this with you, that I haven't explained, but it is the reason we left Germany. If anyone found out about your origin, you would be sent away. We paid much for new identities to remove all trace."

"And there I was, thinking that we were German spies with our new names."

Mama smiles. "That is what I love most about you, Henrik. Never lose your sense of humor."

"You should have told me earlier. I would have understood."

"We felt . . . your papa and I . . . that you shouldn't know, in case you were ever questioned. You give much away in your eyes. You wear your heart in them. And Riki, you must never, never tell Greta. Your aunt was wrong in what she did and I have told her so. We are not speaking. She can be hurtful sometimes; there is a bitterness inside her that grows each year, because she has never known love. Promise me you will not tell Greta."

I nod and she relaxes slightly.

"And what will happen to Papa?"

She sighs. "He is not coming. He is too sick. He will not see the summer."

"You knew he wasn't coming. You kept that from me too."

"Nothing is certain," she says. "I thought that maybe . . . Yes, I thought we might not see him again, but I also had hope. I thought maybe his illness would pass, and that the Jew kidnapping and persecution that happened that night in Berlin would never happen again, that others would step in and we would go back to him. Yes. That is what I thought—that where we are now would be only temporary . . ."

I can see a photo of Papa that Mama has placed on the side cabinet, and I picture Papa in our apartment without us, thinking that we have somehow abandoned him. I am hoping that he is not alone tonight, that Robin is curled up beside him.

"There was nothing else we could have done. We had no choice. We had to come here. Do you understand?"

I don't. Not really. I don't understand why any of this had to happen. I still don't understand why Germany had to change. I don't understand why Papa had to get so sick. I still don't understand why there have to be different rules for Jews. I am about to ask these questions but suddenly the words are drowning in sadness at the back of my throat and I cannot save them.

Mama pulls my chin towards her and does not let go, because she does not want me to look away.

"Your papa loved you. He would be so proud."

I can see that she has tears that are about to fall, and suddenly the sadness is too much, and I throw my arms around her tightly, sobbing loudly now, uncaring that Femke will hear, and suddenly frightened that I might lose Mama too.

"Riki, you must know that your father was my only love," she says, rocking me gently. "He will never be replaced in my heart. Never! You have to know that this hurts me as much as it hurts you. I love him so much. But now we must survive this. It is about looking after you and Greta, and that is the reason I left. If your father had come . . ."

"He could have come," I say feebly, because all strength has left me, and because, deep down, I know the truth.

"Your father is very frail. He has a disease in his body that keeps spreading. It won't be long now. I have already prepared myself for the worst. I have had to harden my heart these past months."

A few days later, when we arrive home from school, there is an envelope on the table that has a German stamp. Mama is waiting beside it. She tells us the news that I have been dreading, and expecting, but it is still a shock. I do not cry this time because anger is blocking the tears, but Greta wails, and Mama has to cradle her and tell her that everything will be all right. That no one else will die.

It is at this moment I feel hatred towards the country of my birth. It is filled with people who have turned their backs on Papa, and let him die without us at his side. I never wish to return.

CHAPTER 11

On the radio an announcer says that Hitler has entered Poland and war has broken out. It has been decided that part of Poland will be in the new Germany.

Mama and Femke are frightened but I am not. I want to fight on the side of the Poles and on behalf of all Jews.

I run to my friend Jonas's place. His whole family is there, which is large. Jonas says that they are moving to Russia because it is safer. He says that if Hitler wins the war with Poland, Jews will be expelled from here anyway. He says that most of his family lives there. I wish I had a large family like his. Jonas says they will be leaving once they have all their affairs in order.

There is a loud roaring noise and Greta and I rush outside to see the German planes flying over our skies. Mama tells us to go inside immediately. Then there is the sound of an explosion. People are rushing past our house saying that part of the town and several villages have been bombed. We run across the paddock to our barn in case there are other bombings. Others follow us from the street. We climb down a ladder into the cellar and pull the trap-door closed behind us. It is a tight space. Greta is squeezing my arm and I have mine around Mama. A father and his son are also there. I have seen them before but I don't know their names. We are all squashed together.

After an hour passes and there is no longer the sound of engines in the sky, we come out again.

Femke and I take the truck to see the destruction of some buildings. We learn that people have been killed. I am shocked at the devastation. It reminds me of the night that shops were smashed in Berlin, but this is worse because these places are not repairable and lives have been lost. The bodies have already been removed.

When we return home, Mama tells us that the school has been closed.

At first we do not know whether it is Germany or Russia that wants our town, because they are splitting the country down the middle: half to Germany, the other half to Russia. Then the German trucks arrive with soldiers and we hear that they have set up an office in the town. Everyone who is a Jew must be registered.

Mama tells Greta and me fictitious details about our "German father." Greta does not look worried when Mama does this, because to her this is the truth. For me, it is the burden of a secret.

Mama tells me later that the surname of Klaus belonged to someone who really lived once, and then died, and their identity was stolen by someone who makes fake identity cards. She says that without the "J" stamped on the cards, we will be safe. She says that she and Papa used all their spare money to purchase the papers without the "J."

• • •

Jonas, Rani, and I watch the German cars go past. It is getting cold again and we wear our coats and scarves and caps and try to sink into them to disappear. I feel sorry for both of them. They watch the cars as if they are watching their futures, as if all hope lies with the men who drive the cars. Rani lives with his grandparents. His father is dead and his mother left for Palestine and chose not to take him.

"Will you leave for Russia too?" I ask Rani. He does not look like most Jews. Rani has red hair, chocolate-brown eyes, and lots of freckles. He is smaller than many of us because he had an illness when he was small. The dark hollows beneath his eyes make him appear sickly. Though, when he plays soccer, his aim is perfect; he rarely misses a goal.

"No. My grandparents are too old to travel," he says.

I do not say that he might have to go. Something tells me he doesn't yet know, and I do not want to be the first to tell him. But Jonas does instead.

"You will have to go," says Jonas. "They will make you. Mama is home packing now."

Rani looks confused.

"But I don't want to go," he says. "I like it here."

I punch him on the arm to distract him, so he doesn't think too hard about it.

"It's all right. Jonas will carry your grandparents on his back and when the Germans move out again, he will carry them back."

Jonas throws his crust of bread at my head and I duck to miss it, and Rani is laughing.

I turn my head so he doesn't see what I am thinking. I am thinking that because of the hateful German army I am about to lose my friends. That life will not be the same without them.

It is Jonas's last day in Zamosc. He and I shake hands and he says he will see me when his family returns after the war.

CHAPTER 12

AUTUMN 1940

A member of the Judenrat—a Jewish council organized by the Germans to administer the work rosters and living arrangements of the Jews—arrives at our door and says that we must take in some Jews who have arrived from the west and require temporary accommodation until they are moved elsewhere.

Femke says that there is no room, but Mama interrupts and says that they are welcome to the space in the barn, and that we have extra blankets.

Many Jews have been removed from their apartments in the town to make way for the Germans who wish to live there now. Near the city, the area designated for Jewish housing is filling up fast, which is why we must house the family until the Germans can make more room.

The family of six enters our house. There is an older couple, their daughter and her husband, and their two boys, who are six years and four years.

Greta and I show the boys around the farm while Mama and Femke talk to the adults. The boys tell us that German soldiers told them to pack their things and leave their house, that someone else will be moving in there. They are sad that they couldn't find their cat before they left, and they think he might be walking around the streets and windowsills looking for them, crying and feeling very hungry. I tell them about Robin and how we had to leave her, and suddenly I am feeling very sad about our cat too. I don't tell them this, though. I only tell them about Robin so that they feel better about leaving their own cat.

Greta asks why they couldn't just stay there and why the Germans couldn't build their own places. The boys tell her that the Germans hate the Jews.

"It is ridiculous," says Greta. "We have the same skin and hair, and some of my friends are Jews."

The boys gaze at Greta as if she is an angel, as if they have never seen anything so heavenly. And in that moment I see it too. Despite the cold, she is radiant like the sun.

Rani's family has been moved to the designated area. There is talk that they will have to move again soon to a much older area. When next I see Rani, he is wearing an armband to show that he is a Jew. All the Jews have to wear one now. I am feeling like a fraud and thinking how Femke said it is still in my blood.

Many of the Jewish shops are closed and the occupants are now put to other work: cleaning, clearing land, and other labor tasks. They will soon be sent to dig anti-tank trenches. Rani's grandparents are two of those people but Rani stays at home while they are out. They have lied about his age. They say he is only thirteen so that he doesn't have to work. His grandmother doesn't think that he would last a week with the rattle in his chest.

But Rani says that his grandfather can hardly stand when he gets home, and his grandmother is too tired to eat. I have heard that many Jews have gone away, and some have escaped through the forest. I tell Rani that maybe he should escape too. I show him the route, which I found by accident one day. It is a pathway that leads into the forest and up to the north. I tell him that many have gone this way to other cities that are safer. That is what I heard, though I can't confirm it. I run home and tell Mama what I have suggested. She says I shouldn't have suggested that. "You don't know if where the others have gone to is any better. They might be caught and if they are—"

"They will be shot," says Femke. "The Germans have started the first executions of Jews who do not follow the rules. They don't care whether they are children or mothers or grandparents."

"That is impossible!" I say with disgust.

"It is true," says Femke. But she doesn't say it in a gloating way. There is softness in her voice. She is not happy about their treatment, despite her views on Papa.

On the following day, when I go back to the Jewish area, Rani's house is empty. The Jews have to report to the officers if, for whatever reason, they are to leave. I believe that Rani's grandparents have escaped while they were at work and that Rani has gone with them. Their little house, which is more like a shed and not fit to live in, has a broken door and a missing window. There is a small pile of wood on the floor. The house is cold and dark and bleak and not like the place they had before, which was bright and clean and warm.

Cupboards and drawers have been left open. I say a prayer to God to look after Rani's family. I don't need a church to do this, and it is just as well since the Germans do not like Catholics either.

Femke has asked me to take the bus to the town to see if there is anyone selling tea. There are shortages of food and, now with the Jews living in our barn, many of our supplies are drying up. Even Polish non-Jews are given restrictions and rules, and the Germans are greedily taking our supplies. We have only a few chickens left and no more pigs; we ate one of our cows and two have been stolen. We do not have the money to replace them.

An officer comes to our door. He is very polite. He compliments Mama and Femke on the farm and on how well they take care of the land. He wishes to take our milk for his officers. Femke is pleasant in return and the man keeps looking at Mama.

"Can I also trouble you for some eggs?" asks the officer, but it is not really a question.

"Of course," says Mama. Greta and I run to get some. We put only the small ones in the basket and hide the other ones under some hay. When we hand the eggs to the officer, he asks, "Are you sure there aren't more?"

"Yes," I say too quickly.

He looks at all of us, as if he is taking a mental photograph, and then he thanks us and leaves. Once the door is shut, Femke complains and stamps her feet.

"They take too much," she says. "How am I supposed to trade for other things once the milk and eggs run out?"

I tell her what Greta and I did with the eggs and she nods her head.

"You must take half of those into the town and see if you can trade them for tea."

Femke takes her milk to the mill in exchange for flour. She has not traded for any alcohol since the war started.

I take the bus to the town that used to look pretty but is no longer picturesque and colorful. The German vehicles and officers have covered the town in gray and black.

I notice that there is a group of people standing in the center of the marketplace. They have their hands tied behind their backs. Some are only children. As I get closer I see that one of them is Rani and I raise my hand to wave, but then I notice several German police officers who are standing there too.

Rani has seen me. He is pale and thin and ghostlike.

The officers are talking to the group, and there is also an interpreter from the Judenrat speaking Yiddish to Rani's grandparents, who do not speak Polish well. An officer begins to yell in German at the group. He is frightening with his hard, brittle words as he tells them they have not followed orders, that they are to be punished.

I stay back in the shadow of the building and watch, and many other people have moved back also, afraid to be caught up in whatever is happening. The officer is telling the group in the center that they must be an example to others so that no one else will try to escape. I am scared all of a sudden that they will be taken to the prison camps that we have heard about: where Jews are not allowed to leave, where they have to work all day, hammering stone.

Some of the older ones are ushered forward. Then one of the police officers walks over to them and—before I have even understood what is happening—shoots a man in the head. The man crumples to the ground. The officer moves to the next one and does the same and then the third. Then they bring more people forward and I am staring, stunned, unable to believe the brutality. It is as if I cannot wake from a nightmare. There are around twelve in all who have been shot, and then Rani's grandparents are brought forward. I see that Rani has screwed up his eyes and he cannot look. The other children are crying for their dead mamas and papas.

Someone else is pulling the bodies away and members of the Judenrat are piling them into the back of a truck, like waste, one on top of another. One member of the Judenrat does not flinch like the others who squeeze their eyes and lips closed when someone is shot. I wonder how hard that man's heart must have grown for him to do such a job, to betray his fellow Jews.

Rani's grandfather is on his knees and he is crying and begging for his wife and grandson to be saved. His wife is kneeling beside him and then it is over. Rani has heard but he has not seen. He will not look. Then there are just the four children, who are screaming.

The officer is angry and tells the other soldiers that children must be shot first in the future. One of the children starts to run away and is shot in the back, and then the officer marches several yards to where the child has fallen, stands above him, and shoots again. The other children are dragged to the center and told to stand still. The girl is whimpering, and the boy is wailing: loud wails that hurt my ears. There are two more shots and then it is just Rani, who has not moved and has his eyes closed still.

I start to rush forward but am grabbed on the arm by a boy some years older than me.

"Are you crazy?" he asks. "Where do you think you are going?"

"He is my friend."

"They will kill you too if you try and intervene."

"But I am a Jew."

"Be quiet!" he says. "You don't need to tell *them*!" The officer walks to Rani and pulls the trigger and Rani falls to the ground, as if he is playacting. The fall is graceful and gentle, like everything else he did in life.

I drop the basket and almost let out a scream but the larger boy has grabbed me around the chest and has his other hand over my mouth. He drags me down the street and behind a building, and keeps his hand in place until I stop resisting. He is big and strong and I am no match.

"Listen," he says. "Their time will come. For now you have to be patient. You have to do as they say." When he sees that I have gone still, he releases me and walks away.

I walk back into the square, and Rani's body has already been discarded into the truck, which is leaving. I pull my cap over my face and notice that the eggs from my basket lie broken on the ground.

When I am home, I tell the others what I saw. I do not care this time if Greta and the smaller ones hear me, for they must know, though Greta still does not know our secret. She cannot. Mama says I must not go alone to the market anymore. I have no appetite and no more tears. The boys and Greta come to my room. Greta rubs my back. She has tears in her eyes for Rani.

The boys are silent. Greta does not say what is in her eyes, not in front of the boys, but she tells me later that she is relieved that we are not Jews, that it is one less thing for Mama to worry about.

Mama bakes the bread and we are given smaller portions to feed everyone.

"But this is not enough," I say. "I am so hungry. How am I supposed to grow taller?"

Everyone stares at me except the older Jews, who look down at their plates. The grandfather passes me some of his but Mama stops him.

"No," says Mama to the newcomers. "Don't feel bad."

I storm into my room with my stomach aching, and I throw myself on the bed. Mama follows me in and lies beside me. She wraps her arms around me and squeezes me.

It has been weeks since I saw Rani killed, and I do not like Poland anymore. I tell her that I wish we had never left Germany, that it would have been safer there. But I don't mean what I say. It is the hunger talking.

Mama tells me to keep my voice down—even the Jews who are living in our barn do not know our origins.

"People know us in Berlin," says Mama. "You would have been given away. No one here knew of Emmett or his background."

I look down at Mama's arms that are wrapped around me and have grown so thin, and remember then that Mama has less food than everyone else.

"Mama, I will try not to complain anymore."

"Oh, my poor boy!" she says. "I am so sorry for everything. I wish that the world were not like this. I wish for you to know a fair world . . . to have a childhood without worry, without hunger."

I fall asleep and when I wake she is gone.

CHAPTER 13

1941

Femke comes home with more news from the town center. It seems that all of the Jews have now been transported to the old Jewish area, where the buildings aren't safe. They have to live in squalor, Femke says, and I remember Rani's house. She also tells us that some of them will be shipped to special camps away from the towns.

Femke recently acquired several new chickens. She and Mama are growing cabbages and spinach and tomatoes in the fields. We have to be careful with the tea but at least there is food. Femke says that she has heard from another person in the town that the camps are not what everyone thinks: that you never come out again. There are rumors that they are killing hundreds of Jews at a time.

Mama says that it is too horrific, that she doesn't believe it. The Jewish family says that they don't believe it either, that no one could be that appalling. Though it sounds too incredible, I remember the shooting in the square and I am not certain of anything anymore.

One evening, there is a knock at the door. A member of the Judenrat is there to reassign the Jewish family, but he tells us to keep the barn available in case there are more people to house. I don't know why anyone would want to live in the barn.

Femke asks where the family is being taken. The official says they are going to the camps.

"Right away?" Femke sounds incredulous.

"Yes," says the young man. "I have my orders."

Behind him is a cattle truck. Through the slats along the side I see many Jewish families standing. There is barely room enough for the ones already in there.

"You mean to say they are being shipped in that?"

"Yes," says the official, a little more impatiently.

I scan the faces and see that one of the people in the back of the truck is my teacher from school. He does not look at me. He is standing at the very back, staring at the road behind and holding a small suitcase, as if he is off to work. I want to catch his attention to wave at him, but he does not look our way.

"Well, maybe they can wait for the next one, where there is room to sit down," says Femke.

The young man goes to the truck and comes back with a German officer.

"What is the problem?" asks the officer.

"The family won't fit in there," Femke says.

"There is enough room."

"Why don't you just leave them alone! They've done nothing to you," she says. He ignores her and calls the names of our barn family from his list, telling them to get their belongings.

I have never seen Femke behave like this, as if she cares what will happen to them.

Mama and Femke escort the family to the door and wish them well. We have got used to the boys playing in the paddocks and the whole family joining us at mealtimes. During the day, the adults have been used for labor and they are thin and worn from the hard work. During the evenings, the father of the boys has been building Femke and Mama a large dining table and extra chairs, in appreciation of their generosity.

The boys are teary and say they don't want to leave. Greta gives them a hug and tells them they are very nice and she would like to see them again one day soon.

As the truck pulls away, Femke doesn't move from the door. Another cattle truck goes past, also crammed with Jews.

"Now are we better off?" she says sarcastically, shaking her head. She looks in the direction of the second truck.

"Bastards!" she says.

After the trucks have gone, Femke stays at the door. It is as if Medusa has turned her to stone.

I ask Mama later why Femke was so protective of the family.

"She is human like the rest of us. She believes in fairness. What is happening to them is not fair."

1942

We are having cabbage and onion pie. It is delicious. Femke has used plenty of salt. We wash it down with coffee that Femke has smuggled in from the Jewish quarter in exchange for milk and bread. We have bought more seed and another hen with the last of Mama's money.

We have not had to house any more Jews, since they are taken elsewhere now. My friend Jasper, the Catholic, and his family were told to leave the house his father built, and they have left for Lublin. One of the boys from school has signed up to work for the Germans. When I ask him why, he says that it is inevitable that we will fight alongside the Germans since they are now our rulers and they will rule the whole of Europe soon.

This makes me angry and I tell him that he is a simpleton. He kicks me in the leg and I hit him in the jaw. The next thing we are punching each other on the ground. It is my first fight in Poland. We are stopped by others who are standing close by.

When I arrive home, I tell Mama about the fight but she doesn't get angry. Femke looks at me curiously.

"It is good to fight for what you believe in, but be careful you don't get yourself killed."

"Your aunt is right," says Mama. "It was brave, what you did, but you cannot let your temper get the better of you."

Then she brushes the hair from my eyes. "You are so like your father, Henrik. You are so passionate."

I do not know what to feel when she says this, but it calms me a little to know it.

Femke comes back from the Jewish area. She often calls at the homes of people she knows to take them some milk, but she no longer asks for anything in return. It seems she has grown attached to some of them. It seems that she has a side that we rarely see.

She is flustered. Her neck is red and her eyes are tormented. There are even tears in her eyes, which I have never seen before. Mama makes her a cup of tea so that she can relax and find her breath.

"Greta," I say, "go to the barn and feed the chickens."

"But I don't want to go. I always have to go!"

I tell her that she must, that it is important, that she can ride my bike whenever I'm not using it.

Once Greta is gone, Femke starts to talk. She tells us what she has seen in the dilapidated Jewish quarter. She says it is worse than anything she has ever seen, and that she witnessed the greatest cruelty just when she thought it could not get any worse.

She says that all the Jews have had to leave for camps to make room for more who will be coming to the Jewish quarter. She says they were herded into the marketplace like cattle and left there for hours, then forced onto the train with only the few possessions they could carry. She saw people shot after they protested that they would not go. She saw children and women die, and even babies.

Femke covers her eyes as if this will block out the images, but I know that it won't. Every day I see Rani's eyes and the look on his face before he died. There is nothing that can block it out.

Mama says it is a disgrace. I see that she is shaking as much as Femke.

"What is to become of us?" says Femke. She grabs Mama's wrist. "You must never tell Greta who she is. It will never be safe."

"One day," I cry in anger, "I will announce it to the world that I am a Jew!"

"Stop it," says Mama. "Please, Henrik, not now. You must control your temper. You must never shout such a thing again. Who knows who will hear it?"

"I don't care."

Mama asks where the people are to be taken. Femke gathered from the gossip in the market that they will be stuffed into overcrowded camps, or possibly killed before they even arrive there.

Chapter 14

The sun is hot on my shoulders. I lean against the fence near the paddocks and draw a picture of the barn. I can hear Greta inside, talking to the chickens. Sometimes we take them into the forest in boxes to hide them from the Germans and the Judenrat.

It is quiet on this day, which makes it all the more strange when I hear the sounds of a motorcar slowing down in the lane at the front of our house. I close up my drawing book and go through the back door to peer from our front window.

A German car idles directly outside our house. Mama is at the side of the house, hanging washing. It is nearly the end of the summer and she is keen to catch all the sunrays that she can for drying. Mama doesn't turn to look at them, perhaps pretending she doesn't see them, and hoping they will drive on.

We have made good use of the farm. Several times, officials have inspected it and approved our work. I think today is another inspection, though these people are different from the others who have come. The motorcar is newer than others I've seen. It is long, shiny, and black and has the Nazi flag on the front. I can see through the glass that the men in the front wear patches on their collars. Two officers are sitting in the front and one in the back.

Many Poles have had to vacate their apartments in the towns and their houses in the villages because truckloads of Germanic Poles have been arriving lately, and they need somewhere to live. These German people who are colonizing Poland are called the *Volksdeutsche*. Some of the local Poles who are not German *enough* have had to leave on foot. We are the lucky ones. It is because of the farm. It is because we are putting food back into the community. Though, at the last inspection, Femke was told that the empty field beside the house will have to be handed in since she does not have as many cows as she did when her father was alive. It will be used for another building site. Mama has told Femke not to protest; otherwise, the Germans might take all of it.

The three men look to the side of the house. They have seen Mama, which I believe is why they have stopped here, because they do not appear interested in looking at the house. My heart is racing. I do not like Mama to be alone and watched. As the men emerge from the vehicle, I walk outside and try and stand as tall as I can. I have grown much taller than Mama, tall for my sixteen years, but still I wish to be as tall as Papa. The men see me and walk towards me to shake my hand.

"This must be the man of the farm," they say, but there is no warmth in these words and I have grown so used to Polish that their German sounds foreign to me.

Mama has seen the car and walks to stand beside me. Two of the men take off their hats. Mama is wearing an orange sundress with straps that tie at the shoulders. She has long graceful arms that are tinted a pale shade of brown, from the sun. Her hair is not done up, not like it was in Germany. It floats about her like yellow streamers.

"Are you the owner of the farm, Frau . . . ?"

"Klaus. My sister and I own the farm."

The third man from the back is checking something on a clipboard. He is going through some names.

"She is here," he confirms.

"And this is your boy?" asks the officer.

"Yes," says Mama.

"It says here there is a daughter," says the third. There is something about this comment that sounds premeditated and Mama has sensed it too. There is a delay before she answers.

"Was," says my mama. "She died recently." And I am suddenly frightened for her that she has lied. I have already seen their methods of punishment for deceit.

The man checks his records. "You need to advise us if there are changes in circumstances," he says. "You need to register the death with the Gestapo."

"I am very sorry," says Mama. "We have been so busy and it was unexpected . . ."

"Do you have the documentation?"

"Mama," I say, before she has a chance to lie further. "Do you want me to fetch it for you?" I have no idea where or how I can produce such fake evidence but stealing the attention from my mother is the only thing I can think of to do.

"Not yet," says the first officer sharply, the one who does not take off his hat. "What happened to your husband?"

"He died in Germany, which is why my children and I returned here."

"Oh, that's a pity. So much death," he says with false sincerity. "What did he do?"

"He was a tram driver in Berlin," says Mama, "until they cancelled some of the lines." The third officer is taking notes.

"Must have been difficult, and such a shame to be widowed so young."

"What is it that you want?" asks Femke, who has walked outside. I sense that she has been listening to the conversation, that she now wants them to get to the point of their visit.

"Our purpose is to make sure that the residents here remain loyal to our leader. We are recruiting for our orientation centers, specifically designed to help the Germanic Poles reacquaint themselves with their German origins. It is especially important for the design of the country."

The officer who speaks is tall with light brown hair and light gray eyes. He wears the gray uniform, and a badge with three leaves is on his collar. His trousers balloon over the tops of his boots, which have been recently polished. The second officer has a badge with only two leaves and the third wears an insignia that looks like lightning bolts.

I hate the first man. He looks at Mama as if he wants to eat her. I do not like the way he pouts his thick, rubbery lips as he speaks, or the lack of sincerity in his tone. His uniform does not make him respectable.

"Well, as you can see," says Femke, "we speak perfect German. Our parents loved Germany . . . Our father was born there, and we are faithful to the Führer."

"Sure you are," says the German with the three leaves unconvincingly. His movements are relaxed and unhurried; it appears he has much time to contend with matters here. He directs his speech to Femke.

"You keep your farm well and we are appreciative of your support. But there is always room for improvement. We are looking for loyal German women for our programs. Your beautiful sister here would be perfect."

"No, please . . ." Mama's clear voice has broken slightly. "I have my son . . . and my sister needs me here." But Femke is calmer and talking smoothly, as if she is one of them.

"What are these programs for?"

"They are wonderful houses with beautiful kitchens. Women are taught so many things. It is a gift and an honor to be selected for them."

Mama is frowning and has taken a step closer to Femke and me.

"Well, I would say that there are plenty of intelligent women from your own country you can employ. My sister looks good, but she does not make for a good wife. She follows the tasks I set for her but she cannot cook, she is a terrible mother, and she does not remember things well. You don't need her."

I understand why Femke is talking falsely. She wants to meet them on their own slippery, slithery, snakelike terms. She wants them to think that she knows as much as they do, that she understands their needs, that she is one of them.

"You don't understand, obviously, that we wouldn't be standing here if we didn't need her."

"Then tell your Führer that my sister is honored by the offer, I am sure, but she is not available. I need her here so that we can keep producing the food that keeps your officers' bellies full."

I can feel much danger in the air and it is dawning on me suddenly that they are talking about taking Mama somewhere far away, perhaps so far that I will never see her again. I put my arm around her.

"You cannot take my mother."

The first officer laughs and the other two respond with grins, though the lightning bolt—the youngest of the three—appears more nervous than amused.

"You look like you are a loving family but we would take even better care of her. She would have more attention."

I step forward then and the officer with only two leaves, who is much shorter and wider than the first, steps towards me.

"Do not do anything foolish, boy!"

The lightning bolt addresses the first man as Herr General and says that perhaps it would be better if they left her and found someone more suitable. That there are still many more places to inspect today, that she is already Volksdeutsche and such persons are needed here.

The general views Mama carefully with his roaming eyes. "She is perhaps too old for the program anyway," he says. "Very well, ladies," and this time he nudges his hat briefly, but that is all. He still does not raise it. The women here are not worthy of his respect. The lightning bolt tells Mama that she must bring documentation of her daughter's death to their office in Zamosc by morning so they can record this in their register.

The men turn away and I sigh inwardly with relief that we have until then to decide what to do. We stand there watching them, since there is nothing else we can do and we are afraid to turn our backs.

"Mama! Mama!" yells Greta from inside the house. "We have new chicks."

There is no time to turn, no time to hide. Greta comes out of the house and stops dead when she sees the car.

"You lied?" says the general viciously to Mama. He then turns to Greta, who takes a step backwards.

The first officer walks briskly towards her and bends down to speak close to her face. We are too afraid to move—we have seen their guns. We have seen what these can do.

"What is your name?" he asks.

"Greta."

"Is this your mama?"

Greta does not need to turn around. "Yes."

"You are very beautiful."

Greta smiles and lowers her head graciously. She is smart. She has seen the way everyone is standing like statues, and she has smelled the fear, but she does not look at me in case that would give her own fear away. She knows she must play along.

"And what is your name?" Greta asks squarely.

The first officer turns to the second and laughs a second time. "What an amazing young girl you are. But you don't need to know my name. Did you know that I have a very important job?"

"No."

"Well, I take young girls and women to live in beautiful cities. The girls there are fed cake and sewn new dresses. The beds are soft and it is always warm in these houses. Do you get cold here, Greta?"

"Sometimes." Greta is always honest.

"Do you want to go someplace where you will have everything you want?"

"No," says Greta firmly. "I like it here." The smile on the officer's face is fixed, shallow, and cold.

I don't think I have loved Greta more than I do at that moment. She has been a loyal soldier and now she has grown to be a warrior princess also.

Lightning Bolt looks nervous. Two Leaves whispers something in the ear of the general, who nods.

"Well then, I think that since the mother is not coming, then we must look to the child, who will no doubt grow to be more beautiful than the mother."

"You will not take her!" says Mama. All frailty from her voice is gone, replaced with the voice of a lioness: low and angry.

The officer holds out his hand to Greta but she does not take it. She turns then and the second officer swoops and grabs her around her middle before she can run.

"Don't do this!" cries Mama. "Leave her! I will go instead."

"Too late," says the general flatly. Mama runs after the officer holding Greta and hits him on the arm. I try to take Greta but the lightning bolt grabs me from behind. I kick him between the legs but then feel a fist to my stomach. The second officer has done this with one arm while he holds Greta in the other.

Mama is hitting him in the face so that he will drop Greta. Femke pulls at Greta's legs but then the third officer holds back Femke's arms. I lie winded on the ground and Femke is restrained.

Suddenly, there is a sound like a crack. The crop that the Nazi general has in his hand is raised in the air so he can strike again, and I see that Mama has fallen on the ground. There is blood oozing from a cut to her face. Femke escapes the arms of the officer and rushes to her sister's side. I rise and run towards the car. Greta is thrown into the backseat while the third officer hurries around to climb in beside her from the other side so that she cannot escape. She is crying and kicking at the door to stop it from closing and one of them has thrown a blanket over the top of her to muffle her screams.

As I get closer to the car, the door closes and the second officer drives the car away. I run after it and see that Greta is restrained in the backseat. She frees herself for just a moment and turns to look at me through the rear window. There is a look of terror and helplessness on her face. I run fast to reach her, hoping the car will stop, but it speeds away.

Something is thrown out of the window. As I approach, I see it is Greta's silver locket. It is lying open on the road and Papa looks out from his photo as if he is a witness to what has happened.

Finally the car is out of my view, but I can still see Greta's face in my mind. Her melancholy and fear have travelled behind the car to reach me. I pick up the locket and start back towards the house, bereft, despairing, and angry. I must get Femke's truck. I must travel in the direction of the town. I sprint home.

When I arrive at our house, there is no sign of Femke or Mama outside, or in the living room. I go to Femke's room and she is sitting beside Mama on the bed.

It seems that when Mama fell to the ground, she hit her head and became unconscious, and she is just now coming around. Femke has Mama in a sitting position against the headboard. She has a damp cloth across Mama's forehead and with another she is dabbing at Mama's wound, which extends from the top of Mama's left eye and across the bridge of her nose to her cheek. There are splatters of blood on the front of Mama's dress.

Femke's hands are trembling badly. Mama is murmuring. I sit on the other side of the bed and hold Mama's hand.

"Mama, can you hear me?"

Mama's eyes are open slightly. She tries to speak but I cannot understand the words. I lean my head in and still I do not understand.

She raises her left arm across her body to touch me, but her right arm lies idle. She cannot open her lips to speak. Then she closes her eyes again and does not respond to any more questions.

Femke calls me from the room and shuts the door. Her eyes are wild and crazy.

"Listen, you need to see Mr. Lubieniecki. Tell him to get the doctor."

"The doctor has gone. He was taken to the camps."

"Just do it," says Femke. "He is hiding in the house." I am amazed that Femke knows this and that I don't. I am amazed at how much adults know. I look at her, mouth open. I know that if the doctor is found he will be taken to the camp.

"Don't stand there," she says. "Go! Run!"

I run from the house and across the field to our neighbor's house. I run fast. I know it is fast because the teachers at school often commented on my lean sprinter's legs, and I have two "first" ribbons from our school sports day, which happened just before the Germans came.

Erek Lubieniecki is a farmer also, though he has no livestock left. When they died, he could not afford to replace them. Now he grows lettuces.

I knock on the door and Jana Lubieniecki answers. She is the farmer's daughter. She never liked me at school. She used to say that I was a show-off, that I liked myself too much.

"What do you want?" she asks. There is just a hint of hostility in the question.

"I need to speak to the doctor."

Jana blinks several times quickly and her lips work back and forth soundlessly. "There is no doctor here. Only my father and mother."

"But my aunt says the doctor is here. He is hiding."

Mr. Lubieniecki's large frame suddenly fills up the space in the doorway. I believe he has already heard our conversation but pretends he has not.

"What do you want, Henrik?" he says softly, carefully. He is a gentle man, and I have never heard him say a loud word to his wife or daughter or even the animals on the farm. Behind him is a small dog, which follows him everywhere. As I go to speak, a large sob escapes my mouth instead, followed by a flood of tears.

"There, there," he says and he is soothing, like Papa. His hand is gentle on my back as he leads me to the living room. The furniture is old and the windows are covered with newspaper instead of curtains.

"Jana, fetch a glass of water," he says. Jana turns reluctantly and returns with a glass as I finally compose myself. I am ashamed that I have broken down, that they have seen me like this, but I am also relieved that I have not done this in front of Femke, because she would call me weak.

"Tell me everything," he says. And I do. It all comes out. All the sadness, missing my cat, Robin, Papa dead, Greta taken—though I stammer sometimes, and speak too quickly. My words pour out like water, even the fact that Papa was a Jew—everything—and finally about Mama, about her cut, about her lack of speech. And then I have run out of breath and Mr. Lubieniecki is watching me intently, and I am suddenly fearful that I have said too much, that perhaps Aunt Femke is wrong and there is no doctor.

"It is safe," he says. "Not a word will be spoken about what you have said. You have my word."

He reaches forward to pat me on the shoulder and I find I can breathe again. He tells me that we both have secrets that we need to keep, that by sharing our secrets, we are bound as brothers. I nod.

"Now, go home and tell your aunt that the doctor will come tonight. I will make sure of it. But not now. It is not safe in the daylight hours."

I nod again.

When I get home, Femke is sitting on a chair. She has her head in her hands. She tells me not to disturb Mama for a while, but I open the door to look at her. She is still sitting, but her head is turned and her mouth is open in sleep, drooping, spittle on her bottom lip.

"Femke, I must take the truck to the town. I must find Greta."

I have been learning to drive the truck around the paddock. Femke has taught me so that I am more useful, so that I can deliver things down the road. More and more lately, her back has been giving her "difficulty."

"No, you don't," she says. "You will not get her back. They will shoot you if you try."

"But I have to."

"No!" she shouts. "Do you want to get yourself killed? And then your mama loses both her children."

I do not want her to see me cry and I go to my room and slam the door. I lie on the bed and cry into the pillow. I cry harder when I smell Greta's hair on the linen: tangy, like rain on grass.

I have no appetite. When I come back out, the rest of the house is in darkness. There is an empty vodka bottle on the table and Femke has fallen asleep with her head resting next to it. I wonder where she has got the bottle from, where perhaps she keeps others, since the local distillery has been closed for many weeks.

There is a knock at the door. It is so quiet that I think at first it is nothing, a creak in the wall. Then I hear it again. When I open the door, the doctor is standing there. He wears a long dark coat, too warm for such a night, and a hat.

Femke wakes up groggily, and then she sees him and is suddenly alert. She pulls the curtains closed before igniting a lamp.

"Thank you for coming."

"I have learned the circumstances from Erek. It must have been terrible." But he says this remotely, as if he has said it many times before. He has probably seen worse things.

Femke waves him inside the house. I remember him. I remember that he has been to our house before, how he treated Greta for a cut to the foot that was infected. And then the Germans came and he was not allowed to practice anymore. That was the last time I heard about him. We thought he had gone. Well, *I* thought he had gone. Femke knew. I now wonder if there are others also hiding whom she has not told me about.

He takes his black bag into Femke's room and checks Mama's heart while she is sleeping. Mama murmurs slightly but she does not appear to wake.

"Out," says Femke.

The doctor does not turn but says, "The boy can stay if he wants to."

He shines a light into Mama's eyes.

"She should be in a hospital," he says. "She has had a stroke."

"What's that?" I ask.

"It's a brain injury. It means that there is a blockage somewhere, stopping blood to the brain."

"We can't go to the hospital," says Femke.

"She is not a Jew. They will probably admit her."

Femke explains that race is not the issue in this case, that she and Mama have kept hold of the farm because they are useful. The sick have to be hidden, she explains. The sick are not part of the German plan. If the Judenrat knows there are now only two people—Femke and me—working our farm, they might put in a larger German family to fill up the space.

He nods to show that he understands. "But she needs rehabilitation and full-time care."

"How bad is it?"

"She may have full recovery but it could be some months. Or she could get worse. Brain injuries are complex and often difficult to cure. Sometimes they repair themselves over time, sometimes they don't. Has she said anything?"

"No," says Femke.

The doctor shakes his head, then takes a small packet out of his bag. He explains that it is sulfa powder. He opens the packet and spreads the medicine across the wound on her face. Mama doesn't move.

"Do you have any iodine?" asks the doctor.

"Yes," says Femke.

"You need to apply the powder again tomorrow and the next day, and then after that, iodine every day. I am sorry I have nothing else. You may need to try the pharmacy in town. Purchase some aspirin . . . say you have bad headaches. They will help too.

"You should encourage her to talk . . . Talk regularly to her to keep her mind stimulated. You also need to bend her legs to exercise them, and take her out into the sun."

Femke follows him to the door.

"I will come back tomorrow night to check on her. I'm sorry . . . there is nothing else I can do."

Femke pushes a banknote into his hand but he shakes his head. She puts some bread and cheese in a bag and he takes this, nodding appreciatively, as if he is the one in debt. Femke turns off the light before he leaves.

After the doctor is gone, Femke tells me that he is hiding in the Lubienieckis' cellar, under the stairs, with his young wife. Femke tells me that our barn doors are open and says to go and close them.

When I return, Femke's bedroom door is shut and I listen through the wall. Femke is whispering to Mama about how much she loves her, and I can hear the tears in her voice. She is telling Mama to remember how the two of them played in the fields and rode horses when they were younger.

It is the following day and Femke has Mama propped up on pillows. Mama has her eyes open but she does not say anything—just stares miserably, vacantly.

"Hello, Mama," I say, and hug her, but she does not hug me back. It is as if someone has stolen her life and left a sack of cotton in its place.

I notice that there is a silver object on the table. Femke explains that the Germans must have dropped it. I look on the side of the lighter and see the initials "DW." I flick it on and a tall flame erupts.

"Can I have it?"

"I suppose," says Femke with disinterest. "I don't want anything which belonged to those bastards." I am fascinated by the lighter and despise it at the same time. I also feel attached to it because it is a link to my sister. I keep it in my pocket and try to guess the owner's name.

CHAPTER 15

Over the next few days Femke and I take turns looking after Mama. We mash her food so that she can swallow it better and we dab her wound with iodine. I grab both ankles and, while she is lying on her back, I bend her knees up and down, like she is walking or cycling. When Femke washes Mama, I am not allowed to be in the room.

I read to Mama some of my books from Germany. Sometimes I make up my own stories. I show her my many drawings. There is one I have drawn of Rani sitting on the fence. He is looking in the distance, his hair catching the breeze. I stop at this one and study it, remembering. Then I get to one of Greta. She is sleeping, her hair strewn upwards across the pillow, her lips pouting even in sleep, her little nose curling at the tip, and her fingers gripping the pillow as if it is going somewhere and she must stop it.

There is another one of Greta. She smiles in this one. I remember I made her sit still and she watched me while I drew her, her large, round eyes curious but calm. There is a slight smile on her lips, as if at any moment she will burst into laughter at something I say. I am remembering a game where I say a word to her and no matter what I say, no matter how funny it is, she is not allowed to laugh. I say "bird" and she bursts into laughter every time. She never gets past the first word.

I go to turn the page to the next drawing and suddenly Mama grabs me with her good arm; her fingers are tightly gripping my wrist.

She is looking at the picture of Greta. There are tears coming out of her eyes. Femke has said not to talk about Greta, has said that it upsets Mama, but I want to talk about her. I pin the picture up on the wall so that Mama can see Greta whenever she wants.

I remind Mama of games that Greta and I used to play and tell her of things that she didn't know we did. Mama wants to hear these things and she stares expectantly, hanging on to every sound from my mouth.

Femke tries to get Mama to talk. Mama's mouth twitches but she won't speak. The scar is a thick scab across the center of her face. Sometimes it hurts me to look at it.

Mama is standing now and walking a bit. Though it is more of a shuffle than a walk. She can walk to the kitchen and she picks up things that weigh very little. Gradually, over days, she begins to help Femke in the kitchen. She does not talk. Although she has tried, her speech is slurred. Femke tells me not to encourage her to talk anymore, because she is embarrassed that she cannot make full sounds. What comes out is half a word, as if it has suddenly frozen halfway through while she is speaking. When she doesn't talk, her face looks normal; however, when she tries to move her lips, half of her face is motionless.

It is this that the doctor says might be permanent or could become better over time. Sometimes at night, I can hear Mama sounding out words in the dark, where no one can see her strange face. But it is not just this change to her face that is most noticeable about her. It is that the light from her eyes has gone, as if their color has been stripped away.

Mama can use the peeling knife with her good hand and hold the potato in her bad one. It takes her several minutes to do each one.

One time when I enter the house, Mama is standing at the sink in front of the little window, washing lettuce. I can see her profile and with the light shining behind her, she looks perfect, as she did before the accident. She is dressed plainly in a black skirt with a cream-colored blouse. She is tall and slender, her pale hair pushed to the back of her neck with a silver clasp. I imagine for a moment what my father must have done when he first saw her. He would have stood mesmerized, like I am doing now.

Two weeks pass and I become restless. After my chores, I wander around the fields until I am at the Lubienieckis' farm. Mr. Lubieniecki asks if I want to help him plant some crops. His last crop was completely taken by the Germans.

It seems a waste to spend so much time, knowing that all the crops will be taken again. I say this.

"I live in hope," he says. "Besides, as long as we grow something, they think us useful and we don't have to leave."

I nod in agreement solemnly. It is like that for everyone. After we finish this task, I come back and do odd jobs. He does not pay me but feeds me, and I think that this is good: there is more food now for Mama and Femke since I won't take as much.

One day in the forest behind our farms he teaches me how to shoot a rifle. He draws targets on the trees and I have to aim. I miss for the first few lessons and then one day I fail to miss at all. He says that I am a fast learner. He pats my head and I remember that Papa used to do that too. Mrs. Lubieniecki is also kind but their daughter still doesn't like me. She says that I was a clown in class and does not like that I come around so often.

At dinner with Mama and Femke, it is always silent. I am not allowed to talk about Greta. Femke says that it is part of the healing and that Mama must get better physically before she is mentally strong enough to talk about her absent daughter. I do not understand this. Femke does not understand that Greta, Mama, and I were together before she became part of our family.

One time I feel so mad towards Femke when she tells me that I am a silly boy for dropping a plate.

"It was an accident," I say.

"It does not change the fact that you are a silly boy."

I hate her at the moment. I think she is mean and tell her that I wish the Germans would take her away in a truck.

Mama looks wide-eyed and shocked. I walk from the room and look for a photo of Greta in a shoebox full of photos from our past—a past that did not include Femke. I take out a photo of Mama and Greta beside a lake. In the photo Greta is laughing at something Mama is whispering to her. I go to show Mama, but before Mama can reach for the picture, Femke snatches it away.

"No!" Femke shrieks, and tears the photo down the middle.

Mama stands up to defend me. She puts her hand up to silence Femke. "Stop it!" she says, which comes out as if it is one word and without the sound of the "t" at the end. But this all happens in a second and in the next Mama has lost her footing, her feet slipping out in front of her, and she falls back hard on the floor on her tailbone.

Femke rushes over to her while she continues to shriek at me.

"See what you have done!"

I want to say that it isn't my fault. But it is. Tears well up in my eyes and I fight hard to keep my emotions under control. Before they spill over, I run out the door, leaving it open, and head into the fields. I kick at the palings of our fence until they split and until my rage subsides.

It is as if Femke wants to erase the memory of Greta. How can anyone forget? I weep for my mother but also for my little sister: loud, fleshy sobs. I miss her so much and there are so many tears it is as if the grief has filled me to the top of my head and is now overflowing. I miss the way Greta would follow me around. I miss the way she tried to copy everything I did and often failed. I miss the way she would tell my stories as if the events of my life were her own. At the time I would get angry at her about this and call her a liar to make her look ridiculous. I would give all my stories and adventures to her now if she would just come back.

After the tears have ended, I return home. There are no lights on and I let myself in through the back door, where the lock is broken. I hear snoring coming from Femke's room. Mama is back in the room with me.

I flick the German's lighter to see if my mother is sleeping. She is lying awake, her eyes staring out at me curiously, childlike. In her hands, she is clutching the two halves of the torn photo. Her face is pink and her eyes are puffy. She puts her arm out to me like she would always do when I was a small boy waking in the night after a bad dream. I climb into bed beside her, my back nestled into her body, and she places her good arm around me tightly. I am enjoying the warmth of her—my body is cold from the night air. I fall asleep and we stay like that into morning.

When I walk into the living area the next morning, I know that Femke has seen us. She doesn't say anything, and I feel pity that she will never fully understand what it is to be loved and forgiven, then loved even more.

CHAPTER 16

We receive a visit from someone Femke knows in the village. Anuska is a Polish Catholic who has lived in Zamosc her whole life. Her children have grown up and moved away. One of them died fighting the Germans at the beginning of the war. Anuska seems to know a lot of things. She keeps us informed. Femke thinks that she could be a spy for the Polish resistance. There is also a rumor that one of her sons is a partisan, that he is responsible for killing Germans and blowing up one of their trucks.

Femke offers her some tea. It is clear that Anuska wants to talk to Femke, but she looks my way. I am surprised by Femke's response this time.

"It is all right," she says. "He can listen."

I feel something close to gratefulness. So many times I have been called a stupid boy.

"I've heard some things," says Anuska. "It is about Greta. She is not the only one who has been taken. I have heard of others across Poland—young women and children, stolen. Have you heard of something called *Eindeutschung*? Children are adopted by Nazi Party members in Poland, to propel the Aryan race. They are taken to orientation centers where they are assessed to see how German they can become.

"Children's racial characteristics are examined. Some who are not German enough are sent to the camps, rather than being returned home. Others are sent to Germany and other countries to be adopted by Nazis, or placed in breeding programs. This is what I have heard but I don't know how true it is.

"I have heard that some of Hitler's officers steal children for themselves . . . and women too."

"That's ridiculous," says Femke.

Anuska shrugs her shoulders and pulls down the corners of her mouth. "That's what I heard."

Femke is unconvinced but I am absorbing every part of this story. It is possible that it is true, because the Germans do many things that we don't expect.

"The children from here . . . where are they taken, do you think?"

"There are camps in the east and the south for the ones they don't want, and the ones they want are sent to the west . . . whether to Cracow first or Lodz, I am not certain."

"And the general who was here . . . do you know where he is from?" I ask.

Femke shoots me a look and then turns away before Anuska has seen. My aunt does not want me to talk freely. She does not want my thoughts voiced. She does not trust anyone, not even Anuska. But Anuska is keen to deliver information.

"Cracow."

"Do you know his name?"

She shakes her head. "No, but someone overheard him giving orders to bring news to Cracow. That's all I know."

After Anuska is gone, I say, "I can go, Femke. I will take the train."

"You will be questioned if you take the train."

"On foot then."

"You are crazy like your mother. There is no safe way."

"But what if I leave through the forest and come in to Cracow from the north?"

"I have heard that the Russians are hiding in the forests. It is dangerous. They will shoot you before they question you."

"Russians?" Whether the Russians are on our side or not depends on who you talk to.

"It is wilderness in there; you will never make it."

But she says this with neither passion nor ridicule—as if she no longer cares, as if she no longer wants to control what I do.

I brush Mama's hair and tie it in a knot, like she used to wear it. It is not exactly like she had it—it is not as tight and neat—but it is pulled back from her face to expose its heart shape. The scar does not look as angry as it did. It is slowly fading into her skin.

I am so tired that I fall asleep beside her. When I wake up, she is lying on her side, facing me, her eyes watery.

"I love you, Mama," I say.

I wipe away her tears with the back of my hand. She nods that she loves me too.

I take Mama a bowl of soup because she does not wish to leave her bed today. I sit on the side of the bed but she does not reach for the bowl. She is not hungry. As I begin to leave, she suddenly grips my arm. I look at her hand—the one on her bad arm. It is much stronger now, her grip firmer.

"Get Greta," she says. I think she has heard what Anuska said. I think she has heard what I said to Femke.

I do not tell Femke, even though I am bursting with the news that Mama has spoken clearly. She does not say anything after this but I am forming a plan. In Femke's cupboard there is a map of train lines and roads in Poland. When Femke is out milking our last remaining cow, I study the map, but it is not detailed. I have no idea how long it will take me to get to Cracow or how to find my way through the forest.

Into my knapsack I put a dinner knife from the kitchen, some clothes, and some food too.

Femke has made a big dinner. I am allowed two helpings of stew. This is rare because Femke is usually tight with food portions. My attempts at small talk sound forced but she doesn't seem to notice.

Femke goes to bed early, just as I had hoped. I lie on my bed still dressed in my clothes and listen for the squeak of Femke's lamp as she winds down the light. Then I wait an hour. Mama lies waiting also, with eyes wide open. I kiss her good-bye. She tries to say something but her sounds have gone again.

"Don't worry, Mama," I whisper, "I will be safe."

As I open the front door some minutes later, a light is ignited behind me. Femke is standing in the entrance to her bedroom. I stand like a trapped animal, frozen to the section of floor in the doorway.

"You will need to take a coat. The summer is nearly over and you have not thought of enough food. You will need much more than you have stolen."

I can't believe she knows.

"Shut the door and come and sit down." She pours two glasses of vodka. The drink burns my throat, but I feel warmer. "You should take a bottle of this for when it gets cold."

"No, thank you. I plan to get there before the end of autumn."

"It will be harder than you think." She pauses. "Henrik, your father was a good man."

"Why do you say those things about him then?"

"Because for years I have wished it were me he took away and not Karolin."

"You should tell Mama this."

"She already knows. She is far too intelligent to be deceived. Why do you think she doesn't fight me about it? Because she feels guilty that she had the life I wanted. I was stuck here taking care of your grandfather . . . miserable old bastard that he was!"

"How did you know I was going?"

"You are a boy. Boys are useless at hiding things. Not like girls."

She goes to the cupboard and takes out a sack. Inside, there are two boiled eggs, pieces of cheese, bread, fruit, and dried bacon.

"My father and I travelled right through the forests once, to the other side. You might come upon others who can guide you through, but be careful of them. Try not to show yourself until you have observed them first. Walk stealthily. Have your wits about you. I have no maps of the wilderness, but once you are on the other side, you must follow the Vistula. It will take you to Cracow."

She tells me about the terrain, about the hills and the waterways and the wildlife.

"If anyone can do it you can, I suppose—someone with your tenacity. You badger everyone till you get your way; let's hope that this works for you in future. Now go, before I cry."

I hug her small, wiry body and this time she hugs me back.

"Come back," she says.

Crossing the fields behind Mr. Lubieniecki's house, I see the lights are still on behind his newspaper windows. I wish I could say good-bye. The night sky nearly disappears as I enter the forest. With only some partial moonlight, I stumble on uneven ground, my knee landing on something sharp, and I reach down to feel the sticky liquid oozing from the scratch. I sit against a tree to wait for the guidance of sunrise, wondering if it is impossible what I have begun, then attempting to put those thoughts from my head when I remember Mama's face. There was belief. I listen to the faint tapping of gunfire in the distance, and the warplanes which sound like a swarm of bees. At some point I fall asleep and wake with the sun streaming through the trees.

It is my first full day of walking. There are few trails in the forest to follow. In the morning the sun must always be behind me, and in the afternoon it must be in front. Femke also said to follow the waterways, which lead to the river. She said noise will guide me eventually. Many more trucks than before are travelling the roads between the cities.

There is a track in the forest, perhaps an old one, and I follow it for a while, weaving through the tall firs and the low undergrowth, sparsely covered with red-and-orange leaves. The air here is free of the battle smoke that travels on the wind.

Several times I stop to drink some water. The forest makes lots of rustling and groaning noises. But my fear is not of anything in the forest—it is the potential for failure that scares me, the possibility that I will die too and Mama will lose us both.

I hear what I think is a car but it is far away and, faintly, the sounds of running water. I can also smell something like rust, but more putrid, and I see a large hole in the earth ahead of me. I walk towards this and the smell grows stronger, and the buzzing of insects is loud in my ears. I peer over the edge and am not prepared for what I see. I draw back to cover my nose and my mouth. The contents of my stomach rise and bile sits at the back of my throat.

In the ground are several people who have been shot. Their skin is gray and in their chests and faces are bullet holes, which look like splashes of black paint. They have been executed and thrown into the space, like garbage. They have not even been covered up but were left to rot.

I run far from the hole, deeper into the forest, and do not stop running for what seems like hours. The tears on my face dry in the wind. Eventually, I rest and the forest looks the same as it did hours before, and I can hear the planes again, and I wonder if I might become trapped in here forever.

People come here to kill or be killed. I have to be careful. I have to walk more lightly.

It is late when I see bright lights through the trees and smell the burning of timber. When I am nearly upon the site, I see that it is a village that has nearly burnt to the ground. Flames leap high into the air from a pyre of furniture, books, and photographs. Smoke hangs in the air like curtains around the remains of burning houses. I hear the sounds of whimpering and see a woman crying. She has no shoes; her shawl is tightly pulled around her shoulders. She is cradling the head of a man while she weeps. She looks up and puts out a hand.

I am knocked in the shoulder by a tall man with a gun. I am wondering whether he is responsible for the decimation, but he helps the woman to her feet.

"Get out of here," he says in a foreign accent. "The krauts will be returning soon and they will shoot you."

As I walk away, I stare past the houses to the village center. I see several more bodies lying there.

I run into the forest, coughing from the smoke and retching from the smell of blood. Deeper in the forest seems a safer place to be, but there is no place that I can escape what I have seen.

The next day I wander numbly, shocked by the treatment of people who have committed no crime.

The skies are gray and I can no longer follow the sun. It is the third day and already most of my food is gone. I walk down a hill that I think must lead to the river. I suspect that I have not been going straight towards the river, but in a zigzag pattern or perhaps in a loop. By the afternoon the sky has become so dark that it feels like night. A loud crack of thunder pierces the sky, reminding me of the bombing of our town. Then the rain comes and it is heavy, and I walk in sodden shoes. The ground is slippery. My clothes, which are plastered to my skin, are like weights around my body. I am so tired. I have had only a few hours' sleep in the past few days.

I can find nowhere to take shelter so I sit once again with my back to a tree. There is much pain in my head. I feel around in my bag and hold out my empty water bottle to catch the rain. I eat the remaining pieces of food and put my coat over me and the bag beneath me to protect it from getting drenched. Bread is stuck in my throat, which feels sore and swollen.

I lay my head against the tree and, unaware and not caring about time, fall into a broken sleep that is interspersed with images of rotting corpses and blood-splattered fields.

When I wake, my mouth is dry and my jaw is so stiff I can barely open it, and my head feels like it will explode. But that is not the worst thing. There is a gun pointed at my forehead. Two boys, perhaps older than me, are talking in Polish. They are telling me to stand but my legs and arms aren't working. One prods me with the gun to make me move faster. I try to stand but my head feels like it weighs too much to hold up.

"He is ill," says one.

"Can you walk?" asks the other one with a softer voice.

"We should take his stuff," says the first.

The other seems to ignore this and asks again if I can walk.

I nod and then fall in behind one of them, while the other walks a few paces behind me. My vision is blurred by the pain behind my eyes, and the light, dull as it is, burns through the top of my lids. I realize that one boy is carrying the pack that holds my drawing book but I don't care.

I don't know how long we have walked but I feel my legs getting weaker and think they may give way beneath me. My skin feels as if it is burning and I take off my shirt.

One of the boys tells me to keep moving. The world starts to fade and I sink to the ground. I feel one arm catch me and then there is nothing.

CHAPTER 17

I dream of Mama and Greta in the fields behind our farm. I dream of Mama's golden hair and Papa smiling and writing in his journal. I dream of our apartment in Germany and I am my age now and Papa has come home from work to find that Greta is gone and blames me.

Throughout my dreams, I see the faces of the boys peering over me and then also there is another: a girl's. I think at first she is Mama, but then realize that this girl is my age and has dark hair. She brings wet cloths and places them on my forehead. She does not smile.

"He might have a disease," says one of the boys standing over me. "We might all get sick. We should carry him deep into the forest and leave him there."

"No," says the girl. "Don't be an idiot."

I go back to dreaming. I dream I am running from gunfire and Rani is there and he is telling me to run faster, but when I turn, he is gone and there are other boys from my school. I know that Greta is in this group somewhere and I call her name but someone says that she has gone back to Germany.

"He is a dirty German." The voice comes from the other side of a wall. I have been muttering in my sleep.

The bed is wet from my sweat and I am covered with a blanket. Through the window I can see the tops of trees and white clouds. When I try to sit up, pain rises to the front of my skull. I lie back down, shut my eyes, and wait for the pain to disappear again. When it is gone, I look around the room. I am in a small bed in a small room, in a cabin of some kind. The floor has wooden boards that are rough and uneven. The blanket is coarse. I hear moving water somewhere in the distance.

I attempt to sit up again, this time rising slowly, easing my head into a vertical position. I am wearing only a singlet and under-shorts. I stand and search the corners of the room for my trousers but they are not here, and neither are my shoes. Something has been pushed against the door so that it cannot be opened from the inside. I climb back under the blanket, weary from the effort of standing.

Sometime in the afternoon, I wake up to the sound of logs being rolled away from the door. One of the boys enters. His rifle hangs from the back of his shoulder. I can see him more clearly now. He is tall and thin with a long face. His shirt and trousers hang off his body like washing on a line.

"Who are you?" His Polish has a Yiddish accent.

"I will tell you if you give me my trousers."

He ignores my request. "You nearly died," he says. "You should be grateful we found you; otherwise, you would be food for the wolves."

The door swings back and the shorter boy enters. He says nothing but has dragged in a chair and moves to sit beside my bed.

"What is a dirty German boy doing in the forest?" he asks.

"I live in Poland. My parents lived in Germany for a while. Are you running from the Germans?"

"What do you think, Professor? Of course we're hiding from the Germans. They have stolen our parents and our homes."

"Welcome to our new home," says the taller, skinny boy, wryly.

"Is this your house?"

"The partisans built it."

"Partisans?"

"Yes, Jews and Poles hiding here, ready to attack the German army."

"What about the Russians? Are they here too?"

"Russians?" they query suspiciously.

"I heard a rumor that some might be hiding in the forest."

"You're not working for them, are you?"

"No," I say quickly, fearful that this might seem as bad to them as working for the Germans. "I am a Jew like you," I say to the taller one. The shorter one sniggers.

"It is true."

"If it was true, you would be cut." He stares at my crotch and makes his fingers into scissors. I am suddenly afraid that he will ask me to pull down my underpants for proof.

"I wasn't . . . My mother . . . she wasn't Jewish—"

"Leave it," interrupts the taller boy. "What does it matter? He is clearly on the run from them. What are you doing this far from the town?"

"I was trying to find the river."

The shorter, stocky one sniggers again. He has ears that stick out like a monkey's.

I tell them about my sister being taken by the Germans and about how I am going to find her.

"You will never find her. She has probably been shipped to the camps by now or killed," says the monkey.

I stand then, my fists clenched by my sides. I am angry. The tall one with the rifle points it at me.

"Calm down, boy."

"I wish to leave now."

"Without your trousers?" And they both laugh this time.

The taller boy goes out and comes back in. He tosses me my trousers and I climb into them, embarrassed by their scrutiny as I do this.

"You know, you would have died if it were not for my sister," says the taller boy.

I remember then the girl in my room. As I am trying to picture her face, I see her through the window, walking towards the house, carrying bundles of sticks in her arms.

"Rebekah!" the tall boy yells from the window. "Your boy is awake."

I am annoyed by the way he refers to me, but he is the one with the rifle so I say nothing.

"Out!" instructs the meaner one, who wears something between a grin and a sneer.

Outside the tiny room, there is a bigger room and a curtain separates it from another private area. There are two cots in the big room, and a fireplace. The place is smoky. There are also a couple of chairs and a table.

The girl is bending down near a woodstove. She has her back to me and I see that her long dark hair has been twisted into a plait. She turns and looks directly at me, curious but not overly so. She has already had time to study me, but this is my first chance to examine her without the haze of illness.

"You should thank Rebekah. Without her you would have died."

Rebekah shakes her head. "Be quiet, Kaleb. I just did what most humans would do," she says.

"Everyone except Tobin anyway," jests the taller boy.

Tobin, it seems, is the friend of her brother, Kaleb, who is the taller boy. Tobin doesn't laugh at this and says seriously, "We have to be careful of everyone. We have always said that. To trust is to fail. And he is a dirty German. He was talking German in his sleep."

"It doesn't mean that he is one of them," says Rebekah. It is as if I am not in the room.

"My sister is right. He is just a boy looking for his sister. He is no threat."

Rebekah is suddenly alert. "His sister? What about that?"

I explain the story of Greta's kidnapping to the girl and she listens intently, her eyes studying me, taking in everything I say as if it is personal.

"I have heard of this," she says sorrowfully.

"You have?"

"Yes, from the partisans. While our country is being repopulated with Germans, many Polish children are sent to camps to see if they are worthy of Germanization. Some are then transported elsewhere, and some girls sent to special centers."

"Germanization?"

"A German purification program. It includes selecting girls to breed with Nazi officers, then taking their babies and testing them to ensure their race is pure."

"Pure *dirt*," says Tobin. And it is Kaleb's turn to laugh but Rebekah doesn't. It is clear from the grooves between her brows that she has not smiled in a long time.

"Do you know where these places are that the children are taken to?"

Rebekah shakes her head. "I don't know . . . perhaps first to camps in the west."

"I believe that she could still be with the man who took her . . . a general in Hitler's army. I believe she is somewhere in Cracow."

Rebekah doesn't say anything. No one believes me. I can see it in their faces.

"If she is a Jew, then it is unlikely," says Kaleb. "There are no processing places that we have heard of there. She will most likely have been taken to a camp or somewhere outside the city."

"She does not look Jewish."

"Neither do you . . . that much. But that won't stop them from putting you in a camp."

I clutch my stomach which has begun to cramp badly. Rebekah recognizes the cause. "You must eat first, before you go anywhere."

"Only a small portion," says Tobin. "And it can be part of your share."

"Stop it," says Kaleb. "We will share the next meal. The boy must eat. We pledged to help our country and that includes its people."

Tobin looks sideways at me. He appears older than all of us, perhaps in the way he takes the lead. Rebekah is closer in age to me.

"We will go and find some meat," says Kaleb.

"Are you hunting?" I ask.

"No, this time we steal." And then the boys are gone and it is just the girl and me. Rebekah peels some onions. We sit across from each other at the table. I am suddenly aware that my hands are filthy and my clothes must smell, but she does not show any repulsion.

"Is there somewhere to wash?"

"There is a stream at the bottom of the rise." She hands me a bar of soap and points from the front door, and I follow the track by which I saw her return earlier. It leads down a slope and into a narrow, flowing waterway. I strip down to my underpants and stand in the shallows to wash myself. Then I scrub my shirt and walk back to the cabin. It is a small log cabin with wooden shutters, like something out of a storybook, and I think of Greta and our stories. I hang my shirt over a log at the front door and enter the cabin shirtless.

"How long will the boys be?"

Rebekah looks up from her task through long dark lashes that surround oval black eyes. I am suddenly self-conscious about my narrow chest, my bony arms.

"They could be hours. They go to the farmers' lands."

"They steal from their own people?"

"They are not our people," she snaps. "They are people who are German enough to be placed there. They are people who care nothing for Jews." There is anger in her voice.

I talk then. I tell her about my papa dying, about leaving Germany. I tell her what happened to Mama. She listens carefully.

"They will pay," she says. "One day, they will pay."

"And your parents?"

"Killed." There is something so final about this statement that I ask nothing more.

"Can I help with the cooking?"

"You can get some water in those buckets. We are always running out."

I get the water, and make several trips back and forth. During the last trip I see the boys returning. They are arguing about the scrawny chicken they have stolen. Tobin says Kaleb was not fast enough, that he should have caught the bigger one.

Tobin takes the chicken and chops its head off like he has done that a thousand times already.

"Let me see your hands," says Tobin.

I show him.

"They are a girl's hands. Get plucking if you want to eat."

"Can't you see he hasn't done it before!" says Kaleb, and he takes the chicken and begins to pluck the feathers slowly. It is obvious that Kaleb is the one without the experience.

"I am fine. I have done it before," I say, and I show them how fast I am at preparing the chicken for cooking. I have Femke to thank for that.

• • •

I don't want to be here amongst these people. But I have no choice. They have saved my life and they are providing food. As soon as the sun comes up the next day, I will leave. But something about the girl casts a shadow of doubt over my departure. The thought of leaving her sunk in such a muddy, desolate place makes me think of Greta, who may also be in a place where she is feeling sad and lonely.

The smell of boiling meat, which is cooked with onion, makes my tongue start to water. It has been days since I have eaten a warm meal. The others sit around the table, though I sit on a log because there are not enough chairs. Kaleb has divided the portions of food.

There are no lamps in the cabin, so Rebekah lights some candles while the boys talk. They have been scouting for German police stations over several nights. They have found one, only sixteen miles away. They plan to steal more guns for the Polish resistance, which will kill the Germans using their own weapons.

"Maybe the boy can get an education," says Tobin without as much animosity now that he has food in his belly. I am eating fast because the food is the best I have ever tasted. It is as if this is the first time I have discovered eating.

"Look at the boy," says Kaleb. "He will make himself sick from eating too fast."

"How old are you?" asks Tobin.

I say I am seventeen. I am actually only sixteen, a couple of months away from seventeen, but I do not tell them this.

"Rebekah is nearly seventeen," says Kaleb with a little more kindness to his voice. "And your sister?"

I pause because my throat feels suddenly tight at the mention of her, but I can't let them see that I am weak. "She is ten." Rebekah

PASTEL ORPHANS

does not look at me this time. She puts food in her mouth and focuses on her dish.

The boys inform me that they are both eighteen. There is some resemblance between Kaleb and Rebekah, but Kaleb is much darker skinned, from the sun.

"So, what do you say to the education?" says Tobin. "Do you want to come with us to kill some Germans?"

"I can't," I say. "I have to find my sister."

"You will not find her. I have said already that she is probably far from here or dead."

Rebekah stands up suddenly, knocking her chair over. "What would you know?" she says angrily.

"A lot more than you. You are here cooking and cleaning. You do not go out there and see what we see. All the killing, all the death."

"Shut up!" says Kaleb. "She knows more than you think. And she does as much as us. Someone has to be looking after things here."

Kaleb turns to me. "You can come if you want," he says, "or you can leave. Whatever you wish to do. I can tell you that shortly we will be heading in the same direction anyway."

"Towards Cracow? When?"

"Maybe tomorrow if we are successful tonight. We are meeting up with the partisans who are west of here. You may wish to travel part of the distance with us until we meet at our other location. We have promised the partisans that we will steal guns. It is our mission."

I think about this. Perhaps it is the only way I can find my way out of the forest, since I have made a mess of things so far.

"But first, as Tobin says, you can earn your keep and help us steal some weapons from the station."

I pause before nodding.

The night is cold and I am glad that Femke made me take a coat. Kaleb goes to light a fire in the fireplace with matches but I offer the silver lighter. He examines it and raises his eyebrows.

"A spoil of war," he says casually. I do not tell him that its real value is the initials of the man I have dreamt of killing. He hands back the lighter and looks at my clothes.

"It will be winter soon. Is that all you have? Do you have anything warmer—hats, gloves, proper walking shoes?"

"I don't intend to be away from home for long."

The two boys look at each other and Tobin shakes his head, as if they know something that they are not willing to share. They then turn their attention to a discussion of tactics. It seems that I am required to spot for them, which means to hide, look out, and whistle if we are unsafe. They ask me to whistle. It is pretty good, I think, but they tell me it needs to sound more like a bird. I practice several times to get it right. I used to whistle on the way to school so it does not take me long to sound how they want me to. Tobin looks at his watch and says that we leave at midnight. There is only half a moon tonight.

They both came from Cracow and went to the same school but the boys weren't friends before the war. It makes sense. They don't appear to be anything alike.

Rebekah moves near the warmth of the fire. I watch her purposeful movements as she brushes the dirt away from the hearth, then from her skirt.

Tobin whispers to me when Kaleb moves away from the table: "Eyes off. She's mine."

I can't believe what he says, as Rebekah hardly makes contact with Tobin and only directs her questions to her brother. Tobin gets up and walks outside to relieve himself.

When I ask Rebekah if she needs help, she ignores me. She does not seem to like me.

Kaleb leans towards me. "Don't mind my sister. She has taken this hard."

"I can't see what other way to take it," I say. "It seems she does not like me here."

"She can appear sour but that is not what's in her heart. You survive or you don't. That's how you have to see it. That's how she is living. That's how we all are now."

What he says sounds reasonable, considering our circumstance. However, something about his statement makes us sound less human—primitive, almost. It is as if we are facing life or death, without any of the good things in between. But Kaleb is kinder than Tobin, who has an edge that makes me nervous—as if at any moment he will change into some other kind of animal.

"So what happened to you?" I ask.

"It is a long story. Now is not the time."

I find my bag and take out the contents. The leather cover of my drawing book is scuffed but the pages are dry and the pencil is still there. I draw the fireplace with the remains of the burnt wood and ash, and the fresh woodpile beside, and the empty chair beside that. I make the chair extra large as if it might belong to a king or a giant, or perhaps a boy who believes he is bigger than he is.

Tobin does not come back in. He is sitting outside smoking a cigarette. Kaleb has joined him now. I can hear them discussing things together. Sometimes my name is mentioned. I continue to draw and fail to notice that Rebekah has moved behind me to view my work.

"It's good," she says, startling me.

I am suddenly embarrassed. "It's adequate," I say.

"Do you have other pictures?"

I turn the pages. Inside are pictures of my mother sleeping after she became sick, of Greta, and of Femke. There are pictures of cows, a caricature of my teacher and friends, and the barn in our fields. Rebekah turns each page over gently as if she is handling something precious.

She stops at the picture of my mother. "She appears to be sleeping."

"She was."

"I don't think she was," says Rebekah. "I think she knew you were there. She is listening to everything. She is not rested. She wishes she could speak."

While Rebekah is distracted—studying the face of Mama—I notice several things about her: the translucency of her skin, her long fingers, and the curve of her back.

"She looks beautiful. What is she like?"

The question takes me by surprise. I have to think about this because I have never had to put Mama in words.

"She is not tall or small."

Rebekah is staring at me as if every word is important.

"What about *her*? What is she like?"

"Oh, umm, she was busy, always busy. She loved my father and my father loved her. She didn't cook well but she got better . . ."

"Your poor mother, to have such a son who does not appreciate her."

"Why?" I say, suddenly offended. I love my mother and this person knows nothing about me.

"If she dies, that is all you are going to say?"

"She is not going to die."

Rebekah stares at me with angry eyes. "Boys are so stupid," she says and walks to the fire, her back to me.

I am confused by her. I don't know what it is that has upset her. I am putting my drawing book back in my bag as the others enter. They tell me that I must be ready in an hour and to get some rest in the meantime. Rebekah goes into the small room that was mine during my recuperation. I feel gratefulness towards her for looking after me, for sacrificing her room, but she is gone and the door is shut before I can make eye contact.

The boys climb into small cots and I lie on some blankets near the fire. Tobin is snoring and I cannot fall asleep. Kaleb stays awake in his cot near the door. Some time later, Kaleb wakes Tobin and then shakes my shoulder, even though I am already awake. "We must go," he says.

As we head out the door, I say that I have forgotten something. Before Tobin can turn to complain, I re-enter the cabin and knock on Rebekah's door. When I don't hear anything, I open it slightly.

"Thank you," I whisper. "For taking care of me when I was sick."

I rush out of the cabin and sense that Tobin is scowling at me in the dark.

We walk for nearly three hours over rough terrain. The boys have been this way several times before but I do not know what I am walking into, what to expect. They carry their firearms in readiness.

We are heading up a hill and I can see the lights of a small village ahead.

"This is it," says Tobin. "See that house over there?" He points, but I do not know which house he is talking about. "That is where the Germans sleep and dream about our women. We will go to that house and steal the firearms, and we will kill them while they sleep."

"No!" says Kaleb. "You know we can't do that. If they wake, we shoot, but only then. We steal food and guns and come and go silently, and hope they don't kill *us*."

The mission is sounding more difficult, and I am suddenly fearful. We spread mud on our cheeks and slowly creep into the town. Only one room in the house is lit.

Kaleb is the tallest and peers through the windows to find where they store the ammunition. He reports back to Tobin and me where we are crouched beside the road, near a fence.

"There is a closed room where I think they must store their ammunition and supplies. There is only one soldier on duty that I can see. But there are other coats hanging on a hook, which means there are probably more men sleeping in another room."

"We have to kill the guard then."

"Stop saying that! If we kill him, the noise will wake them up. We will walk in and tell him to be silent. I will hold the gun on him while you go and retrieve everything you can from the storeroom. Henrik will wait on the other side of the house to alert us if there are others who wake."

Tobin doesn't nod, but the fact that he has said nothing means that the plan is going ahead, and they both stand to walk towards the back door. I follow with a lump in my throat and a heart that is threatening to burst through my rib cage. Tobin uses a piece of wire to unlock the door. It is one of his many skills that he bragged about earlier: breaking and entering. At the time I did not see how he could consider this as some sort of skill or honor, though, watching him now, I am impressed.

As I walk to the other side of the house, I glance through a different window that allows me to see inside from another angle. The German on duty is standing while Kaleb points a rifle at him. There is silence from within. Kaleb and Tobin do not say a word. I need to see if there are other soldiers in the house, sleeping. I walk farther around the building and roll a nearby log quietly to the base of a window of a darkened room. I climb onto the log to peer in. Light from the main part of the house shines into the open doorway of this room and I can see two beds, each with a form lying on it.

Through the doorway I can see that the on-duty soldier has his hands on his head and is facing towards the window where I am peering in. Our eyes meet and the shock of it causes me to hold my breath. Kaleb stays very still and silent as he holds the gun while Tobin tries to pick the lock of the room that supposedly contains the ammunition. But this action seems to be taking a long time. I wonder why there is no key.

The form in one of the beds stirs and then changes position. I duck my head down quickly, then slowly raise it. When I peer in again, he is sitting upright at the edge of the bed. If he turns right, he will see Tobin and Kaleb and the gun pointed at the head of the soldier. Tobin has been unsuccessful in unlocking the storage room door. I whistle to alert the boys, and tap on the glass to divert the attention of the sleepy German. Then I jump off the log and sit beneath the window. I hear the window being pushed open— wood scraping wood.

"Who's there?" says a voice above me, and I hear the click of his gun.

"I am lost," I say. I stretch and twist my neck so that I can just see the tip of the gun an inch back from the edge of the sill. I jump up to grab it, jerking it from enemy hands. It slips through his fingers—which is the last thing he is expecting—and I run back around the house to the other side. By this time, both Germans who were sleeping have no doubt seen Kaleb and Tobin. I have used a gun before and I fire this one into the air to scare the Germans, but I am unprepared for its force and it throws me back onto the ground. Kaleb and Tobin tear out of the back door.

"Run!" they yell without looking at me, and I follow them towards the forest. I do not turn around, but I don't have to. There are German voices at the back door and the soldiers are firing their guns in our direction. We run fast through the forest for thirty minutes or more, until we have all lost our breath.

Tobin is angry. "I told you we should have killed them. There were only three. All we got is one gun from the guard."

I hold up the other one that I have taken.

There is surprise on their faces, which are half-hidden in the night, and then Kaleb laughs as I tell them how I grabbed the gun.

"That was you who took the first shot?"

I nod.

"It seems that the boy has some talents after all," Kaleb says. "You should come and join the resistance."

Tobin scowls and curses.

"Enough, Tobin!" says Kaleb. "Two guns are better than none." But Tobin is not yet over his anger. It seems the key to the storeroom was with one of the sleeping men. Tobin does not put blame on his inability to open the door, but rather on the fact that there was no killing—something I am starting to believe he wishes to engage in more for pleasure than out of necessity.

We return, exhausted, to the cabin. It is still dark, and Kaleb and Tobin throw themselves onto their cots. I take my place beside the fire again but it is hours before I can fall asleep. The excitement from the raid is keeping me awake. I have never felt this exhilarated and it is Kaleb's approving eyes that I remember as I am falling asleep, listening to the wind whistling through the gaps in the walls and shutters.

CHAPTER 18

Daylight. My eyes are crusty and hard to open. It is cold and Rebekah is leaning over the stove, trying to stoke the sparks on the twigs into flame. Once she is successful, she goes back to stirring the oats.

Kaleb is still asleep but Tobin sits at the table, his eyes following the girl.

"We have to eat like horses again," Tobin says to me as I approach the table, as if I might have something to say about it too.

I sit down, just grateful that there is a meal. "If it is good for horses, it is good for me," I say. I sneak a look at Rebekah's face, which is paler today and expressionless, as usual. Tobin does not like what I said. This is written clearly across his face. Opposition, it seems, is something he is not expecting from me, and he is stunned into silence.

Kaleb wakes and stretches, and as he walks past, he pats me on the head like a favorite pet. Rebekah spoons porridge into each of our bowls. It smells good and tastes even better. I remember complaining to Mama about the same food, just like Tobin does, and I wish now that I had never made a fuss.

Tobin eats like a pig, with his snout in his bowl. Rebekah doesn't say anything; she does not even look his way, as if she is used to such manners. If Mama or Femke were here, there would be a smack to the back of his head.

"Why are there no partisans around here?" I ask.

Tobin says that the partisans built the cabin when they escaped to the forest and stayed here until they found better lodgings farther west. Now that my head is clearer I can see the gaps between the uneven timber slats. The cabin was made in haste with crude, miscellaneous materials: uncut pine, stolen fence posts, and train sleepers. The wood oven is small and was perhaps stolen also. The toilet is a hole in the ground behind the cabin. I ask Tobin what time we will be leaving and he says not until the following day. I feel angry because I must get to Cracow to search for Greta.

Tobin complains that we must go back and try again to steal the Germans' guns, but Kaleb shakes his head. "That would be madness," he says. "They will be waiting for us this time."

"No," says Tobin. "They will not think we are stupid enough to try it two nights in a row. It is the last thing they will be expecting."

I see Tobin's reasoning but Kaleb is right. They will be more watchful and nervous.

Later, when Tobin goes outside to relieve himself—which he always does loudly, always close to the window—I ask Kaleb why we are not leaving until the next day.

Kaleb twists his mouth in regret. "Sorry, Henrik," he says, "but we have decided not to leave tomorrow."

"I have to find my sister," I say.

"I'm sorry," he says. "We need more guns and food before we return to the others. We have to find them somewhere else. We have promised that we will return with them."

"Promised who?"

"The partisans. The ones we are working with," he says slowly, as if I haven't understood. "The ones who sent us to search for weapons and return with them. Our mission is not yet complete."

Kaleb sees the look on my face.

"The moment we steal some more we will leave, and you would do best to wait and travel with us. Our base is in the same direction as Cracow. It will be safer for you in a group. Do you want to come to another village with us tonight?"

I think about it before I answer. I think that we were lucky the first time and I'm already feeling butterflies in my stomach at the thought of more danger. But then I remember the rush of stealing the gun, and I wonder if I am capable of doing more. I don't want to go out again, but neither do I want to travel the forest alone. I nod.

"Perhaps you can steal some food while Tobin and I look for guns." He glances around, then talks more quietly. "Listen . . . Tobin is not happy that you are eating our food, but if you contribute, there will be nothing for him to complain about."

"Maybe I should just leave."

"No. It will be fine. I like you here anyway. I think Rebekah likes you here too."

I look across to Rebekah, who does not appear to be listening. She never looks at me and I can't think why he would even say that. She is hostile, in her silence, to everyone. Tobin returns to pace the cabin. He looks at me with something close to menace. I do not like the way his eyes dart around and then suddenly home in on me at times. He is restless, the cabin too small. I am relieved when he finally goes outside again. Kaleb checks his gun and polishes it with a cloth.

Sounds of gunfire ring out through the forest, cracking the air in two and scattering the birds that have not yet departed from the approaching winter. Kaleb walks outside to investigate and I follow.

"What are you doing?" Kaleb asks Tobin. "You are wasting ammunition. We are supposed to be bringing some back, not using it."

"I am testing the gun."

"Then stop it!"

But Tobin ignores Kaleb and fires several more times. I do not want to hear their arguments and I walk towards the stream. There are more shots fired behind me, and then the shooting stops.

As I come nearer to the stream, I can see her through the trees. Her dark hair shines a lighter shade of brown in the sunlight. One long plait hangs over the front of each shoulder. She is bathing in the icy water, wearing only a cream lace slip, like the ones my mother used to wear in Germany.

For a few moments I watch her soap her thin white arms and then feel guilty that I am watching. I step towards her noisily—on purpose—and the crunching of leaves causes her to turn sharply.

As I approach, she looks at me directly. "Do you always spy on girls?"

"I wasn't spying." I wonder how she knows, then presume that she is merely speculating, angry at the interruption.

I take off my shirt and splash some water on my face and neck.

"I want to thank you again for taking care of me."

"It was nothing." She looks at me with eyes half lidded. I detect a hint of regret for something.

"We have to go out again," I say.

"I know," she says. "I heard. It is a stupid idea. We should just leave here. I don't like the cabin. I don't like it here. It is too close to enemy bases. We should return to the house."

"Why don't you tell them?"

"Are you joking? My opinion doesn't count. Tobin holds the power. He tells my brother what to do and my brother does what he is told because he is not a fighter. He is a scholar and a theologian but he is not a soldier, despite what he thinks. He will get himself killed."

"I think he is just looking for ways to protect you both. War limits choices."

Rebekah is silent and goes back to the water to clean the cooking pot and plates.

I take out my notebook and draw a picture of Tobin. I accentuate his ears so that they appear enlarged and elfin-like, and I draw a wide maniacal grin; his exaggerated, round head sits on a small body. On his shirt I draw a small badge with a handwritten inscription: "Head Soldier." He holds the rifle beside him and there is a tag on the rifle that reads: "From the Germans, with our compliments."

Once her task is completed, Rebekah comes over to where I am sitting.

"Why are you here? Why aren't you back with the boys?"

"I prefer it here."

She puts on her dress and I look away shyly. I go to close my drawing book but she touches the back of my hand.

"Can I see?"

Rebekah views the picture carefully, then surprises me by laughing, her mouth wide, before cupping her mouth with her hand. Her teeth are crooked, with her incisors slightly overlapping the front middle ones. For some reason I find this pretty, along with the fact that she is laughing. Her laughter sounds faint and sweet, like a night bird.

"You are quite the artist—or should I say comedian?" She is looking at me, but this time her face is not hard and fixed, but softened, her cheeks round with amusement.

"I don't know," I say, feeling suddenly shy under her gaze.

"Your talent is wasted here."

As she picks up the sack to fill it with the washing, I hear footsteps downstream, and voices. She hears them too. We creep up the hill and hide behind the trees to wait and see who comes.

The men who come carry rifles. They are from the German army, in uniforms different from the ones worn by the officers who took my sister. From where we sit, Rebekah and I look down upon their hard hats, which conceal their faces. I hear them saying in German that they have found some tracks. Rebekah and I retreat stealthily and slowly through the forest for part of the way, so as not to alert them, and then run the remaining distance to the cabin. Out of breath, we announce what we have seen.

Tobin picks up his gun, which is already loaded, and Kaleb loads bullets into his rifle.

"Are you sure there are only two?" says Kaleb.

"Yes."

"They're looking for us. They are scouts. Let's go," says Tobin to Kaleb.

"No," says Kaleb. "We should just wait for them to come. They may not find us. They may just stay along the water."

"We are sitting ducks here. We should meet them at the crest."

But there is no time. "I see them," says Rebekah, who has remained at the window, spying, since our return.

The boys take a window each and aim their guns. "Get down!" commands Kaleb to his sister. "Away from the window!"

There is silence and then a slight rustling outside as the Germans retreat. I think that perhaps they have seen the guns at the window. I am sitting just behind Kaleb, peering over his shoulder. Much of the view is obstructed. Gunfire from Tobin's rifle erupts loudly from inside the cabin, shaking the boards and numbing my ears. Rebekah is curled on the floor, her hands over her ears, eyes closed, teeth clenched. She does not move.

"Wait," says Kaleb, grabbing Tobin by the shirt before he can aim at the other soldier, giving the target precious seconds to disappear from view.

Kaleb is pushed out of the way by Tobin, who rushes outside just ahead of him. I touch Rebekah to break her from the spell and then run after them. One soldier is on the ground, blood seeping from a wound, but he is still alive. The other has gone.

"You idiot!" says Tobin. "Why did you stop me? Now the other one has escaped."

"We should have waited for them to get closer and told them to put down their weapons. We could have captured them alive and taken them to the partisans."

"No, fool! They are better dead."

Tobin runs off in the direction he thinks the other German has gone. Kaleb has already retrieved the gun from the fallen German. The wound is in his shoulder. He is cursing in German and attempting to stop the blood flow with his hand.

"Help me," he says in German. "I will not harm you."

"How can you harm us?" I say in German. "You have no gun and you are wounded."

"What does he say?" asks Kaleb.

"He wants our help."

Kaleb points the gun at him and thinks for a moment. The soldier is not much older than a boy. His helmet has rolled off, revealing his sand-colored hair.

"Ask him what he is doing here."

The soldier replies to my question: "We were told to see if there were any Polish resistance hiding here after our station was ambushed last night."

"But that is miles away. How did you find us so quickly?"

"The gunfire. We were not supposed to come this far but we heard it."

When I tell Kaleb this, he nods as if he is not surprised.

"Imbecile," he says under his breath. He is talking about Tobin, not the German. "Help me take him inside, and tell him that if he attempts to harm us or tries to escape, we will have to kill him." It is hard to believe that Kaleb is capable of killing in view of what Rebekah has said about her brother. It is more likely that he would argue against the necessity of such an act. Still, anything is possible. Circumstances such as ours can change a person.

The German is placed on the floor near my bedding. He is squirming in pain.

"What do we do with him?" I ask.

"We wait until Tobin returns."

The begging, whining, and moaning from the German is fraying my nerves and I take him some water.

"Can we give him anything for the pain?"

"We cannot waste medicine on a German soldier," says Rebekah. She sits with her brother at the table. They look at their hands while I sit against a wall and watch the German writhe.

"What if he dies?"

Neither of them answers. I ask again.

Rebekah stands this time. "What does it matter if he does? How many have *we* lost?"

I say nothing more but look at my hands too. Eventually, the moaning stops and the German falls asleep. I wonder if he is in shock and if he might die.

Tobin returns. His eyes are wild and he is cursing and punching the wall.

"We've lost him." He marches over to the German and kicks him hard in the stomach. Then he kicks him again. The German is winded and tries to vomit, but nothing comes up.

"Enough!" says Kaleb.

"We will have to go now because they will return with others."

"Shit!" says Kaleb, running his fingers through his hair. "This is all because of you, because they heard you firing."

Tobin ignores what he has said.

"We leave tonight," says Kaleb decisively. "We take the German with us."

"What is the point?"

"We take him with us for the partisans to question."

"But look at him. He is barely older than us. He will know nothing. We should just kill him now and save the fighters the trouble."

"No," says Kaleb.

The two argue for a few minutes in Polish. I notice that the German is awake and watching. I wonder how much he understands.

"Gather your things," says Kaleb suddenly to his sister. He turns then to Tobin. "We take the German. I have just as much say."

The two youths face each other; then Tobin shakes his fist in the air before disappearing behind the curtain to pack his knapsack.

I am instructed to take care of the German since I "speak like a traitor," according to Tobin. While the others wait outside, I go to the German's side. The blood has stopped leaking from the wound but he has broken out in a sweat. It is clear he is suffering; color has drained from his face.

"Can you stand?"

"I'm not sure."

I reach down to help him up. He is not tall and he has a young face. I imagine that back in Berlin we might once have been friends at the same school. There is something harmless in the carefulness with which he takes my arm for support, and he does not have the look of those men who took Greta. But there is still no forgiveness on my part. He belongs to the cause responsible for parting my father from us, for Mama's injuries, and for Greta's kidnapping.

It is a dark night and we trip on the pathways that wind between the trees. Tobin walks ahead, then Rebekah, then Kaleb, then me. I have to help the German and it is a task. For the most part he can walk by himself, but occasionally he becomes unsteady and leans into me, sometimes close to fainting.

We walk through the night and into the next day. I am so tired that at one point I stumble. That is when Kaleb tells me he will take over, that he will take care of the German. As the sun rises, I feel like we are the walking dead.

At the edge of a clearing, Tobin tells us to be quiet while he goes on ahead. I watch him circle a white two-story manor house with a tall roof and many attic windows. It has a raised entrance porch and a balcony above this. Around it the grass has grown tall; garden beds are overgrown or dying. I wonder who could own such a house in the middle of the wilderness.

Polish voices travel towards us, and then Tobin walks out the front door, followed by two bearded men dressed in black and carrying guns. Tobin waves us forward, and we enter the front door which is flanked by the two men.

The house is large with multiple rooms. One of the men directs us to rooms upstairs. I lead the German to a bed in an empty room. The German has not said anything for the whole journey, though it is clear he is in pain and badly in need of rest. Tobin follows me in.

"Not this room, you idiot," says Tobin. "You can't lock it."

The German looks close to collapsing and I put an arm around his waist and follow Tobin to a room at the end of the hallway. Tobin leaves while I help the German lie down on the floor inside the small room that was perhaps a storeroom once. I lock the door as I leave and go downstairs. The sound of raised voices leads me to the kitchen. Rebekah is not there but Tobin and Kaleb are talking to the two men. It seems they are leaving.

"But where will you go?" asks Tobin.

"We will go northeast. There is no one to fight here. We will join up with others."

"I will come too," says Tobin.

The two of them laugh: not bitterly or nastily, more affably. "No, you must stay here."

"What about the German?" asks Kaleb. "Don't you want to question him?"

"We seek information about the camps and about the secret slaughter projects, which have nothing to do with planned warfare. He will know nothing about them. He will not know what Hitler's secret army is up to. None of the general army does. We have interrogated before. It is Hitler's secret police who have the answers. If you had captured one of those, it would have been better. You can leave him for the other partisans, or you can do with him what you want."

They wish us luck and begin to leave.

"When will you be back?" asks Tobin

"We're not sure."

"What of Zamosc? Are there partisans there too?" I ask.

"Not yet, but some are planning to drive out the Germans from there eventually."

I tell them quickly of my sister in Cracow, of the orientation centers, hoping they will know something. They look at each other thoughtfully, as if communicating something.

"I'm sorry," says one of the men. He squeezes my shoulder. "We don't know where these ones are taken. We only know that many who are taken to the camps are never seen again."

The two men go, and Tobin and Kaleb discuss the partisans. It seems many hide here and use the house as a base. They do not know the owners. They say that other partisans are coming back here once they finish their fighting in the east, though they don't know how many; they only say that the leader is a man named Eri.

There is lighting here from a diesel generator, and a large tank with water that can be heated. There is even a bathroom with a large bath. It looks like there are things missing from the rooms, like small pieces of furniture that have left indents in the rugs. There is no artwork or glassware; perhaps many things have been looted. I wonder if the owners will ever return and what they would say to find their house in this state. Or perhaps they are dead.

"If the partisans do not return soon, we should go to them," says Tobin. "We should be out killing Germans."

I think that Tobin is a simple, angry boy always looking for a fight.

Kaleb turns to me. "Have you found a bedroom yet?"

I shake my head.

"Then go and find one. There are many. Take your pick."

I fill up a cup with water, drain it, and fill it up again. I go upstairs to where the German is. I unlock the door and peer in. His breathing is slow and deep. I leave the cup beside him, then walk along the hall.

In one of the rooms I pass Rebekah, who is lying on one of the beds, her face to the wall. I take the room next to hers. It has been used before. There is a smell of damp socks and male sweat. The bed is unmade, the sheets are unwashed, and the white cover is stained. But the mattress is soft. Inside a wardrobe are women's dresses and shoes. I am so tired and I lie down to sleep, but it doesn't come. I take one of the dresses from the cupboard to Rebekah next door. She sits up when I enter.

"Here is a dress. It was in the wrong room," I joke.

She shakes her head. "No. I do not wear the clothes of the dead. The people in this house were probably taken away and shot for no reason other than they were Jews."

"Then they would want one of their own to have these so that they do not go to waste."

She thinks about this. I do not wait for a response, but leave the dress on a chair and go back downstairs. The boys are sitting in the living room. Tobin cradles his gun.

In the kitchen there is a large sack of potatoes, some tomatoes, and zucchini. There is also a small bag of salt and flour but no milk or tea. I wash the potatoes and boil them with the other vegetables. Then I ladle the food into bowls that I have washed, since many of the utensils, plates, and bowls have been lying filthy on the floor. The men have not thought of cleanliness. I call the others in to eat, and when Tobin sees what I have done, he swears.

"Do you not realize that you have used too much food? We are miles from supplies here."

"Calm down," says Kaleb. "Tomorrow we will get some more."

I take two bowls upstairs. I knock on Rebekah's door, which is now closed, but there is no answer so I leave the food on the floor outside her room.

I take the other bowl to the German, who is only allowed to leave the room once a day to use the toilet. There is a toilet bowl in his room for other times. I must escort him each time he leaves the room.

When I enter, he is sitting up, his back against the wall. He has taken his clothes off and is sitting in his underpants. There is a bullet hole in his shoulder and around it the skin is inflamed. His face is gray. When his eyes meet mine, I see that any fight he must have had has left him.

"I will die without medicine," he says.

"Can you eat?"

"I'm not hungry. But I need more water."

I return with some water and because he is weak I hold the cup to his lips to drink. I then pass him a few mouthfuls of food before he pushes my hand away and closes his eyes. I leave the bowl beside him in case he is hungry later.

When I get back downstairs, I don't go near the kitchen, where the boys are eating, but to a supply area that was once a sitting room with tall glass doors that overlook a pond. On the shelves and littered across the floor are miscellaneous items: tins, ropes, files, books, German boots and clothing—some with bullet holes—a heater, tools, sleeping bags, and, surprisingly, boxes of ammunition. I wonder if the mission the boys were sent on was simply meant to keep them occupied, to perhaps rid the partisans of inexperienced youths who might get in the way of their fight. I search through the rest of the room and find nothing significant.

CHAPTER 19

That night it is good to have a bed but the creaks in the walls wake me early. I decide that I must leave, but not before I talk to the German. He may know something about Cracow. I unlock his door to find him drowsy but awake.

He asks me if I know where his knapsack is. I look for it in the supply area, the living room, and the kitchen, but it is nowhere to be found. I think that perhaps Tobin has it.

Later, after I make sure that Tobin is occupied downstairs, I search through the drawers in his room. I find a knapsack in a wardrobe and inside it is a water bottle, an empty medicine bottle, and the German's private papers. Tobin has taken the military rations from the German's pack and eaten them; I already found discarded, empty packets under the bed. I take the papers to the German, whose name is Otto Petersen.

"Thank you," he says. I tell him about the empty bottle and he nods. He tells me it is medicine to keep him alert. Tobin has obviously taken this for himself.

"What are you doing with those two? You do not look like part of this group."

I wonder briefly if I should tell him anything but then I do. I tell him everything. He listens carefully to my story.

Then he tells me his. His father was a soldier and he did not know what else to do so he became one too. His father died in service and Otto left his mother, a younger brother, and two sisters back in Munich. His mother did not want him to fight but he had no choice. Hitler has given no one a choice. His family will not receive a pension if he does not serve. He is not happy fighting the war. He does not see the point to it.

"Why change something that was not that bad to begin with? Everyone complained about the economy but Germany was still a nice place to live." Otto says that the Jews did not bother him and Poland did not figure in the minds of most Germans.

"We are not allowed access to much of the information, just the propaganda from the Nazi generals. I've witnessed families torn apart because of their race. We know that the Jews are not treated well."

He says that he has seen many atrocities, and to cope, he has had to turn away and pretend that he does not see. He calls Hitler's personal army "Hitler's dogs," though he only says this to those he trusts; otherwise, he will end up with a bullet to his head from one of his own. He says that he trusts me.

I show him the lighter and ask if he knows who might own it. If he recognizes the initials, he doesn't show it. I do not forget that he is the enemy. I return the lighter to my pocket.

"I too have heard the stories of young Polish women being captured and paired with officers to fuel the Aryan race, but I know with more certainty about the stolen children."

"Do you know where they are taken?"

"One day we went to the house of a senior officer and were asked to wait outside. There were little girls and boys playing in the front yard. We were told they were part of a program to Germanize the occupied territories."

This news excites me. "Do you have the address?"

"No, but I can show you; and it is not the only house that has children. There are other places that house them—often on the outskirts of cities, where the officers reside." He says that he will draw me a map if I get him something to write with.

I go to my room to get my notebook and pencil, and I see in passing that Rebekah's bed is made neatly and the dress I left for her is gone from the chair. When I return, Tobin is waiting for me outside the prisoner's door. He does not move to let me pass.

"What are you talking to the German about?"

"He thinks he knows where my sister is."

"It is a trick. He lies so that you do not kill him. So that you will protect him."

He has seen my book and grabs it. I attempt to take it back and in the scuffle it falls open on the ground, displaying the page with my drawing of Tobin.

Tobin picks up the book. "What is this?" he asks. But he already knows. He is quite recognizable, even in comic form. "Are you making fun of me?"

I do not know what to say. He drops the book, pushes me against the wall with his stocky forearm, and with his thick fingers, grabs me around the throat. He is stronger than he looks and I am unable to pull his arm away.

"Leave him!" shouts Rebekah, who appears in the hallway.

Tobin looks at her, then slowly releases me, but not before giving me a parting shove.

"You are lucky, you little bitch, that you have your brother; otherwise, you would keep me warm at night," he says vehemently. "You think you are better than me and you ignore me. You are nothing but a stupid Jew, and it is because of you my country is ruined."

"It is her country too," I say, surprised by the forcefulness of his words, surprised by the slight against Jews.

He turns back to me and takes a swing, but I duck and he plants his fist in the wall. I punch him in the stomach but the hit is not strong enough; the muscles in his stomach are solid, like bedrock. He swings again and hits me in the ear and then again in the side of the nose.

Kaleb arrives before Tobin can do any more damage to me. He pins Tobin's arms behind him while I pull away. Tobin struggles violently, screaming that he will break both our necks, but he is unable to free himself from Kaleb's firm hold. Kaleb is tall and thin, but as I have just discovered, he is also very strong.

"Stop it, you idiot," he says. "We are on the same side. What is wrong with you?"

"The boy is a traitor. He is siding with the German. They have been talking, conspiring. You cannot trust him."

"It is you I do not trust," says Rebekah to Tobin. She is suddenly forceful in a way she has not shown before. Then to her brother: "He is loose: a wild beast who will fail us all. Look at his face. He is mad! He hates us!"

"Shut up," says Tobin. "You think you are better than all of us. You look down your nose even at your own brother."

"Be quiet!" yells Kaleb, who looks at me, then back at Tobin. "Henrik is one of us. You don't have to fight him. I think we must all get some sleep. I think that sleep will cure the anger."

"Henrik," says Kaleb. "It is probably best that you do not visit the German again tonight." He picks up my drawing book and passes it to me. Some of the pages are bent.

I storm off to my room, frustrated that I am bound to these people. I slam the door and lie on the bed. My nose is hurting and my ear is buzzing from the blow. I am exhausted but I am too old to cry now. Or perhaps some of my grief has been cured by the act of survival. All I know is, at the first opportunity I want to kill Tobin myself. He is an enemy to us all.

But now, there is renewed hope that I will find my sister, and that hope lies with the German.

CHAPTER 20

Rebekah is naked from the waist up and we are lying on a bed. She is on top of me, pressing her breasts against me, and her mouth is covering mine.

"Riki!"

I wake suddenly to morning light, which pierces the gap in the pale lime-green curtains, and Kaleb standing over me.

"What are you doing?"

Under the sheet my penis is leaking and the fluid has seeped into the fabric that lies across the top of me, leaving a small, dark, sticky stain.

"What's this? Up to no good."

"Quiet," I say, coming fully awake now. "Please get out of here."

Rebekah walks in and asks what we are talking about, and I grab the area of sheet to hide the results of my dream.

Kaleb looks at me and I want to throw something at him. He winks to say that the secret between us is safe.

"Go away," says Kaleb to Rebekah, still smiling. "This is not your business."

Rebekah throws her hands in the air.

"Boys are such idiots."

When she is gone, Kaleb laughs and jumps on me, punching me.

I tell him to go away and turn to the wall so I can imagine Rebekah again. If he knew I had been dreaming of his sister, he would probably hit me harder.

But he stays.

"When do you think you will go?"

"Soon."

"You know if you wait, the other partisans will have maps of the roads and German bases so that you can get to Cracow more safely."

It makes sense to stay, but I am feeling that time is slipping through my fingers. Kaleb is constantly finding ways to keep me with them, though what he says is logical. I need direction.

"I am sorry about Tobin," says Kaleb, changing the subject. "He will be better today."

I do not tell him about the conversation with the German. I think I must keep that information close. Perhaps I can't trust Kaleb either.

"What is wrong with Tobin?" I ask carefully, testing their friendship.

"Lots."

This causes me to laugh.

I go downstairs sometime later. I am always thinking of something new to draw and I have run out of pages in my book. I look for paper in what was once an office and find loose sheets in a desk drawer. I take the sheets and tuck them between the other pages of my drawing book. On the desk there is a square patch that has less dust than the rest of the surface, perhaps where a typewriter once sat.

Rebekah is sitting outside at a small, round table on the terrace. The pavers are cracked and weeds grow through. The air is crisp and the sun is weak.

She holds her hands together in a ball. When she opens them, a butterfly rises and flutters away over some low bushes towards the sun. Rebekah's face is radiant, as bright and white as if she is feeding light to the sun, instead of the reverse. She turns to look at me. Her mouth is open so that her teeth are just showing. She is not smiling but neither is she scowling at my intrusion on her moment. I am suddenly guilty as I remember the dream from this morning.

"It is a perfect morning," she says.

"Yes, but aren't you cold?" The weather is turning and there is iciness to the air when we stand in the shadows. Rebekah has no coat and wears only sandals. I remember that in the cupboard there are warm clothes that would fit her too.

She doesn't respond. She is somewhere else in her head perhaps. I sit on one of the white iron chairs and imagine we are at this country manor on holiday.

I am disappointed when the boys join us. I am enjoying the time with Rebekah, even just her silence.

"We are going out hunting. You should come and learn some things."

I don't want to go. I want to stay close to Rebekah. I want to speak to the German.

"What is it that we hunt?"

"There are boars here and perhaps some elk. If we don't shoot anything, we will walk to another village and steal."

"But the nearest village is miles away." I am wondering why anyone would build a house so far away from everything.

"Do you have something better to do?" asks Kaleb. Yes, I want to say, but can't. I don't want to sound ungrateful. After all, Kaleb has been kind.

The gun I stole has been taken by Tobin. He carries it in the back of his pants, as if it is his prize, not mine. But he also carries a rifle and a sharp hunter's knife.

"What do I use to hunt?"

Tobin goes inside and comes out again with a kitchen knife.

"Don't I get a gun?"

"No, we won't be using guns . . . only to protect ourselves should we come across Germans," says Kaleb as he shoulders his rifle.

We wander the forest for an hour, marking trees so that we don't get lost. Tobin begins to whistle loudly behind us. Kaleb turns around angrily.

"What are you doing? Have you lost your mind? Do you want the Germans to find us again?"

Tobin begins to laugh and I wonder at his inability to care.

I see a slight movement between the trees. "Look," I say and Kaleb has seen it too.

A wild boar stands a short distance away. He has seen us before we have seen him and he takes cover behind a low thicket.

"Be still," says Kaleb.

"How do we catch him?" I whisper.

"I don't know."

I have the urge to laugh because neither of us are experienced hunters.

"We have to surround it," says Tobin. "Or I can shoot it."

"No," says Kaleb. "We have already seen the result of that. No noise."

"It is a stupid rule." He thinks about it. "If at the end of the day we have no meat, then I don't care what you say; I am shooting any animal that comes across our path."

Kaleb watches him steadily.

"You," says Tobin to me, "go around to the other side. Have your knife ready and go for the heart. When I whistle once, be ready to stop it."

"Me?"

"If the rabbi here wants to do it the hard way, then so be it," says Tobin, inclining his head towards Kaleb.

I spy the boar, which is not large but not small either. I have heard they can be fierce.

"We will be chasing him . . . right on his tail," says Kaleb.

I wonder if I have the short end of the plan.

The boar seems to have lost his focus on us; perhaps he is blind, or perhaps we have been still long enough that he forgets we are here. Perhaps he knows we are not experienced hunters.

I creep around to the rear of the boar, only several yards away. His nose is switching and he grunts softly: a warning. Tobin has covered the other third of ground. While we wait for Tobin's command, I watch the beast; his mangy charcoal coat and his long snout and teeth scrape in the soft earth of the forest floor. I would like to draw him. Perhaps I will have him wearing the uniform of a German general. Then Tobin's whistle sounds and he and Kaleb rush forward. I have not really thought of how I will stop the boar; I have been thinking that somehow the others will arrive in time to help.

The creature bears down on me without seeing me, running without thought, mowing down the clump of trees that have been my disguise and everything else in his path, including me, throwing me backwards onto the ground. He does not stop to gore me, thankfully, because he has smelled the chase of others on his tail. I lie, winded, with my knife still poised.

Tobin has managed to jump on top of him. The boar lets out a squeal that seems louder than a rifle shot before he bites down on Tobin's arm, breaking skin. Kaleb grabs him from behind while Tobin stabs at his snout with his free hand. His teeth are no match for the knife and he is forced to release his piercing hold on Tobin. The creature wriggles free from Kaleb's arms and runs into the forest at full speed, snout bleeding.

"You imbecile!" screeches Tobin at me. "Why didn't you catch it?"

"Don't be a fool," says Kaleb in my defense. "He did not stand a chance. In any case, Rebekah may not eat swine."

"Will you?" I stand bent over, my hands resting on my thighs while I catch my breath. I am thinking about what Kaleb has just said. I am thinking about Papa.

"What?"

"Eat swine?"

"Yes. I think that God will forgive me this time, that he makes exceptions."

"And what about the rest of us then?" I ask jokingly, without spite.

"Did you not know? The rest of us are doomed!" says Tobin.

"I did not mean it that way," says Kaleb, embarrassed. "God watches over all of us."

"Even the Führer?"

"Maybe not the Führer."

Kaleb shares the joke this time.

Tobin looks away sourly, as if we are fools, and examines his wound. We head deeper into the forest to look for the beast. I have not quite recovered; my chest and ribs are sore. After another hour of walking, Tobin is seething.

"We should have shot the swine," says Tobin. I am starting to wish we had also.

Kaleb confides to me that he is glad we did not catch the boar, which would have offended his sister. He makes light conversation quietly so as not to scare any more of the wildlife. He talks about the villages around the forest, and about the days when he and Rebekah would go on holidays to a lake where they would swim and bake in the sunshine. He says that Rebekah was afraid of the water and would stay in the shallows. He says that she was sick often with a bad chest, that she wasn't allowed to stay in the water long or play outside much. He says that she had recurrent infections.

"What will you do after the war?"

"I will study to be a rabbi."

"You'll be a preacher then?"

"No, a teacher."

"What do rabbis teach?"

"The ways of our faith: 'Those who are wise shall shine like the brightness of the firmament, and those who turn many to righteousness, like the stars forever and ever.'"

Kaleb tells me that during his bar mitzvah he had a spiritual awakening, as if God was calling him for something. He was so moved that after this he would study the concepts of the Torah most nights.

"I've always enjoyed discussing ideals and ethics with my father and friends. And I especially like helping the young ones find their faith."

I tell him that what he is doing now is far from his plans. But he does not think that it is very far from his original plan at all. "It is merely an intersection," he says, "before a straight road presents itself that will lead to justice."

It is then that I see movement just to my left. I think it might be a hare. I walk stealthily towards it and see that I am right. Its whiskers are twitching wildly; its eyes are fixed. It knows I am there. I inch closer and then it is off and I make chase, jumping high over thickets and weaving through trees until I am upon it, one hand and then the other catching its hind legs. It tries to wriggle free, its back legs churning the loose earth and dead leaves around it.

With one twist I break its neck, as I have seen Femke do to the hares she caught in traps set in the forest. The others have heard the commotion and followed me a short way; they wait as I approach with the kill, then examine it.

"It is too small," says Tobin.

"It is better than nothing," says Kaleb. He turns to me. "Where did you learn to run? You should be running for Poland."

"Or running from Poland."

Tobin is impassive. At least his former bad mood is gone now that he knows there will be meat to eat tonight.

Kaleb chuckles. "Riki, you can steal guns, run fast, and catch small animals. Do you have any other skills we should know about?"

We return with the hare and Tobin walks on ahead. I ask Kaleb about Tobin and how they became friends.

"We grew up in the same town but we hardly knew each other before the German invasion. Tobin's father was killed by Nazis at the start of the war for refusing to give up his valuables in a raid on his home. Tobin had to leave school early to work in a factory to support himself. We have little in common other than we were forced together through circumstance."

When Kaleb and Rebekah lost their parents and Tobin lost his job and then his home, they fled together. Many others were killed but the three of them escaped and found the partisans, by chance, in the forest house.

"You just have to give Tobin room. It is good to have him on our side."

Anyone who needs excuses, I think to myself, *is probably not a worthy friend.* I do not trust Tobin. There is something bad about him, something that cannot be tamed.

We come to the house in the forest, which seems to be off the Germans' radar. It is not part of any village and is apparently located far enough into the forest to not attract attention.

It is then we hear the hum of aircraft high above us, heading east.

"What about aircraft that fly over? Can't they see the house?"

"One house in a Polish forest is not the concern of the Luftwaffe," says Kaleb. "I think they have their sights set elsewhere."

CHAPTER 21

It is early. I am keen to speak to the German. I pass Tobin's room and notice that he is missing. I take the opportunity to unlock Otto's door but see that he is sleeping heavily and decide to let him rest.

As I lock the door again, I hear sounds from within the supply room below me. I creep downstairs and watch secretly from behind the door to see who it is. Tobin takes out a key that is hidden in a book. The key unlocks a metal box that has been hidden under clothing, and he retrieves a small brown bottle from it and empties the contents into his hand. He takes out a bandage for the wound on his arm. He turns in my direction and I draw quickly back, closing my eyes and hoping that he has not seen me. I disappear into the next room and stay there until he is gone.

Later that morning I check to see that Tobin is outside before I open the secret, locked tin box. Inside are bottled painkillers, powders like I have seen used on Mama's wound, and needles fixed to small tubes. These tubes contain morphine: something my papa once took for his pain. I take two of the sachets and two of the tubes and hope that Tobin does not notice them missing.

Upstairs, the German has not touched his food. When he sees the medicine, his eyes open more widely. Otto takes the tube of morphine from me eagerly, snaps off the cap, and inserts the needle into his arm. He does not wince from the piercing; it is nothing compared to the pain in his shoulder. After this, I apply some of the powder to his wound.

He is appreciative. Medicine is better than gold. I hear the sound of heavy steps downstairs. I cannot be caught with the German while Tobin is around. I return to my room.

It is late at night. There are murmurings in Rebekah's room and shuffling noises. Something slides along the floor, then there is a crashing sound.

I go to her room and knock softly, and when there is no answer, I turn the door handle. Tobin is on top of Rebekah on the bed, pulling at her dress. I switch on the light and see that he has his hand clasped over her mouth. A lamp lies in pieces beside the bed.

When he sees me, he jumps up quickly.

"What are you doing?" I say.

"It is none of your business. Get out!"

"Rebekah?"

"He is forcing me to be with him."

Tobin smiles. "I was only trying to kiss her." He puts his arm around her. "See! We are good friends."

She shrugs his arm away violently and turns to the wall so that I cannot see her face.

"I don't think she wants you here," I say. "You should get out."

"No, you should get out!" He does not say this loudly but in a menacing whisper, and I realize that he does not want Kaleb woken.

"I think I will call Kaleb," I say. "Maybe he would like to know about this."

Tobin says nothing but stares at me through cold, glazed eyes that make my neck tingle. We stand close, facing one another.

He is the first to turn away, towards Rebekah. "Prick-teaser!" he says, under his breath. "You have led me on, you know you have!"

He pushes past me, butting my shoulder with his own. It is a short, sharp pain replaced quickly with relief that he is gone.

Rebekah sits facing the window, her hands in her lap. I go to stand beside her. When she looks up at me, I see that she is ashamed, that perhaps she is thinking she is somehow to blame. I tell her that she has done nothing wrong. That it is all in Tobin's head.

"Do you want me to wake your brother?"

"No," she says quickly. "It will be too ugly. It is best to say nothing. I can handle it."

I do not want to say anything further but it is clear that she is no match for someone like Tobin. He might be small but he is a powerful ball of muscle. There is also something that tells me he would fight to the death, even without a cause. What is to become of her in the company of such a madman?

"You must tell Kaleb once I am gone," I say.

"You're going?" she says, as if she has forgotten.

"Yes, I must find my sister."

She looks down. "Yes, you must."

We have each been sent in different directions to steal some food. It has been a long day; I have been travelling for hours and I am exhausted. I have taken a sack of grain and milked a cow, returning carefully with the bucket so as not to spill a precious drop.

I am allowed to take the German some food, but only small portions. He must eat with his hands. He is not allowed a fork for eating or a pencil for writing; these could be used as weapons. Otto says he is feeling a little better but he needs a doctor to tend the wound if he is to fully recover. I see that the area around the bullet hole is still inflamed and his skin is hot to the touch. The powder can't cure something this serious.

Tobin has been pacing angrily. He is anxious for the partisans to return so that he can fight with them: "Fight with real men," he says.

The reason I have not yet left is that I am planning to take the German with me when I go, and I am waiting for Otto to improve. He has promised that if I help him get to Cracow, he will help me. He shows me a picture of his girlfriend in Cracow, who is the daughter of a German officer. She is standing beside her father, who wears the Nazi uniform. Otto has reminded me that he is the enemy. He sees the change in my expression at the sight of the officer and quickly puts the photo away. He explains that the girl, Emelie, is his Polish girlfriend: one of the new Germans. He shows me letters from Emelie which are very personal and explicit, recounting the nights they were together. My cheeks are reddening and I have to stop reading. But, he admits, Emelie is not his real love. There is another girl in Germany who he has been in love with for a very long time and hopes to marry.

Otto believes that he can find out the location of an orphanage and the addresses of officers from Emelie, who might have learned these from her father. I show him the lighter again and he examines it. He still does not recognize the initials and I believe him this time.

I do not need the maps from the partisans. I need Otto. I am scared now that should the partisans return before Otto is well enough to travel, he might be executed. Do I take Otto now and risk him dying, or do I wait a few days for him to get better, and hope the partisans do not return?

Rebekah and I talk more freely now and sometimes she will even talk about her family, but only about the good times. She talks about Hanukkah, which is due to happen soon, and how normally they would light candles and have lots of family visiting and there would be children everywhere. She says that it is a weeklong celebration of rich food, where plates of food constantly replace the empty ones. There is singing and her grandfather plays the violin. She says that although he can play well, his mind is going and he does not always remember her name. She says she misses the busy house.

Then a gray cloud passes across her face and she no longer wants to talk.

I help clean up after dinner and Tobin doesn't like this. He does not like that I spend so much time in the kitchen with Rebekah. I wonder if I can trust her about the German. I think that I might miss her when I am gone.

But my plans to leave are dashed when the partisans return. They appear out of the forest in the middle of the day, their faces muddied, their clothes dark with sweat and blood. There are eight of them and they are solemn and tired and do not speak.

Tobin greets them excitedly. He is very familiar with them. These were the first ones to help him and Kaleb and Rebekah when they escaped into the forest.

Tobin follows them inside, on their heels like a puppy, barking orders at Rebekah to boil water for washing, and to boil the vegetables and slice some bread.

"Is there no meat?" asks one of them. These are the first words spoken to us.

"Not today, but later we will hunt," says Tobin.

They go out to the rear of the house to use the water basin. They strip down to their underwear. There are six men and two women. I am too embarrassed to stay and too embarrassed to walk away, but the women do not seem to care that anyone else is present.

Tobin asks them questions. A couple of them respond that they have killed many, but generally he is ignored.

Rebekah pours boiling water into the outdoor basin. The partisans wash themselves with the soap that she has brought them. They do not look at her, nor do they thank her. Exhaustion is etched in their faces: their eyes sag, their expressions are dull. Most disappear upstairs and I remember the wardrobes with clothing, and wonder if I have taken one of their rooms—if we all have.

Several reappear wearing clean shirts. Kaleb and I take buckets down to the river to refill the water tanks.

When we return, Tobin is showing the partisans his German prize. Otto has been brought downstairs and he sits in a chair, his arms tied behind him. I know he is aware that I am in the room, but I can also tell that he is resisting the urge to look at me directly.

Eri is the leader and speaks some German but Machail, another partisan, is fluent in the language and does most of the questioning, relating Otto's answers back to the rest of us. It seems Otto has lied to the German army about his age; he is seventeen, not nineteen. Eri punches him in the stomach and the boy retches, but he can't lean forward because his torso is bound to the chair. I turn away and Rebekah sees me do this and looks down at her feet.

All of us watch the questioning. Spittle sits on Otto's chin and his eyes keep closing involuntarily. I am tense with fear. I want to say something but Rebekah touches my hand, then draws away again. Did she mean to do that? Is she afraid that I will attempt to stop the interrogation? I am unsure. I notice that from across the room Tobin is looking at our hands—at our point of contact.

It is revealed that Otto is part of a reconnaissance group that scouts the towns after Hitler's Schutzstaffel, or SS, has been through, to clean them up and to place any villagers left behind on trucks to a camp in the west. They are little more than scavengers, says Eri. After an hour, the questioning stops.

"He is just a child, barely off his mama's breast," says Machail, who looks too frail to be a fighter himself. "He knows nothing that can help us."

Eri instructs one of the other men, a former medical student, to get rid of the bullet in Otto's shoulder and stitch him up. It seems they will treat him as a prisoner of war and perhaps offer him up to his unit as part of a negotiation. Though, after some discussion, they conclude that it is unlikely the Germans will negotiate; Otto may be more useful on one of their missions instead. Tobin looks disappointed. I think he was hoping for an execution.

Otto is taken to another room and I follow; the partisans take no notice that I am there. In their eyes I am just a child. A man and a woman are to perform the procedure. They instruct Otto to remove his clothes and lie on a table. The room was once a formal sitting room like the one we had in Germany, where grown-ups would sip their brandy and wine. Today it is an operating theater. The partisans have their own supplies of medicine in their bags.

"He is doing well, considering the wound," says the woman.

I do not volunteer that he has already received some treatment. The man, known as Danii, swabs the wound, which is inflamed around the edges, then begins to cut with a small scalpel. The woman puts a wad of cloth in Otto's mouth for him to bite down on.

"Shouldn't he have morphine?" I ask.

I am about to tell them that Tobin has a tin with medicine.

"We don't waste such medicine on a German. Why are you still here?" asks the woman called Ailsa. Both are now interested in my presence.

"Get out!" says Ailsa. She is stocky, with a square-shaped face.

"Wait!" says Danii. "He can watch. It is a good thing for others to learn, in case we are blown up and someone else needs a surgeon."

It is a joke, in part, but Ailsa does not smile.

"Fetch the morphine," instructs Danii.

"We shouldn't waste it," says the woman.

"We have enough for now," he says.

She begrudgingly retrieves some morphine from her own bag, not the supply room. I wonder if Tobin has stolen his secret stash from the partisans. She roughly pierces the skin on Otto's shoulder and pumps the needle with less-than-gentle hands. Danii cuts the bullet out. It is deep and nestled in bone. Otto whimpers slightly but his body is steady. I am not squeamish; rather, I am fascinated. They patch the wound, then sit him up.

I offer to take him upstairs and he leans on me heavily.

Ailsa eyes me curiously. "Children! They can't tell good from bad," she says humorlessly.

I lay Otto back on some blankets in the tiny storeroom.

"Thank you," he whispers and then he is asleep.

Eri is not content with vegetables. He has come from the forest with a dead deer. Rebekah and I must cut it up. I have never taken apart an animal this large before and neither has Rebekah. The same woman who helped with the surgery seems to know about this also. She instructs us to gut the torso while she watches. Rebekah rubs her nose with the back of her hand and accidentally smears blood across her face. She has gone pale. She does not like the sight of blood.

"Can you get the stove ready?" I ask her so that she doesn't have to do this.

Ailsa chops the limbs with her axe while I skin the pieces. When we have finished, I carry the pieces in sacks into the kitchen, where Rebekah is waiting. My hands are sore.

We boil only a portion of the meat in spices with potatoes. We make a feast and take plates of food to each of the partisans, who are now talking in the sitting room, draped across chairs and couches. There is only a faint smell of sweat now that they are washed.

Rebekah, Kaleb, and I do not take large portions. It is clear that the partisans have that privilege now. Tobin, however, takes the same as the newcomers.

Now that they are clean, I can examine their faces as new subjects to draw. The men wear beards and the women have cut their hair short. Their faces and lower arms are browned from their work; their necks and upper arms are white.

Tobin is transfixed by the men and the accounts of their attacks. They tell us that they have lost ten of the partisans during recent skirmishes, and were lucky to escape the blasting of a metal factory, which has been turned into a German munitions factory. They say they had to sacrifice some of the local Poles who had been working there.

"These are the trials of war," says one. But it is said without emotion. These people seem devoid of sentiment.

They have been travelling for six weeks and plan to stay here for several weeks, since the manor house is a secluded base to work from, nestled in difficult terrain. A track that led here from a village, before the war, has become overgrown, and its entranceway is disguised. It is unlikely that Germans will bother them here.

I am disappointed that they are staying because it means I cannot escape with Otto as easily. They have someone on lookout twenty-four hours. They are planning to head southeast eventually, because they hear there will be more trouble in Zamosc. I listen carefully as they tell of more Jews being taken and farms stolen.

Kaleb tells them that Zamosc is where I am from. They are interested in this and question me on business there. I am pleased to tell them all the information I know but am suddenly concerned for Mama and Femke, and I wonder if I will be back in time to help them.

Upstairs, I discover that my things have been moved to Tobin's room and Kaleb's to Rebekah's. The partisans have taken over the other three rooms. They are everywhere, filling up all the spaces in the house so there is nowhere for privacy. The house is suddenly smaller. But there is relief at least for Rebekah, who has the safety of her brother.

I am grateful that Tobin is rarely in our bedroom as he likes to be close to the partisans. He stays up late with them and returns to the room a couple of hours before dawn.

The partisans have many meetings over the next few days. The rooms are filled with cigarette smoke and a metallic smell of weaponry. Tobin is there and Kaleb sometimes, and sometimes me. They study maps marked with German stations, train lines, camps in the east, trade routes, and factories. They know where they can steal explosives. Several of the partisans leave early one morning to get these. They may be gone for several days.

In the meantime, the rest of the group will travel to a German village many miles away. Kaleb and Tobin will accompany them. I am told that I must stay and guard the house with Rebekah.

With so many gone, this would have been a good time to head for Cracow, except that Otto—who was meant to go on the mission with the partisans—has a fever and might not last our trip. He has told me that the journey will be long, treacherous, and cold. The weather is already turning. There are frosts in the morning and I am wearing my coat to bed.

The group leaves while we are sleeping. I check on Otto, who is still burning with fever. Rebekah puts cold cloths across his body; then we both spend the rest of the day cleaning the house and the partisans' clothes. I resent that I am reduced to performing these domestic duties instead of searching for Greta.

Once the chores are completed, Rebekah disappears in the direction of the river and I sit on the back terrace with my sketch-book. I sharpen my pencil with a knife and, from memory, draw a picture of Eri. He sits on a tree stump cleaning his rifle. I draw his deep frown lines, and a cigarette, half finished, hangs from his mouth.

Rebekah startles me. I did not hear her come up behind me with the buckets she carries to fill the water tank. I offer to help.

"It is too late. I have walked all this way anyway. You can go back and get some more if you want."

She disappears into the kitchen and I follow her.

"Actually, we have enough for now," she says. "Keep drawing. It is a good record to have."

I return to my drawing and she comes to watch this time. I am aware of her gaze and find it difficult to concentrate now.

"Do you have one of me yet?"

"Yes. Do you want to see it?"

She nods and I turn back the pages so that she can see the one I have drawn of her at the cabin table, her head bent.

"It is good," she says. "But you have made her too pretty."

"No," I say. "It is exactly as you look."

She blushes and it is the first time that I think she might like me. The thought hurts, knowing that I plan to leave her. We are interrupted by the return of her brother and the partisans, one of whom is missing. They wash at the basins, their faces grim. I am afraid to ask how their mission went because there is no hint of celebration in their expressions. Tobin arrives soon after with teeth gritted. He does not wash, but instead marches inside and up to his room, where he slams the door.

Rebekah and I follow Kaleb inside. We learn that they were all lying in wait to ambush some German officers. They were supposed to wait until the truck carrying several of the officers was nearly at a checkpoint where the group was hiding in bushes beside the road. But Tobin started to shoot before they reached the checkpoint and this alerted them to stop their vehicle.

The partisans fired at the vehicle, eventually killing the four Germans, but they lost Machail, who is now buried in the forest. Eri has told Tobin that he will not be accompanying them on the next mission. That he needs to grow up first.

While the partisans gather in the dining room for their meeting, Tobin, who is now excluded, storms around the house looking to pick fights with Rebekah. I learn from Otto that Tobin went directly to Otto's room and kicked him in fury. I am so enraged with Tobin, I confront him on this.

"Who do you think you are?" shouts Tobin.

"A human, unlike you."

He shoves me hard and I fall backwards onto the ground. I stand to face him again. I will not back down. I am ready to fight, but the noise has alerted one of the partisans.

"That is enough," the man shouts at Tobin. "Don't you think you have done enough damage today?"

Eri arrives and the two men glare at Tobin, who curses and heads to his room.

I decide not to mention that Tobin has kicked Otto, since the partisans are unlikely to share my sympathy.

It is the night of the next operation and the men are leaving Tobin behind. He is angry and says that the partisans are stupid Jews who don't have any idea about real fighting. I do not like this talk—considering he is the only non-Jew amongst us—nor that he carries his gun with him to every room.

"Why don't you leave to fight the war elsewhere?" I ask.

"I might just do that," he says, sneering. "I might even tell the Germans about this house full of dirty Jews who can be taken to the camps."

Rebekah looks down. Her hands are trembling and to stop them she grabs the edge of the table.

"You shouldn't say things like that," I say. "We are all on the same side."

Tobin clenches his fist and I think he might hit me. I am ready if he does, though my chances of beating him are slim.

"Just go away," says Rebekah, distracting him.

"See! You need a girl to fight your battles." He turns and walks out the front door.

My heart, which was racing, slows to normal pace.

"He is mad," says Rebekah.

Before the group leaves, Kaleb is told to stay and I am told to come. I am relieved that Kaleb agrees to remain behind because I would not have left Rebekah alone. Kaleb seems happy to let me go this time.

Before we go, I am given a short gun that is heavy but can be fired from one hand. I tell Eri that I am not used to fighting, that I have only had brief target practice.

"No matter," says Eri. "You will get used to it."

The walk is long. It is four hours, and I wonder how these men do it sometimes, night after night.

The men are crude and treat the women the same as men. The two women, Ailsa and Martha don't care; they are just as lewd. Ailsa squats to urinate beside the path. She is not bothered that we can see.

We come upon a path that leads through several houses. We must be quiet because many of the Polish residents are "German snitches" now and they would give us away. The faint smell of gunpowder hangs in the air, and in the distance, there is the familiar hum of German planes.

In this village there are no German bases, but there are people here who are known to be spies. We have come to interrogate them, as they have information. It is late and we hear no noise from within the little house we have stopped in front of. Under the moon it looks peaceful and pretty, and I can't imagine that bad people live here.

Eri takes a key from his pocket and with lightning speed opens the front door. I am curious as to where this key came from, but uncertainty and apprehension override curiosity when I am nudged in the back to move forward. We attempt to file into the dark house stealthily, but the floorboards creak under our steps. There are five of us: the two women, Eri, Danii, and me.

Immediately, the house is flooded with light and an old man points a gun at us from his bedroom doorway. He wears a long shirt over trousers and slippers, but he does not look sleepy. It is as if he has been waiting for us.

"Put the gun down," says Danii. I understand that I am here to help translate from German to Polish, and from Polish to German, to replace Machail. Eri speaks some German but not as well as I do. I am here in case he does not understand something. The women are here for backup. I am told they are good with their guns.

"Put down the gun," says Eri, his voice deep and steady. "You kill one of us, there are still four to finish you and your wife."

I feel my bowels loosen slightly. I know what he is capable of. I know that this threat is not idle.

"My wife isn't here. She is staying with our daughter who has just had a baby."

"I doubt that. Put the gun down."

"You will not kill us." He has betrayed his own lie with that "us."

"Not if you put the gun down."

He puts the gun on the table and moves to a chair. He sits down gingerly, as if bending is an effort.

"Where have they been taken to?"

"Who?"

"You know who." Eri takes a chair and sits in front of the old man. It is a tactic that Tobin used on me, perhaps taken from the partisans, who use it to interrogate face-to-face, to encourage conversation.

"I don't know anything."

"You are a spy. You know everything. The family who lived in this house . . . where were they taken?"

"I told you: I don't know."

"Get her!" Eri orders.

Ailsa goes into the bedroom, opens a cupboard door, and grabs the man's wife, dragging her from the room. Ailsa shoves her hard and the old woman falls.

"You said you won't kill us," shrieks the old man, looking at his wife on the floor. He speaks no Polish. He is one of the new Germans placed here to spy.

"I said I would not kill, but I said nothing about not harming either of you."

The wife is whimpering on the floor. The old man tries to snatch his gun off the table but Eri is quicker, lunging forward to grab the old man's wrists and slamming them on the table. There is the sound of bones hitting wood and the old man cries out loudly.

"Silence," says Danii. "You will wake the neighbors."

"It doesn't matter," says Eri. "We will tell them that there is a spy amongst them working for the Germans."

Eri points to me. "Sit the woman in the chair and hold your gun to her." To Martha he says: "Search his papers." And to the others: "Make a noose from the ceiling."

The woman appeals to me for help. She says that her back is sore but I ignore her. In fact, I only glance at her eyes once, and then I hold the gun at her without really focusing. Perhaps it is the adrenaline running through me that I feel no sympathy towards the begging couple. Perhaps it is Eri's hate, which has spread to me, or perhaps it is my memories of Rani and the shallow grave in the forest.

"Now, old man, unless you tell us where the family who lived here was sent, I will get my boy here to shoot your wife and then I will hang you."

I see that Danii has strung up the noose over a beam like he has done this many times before. I wonder how it is that someone who heals can also assist with an execution. But then, here I am holding a gun on an old woman. It is not so strange in war.

"I know nothing."

"Shoot the woman in the knee!" instructs Eri. It takes a couple of seconds to realize that he is talking to me.

I focus on the knee but I can't pull the trigger. It must be several seconds before Martha pushes me out of the way and shoots the woman. The old woman shrieks in pain and collapses on the floor.

The female partisans seem more ruthless than the men, as if they have much to prove to the German army of men.

"All right," says the man, crying now and begging us to leave his wife alone. I feel ashamed that I have not done anything yet, and ashamed that someone else had to, and ashamed also that I am part of such violence.

"The family you speak of was sent to Auschwitz."

"What happens to the Jews there?"

"They are kept safely in prisons until the end of the war. They are well cared for."

"I don't believe you." Eri points his gun at the wife.

"Stop!" yells the man, looking at his wife. "Please don't kill her. I will tell! I will tell everything!"

Eri sits back down in front of him.

"Most of the Jews are there to work."

"And others?"

The man pauses. "Some are used in experiments."

Eri looks at me quizzically and asks me to repeat the translation, as if he can't at first believe it.

"What sort of experiments?" he asks the man.

"Medical. To test medicines and drugs."

"Do they feel pain?"

The man swallows hard.

"Do they feel pain?"

"Yes! Sometimes!" says the man, and then quietly to his lap: "Sometimes, they feel pain."

"Have you seen this?"

"No, but I have a son who works there."

It now makes sense that he spies. He has Germany in his bones. He is a Nazi.

"But it is for good," says the spy. "My son says that with such tests they will discover cures for diseases."

"For Jews too?" asks Martha cynically.

The man doesn't answer. He looks into his hands and then at his wife.

"I thought not," says Martha, who kicks him hard in the leg. The man barely flinches because he is too preoccupied with his wife's pain.

"Are the Jews being killed there?"

"Some."

"How many?"

"I don't know. A few. Only those who make trouble."

"And how are they killed?" asks Eri calmly, like he is just going through the motions, as if he already has the answers.

"Some die from their illnesses; sometimes they are shot or hanged. Others, I believe, are gassed."

"You believe?"

"Yes. This is being tested more widely across the camps." It sounds like he is telling us something that he read in a newspaper.

"But," he says, suddenly remembering, "many are killed humanely, with injections." The rise in his tone suggests that what he has just said will somehow be seen as something good, as if it will somehow make a difference to his current position.

"Can you explain to us how the killing of people because of their race can be humane?" asks Danii, not calmly like Eri.

The man cannot. He cannot even meet Danii's gaze.

"The family taken there from this house—the Aronofsky family—where are they?" asks Eri.

"All dead. All the first shipment is dead."

Eri stares at something on the wall. He does not say anything for several minutes. These are long and painful minutes and no one says anything. The others are used to Eri. The old man's eyes keep darting sideways in the direction of the noose.

"I wonder if you would make us some coffee," says Eri suddenly and politely to the man.

The old man is surprised. He was expecting a bullet to a part of his body, as was I.

"Yes, of course . . . coffee. It is cold tonight, yes?" says the old man. He stands up cautiously, nervously, waiting for Eri to confirm these instructions, but Eri says nothing and the man then continues towards the kitchen. He glances at his wife, who has gone quiet on the floor. I believe she has fainted from pain and shock. No one bothers to check.

We watch the man open a tin and scoop coffee grounds into a pot on the stove. I do not want coffee. I do not understand what Eri is doing. He lights a cigarette and relaxes back into the chair. Perhaps he is allowing himself time to think what he will do. I notice that the others stand fixed, like statues. Their guns do not waver.

When I look at Ailsa, she is smiling and it is then I understand. They are playing with him. Eri has designed this. He is torturing him with time—time the man has to think about the noose and his impending death.

A flash goes off. A bullet passes through the middle of our group, but miraculously misses us all. The old woman has pulled a gun from her dressing gown pocket. Martha fires several times into her head.

The old man, who is not as frail as he made himself appear, has slipped out the back door. Ailsa fires her gun at the doorway but he is already gone.

"Quick, after him!" calls Danii.

I walk to the window as everyone but Eri rushes after the escapee, who runs along the narrow road, calling for help. I see that lights in the surrounding houses remain turned off, and curtains stay closed and still. Everyone is too afraid to look outside their windows.

I close one eye, aim the gun at the running man, and pull the trigger. The weapon jumps in my hand slightly but I have control of it. The old man crumples to the ground.

Eri gets up from the table to stand beside me at the window. We watch as Danii bends to check that the man is dead before returning to the house. Eri turns and looks at me as if he is seeing me for the first time. He nods. It is gratitude and commendation.

I think how easily death can happen, how easily I can make it happen. My body is trembling slightly, but there is no regret, only numbness. It is but one life for the many, perhaps hundreds, who have died in the camps. That is what I tell myself. That is what I will tell myself if I have to do it again.

"Let's go," says Ailsa excitedly as she rushes back in.

"Not yet," says Eri, taking a seat again. "Let's have our coffee first."

It is only the next morning that I learn the Aronofsky family is Eri's family. His immediate family as well as his aunt, uncle, and cousins are now all gone. Kaleb tells me this. He also tells that Eri and the others have been talking about my aim on the man who fled, that I would make a good partisan.

The town we visited has no more Jews. Most of them were massacred by German police. Some, like Eri, escaped. He had argued with his parents and cousins about returning to the village after it was raided the first time. While he escaped farther into the forest, his family returned to their house—and shortly afterwards were taken to the camps. He later learned that one of the new residents had a close affiliation with the Germans.

This was the man I killed.

It is getting colder now and I am disappointed with myself that I have not left earlier. Next time the partisans go on a mission, I plan to leave for Cracow.

Rebekah tends to sit closer to me now, as if I have passed some test that allows her to. She talks about her childhood. About how Kaleb and she were very different, how Kaleb was always quicker and cleverer. How childhood illness made it difficult to meet people and make friends. How the war has brought her closer to her brother. But even with this new openness, her words are measured. When I question her about her parents, she goes quiet and finds excuses to leave. These questions are obviously painful for her. I know from living with women that while they say much, they will only reveal the things they want to, that they carry many secrets.

The rest of the partisans return with explosives. They have also brought with them wine and whisky and more vodka. Again there is much washing up and much feeding of them while they are hungry. They wear packs that carry the materials they need to make bombs.

But this is to be no early night of rest. It is an occasion to catch up with old friends, and I am considered part of the group now. Tobin is there too, though it is as if there is a window of glass between him and us that might shatter any moment. When Rebekah and I go to collect more water for the washing tank, Tobin says to us under his breath that we are nothing but slaves for the Jews. There is malice in these words.

But I am not the only one to hear this. Martha has heard and she whispers something to Eri.

Eri instructs Tobin to carry logs into the house. He is slow to respond and only does so when Eri takes a step towards him. The other partisans are silent and watchful. I believe they are now aware that Tobin is unsteady, that perhaps he is no longer to be trusted.

This night there is no mission. It is time to celebrate the reunion of the partisans after their successful missions. Eri seems more lively and happy to have everyone back together. He pats me on the back and passes me a glass of vodka. I take a sip and cough and everyone laughs. I still do not have a taste for the burning liquid.

We have built a small fire outside and we drag chairs from the house to surround it.

Eri talks about the killing of his family, how he returned to find them gone. He also talks about the couple who was just killed. Once the German police find out, they may come looking for those responsible. He says he is looking forward to it if they do. He says that they hate to be outsmarted; humiliation for a Nazi is worse than death. He says that it is best to stay a few more weeks only, and then move east. They should be able to recruit more partisans for their attack on the invaders.

The men are drinking much and I see that Rebekah laughs at her brother, who has joined in. Her smile is wide and serene, her eyes glinting from the flames. I am feeling warm and funny inside from the vodka. I tell her that she is very beautiful when she smiles but she shyly walks closer to her brother.

I am an idiot for saying that.

Eri is sitting on a chair and Martha sits on him. She turns her head so that they kiss passionately. When Eri realizes that people are watching them, he puts his hand on Martha's breast. The men, and even Ailsa, cheer.

Tobin drinks but he is watching everyone as if they might turn on him, or perhaps it is that he looks for someone to blame for something. But he is at least calmer tonight. He is not wearing his usual rage. The alcohol has made him dull and lonelier still. From an outsider he would draw sympathy.

Eri and Martha disappear into the house. Eventually, the rest of us straggle inside when the fire dies and the cold seeps into our bones.

I crawl into bed with heavy limbs. It feels like the floor in my room is moving and I am relieved when my head finally rests on the pillow. Tobin is snoring loudly in the bed across from me.

Down the hallway I can hear the rhythmic squeaking of bed-springs, the grunts of Eri, and Martha's gasps. I wonder if Rebekah is listening also. My own bed sways with wine and vodka.

The partisans are planning another mission. I am asked to go also.

"We will leave Tobin to watch the house with Rebekah," says Eri.

I say nothing but Martha has seen Rebekah's face. She understands. She knows that Tobin is a predator.

"We should leave the boy this time. We need someone who is a good shot to watch the house. Tobin is strong; we will need a donkey to carry the explosives."

Eri looks at Martha. The smile is brief but I have caught it. Tobin is something of a joke between them, perhaps all of them. The looks Eri and Martha give one another are a code. There are no hugs or kisses this morning. They are bound by forces that over-ride love.

I am relieved when at lunchtime they begin to pack for their mission. The journey will take them many hours and they hope to be back just before dawn. Once they are gone, I can release Otto, who is now recovered from his illness, and we will leave together.

I go to Otto to tell him what is happening and he sits up enthu-siastically, talking rapidly about where to go first. He tells me that I can trust him when we get to Cracow, that he will always be grateful and will never give me up. That perhaps after the war I can come and stay with his mother, brother, and sisters. He has affirmed our friendship.

I look at his light skin and think that even to look as Hitler wants does not make things better. That life is hard whatever your color, whatever your race. We shake hands, positive about the future, positive that we will succeed.

But then as I pass Rebekah's room, I also feel regret. After I am gone there will be no one else to look out for her. I hope that Kaleb will watch out for his sister, but his enthusiasm seems to grow towards the partisans and their plans.

My hopes are suddenly dashed when I see that Otto is with the partisans as they begin to leave. They think that Otto might be useful, in case they need a decoy. In case they have to use him as a cover. They tell him that if he tries to escape, they will put a bullet through his head.

I watch Otto leave with the partisans. I watch the best chance to find my sister disappear behind the trees. I sit for a moment to reflect on my bad luck.

Then I remember how the partisans sleep through the day after their night missions. Perhaps tomorrow will be the time to go. I am determined to make this work. I just have to hope that after such a long walk Otto is well enough to go. I have to hope also that he is not shot by either side.

I cannot leave without telling Rebekah. I go to her room to tell her of my plans. She is wearing the dress I left for her. She has finally decided to wear it. It is pale green with flowers and long sleeves with cuffs. She is very attractive with her dark hair and smooth, light olive skin. She wears a cardigan of light green over the top of the dress. After she hears my news, her eyes are fixed and wide. I see a flash of shock and disappointment before she is once again composed.

"When?"

"I must leave tomorrow," I say.

"I thought this would be coming," she says.

"I will leave in the morning after the others return, while they are sleeping."

"You could leave now."

I find excuses: "I have no flashlight. I do not know the terrain like Eri. Last time I attempted to travel at night I got lost and nearly died." I cannot mention that I am taking Otto. I do not know how far to trust her.

Rebekah nods.

"Do you mind that I am leaving?"

"It is your right to do what you have to. Will you take the German with you?"

I look at her with an open mouth. *Has she heard us talking?* I wonder. I know that she has some knowledge of the German language.

"It makes sense," she says. "If you leave him here, Tobin will shoot him eventually. I think Otto will be grateful, and for that reason I think you can trust him. And I am sure that since he knows Cracow and the countryside, he can guide you. It is all right. I will say that I saw and knew nothing. The two of you can slip out. If I have to, I will make up something; I will say you have gone to the river, and no one will check on the German. You and I are the only ones who do."

I wonder what will happen to her when I am gone.

"What will you do?" I ask. "The men are talking about going east to fight. Kaleb has talked about this too."

"I guess I will have to follow them but Kaleb has already said that he must find a village, a safe place to hide me."

"But surely he won't desert you in a village if you don't want that."

"No, he won't, not if I ask him not to, but that doesn't stop me from being a burden. It's not that he doesn't love me; it is just that he is able to set aside sentiment. He is prepared to make sacrifices, even sacrifice himself, in his quest to find greater good. I also know that he fears for me if I come with him. Without me there, he can focus fully on his task. He has a taste for this; he wants to free our country. He wants to commit to the cause. While I am with him, he is restricted. You have relieved some of the burden on him by looking out for me here."

It is brash of me, but I can't stop my next words; it is as if they need to be said: "Do you want to come with me?"

This has surprised her. She actually pauses as if she is thinking seriously about it.

"I should stay with my brother for now. He is the only family I have left."

"Of course," I say. "You must stay." As if my suggestion was ridiculous.

Then she does something I am not expecting. She takes my hand in hers and bites her lip before she speaks.

"I will miss you," she says.

It is a shock to me. She has seemed so impersonal and mistrusting of everyone for most of the time. She has shown no affection, not even to her brother.

"I will miss you too," I say.

I am about to leave when I remember something—something that I have been meaning to tell her.

"You asked me about my mother. Well, I want to tell you this . . .

"My mama is everything good. She is beautiful on the inside and out. She always talked to us as grown-ups and she found something good in everything we did. She spoke softly and gently, like our ears needed respect, and she carried the worries of the world on her shoulders so that we did not have to. She never once complained. Even when we had to leave Germany, even when things got hard and food was short or the day was cold, she never once said aloud: this is bad or horrible or terrible. She would light up the room when she walked in, not like a bright starry entrance, nothing like that, rather like the soft light of a candle; it was so subtle you hardly noticed it until she left again, and then you would realize that the warmth was missing."

Rebekah considers me a moment and then leans forward to kiss me on the cheek. Her lips are soft. "I wish I could meet her. Good luck, Riki."

She leaves me then to stare out the window towards the fading sun. She does not come down to cook dinner that night. I take the opportunity to fill up my knapsack with food, and another bag for Otto. I also take some of the medicine from Tobin's secret stash.

There is an ache in my chest as I pass Rebekah's room to reach my own. It is wishful thinking that I might see her again, that she might open her door. But there is no light coming from within.

I lie on my bed to sleep but I am too restless and sleep is brief. Most of the time I stare at the charcoal air around me. Then there is a sound. It is the sound of muffled crying.

Chapter 22

The sun is not yet up and I am pacing outside the house, staring at the trees, afraid that the partisans will return without Otto. I have already decided that if Otto is not with them, I must leave as planned. There is no more time to wait.

Then the women and men enter the clearing, and at the back of the group walks Otto: small, beaten looking, but alive. I smile as they enter but it is a smile of relief, not of greeting. Kaleb is excited. He tells me how they blew up a German car, and shot the occupants as they tried to escape the burning vehicle. One of them was an SS general.

Part of me hopes that it is the same general who has stolen Greta, yet at the same time I need him alive because he is perhaps my link to finding her. I imagine what I will do when I find him. I think that I will be like Eri; I will tie the general to a chair and hold a gun to his wife's head until he tells me where to find Greta. This has been in my thoughts for days.

Martha says that Kaleb was very brave and I see that Tobin says nothing, his lips pinched together. He does not look at the others. Some of the men pat Kaleb on the back. I think that if there was any doubt whether Kaleb would join them or stay with his sister, there is none now. Rebekah sees everything I do, and she forces the corners of her mouth upwards supportively and congratulates them on their successful mission.

I am asked to take Otto to his room. Once it is safe to talk, I tell him of my revised plan. Despite his exhaustion, despite the distance he has already travelled, he is still anxious to go. It may be his only chance to escape.

Rebekah and I cook the group breakfast: bread and boiled eggs. They drink black coffee as they talk on the terrace at the back of the house. It is around seven o'clock in the morning now and they are not looking tired. They are fuelled by their success and still laughing at the surprise on the face of the fat general. This is description enough for me to believe that it is not the same general. I am relieved to have the chance for my own revenge, not just for taking Greta, but for Mama too, who lost her independence, her dignity, and something more precious: her daughter.

It is almost nine. I am beginning to despair that I will not be leaving today because while most of the partisans have gone to bed, others like Eri and Kaleb do not seem tired at all. Eri and Martha are cleaning the guns again, something they seem to enjoy, and Tobin is sitting gloomily against the house, watching them.

I go in search of Rebekah and find her outside, sitting at the small table by the front door, darning some holes in the socks of the fighters. I sit beside her. She has seen my worry.

"You can still go. They won't know you have gone if you leave the front way. I can watch out here and distract them if I see them walking around. They never check on the German and I will tell them you are washing at the river."

I consider this. My stomach is jumping around so much I think I will be sick.

"But won't there be someone on duty watching?"

"Who do you think has volunteered today?"

Rebekah has thought it all out for me.

"All right then. I will go fetch Otto and exit by the front door."

She nods and my chest is rising and falling fast. I go to my room to collect my things but notice that the gun that was given to me by Eri is missing from my side table. I search the bedroom and the storage room and the kitchen, but it is not anywhere. There is no more time to search.

I open the door for the German. He stands ready to leave, holding the two sleeping bags and ropes I hid in his room earlier. There is a strong smell of urine from his pot, which won't be emptied today. I whisper that we must be quiet, that some are still awake. We slip quietly out through the front door. I am surprised and disappointed when I do not see Rebekah there. We enter the forest from the estate's clearing and stop behind a tree. There is no one watching.

"We must walk fast," says Otto. "We must build up distance."

We walk fast and silently, weaving between the pines. The sun is weak today, the air is cooling, and steam rises from our breaths. I am grateful for the coat in my bag.

"Did you bring a gun?" he asks when we are minutes away. I tell him that it has been taken, how I was unable to find it. Otto looks disappointed.

We walk for several more minutes and then we hear the crunching sound of steps on fallen leaves. Tobin appears from behind a tree.

"I knew it," says Tobin. "I knew that you were a traitor."

"Tobin!" I say. "Otto is helping me find my sister."

"Do you really expect me to believe that?"

I am thinking that he will instruct us to return to the house, but instead he waves his gun to indicate that we should walk farther from the estate and deeper into the forest. Fear is building within me.

"Why don't you take us back? I will explain everything to Eri also."

"Keep walking," he says.

And then there is an explosion. At first it sounds like it is in front of me, and I put my hands over my head and crouch, by instinct. Then there is movement at my side as Otto falls to the ground, his face sideways in the dirt. There is a hole at the back of his head and part of his skull is protruding where blood oozes. I see that one of his eyes is still open. I scurry to his side.

"No," I whimper. I turn him over but his eyes are vacant as he stares at the gray above us. I feel rage building within, and tears sting my eyes.

"You could have just let us go!"

"I shot my own father and said it was the Germans. That makes me capable of anything. Did you actually think that I would let the German leave alive—or you, for that matter?"

I am thinking that it is here that I will die. Mama will not know. No one will know. Otto and I will disappear without a trace. It is a moment in time that is suspended by its sheer gravity.

"Let me go!" I shout. "I've done nothing to you."

Tobin laughs then, bitterly. "You are a Jew. You do not deserve to live. I am leaving here too—to join the German army so that I can kill all the dirty Jews I want to. So that I can tell them of the partisan plans. Our country was taken and destroyed by your kind, not the Germans."

"We are the same," I plead. "You and me, Tobin. We both want to live in our country with freedom."

"This isn't your country, but you will be buried here. Of that I am sure."

"You make no sense," I say. "You kill a German and now me. You do not know what side you are on." I spit at him like I have seen men do.

The corners of his mouth flicker. Humiliation is his weakness also.

"Get on your knees and put your arms behind you."

I do so and he steps forward.

"This is for no one but myself."

He closes one eye and sights the rifle with the other, taking aim at my forehead. I close my eyes and pray. I think of the angels on the stairs and then of Mama, Papa, and Greta. I then open my eyes at the last second to see a bullet flying out from the front of Tobin's chest, and to hear it whizzing over my shoulder. He falls forward, stiff like a doll, and I have to lean out of the way or else he will land on me.

Behind him several yards stand Eri and Kaleb, and behind them stands Rebekah.

"You should have said something," says Eri.

"You would not have let the German go," I say.

"You're right, we wouldn't have. But this nearly cost your life. We should shoot you too." He is aiming his gun at me. I look at Rebekah for signs of guilt and betrayal but her gaze is steady.

Suddenly Eri laughs and puts the gun down.

"You don't know how much I wanted to do that to the shit-eating Jew hater." He nods towards Tobin.

And Kaleb starts to laugh too. I am too nervous to laugh but I feel some of the tension leave my body.

"I saw Tobin following you," says Rebekah. "I had to tell them."

"Now, I have learned that you want to go to find your sister," says Eri. "I do not like your chances. For a start, the forest is the devil's asshole. It is winter. Soon, there will be snow and ice and nowhere for shelter. It will take you two weeks, if you are lucky, to navigate your way—possibly longer with bad weather."

"Here is a compass." He walks over to me and I stand up. He also has a hand-drawn map of the forests, which he says he doesn't need since he knows it as well as the freckles on Martha's back. He places them in my hand firmly, then pats me on my shoulder. He is large, burly, and dark and I think it is possible that he will win the battle of Zamosc; if anyone is capable of it, he is.

"You should go south and stay near the base of the mountains. Then north to Cracow from there. It is longer but safer. Follow the cattle trucks that are going to the camps. They will lead you to Cracow also.

"You are a good boy but there is still a lot you don't know. I will not be surprised to find your frozen body alongside that of your little friend."

I presume that he is referring to Otto, lying dead in the mud.

Eri, curiously, places his hand against Rebekah's cheek before turning to leave.

"Make sure you bury the bodies, and *Zol Got dir helfen*," he says.

When Eri is out of earshot, Kaleb comes over to me. He reveals that Eri has just sent God with me also. "I have enjoyed your friendship. You would make a good fighting companion. Once you complete your quest, perhaps you will return." He peels off the rifle that is hanging from his shoulder and hands it to me. "Take this."

"But don't *you* need it?"

"Not now that Tobin is gone," he says, grinning widely. "I have his now. It is better."

Then Kaleb reaches for Rebekah and they clutch each other as if for the last time. He stands much taller than she does, leaning over to cradle her small frame. Rebekah cries and grabs the sleeves of his shirt.

"Please don't get yourself killed," she says. Look for me in Zamosc."

And it is then that I see: Rebekah is dressed for travel and she carries a knapsack. She is not only coming with me, but she hopes to return to Zamosc with me also.

"Promise me that you will take care of my sister."

I look to both of them, confused, wondering if I have missed a part of the conversation. "Of course, but are you sure about this? About being separated?"

Kaleb reaches for my hand and squeezes it to reassure me. He does not cry. He is full of belief, both in himself and in others, and for that I can admire him. And then he is gone. Then there is just Rebekah and me. She looks at me cautiously.

"It is still all right if I come, isn't it?"

I nod, frowning, wondering if it is fair to put her in danger.

"You are unsure, though, aren't you? About whether I am capable."

"I am sure as long as you are."

"Yes, I am. There is nothing for me here. My brother wants to fight. I have no home except this forest house, which is someone else's. And once Kaleb is gone, I have no one. I don't want to hide for months in a cellar or attic somewhere: waiting and hoping every day that I won't be discovered, wondering if someone will reveal where I am."

We dig a shallow hole with our hands and roll Tobin in. Then I dig another for Otto, deeper. I take his identification papers and his photos and letters and place them in my bag.

I say a few words in my head: *You will not die here for nothing. I will tell people of your bravery. People will know who you are.*

Rebekah walks over to stand beside me. I look at her. She is small and slender, her features fine. I am grateful for her company and I will honor my promise to take care of her.

PART TWO

Rebekah

CHAPTER 23

It seems that everything is against us. First, Otto was caught by Tobin and killed, and now the weather is about to turn.

In the next day it will snow. I don't know what the future holds, but this is my choice now. I must survive. I must help Henrik find Greta.

It is ironic that we are both separated from our only siblings—but Kaleb and I parted willingly, while Henrik searches for the one he lost.

Kaleb and I spoke often of his need to fight. I do not blame that about men. Kaleb is a man now.

It feels right to walk beside Henrik, who is smart and thoughtful. He does not tolerate fools and he is good at most tasks, even ones he has not done before. But his real talent lies in his art. It is incredible and such a shame that more people cannot see it.

I used to play the piano. Mama and Papa said that I had a talent, and that people would pay to see me play one day. Of course, that is what they said: the parents who raised me, the people I lost. It is perhaps not the case. Many were more talented than I.

When our parents hid Kaleb and me just before the Germans came, it felt like a game, as if it wasn't real. But then we heard our parents scream and the sounds of our cousins being dragged from their hiding place, and suddenly my past life was over. Long after dark, long after we heard the cars leave, we came out from the secret attic. Kaleb told me to cover my eyes and said he would lead me. He did not want me to see what he saw. But I couldn't help it; I looked.

Kaleb and I then crept through the sewers and hid like rats until we made it to the forest. Inside the forest we met Tobin, who said his father had been murdered by the Germans—which now I know was a lie. We came upon the partisans, who took us to the large manor house. But we were not treated as children. We were all given tasks. Ours was to travel to villages and steal as much ammunition as we could. Our last mission failed but I believe now that we were meant to go there, and we were meant to find Henrik. Another couple of nights—sitting rain soaked, bedraggled, and hot with fever—and he would have died.

Henrik's vulnerability drew me protectively to his bedside: the fear that he would be discarded like so many in this war, thrown by Tobin to the mercy of the forest. I sat and cared for him through his fever. This bothered Tobin, and even Kaleb sometimes. They did not trust him but I sensed right away that we were on the same side. I could see only goodness in those dark blue eyes.

We walk closely but do not talk much. Henrik stops often to look at his compass. He is bright and quick and fascinating. He has walnut-brown hair, a long straight nose, and a jawline that angles sharply towards a pointed chin. He has long limbs and broad, bony shoulders, wiry and athletic. If not for his dark eyebrows and his thick black eyelashes, he might pass for Aryan. When he sees that I am studying him, I look away. His look is too intense sometimes, as if he is trying to read my mind.

"We have to walk until dark. Have some bread!"

I shake my head. "Just water. I can wait." I pull out my tin flask and take a sip.

Eri said to head south and stay in the shadow of the mountains. He also said to keep well south of the river. He said the river is a good guide when we near Cracow, but we are more likely to run into the enemy along it.

But it will be days before we even reach the mountains. We have walked for six hours and already the exertion has made me nauseous, and my calves are burning. Some areas of ground are like slush: muddy and slippery. The scratchy undergrowth catches us as we pass by.

As we walk, we collect tinder and store it in our bags so that we can light a fire. Once the snow is here, such wood will be hard to find.

It is late afternoon and the sun is nearly gone when we come to a hollow. The hollow is deep and shaped like a bowl, and is surrounded by long, dying grasses. We have two canvas sleeping bags, which Kaleb has given us.

I need to urinate and disappear behind some fallen brush. Henrik understands what I am doing and walks in the other direction, his back to me. Sticks of hard grass scratch my flesh.

Henrik flicks the lighter against the wood and on his third attempt we have fire. The lighter belongs to his sister's kidnapper. I wonder if the German returned to look for it, but I don't say this to Henrik, who has probably not considered this. I do not want to put more worry in his head.

The sun has set earlier today. The days are shorter now. I can feel the air growing cooler around me.

We share a piece of cabbage pie that I had secretly set aside for this journey, and I watch the wood burn. Henrik's face is deep in concentration as he nurtures the flames, stoking embers and adding twigs. When he looks across the fire at me, I suddenly realize that it is just the two of us now against the world, against the odds.

"What was it like growing up in Cracow?" he asks.

"It was good until the ghetto."

"Did you live there?"

"No. Mama and Papa refused to go. That's why they were killed. It seemed such a waste at first, and I thought we should have gone. But Eri says that it is an awful place: Jews are trapped, some are killed."

I can tell that Henrik wants to ask more questions but he politely refrains.

"My family was not wealthy but they weren't poor either—like yours, I suppose. Papa was happy working in partnership with his brother, who owned a fabric store, and Mama was a dressmaker. They had big plans for their children, though. They wanted Kaleb to study medicine and me, music, which is why they bought a piano."

"Is that what you want to do?"

"I guess so." I wasn't overly interested in music, and Kaleb did not want to study medicine. I wanted to be a nurse, though I did not tell Mama and Papa. I did not want them to be disappointed.

Henrik tells me that his mother is a piano teacher and that she could help me. He tells me about his life in Germany. I try to imagine his life, which sounds like it was grander than mine. I wish that things could go back to how they were in our apartment, before the war.

We lie on either side of the fire. I close my eyes but can't fall asleep; there are too many noises. I think the enemy is out there somewhere and wonder if we should put out the fire. Eventually, it is just a glow and Henrik has closed his eyes.

• • •

At some point I must have slept because there are shards of light shining through the trees, telling me that it is morning. Pieces of sunshine barely squeeze through the gray. Henrik is up and walking around, looking at his compass and checking the map.

"We must stay as far from the towns as we can," he says, steam rising from his mouth as he speaks. I like the sound of his voice, which is low and gravelly and similar to the voices of the men who would smoke with my father after the children were all in bed.

We share a piece of bread. I feel hollow inside. I know that we must conserve the food. I make Henrik's piece slightly larger than mine.

We roll up our sleeping bags and tie them with rope to our backs. Henrik helps me with mine.

The terrain is difficult and marked by endless small hills; we always seem to go steeply upwards before we go down. I wear trousers but Henrik is in shorts, and I tell him that he must change because his legs are covered in scratches. Eventually, he agrees. It is hot as we walk but cold when we stop.

A light rain is released from the sky. It is time to stop, he announces. This time we need cover. Henrik builds a small hut using fallen branches that can bend. He threads them through one another to make a wall. He grabs more leafy branches and throws them over the top. We crawl in through a narrow space and sit squeezed together in our sleeping bags. There is no fire tonight, and during the night small drops of rain find their way through the gaps.

By morning, the rain is heavier and we trudge through mud with sodden shoes. Henrik walks with his bag under his coat so that the twigs will remain dry until we have a dry space where we can light a fire.

For much of the day the clouds are dark, making it difficult to tell the time. It is sometime late in the afternoon when we come upon a small cave. A piece of rocky shelf juts out from just above the low opening, like an awning. I am suddenly afraid that there are wild animals at the base of the mountains, perhaps in here.

Henrik flicks the lighter to view the empty space. It appears abandoned. In the corners, animal bones are scattered, and there is a smell of decay. It is large enough for several people, though the ceiling is not high enough for us to stand. We sit inside, grateful for shelter with a dry floor.

The weather is relentless; the rain clouds have opened their doors to full. We decide to stay for the rest of the day and into the night. Henrik wears his father's watch but it is not working. The front of the glass is cracked. He says that it was damaged when he played soccer in Zamosc but he did not want to take it off. We have no idea what time it is.

We take off our shoes. My feet are blistered and Henrik's, I notice, are bleeding; the soles of his shoes are almost completely worn through in patches.

We have some onion and bread and I have filled up both our water bottles in the rain.

With tinder, Henrik makes a fire, but it is small and may not last long. He takes his trousers and coat off to place beside the fire and I see that he has many bruises on his legs from the times when he has slipped. When I take my outer clothes off, I see that mine are the same. He says that we must lay our clothes, socks, and shoes beside the fire to dry them while we can. In just our underwear, we climb into our sleeping bags. I am aware that we are nearly naked but this is no longer something that worries me. I am too hungry, cold, and sore.

The fire is still going when I fall asleep. This is the first time I have slept for more than a couple of hours. When I wake, my shoulders are stiff from the heavy backpack and the hard ground, and my legs are aching. Henrik is still sleeping. My clothes are not yet dry but I put them on anyway. I am just rolling up my sleeping bag when I hear the crunching of footsteps on frost-covered leaves just outside the cave.

I poke Henrik awake. His eyes open halfway. He is having difficulty waking. I put my finger to my lips and point outside. He hears the noise and suddenly he is alert also. He picks up the rifle from near his bag.

There is a low grunting as the bear comes into view only yards away. He is dragging the remains of a small animal. We have invaded the home where he plans to sleep for the winter. He sniffs the air, then growls. He is just as shocked as we are. When he opens his mouth, I can see his sharp teeth. His fur is dark brown and he is young. I wonder if, like mine, his parents were killed in the war.

Henrik picks up a rock and throws it at the bear. He retreats slightly but it doesn't deter him; he will not give up his home without a fight. The bear sizes us up, thinks that he will be the clear victor, and steps forward on his large paws.

Henrik aims his gun.

"No!" I say. "Just shoot in the air."

He shoots to the side of the bear, which startles the creature enough that it runs out of sight. He has left his kill, but he will not retreat for long. We sense that he has not gone far and take the opportunity to pack our things. Henrik is fast and nimble, and he is dressed in seconds.

"All right," he says. "Let me go out first and see where it is. If I have to, I will kill it."

I nod. This is about survival for us, the same for the bear. Henrik creeps out.

"I can see him. He is behind some trees but he is coming back. Come out straight away!"

The bear is on all fours at first and then he stands and growls. I hurry towards Henrik, afraid to see if the bear has followed, fearful that he is on my heels. We run through the forest, weaving through the trees. Henrik turns often to see if the bear is following, but he is not interested in us. He wants his dinner and his home. He can have them.

We stop to catch our breath, and discover that I have dropped my sleeping bag. "We can't go back," he says. "We will just have to make do. We have to try and beat the weather."

And then as if God is teasing us, he releases his powdery snow.

CHAPTER 24

It is freezing this night, like the many nights before it, and Henrik makes another shelter. We huddle together in the one sleeping bag. Our bodies are warm together but by morning Henrik's body is stiff and cold like mine.

The walking is difficult, our steps heavier as our feet sink in deepening snow. Our clothes are damp. Walking keeps us warm. There is only a small portion of food left. Henrik makes a small fire and we roast two potatoes.

We eat them slowly. When I have finished, my stomach is still empty and I wonder whether we should eat the rest of the bread.

We wait till morning and finish the bread.

Over the coming days, we pass several villages and are careful to remain unseen. I am relieved to see that life continues, with people performing their ordinary household duties in their ordinary surrounds, seemingly untouched by invasion, seemingly trustworthy. Though trust is no longer something I take for granted. It must be earned. Trust is something rare and precious.

We hide behind the trees to spy on a house. A man chops wood. Henrik says that when the man goes inside, I am to stay while he tries to get some more food. We wait until the man enters his house.

I watch Henrik step into a curtain of snow; the weather is slowly worsening. I can just make out his dark figure as he disappears around the side of the house. It seems like a long time before he comes back again. He is carrying something gray in his arms. He is running.

"Run!" he yells.

There is a man behind him and together Henrik and I run blindly through the forest, uncaring about the direction. I am lagging behind Henrik because I am carrying both our packs, even though they are lighter now with less food. When we eventually stop, the man is no longer in sight. Henrik holds out several apples and a woolen blanket.

"Here," he says, and puts the woolen blanket around my shoulders. His nose is red and we breathe heavily from the chase.

Not long after, Henrik searches in his pocket for something, then curses in German.

"What is it?"

"I have dropped the compass." He heads back a short distance to search, following our footprints and using his feet to brush aside the powdery white surface. But he returns without it.

"We must keep moving forward. We will ask for directions at the next village, as I think we should already be turning northward."

My legs feel like two large weights hanging off the end of my body. My head aches and my menstrual period has come. Every so often I sneak off to replace my rags and wipe the soiled ones in the snow.

Henrik thinks that perhaps we should walk at night now. He uses the lighter to light the way. I walk in his shadow. We have already eaten the apples. Then suddenly the light disappears and Henrik says there is no more fuel.

We continue walking, at my peril, unfortunately. I do not see the dip, which is hidden beneath the snow, and my foot slips awkwardly against the ground. I feel something give in my ankle.

Henrik helps me to stand but I cannot put any pressure on my left foot. I have twisted my ankle. I wince when I try to walk.

"We will have to stop then and try and walk tomorrow," Henrik says. "Maybe a night of rest for it to repair."

I do not tell him that one night is unlikely to fix such an injury. This has happened before, and I used to own a pair of crutches for such occurrences. My bones and muscles are weak, and I was too ill to exercise as a child.

Henrik does not make a shelter this time; he does not have anything to make it with. Much of the bracken is hidden beneath the layers of snow. He spreads the sleeping bag on the snow and we lie in it with the woolen blanket over the top of us. At some point I sleep and dream of my bed back in Cracow. I dream that Mama has made a berry pie, which is hot from the oven, and the fresh cream is melting over the top.

When I waken, my mouth is dry and my lips are cracked. I reach out and put some snow in my mouth.

Henrik checks my ankle, which has swollen. His face is grim and wan. His eyes are puffed and bloodshot. He has more to worry about now and I am the cause. I want to be the one to hug him and tell him that it will be all right, and I cover my face to stop the tears.

"Hey, what's this?" He pulls my hands away to reveal my sorrow.

"I am useless. I am so sorry. I should not have come."

Henrik takes my hand and chooses a tree to sit by and lean his back against. He pulls me down between his legs, placing his arms around me, and I rest my head on his chest.

"I am so glad you came with me. Don't cry. It will be all right. We will get through this. It isn't far now. Soon, we will be returning to Zamosc with Greta, and Mama and Femke will take care of you too. Eri will kill plenty of Nazis and drive them out of the villages. We will all be free."

He strokes my head until my tears stop falling. I am exhausted and, with my head against his chest, I can hear his beating heart. I think I am falling in love with him, and this is the last thought I have as I fall asleep.

It is afternoon when we both wake. Henrik tears off part of his shirt and binds my ankle. There is no more dry tinder to start a fire and no lighter to light it with anyway.

"I am going to the next village to see if I can get some help."

"Who will want to help a Jew?"

Henrik bites his bottom lip, and this makes him look like a small boy. But he is not a small boy. He is almost a man and very brave. I have never met anyone like him. He is funny but he is also very serious at times, which makes me feel safe.

"I don't want you to go. What if you hurt yourself?"

He does a little dancing shuffle in the thick snow. "Look! Unlike my companion, I have two good legs! There is no fear of that happening."

I laugh at the way he lightens the load of worry with his comical drawings and his buoyancy. He is like a raft in the sea of despair. But my smile quickly goes when I wonder if he will come back. He buttons up his coat and leaves the packs, but not his rifle.

"I will be as quick as I can. We need food and we need a place where we can be out of the cold, just for a little while. We have been in the wilderness for long enough."

And then he is gone.

• • •

The sky dims quickly until there is no light at all. I listen to the sounds of the forest. It is mostly the quiet noises of wildlife that I hear, though occasionally, very faintly, I think I hear guns. Then there is the groaning of planes in the distance. There is a war going on outside the forest. Sometimes amidst the trees this is easy to forget. I start to see shapes in the dark. Sometimes I imagine they are German soldiers. There is the sound of a truck in the distance. It is the sound of civilization. I do not know how long it is before I hear footsteps. I stay very still. The footsteps get closer and then Henrik whispers my name.

"I am here," I say.

Henrik follows my voice to reach me in the dark.

"I have found someone who can help us. There is a family in a village."

Henrik tells me how he spied through the windows until he found people who appeared kind: parents with small children. He thought they might be understanding and helpful.

"Are they Jews?"

"No," he says. "But they say they hate the Germans."

"Do they know that I am a Jew? That you are part Jew?"

"Yes, I thought that it was necessary to spell out such things."

Henrik tells me that we are only a couple of days' journey from Cracow, and we should travel close to the roads now. The family has offered some supplies.

He hands me a large stick, which I lean on with one hand, and then he supports my other side. We come to a narrow part of a stream; its banks are frozen and pieces of ice float past us. He carefully balances himself in the flowing water and then lifts and carries me over one shoulder. Then we are near a road. There are several lights ahead and we arrive at the village, which is nestled into the forest. It is pretty and peaceful. The planes have stopped temporarily.

He knocks softly on a cabin door. The houses, though basic in many ways, are raised from the ground and have electricity. A man answers. He does not smile but opens the door wider to let us in. There is a woman there, and two children sit in nightgowns beside the fire. The woman smiles nervously. She is small and matronly and moves forward to help me sit down. The man's smile appears forced.

The woman ladles some soup into bowls. It is watery but warm, with much flavor, and there are small bites of meat. After this we have some black tea. I am very grateful.

"Thank you so much," says Henrik. "We will be gone in the morning."

"Where are you from?"

Henrik talks about the trek through the forest. He does not talk about his sister or Eri, and I am relieved because, like me, he knows to keep most of his cards close to his chest. He gives the name of a town to the north, one that I am not sure exists, and says that we were heading there but somehow got lost.

The man and woman are equally guarded. They say nothing of themselves. Henrik queries whether there are soldiers in the town.

The man pauses slightly. "No," he says. "There were, but they have done their damage and gone now."

The woman takes the two children to bed. I smile at the children and they wave as they leave the room. The woman returns with a fresh bandage for my ankle, which she wraps up tightly.

"You should be resting this," she says warmly. "Otherwise it won't heal."

We talk for a while about the war and they advise us of the progress that Germany has made into Russia. I want to cover my ears. I do not want to hear any of this. Shrill voices come from a radio they have left on. I understand some of the words: "victory," "loyalty," "honor," and others that German spokesmen are fond of using.

Then it is late and I feel sleepy from the warmth of the fire. The couple says that we can lie here near the warmth. Henrik tells them again that we will be gone before sunlight.

I do not know how long I have been sleeping when I awake to the sounds of a truck coming down the road. Henrik is sleeping heavily. The trips back and forth to collect me have exhausted him. The house is some distance from the rest of the town. I wonder why the truck is coming this far, to where the forest ends. There is something about this that disturbs me.

"Henrik," I whisper. "Wake up! There are people coming."

The sounds of noisy slumber stop and I know that he is now listening too. We do not need to pack our bags; they are ready for us to leave. We made sure of it.

"We will go out the back way," he whispers, "straight into the forest."

We creep towards the door, but there is slight movement ahead and the room suddenly appears under a cheerless, sallow light.

I am in front of Henrik. I stop dead in my tracks.

"You have to stay," says the man calmly. He stands at the back door to block our way. "The Germans are here to collect you."

"Why did you tell?"

"You should have been gone a long time ago."

"Let us go," says Henrik. "We are hurting no one. And you will always be in our prayers."

The man grins. "I do not need your Jewish prayers."

We can hear the voices of Germans now and the shutting of doors. I can hear their footsteps crunching in the snow. I feel Henrik shifting behind me, and something slides across my back.

"Please," I say.

"Please," echoes Henrik.

The man shakes his head. "It is for the best that you are taken to be with your own kind."

"They will kill us," I say, pleading.

"They will take you to a safe camp."

"It is not true. They have been lying to honest Polish people. Those are places where they slaughter Jews."

The man hesitates. He sees the pain in my face and it distracts him.

"You must wait here for the Germans. They will decide what's best."

"Then I am sorry," says Henrik.

"What for?" The man is humoring him.

The sound of Henrik's gun deafens me, and the man drops his own gun and clutches at his thigh before sinking to the floor. Henrik tries to drag him out of the way to get through the doorway, but the man makes himself into a dead weight so that he is difficult to move. He then grabs at our limbs as we scramble over him, but we slip through his weak grasp. Henrik drags me by the arm to hobble faster across the small yard, the pain in my ankle still raw. I hear the Germans circling the house; they have not yet seen us. We enter the forest in the direction from which we have come, in the direction that Henrik knows.

"Halt," yells an officer, and then there is gunfire that lights up the trees around us like candles during Hanukkah.

We run and run, and I bear the pain, until we reach the river to hide near the frozen banks under frozen branches. Our previously warmed bodies become chilled to the bone again as we watch the Germans shine their flashlights onto the stream. The lights pass over us but we are disguised by the branches. They do not try and cross. They do not want to get their shiny new boots wet, or their feet frozen. They return to their truck while we stay hidden for several more minutes, until it is safe to come out.

We must keep moving. Our wet clothes will turn to ice if we stay still.

• • •

In the morning, Henrik steals some dry wood from another village farther upstream. He starts a fire using some sheets of paper from his book. It has, astonishingly, stayed dry from being inside his shirt, wrapped in heavy cloth.

We warm ourselves by the fire until our clothes are dry. My ankle is neither worse nor better. Henrik checks the place in his art book where he has been marking the date.

"Happy Christmas!" he says.

"Happy Hanukkah!" I say, though it is a couple of weeks late.

"What would you have been doing during Hanukkah?"

"Lighting candles, praying, telling stories, and eating lots of sticky, sweet, doughy cakes."

"Stop," he says. "You are making me hungry." And both of us are silent while we imagine the food.

Henrik says nothing. Much of his former motivation is missing. He sits a short distance away, his eyes glazed. There is a change in him. Sometimes he looks up through the trees, in the direction from which we have come; before, he was always looking in the direction we are headed. I try to think of something to say that might shake him from this mood but can't find any words. Today, everything seems a little grimmer. Some of the fight has left him.

"I am sorry," he says.

"What for?"

"For bringing you here. You should have stayed with your brother."

"That would not have been any better." And then I say more quietly, "I wouldn't have been with you."

He looks at me. His face is patched with grime. He reaches over and takes my hand. I am hoping that he feels the same. Then it is as if this touch has ignited something within him, and he stands to brush off the sleet.

"I know we are both tired, but we have to keep walking." He steps towards me. "Here, lean on me. I will carry you the rest of the way if I have to."

"You don't have to," I protest. "Just the stick will do."

He puts his arm tightly around my waist and he shoulders both our packs.

"I think we might be there before nightfall."

And then we are walking, warming up, though my throat is sore and my head aches. I do not say anything. I must get through this. I must not let the illness beat me, or our cause. There is a weight to my chest. This is the first symptom of a chronic illness that lies buried within me, always ready to return at some point when my resistance is low.

We trudge slowly in mud, slush, and snow. Although our legs are heavy, our heads weary, we do not stop. The sound of commercial activity grows louder as we reach more densely populated towns. It won't be long before we reach the place of my birth.

I feel trepidation, because the closer I get, the clearer my memory of the night I disappeared. I think of my friends and relatives who are in the ghetto and wonder whether there is any chance I will see them alive again. I remember the heartache of my mother sewing yellow stars onto the front of our coats, her tears making dark stains on the fabric as she did this.

We relocated within the city to the Jewish quarter of Kazimierz, into an abandoned apartment. But then we were ordered to leave there and move to the ghetto in Podgorze, another district of Cracow. I remember watching my neighbor load his horse and cart full of his belongings, his three little daughters also sitting in the back. I remember my father watching from the window, saying that they couldn't make us go.

My father was well respected and well connected. He had many friends who weren't Jewish. We were fortunate, to a point: able to hide in the cellars and attics of friends around the city.

Always hiding like mice, always wondering what had become of our friends. He and my mother would fight often. She missed her family and believed we would be better off in the ghetto; she thought we would at least have company there. But we began to hear things about people being taken or shot. About soldiers appearing at front doors without warning, and families split apart. We were always relying on the generosity of others. This was hard for my father. His independence and his ability to support his family were everything to him.

Henrik and I leave the forest and find a road. It will not be so easy to disguise who we are. Henrik sits down behind snow-covered bushes to discuss a plan.

"We must not look like we are travelling. We need to hide our packs and the rifle and we will pick them up when we return. There is an address on the letter from Otto's girlfriend in Cracow. We can go there first."

I tell Henrik that the address is on the other side of the city. We have to cross the city looking like beggars. I tell him that I do not think we will make it without being stopped.

"We stayed with a family for a while," I say. "They looked after us until they thought they were being watched. We could go there for a night." There is a selfish motive to my suggestion: I do not think I will last another hour of travel.

"So they asked you to leave?"

"They had to. They had their own children to consider."

"How do you know they will accept you now?"

"I don't. But we can try." I cough. It hurts.

"Are you all right?"

"Yes," I lie. "They may not take us in. They may be too fearful."

He thinks about this while we bury the packs. My fingernails are chipped and caked with dirt. I imagine my face is as grimy as Henrik's. Our clothes are muddied and wet.

"We have to wash."

GEMMA LIVIERO

"Yes," says Henrik. "Stay here. I will find something."

Every time he leaves me, I think he won't return. Being separated gets harder each time. It is like we have never *not* been together. But it is not like brother and sister. This is something more.

I stay behind some trees. I see much from my hiding spot. There are vehicles and carts going in and out of the city. There are houses along the main road. Some people are walking and some, cycling. I am envious that they do not have to hide.

CHAPTER 25

I am getting anxious. Henrik still hasn't returned. The thought of another night in the forest fills me with dread. I begin to over-heat and peel off my coat, then shortly afterwards slide back into it when a chill creeps up my spine. My body cannot decide if it is hot or cold.

It is dusk when he returns.

He has everything we need: soap, clothes, a coat that's too big for me, and a stick to help me walk. The clothing looks clean and warm. He helps me back to the icy edges of the river, and we use the soap to wash our hair and faces and hands. I pull my hair back into a tight bun. Henrik dangles a silk scarf in front of me.

"For class."

He has become quite the thief.

We turn away shyly from one another to dress ourselves. Henrik's pants are too short but the shirt fits well across his shoulders. Over this he wears a jacket, and a cap is on his head.

"How do I look?" he says, and struts around with an exagger-ated German soldier's walk. Despite how ill I am feeling, he still makes me smile. I feel better when I do.

"Now we have to think of new identities. If anyone asks, I am Otto and you are . . . Emelie, Otto's girlfriend." He pulls out a photo and papers. It is a picture of Otto. "I can pretend I am Otto with his identity papers and say that I am on military leave."

"You don't look anything like him," I say, studying the photo, remembering Otto's boyish stare.

"I will wear my cap low."

The plan is not even close to tight but we have nothing else.

"Once we are there, with your friends, we will find out if they know of any safe houses, and perhaps they will know something of where my sister has been taken.

"For now, we will stay well back from the road. If we see a vehicle, we will walk towards a house as if it is ours. We will even walk right through the front door if we have to."

We stay in the shadows till dark. We have trained our ears to listen for footsteps. We can hear the sound of cars from many streets away. We are careful.

Then we are in the city and it is dark and we slide along back streets and pass amongst people undetected, for the most part.

I know my way through Cracow. I am useful this way. We arrive at a familiar house, and I knock softly. A woman whose name I can't remember opens the door, releasing the light from the hallway.

She does not appear to recognize me at first, and then she does. She offers a wary smile and calls her husband to the front door.

"I am wondering, since you helped me that last time, whether you can help again . . . just for a couple of days."

"No," says the man in a gruff voice. "You should get out of the city."

There is a hollowness to his tone, as if he has nothing inside of him, as if he has been emptied of feelings. He tells his wife to close the door.

"Please, Irena," I say, suddenly remembering her name.

"I'm sorry, dear," says Irena. "It has been a very tough war. We lost our son in the fighting and it would not seem right if we took in those like you."

Like me! I think, as if I am somehow the cause for their suffering. I want to shout "but we are the same" but I say nothing. I feel Henrik nudge me in the back. He wants to go. All I say is: "I'm sorry for your loss."

"Rebekah," she says as I turn to leave. Her husband has already returned to the depths of the house. "I remember you were a lovely girl. I wish you luck . . ." And then her voice breaks and she begins to shut the door.

Henrik thrusts his foot forward to block the door from closing.

"One thing," he says. "Can you tell me where this street is?"

The woman squints at the map that Henrik is pointing at before taking her glasses from around her neck and putting them on. Henrik passes her the map and she holds it towards the light.

"If you keep going up that road, you will reach the village. Turn right at the factory."

Henrik snatches the map away from her. She takes off her glasses and looks at Henrik disapprovingly, as if she has found another reason not to help us. "Why do you want to go there? It is full of Germans, like everywhere else in the city."

"None of your business," says Henrik in a cold-sounding voice.

"Bastards!" he exclaims as we walk away, and I touch his arm to silence him.

"You should not have shown her where we are heading."

"I didn't. I showed her a street far from where we are going, in case she contacts the police." He is right not to trust anyone, even Irena, who was kind once. It is an unkind war.

Henrik puts his arm around me and we hobble along like man and wife, down the main streets. We are headed towards the address of Emelie's house on the outskirts of Cracow but it is too far for us to get there tonight. We are both exhausted and I am ready to collapse.

"You must rest. You need to put your leg up. We need food."

"We can just go back to the villages. Maybe sleep in some bushes."

"No," says Henrik. "We will keep going a little longer."

The streets are emptying. It is dangerous for us to still be out and my heart races every time we see anyone. Everyone is the enemy here, all those who would see my family gone or dead. Suspicion has become a part of living.

We walk near the river until we find a small boat to steal. I remember this river, with its rim of frozen, winter-white bushes lining its borders. In another couple of days the river will be covered with a blanket of ice. Henrik rows us across the water. It takes much effort for him to cross the current, which carries us swiftly away from our destination and towards a well-lit bridge stationed with guards. It takes many minutes before we reach the other side of the river. We pull the boat into bracken and hide it for our return.

We walk as far from the road as possible. Some trucks pass and their drivers look at us, but they are thankfully not curious enough to stop. Only once do we see an official vehicle, and when we do—true to Henrik's plan—we walk towards the front door of the first house we pass. But the car does not seem to notice us; it passes just as we reach the door and we continue as before.

It is as if the war hasn't found the city; it is as beautiful as it was before. I point across the river. "There is the ghetto, across that bridge."

We reach a part of town once known as the Jewish quarter—before its inhabitants were relocated to the Podgorze ghetto—and pass a row of abandoned workshops. Hanging on a wall outside are the remains of a printing-works sign. There are no lights on and the windows are smashed. Henrik lifts me through a gap and then climbs in after me. The lights are on in apartments nearby, which Germans have taken over. We have managed to dodge the German military, which patrols the area, but my throat hurts more from suppressing the noise of my cough. "We will sleep on the ground here," Henrik says. "And before sunrise we will continue to Otto's girlfriend's house." He points to streets on a map, and I follow his fingers and confirm that we are going the right way.

"If we follow this road and turn here, we will reach it."

I fall asleep and wake early to the sound of the city rising slowly, like a giant groaning beast. Engines purr close by. I do not want to rise. There is so much pain it is difficult to place where the worst is coming from. Henrik is keen to move and jumps up to spy through the windows, adjusting his pack.

"I can't," I say. "You go ahead. I know the way. I will meet you there." I put my head back down. All I want is sleep, and to forget for a while. In my dreams there is no pain or loss.

He looks at me, concerned, touching my shoulder and leaning in towards me. He is so close to me that I can see the tiny red blood vessels around his circles of marbled blue.

"No," he says. "We must keep going. We must never say die."

We reach the outskirts of the city as a bright red sun surfaces gingerly on the horizon. My mouth is dry.

There are now some vehicles moving, and each time we hear one we scramble into the trench beside the road.

"Are you sure we are going the right way?" asks Henrik.

"Yes," I say.

Ahead there are formidable manor houses. The one we seek is set well back from the street. We creep beneath the side windows of the house, and since we cannot hear any sounds yet, we take the chance to run to the rear of the property, towards a barn. There is a padlock on the front door so we go to the back of the barn. To cover up the noise, Henrik waits for the sound of a passing truck before smashing a windowpane. He reaches inside to release the lock and clears the jagged pieces of glass at the window's rim. He wriggles in first and pulls me through by the arms. I am close to a dead weight. Every part of me feels like it has been filled with lead. We climb a ladder that leads to a loft. I think I might be sick, but there is nothing in my stomach.

"What now?"

"We wait and watch from the window to see who comes and goes."

There are sacks of food stored here. Henrik pulls out two oranges, bites into one—skin and all—and passes me the other. When I don't take it, he peels it for me. My arm is heavy when I reach out to take it. Then he opens a sack of flour and takes a mouthful. I do not want to eat.

"You should have some. It makes your belly feel full. Are you all right?"

"Just tired."

"You must eat."

"Later," I whisper.

I put my head on a sack of flour. I think how tragic it is that we have had to break into someone else's home, and that I might die in a stranger's loft. I stare through a tiny glass window, which lets in a melancholy light that seems to say: *What are you doing here? There is nothing for you here.*

• • •

Henrik has disturbed my dreams again by moving around the loft. It is late afternoon. I feel my bowels move so I drag myself down the ladder, unbolt the door at the back of the barn, and walk outside in the slush to relieve myself. I can smell that he has already done the same and covered it with snow. I crawl back up the ladder to my sleeping place in the corner of the loft.

"There are only women in the house. It looks like there is a mother and her two daughters, and their housekeeper."

"What if they come out to collect food here?"

"That's what I am watching for. If they come, we will climb down from the loft and hide in one of the stalls."

There are several compartments below us where horses were kept, though there are none there now. One of the stalls now has a broken window. I am hoping this isn't noticed. These people living here are probably not the true owners. For one moment I hate the girls who live in this expensive home.

"We're safe for now," says Henrik. "We'll sleep. It looks like you need it. Are you sure you are feeling all right?"

"Yes."

"You look gray."

"I'm fine."

Sometime during the night I wake and try to catch my breath. My chest hurts each time I cough, and my breath is raspy. Henrik doesn't stir.

In the morning I see the woman and her girls leave the house. There is a fine mist across the snowy paddock and the smell of cut pine pervades the air. At another time this peaceful scene would have been free for everyone to enjoy. But during this war we can only borrow someone else's view—someone who believes they are more deserving.

I do not disturb Henrik. He wakes late and apologizes for sleeping so long.

"That is the best sleep I've had."

I tell him the girls have left.

"I have a new plan."

Henrik is always thinking.

"I am going to copy Otto's handwriting and write to his girl-friend, Emelie. I am going to say in the letter that 'Henrik and Rebekah are friends of mine and could you help them? They saved my life.'"

"You have to tell her Otto is dead. It is only fair."

"I will, eventually, but keeping him alive in this letter might be the only way to get her to help us."

I agree because part of me does not care, the part of me that feels so ill. I try to stand but lose my balance and Henrik, as quick as ever, jumps up to catch me. He feels my forehead and looks at me with deep concern.

"You are very ill. You have a raging fever and need medicine."

He opens a sack containing sugar and scoops some up with his hand. "Here, put this on your tongue."

"How will that help?"

"You must have something, at least for energy."

He gives me a water bottle that he has filled with snow.

"How long have you felt sick?"

"Two days, I guess."

"I'm sorry. I thought you were just tired."

This is what I wanted him to think.

"Lie down and stay down," he says. "I will take care of everything."

"How are we going to get Emelie's attention? She must be the older girl."

"I don't know. I might put the letter from Otto under the front door, along with a message asking her to come to the barn and not tell anyone."

His idea carries much risk but I am too weary to question anything.

Henrik writes the letter, copying Otto's handwriting. It takes him several attempts. He uses some loose paper from his drawing book that is always inside his shirt, as if it is an extension of him, a limb he can't do without.

It is almost dark when he completes the task, but before he can take further action, he is startled by movement at the back of the house. The younger girl, who is perhaps twelve, wears oversized snow boots and crosses the paddock towards the barn.

"Hurry!" says Henrik. "Climb down into the stalls."

We hide behind a wall and watch the girl walk through the doors and climb the ladder to the loft. A short time later she climbs back down again.

"I must speak to her."

I grab his arm and shake my head. I believe he will frighten her, but he ignores me and steps towards her. I follow behind, clinging onto him. My breaths are short and loud. She hears this and turns.

"Hello," he says brightly, in Polish. The girl looks like a frightened rabbit. She says nothing. She holds a basket full of apples and oranges. I notice that many of the apples have bruises.

"I don't think she understands."

Then Henrik introduces himself in German and at this the girl lifts her head slightly, her interest piqued. "And this is Rebekah. We are good friends of Otto, your sister's friend."

The girl does not say anything and I suddenly wonder if we have the right house. Because war changes much, including addresses.

"Do you know Otto?" I ask, and the girl turns towards me. She watches my mouth, curious at the wheeze in my voice.

The girl nods. "He is my sister's fiancé." We have made some connection and she doesn't appear as if she will run.

"Otto asked us to come here and see Emelie," says Henrik. "We are on a special mission and we are not to tell anyone our plans, except for Emelie."

"Mama can keep secrets."

"No," says Henrik quickly. "Otto gave us strict instructions to speak only to Emelie." And then he corrects himself. "He said you were a lovely girl and could be trusted also."

I can see that the girl is thinking hard about this, absorbing our words. Her eyes dart towards the corners of the barn. She remains suspicious.

"You are quite safe," I reassure her in broken German.

"It is simply a message that we must give to your sister, and we must tell no one else. Here," says Henrik, passing her the letter. "Can you give this to Emelie when no one is looking and then tell her to come to the barn when it is dark? She can pretend to be getting some more food or going for a walk. Do you think she can do that?"

"Yes," says the girl. "My sister is eighteen. She can go wherever she wants."

Henrik takes a step forward and the girl steps back.

"What is your name?" I ask.

"Maud."

"That is very pretty," I say.

"I like your name," she says to me. "Are you German?"

"Yes," says Henrik before I have a chance to answer truthfully.

"So are we. We came here to live with Papa, who works here, but I want to go home. I miss my friends."

"So do I," says Henrik. "I miss our home, my parents, and my cat. I can't wait to go home."

And I can see that trust has washed over her like a summer shower.

"So, can you take that to her now and tell her that she must not tell anyone? That she can trust what Otto says, and she can also trust us."

"Yes," says Maud.

She opens the door, takes one last look at us, and closes it again. Our fate rests completely with her.

We climb back into the loft and I am relieved to lie down again. I want to sleep but the excitement of our current predicament is suddenly too great.

"Do you think we can trust her?"

"Yes," says Henrik, and I love the way he can give a definite answer, as if he is willing it so, or as though he knows much more than any of us.

"How are you feeling?" he asks.

"Not good," I say. There is no more point to lying. We have done as much as we can for now.

"What do you think it is?"

"I have a weak chest." This is what Mama used to say. "I am prone to chest infections."

"How is it treated?"

"Just medicine and rest." I don't tell him of Mama's warm herbal drinks, or the ground seed paste and leaf oils she spread across my chest, or the steaming, salty baths used to clear my lungs. There is no point.

"Then we must get medicine."

Long after dark, a light comes towards us across the snow. We wait for the doors to open to see who it is before we climb down from the loft.

The girl takes off the scarf that is wrapped around her face and neck. Emelie is a pretty girl with curling, honey-colored hair. Her eyes are wide with curiosity. She holds the letter in one hand.

"Come! Sit!" she says. She does not appear fearful. The letter is enough to make her trust us.

We sit on the hay bales in one of the stalls. She lights a kerosene lantern and hangs it on the wall.

"Are you Polish?" she asks.

Henrik says that he is German but asks, for my sake, if she speaks Polish. Emelie says she can speak German, Polish, and English.

"I have not heard from Otto for a long time. You cannot imagine how good it is to hear that he is alive."

I feel a lump in my throat and have to look away. But Henrik is a professional now.

"Yes," he says. "He is a good man. You must know that."

"Yes," she says. "I do. We plan to get married."

I wonder if she is lying, or if this is her fantasy, because Henrik has already said that Otto admitted she was his temporary girlfriend. His real love lives in Germany.

"Now tell me what it is you want. Otto says that you need help and food and that you are trying to find your sister." She is looking at us carefully while she says this. "I must say I am rather surprised. I would not have believed that Otto could be disloyal to his unit and help others on the run. But there you are. You never really know anyone. Are you Jewish?"

There is a pause. And I am wondering what Henrik will say.

"Yes," he says. "In part, but Hitler's dogs do not know this about my sister." Then he realizes his mistake. He has forgotten that he is talking to one of Hitler's people.

"Sorry," he says.

"It is all right," she says. "Mama complains about him all the time, though not outside the house, and certainly not to Papa. Even Otto did not understand the need for war. But you must know something about me before we go any further. Firstly, I want to help you because if Otto thought you were worth helping, then you must be good people. But secondly, my father is Oberführer Scherner. He works for the Führer. I don't know what his duties are and he doesn't spend much time at home, but I do know that it is dangerous in this city for people like you. It is full of Germans now and the Jews are trapped."

"Yes, we have heard about the ghetto."

"It makes sense that Jews should live in a place together," says Emilie. "But then they were driven out of their own place and into another; the people who lived across the bridge swapped places with them. And then Hitler's men turned the ghetto into a prison.

"I still see trucks go across the bridge carrying Jews who have been found hiding in the city, as if they have committed some crime. I've seen small children carrying all they can in their little suitcases. Otto said that it doesn't make sense. We talked about this in secret.

"The ghetto is a dreadful place from what I've heard," she says in a way that suggests she wants no knowledge of it. "The sanitary conditions are not the best, with people so crammed together."

She appears open and honest, and yet there is something underlying the things she says that bothers me. Something that does not seem sincere, but it is nothing I can define as yet. I sense a shallowness to her words, a disconnection to the meaning behind them—perhaps because they are someone else's words, maybe Otto's, and are now chosen just for us. Could it be that she is more disgusted by the state of the ghetto than the cruel reasons for it?

"And what of your father? Does he say anything about this?"

"No," she says. "He shelters us from what he does. He is a good father to us . . . So, what is it that you need? You cannot stay here forever but I will help you with some food and clothes, and if there is any information that I can find, I will do what I can."

"Rebekah is ill," says Henrik carefully. He does not want to frighten her away. "She has a chest infection."

"Is it bronchitis?" she asks.

She does not wait for my response.

"Mama had that last year and with special medicine she was better within a week. There is none here but I can forge a note from my father and take it to the infirmary."

Henrik looks giddy with excitement but I am too tired to be grateful.

"By the looks of things," says Emelie, "another week and you will be dead without medicine."

Henrik is alarmed by this. "Surely not."

"That is the trouble with men," says Emelie matter-of-factly. "They do not notice when women are troubled. If you can wait till tomorrow, I will bring what you need. I cannot come back tonight but tomorrow everything will be delivered, and then I will ask around about the children."

I wonder if her questions will arouse suspicion, and pray that her bright and talkative personality, along with her position, will quell any doubts. It is perhaps a blessing for us, for once, that we have found a possible ally in someone whose father is a favorite of the Führer.

CHAPTER 26

It is a bad night. I am feverish and Henrik can't sleep because he is worrying about me. He creeps outside to wet a piece of linen in the snow. He holds this to my forehead. My head feels as if it might explode each time I turn it. Everything hurts.

I keep apologizing for being a nuisance and he reminds me that it is good that he can repay his debt. Though it is he—he says—who should apologize, for not realizing that I was so ill.

Some light comes through the window but I cannot make out his features. I know that he is sad, though. I can sense it.

It is late morning when Emelie returns. Her mother and sister have left the house. She is carrying a basket full of bread and cheese and pastry filled with egg. And there is medicine. I have to swallow tablets with water and this is difficult with my throat so dry and tight.

Henrik does not look at the food even though his belly is empty.

"Will your sister say anything?"

"No," says Emelie. "I have threatened her with death."

There is something I trust more about the younger one. I think Emelie may only be helping us because this is the most exciting thing that has happened to her in a long time, lonely and bored in a place far from her true home.

Emelie touches my coat.

"We need to get her out of these damp clothes and bathe her. Then we will cover her with blankets because her hands are frozen but her head is hot."

Emelie disappears and reappears with gray woolen blankets and a pillow. I am stripped down to my underwear and wrapped in blankets that are coarse and smell. I think perhaps they were once used for the horses but I don't care. I lie down and put my head on the soft pillow.

"It will probably take a couple of days before you notice any difference. I will be back to check tomorrow." She leaves. She is not hard, but she is not warm either. She is honoring a fake promise by a boyfriend who did not feel the same way she feels, and that alone is cause for us to be grateful.

Henrik breaks off some pastry and hands it to me but I do not take it.

"I will save some," he says.

I can tell that he is ravenous. He climbs down the ladder. I know he does not want to eat in front of me. When he returns, I smell pastry on his skin.

Over the next two days I get worse and then get better, and then worse again. Henrik is beside himself with worry. I tell him that perhaps he can leave me while he searches for his sister, but he won't leave my side.

One night it is raining hard and there is a storm. Every time there is lightning I see his face. I shiver hard. Henrik wraps me tightly in the blanket to keep me warm and then rests me in his arms while he leans against the wall. Together we watch the lightning outside the window.

I don't know why, but suddenly I am crying. Perhaps it is the very goodness of him that makes me cry. Perhaps it is the way he cares for me. After Mama and Papa died, I thought there would never again be anyone to hold me when I was sick. Kaleb and I were close, but we were drawn closer because of war; before the war we were different. We lived different lives. He loved his books and discussions with friends and I loved being at home, baking with Mama and listening to her sing. It was Mama who was the musical one, not me.

I begin to talk. I need to let it all out, to tell someone. To record the life I had, before it is lost forever when I am dead. I had a journal once but it was probably dumped or burnt. I tell Henrik everything.

The night my parents were killed, we had been living in the attic for seven weeks. We would sometimes come out and eat with our hosts, the Steiner family. They were kind and had children of their own. At first, it was difficult for the Steiners, knowing the danger they had put themselves in, and having to find extra food, but then they got used to us there and took pity on our plight. It was cramped. We had my two small cousins living with us also, but we made the best of it. We had mattresses on the floor. Being too tall, Papa could not stand fully. Sometimes, there would be a knock at the door and we would have to remain silent in the attic. We could not move. The Steiners had friends who called on them unexpectedly. Some of the friends had contacts in the SS. There were times when we had to stay still for several hours. Mama's legs would cramp up and Papa would go red in the face from anger. There were no windows, only tiny vents, and we craved fresh air.

I will never know why the German officers chose the town house to raid. I think that perhaps one of the Steiner children may have mentioned us accidentally. But the knock we heard at the door that night was different than previous ones. This time it was hard and sharp. Only my brother and I had time to climb back into the attic. My papa pulled the ladder away and shut up the hole. He and my mama didn't have time to climb up themselves or push our cousins through, who were playing in another room.

Kaleb and I listened as Hitler's men burst impatiently through the door, ultimately breaking it. They yelled in German. Our bene-factors were shot first. We heard the men ask some questions, and then I heard Mrs. Steiner die, and then Mr. Steiner. I heard the Steiner children whimper and tell the intruders that they had peo-ple, my parents and cousins, in a back room. They did not have time to tell about the secret room above their ceiling. There were more bullets and then no more sounds from the Steiner children.

Then I heard their steps. I can never forget the sound of their boots on the wooden floor. It is something I will hear forever. My father begging them to take him and allow my mother to live instead. My mother sobbing, then screaming as the children, my cousins, were being dragged from another hiding place. And then the round of gunfire and the silence that followed. I heard them smashing furniture and tearing doors off wardrobes to check else-where, and finally the German voices giving orders to leave. They did not think of the attic. It would have been considered uninhab-itable. In another time, we would have agreed.

Kaleb and I stayed in the attic for hours. We lay on our stom-achs holding hands, staring at each other, and praying silently. Kaleb was the first to open up the hole, to climb down into the horror. I climbed out also and fell into his arms.

In the dark we could see bodies on the floor, some lying across one another. We did not dare turn on any lights but Kaleb shone a flashlight across the room. He tried to cover my eyes but it was too late.

We saw the Steiner children first, who were directly beneath us. They never even had the opportunity to point at the ceiling, so quickly were they killed. The girl was still gripping her mama's skirt, the boy beside her. Mama and Papa had both fallen forward. They had been on their knees, I think, when they died. They had fallen across each other, and our tiny cousins—Mila, four; and Sarah, two—had multiple bullet wounds. Mama's eyes were still open.

Then I started to cry and threw myself on my parents. Kaleb pulled me away; we had no time to grieve. I followed Kaleb into the sewer, a place he had discovered as a boy, and we followed that across the town. Once outside the sewer we did not stop running until we reached a forest. Kaleb thought our best chance was to head east. We had no plan, no clothes, no food. That was when we met Tobin, who showed us the manor house.

I cry now for my parents. Lying in Henrik's arms, I am able to grieve. It feels good to tell someone, but not just anyone. It feels good to tell Henrik, who is someone with the ability to understand.

I feel that death is hovering. At one point I don't think I will recover at all. And at another point, I don't care.

Henrik tells me that he loves me, that he doesn't want me to die, and I squeeze his hand in reply.

Then one morning I wake up and the aches are almost gone, and I can breathe out and hold this breath longer than before. I am hungry, so hungry. I eat bread until I cannot fit any more in, and sip some milk.

Henrik and I stare at each other. I am slightly embarrassed that I was so open with him during my convalescence, but not regretful. He holds my hand and then kisses my cheek. There is no need for words. I belong to him and he, to me.

"It is my birthday today," he says.

"It is mine in three days," I say.

And we laugh because it is good to feel good again.

My breathing is still labored each time I exert myself. Each night, Henrik disappears to search the town for his sister in locations, identified by Emelie, where new Nazi families have arrived. He spies in windows and at schools, watching, hoping. We have been in the loft a month now.

Both daughters come to the barn to collect food, sometimes when Henrik isn't there. Maud has been told not to talk to us, but she can't help it. Sometimes she climbs the ladder just to say hello. She is more sensitive than her older sister. There is something wiser and deeper about her. I wonder what she has been told about us—I sense some fear in her also. I wonder if this has come from Emelie, to keep her away.

"Are you still sick?" she asks in German.

"Better," I say.

She nods, appearing happy with this response, before retreating quickly. We never see the mother, who Emelie says prefers to stay indoors. Sometimes the housekeeper comes to collect food when Maud isn't home. At these times we have to grab our things and hide in the stalls.

Emelie brings another lead when she delivers food, reporting that there are several homes where some senior officers are housing children. She has found this out from a friend of her father's, an officer, whom she met in the street. The officer also told her that the war is going well, that Germany will take over Russia, though it is a tough fight. Stalingrad is resilient but it will soon weaken. Germany will win the war. She sounds almost proud when she says this but, of course, we cannot say anything. We are indebted to her.

"What if you do find your sister and this officer is right about the war? What will Jews do?"

We have not considered this. We have not thought about the future of Jews if Germany should win. Some of the hope leaves Henrik's face for just a second. I think of Eri and his band of partisans.

When she leaves, I wonder also what Jews will do.

"It is propaganda," says Henrik. "The Germans make up stories. My papa used to recite the things Hitler and his dogs would say so that the people would stay on their side. He used to read articles in the newspaper. It was full of lies, told to twist the thinking of weaker-minded Germans . . . Germans who want to believe anything."

Henrik always has a positive view.

Emelie has drawn a map of where she thinks some of the children are housed. She has been told of a family with adopted orphans. Their home is not far from where we are.

Henrik has previously shown her the lighter but she still has not heard of any general with those initials.

I offer to come even though Henrik says no. But I insist. I am desperate for fresh air. Finally, Henrik agrees.

"You will need better clothes," suggests Emelie.

She comes back with a dress and a shirt and trousers. The dress is oversized but it will do. It is woolen with long sleeves. She also has brought me tights and shiny shoes. The clothes are expensive. The shirt and trousers fit Henrik well; he must be the same size as the girl's father. Then the girl pulls out a wig. It is fair and curly. She studies my reaction.

"She looks too Jewish."

Emelie pulls my hair tightly back and pins it to my head, then puts the wig over the top. She holds up a small mirror so that I can see. The wig makes my face look small. It is too much hair.

Henrik laughs and I love the sound. It is soothing. It is as if we are simply playing dress-up and this is not about life or death.

"Do I have to?"

"Yes," says Henrik. "You must look Volksdeutsche."

"But what do we say we're doing if we are caught?"

"You can say that you are visiting your cousin," says Emelie. "Use my name if you have to. They won't check. My father is important and he is never around."

"But that is dangerous for you."

She shrugs her shoulders. Danger hasn't really occurred to her.

"If they come and knock on the door to check, then I will say I have no idea who you are. That you must have broken in and stolen our food."

She is direct and sure of herself. I wonder then, as grateful as I am, whether perhaps she would have been the right girl for Otto, who seemed more sensitive and questioning. She has been raised a good German. She would make a good fighter because she is unemotional. She is doing what she has to, but at the same time enjoys the risk. Perhaps she is like her father; God forbid we ever meet him. I wonder whether to her we are just a game or a distraction—a way to pass the time to dispel the boredom, as if the war is not going on, as if life will always be good for her.

Henrik agrees with her idea.

I am still weak from illness but my chest no longer rattles.

Outside the air is cool and fresh. The sleet is thinning. We carry baskets with food as if we have come from the grocers, though we look odd without shoes for snow. Several vehicles pass us by, and

Henrik waves and nods at the occupants. The more confident we appear, the better it is. We must not look down.

Another vehicle passes bearing the Nazi flag. I feel my heart racing again and clutch Henrik's arm. I see that the men inside wear uniforms with insignias on their collars. Henrik waves again and they do not stop.

We find the address where some of the children have been taken. Outside is a garden with children's swings. The ground is slippery from the melting crusts of snow. We wander past a couple of times until we hear laughter. Henrik stops to listen. We walk slowly past again. There are four children, all around the age of six. None of them are Greta.

We go to the next address but there is no one home.

"We will come back tomorrow," I say.

We go back the next day and there is still no one there. Henrik creeps towards one of the windows. "There is no one living there."

"We will go back to the other house," I say. "Perhaps the older children were inside."

"We can knock on the door and I can ask for a name and then say I have the wrong address."

Henrik does this while I wait on the path.

"Oh, so sorry," says Henrik to the occupants. "My sister is useless with giving information."

"What did you say your name was?" asks the owner of the house.

"Scherner," says Henrik.

"I know that name."

"My father is an officer."

"All right then."

"You have lovely children. Four, is it?" Henrik can see them through the doorway.

"Yes. Four is enough."

And they laugh. I am amazed at how easy Henrik is with people and how easily they reveal themselves to him. He is special, golden almost.

Henrik shakes his head at me and we return to the loft after dark. He doesn't say anything but I can sense his disappointment. It has been weeks now and we have gleaned nothing.

"It is finished," says Emelie. "I have run out of addresses. I do not think your sister is here."

She says this offhandedly, as if a dance hall has closed for the evening and she is wearily glad that the event has ended. It is clear she doesn't know pain, that she doesn't understand what it is to lose someone. Not yet anyway. Though, even as I think this, I also think of Otto.

We hear the sound of a car. It is close. Emelie rushes to the window.

"Papa is home," she says excitedly. "I must go to see him."

"Perhaps he will know something," says Henrik.

"Perhaps," she says, but she is not really listening. We are suddenly no longer a priority. "I must go."

She runs. We peer over the windowsill and watch her father step out of the vehicle, dressed in full SS uniform. His buttons and boots shine. Even from a distance we can see that he is tall and commanding; he is also frightening, and my heart quickens.

Emelie does not come back the next day, or the day after that. We can hear much laughter coming from the house, and a truck arrives with food parcels and clothes. We watch it unload.

When Emelie finally does come out to the loft, she is beaming.

"It is so good to have Papa back."

I don't know why but I am starting to feel uncomfortable around her. I notice that she is wearing a gold chain.

"That is nice," I say.

"Thanks," she says, but she does not meet my eyes. She holds on to it a little tighter. She does not like me looking at it.

"And that is a beautiful dress."

The dress is silk and long.

She has brought some more food and some news.

"Father spoke about the children taken from their parents. He says that they are taken to be looked after. Well . . . maybe not all of them."

"What do you mean?"

"They have to be racially tested first."

"What do you mean?"

"I don't know the process, but if they are German enough, they are sent to the families of officers to be raised, or to centers in Germany and Norway and other places."

I can see that more light is draining from Henrik, as if a candle is slowly fading.

"There are centers in Lodz and other cities where the children were taken first. She may still be at one of those."

I think that it is unlikely. It has been months, though for Henrik's sake, I will not give up until he does.

"And what if they are not *German enough*?" There is a slight sarcastic edge to Henrik's voice and I see that Emelie has picked up on this also.

Her tone is belligerent when she responds. "To the camps, of course."

There is no doubt now that if it weren't for Otto, she would not have helped us; we too would be rotting in the ghetto or the camps.

"Papa is sending word to Otto's army group to see how he is. It is so good to have Papa back."

"How long is he staying?"

254

"Only a week. You are lucky we don't have horses; otherwise, he would be here every day. He loves horses. We used to ride together."

She seems more fickle and airy the more I speak to her.

"Anyway, I will try and find out the addresses of these centers. But you can't leave during the day. Papa might see you."

I think this comment is more for her sake than ours. I can't imagine what her father would do if he ever found out she had housed and helped us.

"Rik," I say.

"Yes," he says in the dark. The moonlight shows his face in a hue of blue. I touch his cheek.

"Are you all right?"

For hours now Henrik has been tossing and turning. Each night we lie with our backs together. My cough is almost completely gone, no more trying to muffle it with the blankets.

"I was thinking about our families. I was thinking about how you lost your parents," he says.

I do not say anything.

"What do you think will become of us?"

I am shocked by the question and I look at his face. He turns from me and sits up so that he is a silhouette in the window. There is a white glow around him from the moonlight. The barn creaks and complains against the heavy warm wind that is brushing aside the cold weather to lay a pathway for spring.

"I don't know," I say.

"Do you miss your parents and your brother?"

"Terribly," I say. "But I keep thinking that through all the loss one good thing might come. If we can return your sister to her mother, then somehow a bit of the pain will go away."

He turns then so I can't see his face, which is fully in darkness.

"You have been wonderful, you know. You have suffered with the ankle and then this sickness and still you are here supporting what I must do. If I didn't have you . . ."

"There was never any question. What else was I going to do?"

"I can't wait for you to come home with me! I want us to get away from this country . . . perhaps to emigrate to America or Australia, all of us together. Germany has turned its back on me. I will not live there again."

I put my hand on his arm.

"I really want that too."

He puts his hand over my hand and I can feel his eyes burning into mine, caught in the stream of light.

CHAPTER 27

In the early morning, I hear the sounds of car doors opening and closing and a motor starting. I am the first to hear the barn doors open and Emelie's footsteps. Looking outside, I can see that her father has left early for somewhere.

"Henrik," I say. "Wake up!"

Emelie's head appears above the ladder. From the frown on her face she has something on her mind. She climbs into the loft and sits on a chair she had placed earlier so that she didn't have to sit down on the floor and spoil her nice clothes. Her lips are thinner today, her chin raised higher.

"My father informs me that Otto is missing."

"Oh," says Henrik. "Do they know anything?"

"Only a few details. Another soldier reported that he was shot and wounded two months ago when they discovered some partisans who had been raiding the villages. Where did you say you saw him?"

"It was around that time, I think."

"You said it was Christmastime when you last saw him. Where was it?"

"In the forest."

"And he was alone?"

I wonder now why she hasn't asked these questions sooner.

"He was with the partisans."

She stands up angrily. "What do you mean by that? Was he captured?"

"No. He was a free man. We were staying at a house. He had befriended us all."

"You are saying that he had befriended the resistance . . . the enemy. He would be shot for that!" she says.

"Well, perhaps he had joined the partisans. I do not know exactly."

"No, Henrik," I say. "Enough." I cannot take this deception any more. I do not want word to get out that Otto was a deserter or betrayer. He deserves more than that.

"Otto is dead, Emelie," I say. "He was killed by a madman who had no allegiance to anyone but himself."

"Dead?" The query is venomous.

"He was captured at first and Henrik tried to help him . . ."

"You lied to me!" she says. When I try to tell her that Henrik had helped Otto escape from the partisans, she is no longer listening.

"We were going to tell you," I say, "but the letter was the only way to get you to help us."

"So you forced Otto to write it. Probably with a gun!"

"No! I wrote it."

Emelie looks at Henrik, her expression blank as if she can't quite believe that she was duped.

"I'm telling my father. He will be back tonight. You have all day to run now if you want, but eventually he will find you. Soon all the Jews will be gone from here. It is something to be thankful for!"

To have been duped by Jews is perhaps worse than the truth about Otto's disappearance.

"Wait!" says Henrik. "Otto told me something before he died. He said that he loved another back in Germany. He said you were a spoiled little girl but that he had to be nice to you because of your father's seniority, because you would tell your father if he wasn't."

I can see that this revelation hurts her initially but I do not think it will scar. She is shallow enough not to believe it, or perhaps she is fickle enough to find another to quickly replace Otto.

"Thank you for your help," I say, because we cannot forget that I am alive because of the medicine, shelter, and food.

"The clothes weren't mine anyway. Papa brought them back from the camps. They were taken from the Jews. Even the dress I wear now has come from the camps, and you should see the one that Mama has."

She is cold—far colder than I thought—but what we have done to her is perhaps just as cold. It is all part of the fight.

There is no cover of darkness but Henrik is not afraid. We change into the clothes that Emelie had brought for our earlier disguise, grab several oranges, and exit the barn at the rear. Henrik throws the blankets and clothes we arrived in into the fields next to Emelie's, in the opposite direction from where we are headed. He hopes that after the Gestapo has been alerted to our existence, their military dogs will find these and the guards will think we are heading west.

A vehicle with a siren blaring passes us on the street and does not take any notice of us. There does not appear to be anyone searching for us. Not yet.

In the afternoon we stop in a garden shed to eat an orange. Amid the smells of wood rot and earth, we peer through the slats and wait for the sun to fall.

"Do you think Emelie will tell her father that she helped us?"

"No," says Henrik. "She would not risk punishment. She will say that there were Jews or criminals of some kind hiding in their barn, stealing from them. That is all she needs to say."

"You should not have said those things . . . They weren't true."

He turns to me. "About what?"

"Otto deserves more than a deserter's burial. Can you imagine his family finding out what you said? Such a lie is too great."

"They are the enemy," says Henrik.

"But he was also your friend."

"I do not know that for sure. I do not know anything."

"You said yourself that you trusted him."

"How do I know, now that I have met his girlfriend, if he only said those things to escape and would have ratted me out?"

Henrik has changed. Some of his trust has gone. Perhaps he is growing harder, like the partisans. After what we have seen, we can never again be who we were.

But I cannot believe what he says about Otto. There was something trustworthy about him, and Henrik knows this too. I hope it is just his anger talking. I hope that he will return to the Henrik I first met. I don't like our fighting.

Once the light has dimmed, we creep behind houses towards the city lights. One time, we encounter a barking dog who alerts the elderly house owner. The woman steps out from her back door to yell at us, thinking we are thieves, and Henrik, casual as always, apologizes profusely for the intrusion and wishes her a good night. She watches us until we are out of sight.

As we near the city center, there are checkpoints ahead and more sirens sounding. A horse and cart, carrying sacks of vegetables, stands at the edge of the street; the owner has left it to deliver some goods. While he is distracted by his task, we climb into the cart to hide under empty potato sacks. It is only seconds before the driver returns and climbs into the vehicle. Several long moments seem to pass. My heart is pounding with fear that he has noticed something different about his load. Henrik squeezes my hand and the driver suddenly orders the horse to move, and the cart bounces briefly forward before rattling into steady motion. The driver rides past the guards, mumbling his German greetings. After several minutes of travel, when we are well past the checkpoint and into the city streets, Henrik raises his head to peer over the sides.

"When I say jump, *jump!*"

He gives the command.

He jumps but I do not have the nerve. I am worried that my ankle won't support me. The cart, though slow, is still moving. He runs after it.

I crouch near the back of the cart, one foot on the edge, and then suddenly the driver sees me and he comes to a stop. I climb down.

The owner steps out of the cart to yell at us. Henrik grabs my hand and we run down a lane before stopping to hide behind some bins.

We are both panting from the effort.

"Don't ever do that to me again," he says, but he is wearing a small smile. He reaches for my hand. "When I say jump, next time *jump*, or you will kill us both!"

We are friends again. His anger is gone after the thrill of our close encounter with capture.

We choose the streets carefully. By now, Scherner will have informed the police and they will be looking for thieves on the run. Premises and streets will be searched. Every time we hear the blowing of a whistle, my heart races. They will not stop looking until we are caught.

I wrap a scarf around my head and Henrik wears a hat that he has stolen. He holds my hand and we pass another couple in the street. Henrik says hello in his perfect German and then kisses me awkwardly on the lips as part of our disguise.

"Where are we going?"

"I don't know," says Henrik. "I will know it when I see it."

We are nearly at the end of a long street. Every vehicle that passes us causes my hands to tremble. A policeman turns the corner and Henrik pulls me through a café door.

"Act German. Act like you deserve to be here."

I hold my head higher but I keep the scarf on. We slip into a corner booth. There are several other patrons. A young girl comes to serve us at the table. We order coffee and sausages and onions.

"How will we pay for this?" I whisper.

"We won't. We just have to stay here for as long as we can."

I can smell the coffee and the food. The smell is delicious and my mouth waters. When the food arrives, it takes much control not to gulp the coffee and shovel the food into our mouths greedily. I take tiny bites and close my eyes each time so that I can savor the taste and cement the memory.

We talk quietly, but all the time Henrik sneaks glances at the owner, who occasionally looks over at us. A smartly dressed man walks in and stands beside the counter. The café owner and man greet each other with smiles that appear genuine and intimate. This customer, it seems, is a regular here. The owner takes a cake box from below the counter and hands it to him. They do not engage in conversation but as the man walks away, the café owner says, "Give your wife and little ones a kiss for me." The customer nods, then walks briskly past us towards the door, casually glancing in our direction. The man looks familiar.

"I want you to know that if this is my last meal, I am glad it is with you." I do not know what has come over me; perhaps the enjoyment of my food makes me talk this way. But I feel it is important that Henrik knows this.

Henrik smiles. "I want you to know that in a couple of months I want you to be in my home with me, laughing about our escape."

This is the reason why I love him. It is his thirst for life and belief in the future. I think: *How can anyone not fall in love with Henrik?* And in that moment I am grateful that out of all the girls in the world, I am the one who is his friend.

Then the other patrons are gone and the owner is cleaning up. The girl has taken off her apron and says good-bye to the owner. The tinkling of the bell above the café door as she leaves suggests we should also take action. The café owner saunters over and Henrik tenses slightly, but it is something that only I can recognize; the way his lips twist slightly and his hair falls forward on his forehead, it is as if he is thinking hard about something.

The owner introduces himself as Gottfried Schlick.

"Are you new here in the city?"

"Yes," says Henrik. "We are staying with the Scherners."

The café owner says that he is familiar with the name.

"My uncle is responsible for logistics here, in particular the transfers of Polish children."

"Ah yes, the children," says the proprietor.

"Do you know of them?" asks Henrik, trying not to sound too interested.

"I presume you are talking about the orphans?" Henrik nods. "We used to see about a dozen of them marching by the café. Sweet things. Such tragedy, yes? Parents killed in war."

I think that the propaganda is working well. I wonder how many children were stolen, and know that Henrik is thinking only of one.

"What do you mean: *were?*"

"They left two weeks ago. I heard that some have been sent to Germany for adoption."

I fear that perhaps Emilie knew this all along.

Henrik has gone quiet. The man speaks Polish and it is easy for me to continue the communication.

"They weren't orphaned," I say.

"What do you mean?"

"They were stolen."

I cannot stand the ignorance of these people. These people who were once my people. Henrik throws me a look. It is one I have not seen before. It is stern and disapproving. I try to deflect the comment, and lighten my tone. "The orphans will no doubt be adopted by kindly German parents, who will teach them good German ways, no?"

"But you said *stolen*."

"She meant stolen by war."

"Ah, I see."

"Are you still open for one more coffee?" Henrik asks the man, who says that he is.

"Get up," says Henrik when the man is behind the counter again. "We have drawn suspicion now and we have to get away. Don't run yet; just walk."

The bell on the café door sounds again as we leave, and I turn to see that the owner is following us. We head for the corner of the street, breaking into a run.

"Wait! Don't be afraid. I know who you are."

I slow down to a walk but Henrik pulls my arm. "It's a trick."

Something about the man's voice has made me want to stop. I whisper to Henrik that I think Gottfried is a Jew. Henrik holds his hand in his pocket, where he holds a dinner knife he stole from the café, just in case.

"What do you want?" he hisses to Gottfried.

"I want to help you. I think I understand something. Please . . . come with me."

We can hear cars coming closer and shouts in German coming from the direction we were heading. Henrik nudges me back towards the café. We have no choice now.

We enter the café and Gottfried locks the door behind us. I think at that moment we are doomed, that perhaps my instinct has killed us.

He leads us through a door to a back room. There are others there: a man and woman.

"You are Jewish, no?" says Gottfried.

"What is this?" asks Henrik.

"I knew the moment I saw your eyes," he says to me. "Jews cannot hide the sorrow." He turns to Henrik. "You . . . I'm not too sure of."

He introduces us to the man and woman in the room: a young married couple.

"These two have escaped the ghetto. This is a safe house for those on the run, those who are not welcome to enjoy freedom. I give much free food and coffee to the German officers, so they never search my place. And they come to the café often. Sometimes, I invite them to play cards with me."

Henrik looks at me quizzically. "How did you know to trust him?"

There is an inflection in the way Gottfried says certain words that reminds me of the voices of my father and uncles and grandfather. But I do not say this. I think that Gottfried might not want us to know that he is Jewish. So I say to him: "The man who came in earlier lived on our street. Last time I saw him he was being escorted to the ghetto. You appeared too familiar with him not to know of his history."

"Your girl here is smart, yes?" says the owner to Henrik.

Henrik looks at me as if I am suddenly more valuable.

"Who are the people who stay here?" asks Henrik.

"British, French, Dutch, many others—from ghettos or battle-fields, or from the resistance. People move east or west from here, wherever they think they will be safe.

"You both can stay the night here. There are beds and a wash-basin behind this wall." He slides the wall open to reveal a secret bedroom. "But you will have to share it with these two for tonight."

Henrik and I listen as the man and woman talk about the con-ditions in the ghetto, about how several families are squeezed into one room. How the Germans took away the doctor and people never saw him again. How there is a secret tunnel by which some people have escaped, but there are some who are too afraid to leave and believe that it is only a matter of time before they can return to their old homes.

Gottfried says that he has heard a rumor that the ghetto will soon be closed completely and all inhabitants forced into the camps. I wonder then about some other cousins there.

"Did you know the Rozenweig family?"

The couple remembers the name but describe the place as cha-otic and say it is difficult to know if people are still there; so many have been sent to the camps and others have been taken away for reasons known only by the Gestapo. The woman describes how sometimes people are taken to another part of the town and shot, their possessions stolen. "The bastards are doing it for sport," says the man. These words fill me with hatred and hardness, leaving no room for sadness.

"Are we losing the war?" asks Henrik.

"No," says the woman. "The Russians are standing firm in Stalingrad. The Germans have lost battles in other parts. They are not as victorious as they report on the radio and in the newspa-pers. The Western allies will not stop, and the resistance will not give up. Do not lose hope."

Henrik explains to Gottfried why we have come to the city.

"I know more about the stolen children," says Gottfried. "I know they are not only orphans, that many were taken from their families."

"You do?" This has Henrik's full attention.

"Yes."

The café owner is quiet for a moment.

"I know of a small orphanage. It is a house with a fenced yard. Children being brought there were anywhere from babies to the age of ten. I remember that they were all pale haired. One of the women who worked at the orphanage brought a couple of them in here one time. She said she was a nurse but she acted more like a prison camp supervisor."

Henrik asks him to describe the children.

"They were two little girls, around the age of eight, I guess."

Henrik doesn't flinch. This information seems more solid, more truthful, than the leads from Emelie.

"The woman said that the girls were being given a special education. They had lost their parents and were being taken care of. They would then be adopted by suitable German couples who had come to colonize Poland, or perhaps they would go back to Germany."

"And the other orphanage you spoke of . . . where is that?"

"It was a larger place but it has closed down now. The children are all gone. Many were Jewish."

Henrik explains that he has spied on many homes of newly arrived Aryan families who have several children.

"Can I have the address of the small orphanage you mentioned?"

The owner writes the address down and describes where it is.

"You will see nothing now. The children will be asleep. You would have to look in the morning, but that is not wise either. Not after what you've told me. The Germans will be on alert." He pauses to think. "Perhaps I can ask. I have had to deliver food there before. Maybe I can see if they require anything and then have a poke around."

"Would you?" Henrik sounds eager.

"Of course," says the café owner.

CHAPTER 28

Gottfried is up early making dough. He boils some meat for the stew that is to be served at lunch. We eat freshly baked bread, steam rising as we break pieces apart. The bread is washed down by more coffee.

"I'm not always a baker . . . in case you were wondering." And he casts a look at the other couple, who seem to already know his secret.

"The Germans have stolen much art and coin and many jewels from their raids and from their prisoners, but they are not so clever that it is hidden from dexterous hands such as mine. I am experienced in black market activities. My contacts tell me of recent plunders and I steal from the German looters who are looking to get rid of their spoils quickly. It does not sound like an honest living but before you judge me you should know it is my way of helping those it was stolen from. I use the money to buy food and keep this business profitable and then sell food to the Germans. They pay me and I use the money to house those who need help. You know, not all Germans are bad people. Look at me: I am German also." He looks at me to see if I might question this.

"Helping people sounds very honest to me," I say.

"I like this girl!" he announces to the air, and I am suddenly embarrassed that I have been so forthright.

"Where do you keep all these goods?"

"That is information which is best kept my business, dear Henrik, but before the items change hands, they are kept safely stored away from here."

"Do you have any family here?" I ask.

"My wife left me years ago when I was a fat, poor baker. My son is dead."

"I'm sorry."

"Don't be. It is because of this turn of events that I am doing what I do now."

The young woman speaks up. "You have saved many lives. I will be sure to tell England what you have done."

"Just wait until you get there, though," he says, and laughs deeply.

"Who is the girl who works for you?" I ask.

"She is the daughter of a friend of mine. She brings messages that tell me when to expect someone and at the same time gets paid well for serving in the café. She sees nothing." Gottfried covers his eyes and grins. "It is best that way, should she ever be questioned."

"Is Gottfried your real name?"

"Of course not."

And we all laugh.

The next day, the baker, true to his word, leaves the café on our behalf, taking some pastries with him. He returns with news.

"Many of the children have been transported, mostly the very young, because they are more in demand. There are two older ones there."

"How old?"

"Around seven or eight perhaps, maybe a little older: a girl and a boy."

Henrik stands up as if he will run.

"Calm down, Rik. There is no guarantee that it is your sister. And there is no point to going there now, unless you want to get caught."

Henrik rushes from the room and returns with his drawing book. He hurriedly finds a picture of Greta and holds it up to Gottfried.

Gottfried leans in to examine what it is that Henrik so desperately wants him to see.

"Is this your sister?"

"Yes," says Henrik. "Did you see her?"

Gottfried squints. "It is difficult to say . . . I only caught a glimpse."

"I must see them. I must know."

"Yes, and you will, but there is a thing called timing. Bad timing has wiped out armies. It has killed those who are too impatient, too desperate for answers, who use their hearts instead of their heads. You will always get your moments, but you have to measure them carefully."

I like this man the more he speaks. He is as wise as he is kind as he is sharp.

"Tonight they will have their evening meal around six o'clock. I found this out from the charming housekeeper, who seems to have an eye for me. Not that I like to boast." He winks. "So wait until then. You must go alone and leave the girl. She will only draw attention."

Henrik nods.

"Go to the left side of the house. There is a dining room there. You can peer in and see if your sister is one of them."

All day Henrik paces the room. The other couple is leaving that night. They are heading west. Gottfried has another contact in the place they will travel to. It seems he is part of a wide network of underground traders and resistance workers.

Henrik is back from the orphanage and now lies on the bed staring at nothing. He does not speak. Gottfried is out serving customers and the couple has left.

"Are you going to tell me?"

"I already did."

"You said that she wasn't there, but did you see anything else?"

"I would have told you if there was anything else!"

"You don't have to snap at me. We are on the same side."

"I know," he says more softly, his chin resting in his hand. "But . . ." He is thoughtful for a moment. "There were only a couple . . . younger than Greta. The boy was crying and eventually a woman came in and took him out. The girl was left to finish her soup on her own. The look on her face showed that she was terrified. I could tell she didn't like the place. When the woman came in, she jumped. I know that Greta wasn't there. She would be looking after these younger ones if she was."

Gottfried comes in. He has already heard.

"Sorry you didn't find her," he says. Gottfried then tells us that many people have been transferred from the ghetto to a labor camp farther south, to work in the quarry and factories.

"Maybe she is there in the camp," I say.

"The camp is for workers," says Gottfried. "Many from the Podgorze ghetto are taken to work there—families, children. But those from outside Cracow are sent elsewhere."

"Where are they sent?" says Henrik.

Gottfried seems reluctant to answer and scratches his head anxiously as if regretting the telling.

"There is another camp called Auschwitz not far from here where many Jews and other prisoners are taken."

"I have heard of this," say Henrik. "I have heard they perform experiments on the prisoners." He explains what he learned on his mission with Eri.

"It is not a good place," says Gottfried. "I do not think anyone should go there if they don't have to."

"But what if she is there? What happens to the young children? Surely they are cared for!"

"I have heard stories from the guards there . . . The conditions could be better."

"I must go. How do I get there?"

Henrik doesn't see it—perhaps he doesn't want to—but I do: there is something Gottfried is holding back.

"It is difficult. You run too great a chance of being caught. You will not get very close. It is too well guarded."

"I will go, regardless."

Gottfried pauses. "You can't go there."

"If it was your child or sister, would you go? If you were me, would you go?"

Gottfried closes his eyes and does not say anything for many seconds.

"I can't stop you," he says finally.

"Can you help us?"

"I don't know."

Gottfried says he needs to think.

Gottfried comes into our hidden room.

"I am not sure you will find your sister there."

"But you are not sure that she isn't there."

"No, I can't say. But I can get you to the town near the camp. That is all."

"You will do that?"

"Yes," he sighs. "I can tell that you are determined, Rik, that you are the type of person who would rather die trying than not try at all."

Gottfried is right. Henrik does not give up anything easily.

"I can drive you most of the way to the camp and hide you in the back of my truck. I can leave you on the outskirts to spy but you won't be able to get close. There are thirteen-foot fences and barbed wire. There is a spindly birch forest where you can spy from but it will be dangerous. I do not recommend you do this but I can see that you will go no matter what I say, so I can be of some help. You will need binoculars." He slaps his thighs, something he does often when he is thinking. "And then what if you do see her?"

"Then I will think of something."

Gottfried shakes his head gravely.

"I think you will get yourself killed."

"I am coming too then," I say. "I can help."

"You, even more than him, should not go near that place."

"I have to go." For Henrik, I have to go.

"You can't come, Rebekah. I do not want to put you in such danger. You have done enough to help me. You must stay here."

"No, Henrik. I will not."

He meets my eyes and knows, like me, that we are joined now in this quest to find Greta. That no matter what he says I will follow him.

"Is this true? You are going too?" says Gottfried.

Henrik turns away.

"Yes," I say.

Gottfried shakes his head solemnly, sadly.

"I will drop you both off, but I can't stay with you, even for a minute. Any unexplained activity is considered illicit. Everyone is guilty until proven otherwise.

"It will be four days before I can return. If I come back sooner, any guards who see me pass will query. I can pick you up at the same point I leave you but if you are not there, then I will keep driving back. Do you understand all this?"

Today we stay hidden in the secret room. Gottfried has told us that the police have stepped up personnel, have added more check-points, and are searching more homes. Several policemen come into the café. Henrik and I are frozen with fear while the police are there. I think that at any moment they will enter our hidden sanctuary. My chest hurts from the tension.

The visitors are not keen to discuss their work at first. They prefer Gottfried's cakes and light banter. Though, as the policemen leave, they ask whether Gottfried has seen any suspicious persons in his café or on the street: in particular, teenagers. Gottfried volunteers that he did see several children come into his café. They stood for a few minutes inside the door as if they were hiding, and he overhead them talking about the Ukrainian border. He tells the officers that they looked scared and says that he gave the teenagers the bread they ordered but they then ran out without paying. He says that he ran after them but they were too fast. He thought he saw them get in a vehicle, a truck, at the end of the street. Had he known there were children on the run, he would have given them more cake to keep them here and then sent a message to authorities straight away.

Gottfried is so convincing that I start wondering if it is true, until he walks into our little room and winks at us. "Stupid krauts believe everything I say." And there is that laugh again, the one that is so infectious that I am now smiling with relief. Though, I notice that Henrik isn't. The war is changing him. Once upon a time, I think, he might have fallen over from laughter. But at least he is drawing again. At least he is still in there somewhere. Finding Greta is just as much about saving Henrik as it is about saving her.

That night, after the café is closed, Gottfried unlocks a cabinet and pulls out several maps, including one of Auschwitz. He marks places such as the heavily guarded areas and where the women and children are housed in the camp. He points on the map to a place where many of the prisoners congregate: a central point where they are chosen for certain duties.

"How do you know it so well?"

"The guards there love to talk, to boast. I have an agreement with some of them. They pass me loot and I sell it and return half the money to them. Although rarely is it half—I keep most for me. I tell them: 'The black market, it is not as lucrative as it used to be.'" He shrugs his shoulders and raises his eyebrows as if he is reliving those conversations. "They can't say anything. They can't prove anything and they wouldn't dare try. They would be imprisoned themselves."

"You could get caught," I say.

He laughs off the suggestion. "And miss out on such enjoyment as to swindle a German who is swindling a Jew?"

His run to the camp is scheduled for the following day. His cover is that he will deliver fresh bread and cakes for the camp commander, which he will bake during the night. Before it is daylight, we must go outside and hide in the back of his truck.

Gottfried is experienced at smuggling people. He has designed some crates with a false bottom a foot above the floor of the crate and openings at the base on either side. With several placed together, they are long enough to hide a person. He fills the empty cavities above the crates with bread and pastries, cleverly concealing the person hiding underneath. We are to lie still in the hollows for an hour, over bumpy roads. Gottfried says that he has never been inside the camp where the prisoners are; instead, he drives into a rarely used barn in one of the rail yards outside the camp. There he can load up with goods: dresses, jewelry, leather bags, and other belongings that the guards have brought in sacks. He hides

276

these underneath the crates, just as he is hiding us. There might also be a silver frame, clock, or watch. Small things. Gottfried says that he only takes the best clothes: only silk dresses and shirts, or tailored suits and new shoes.

Then he hands over to the guards the money from the items he has already sold. After this he drives farther up the road to deliver cakes to the soldiers who meet him at the entrance to Auschwitz, but he does not go inside and has no desire to do so. Something about the place suggests permanency, he says.

Or a doorway to the afterlife, I think.

"Have you ever smuggled people from this place?"

"It isn't like the ghettos, where smuggling is easier. The camps are more difficult. Once people are in the camps, I can do nothing more." Then he remembers Henrik and what he plans to do and lifts his tone slightly. "Though, of course, that isn't to say it can't be done. Perhaps you will be the first after all."

He points to an area on the map that is west of the camp. "This is a wooded area where you can hide. There is a small white house and barns which will help to block you from view. As far as I know, no one lives in the house. Many residents nearby were told to leave when they began work on the camp.

"The area around the camp is heavily policed. The people still living there are employed by the Germans, or they have special documents that allow them to live there. It will be a miracle if the guards don't see you and an even greater one if their dogs don't." He pauses to see the reaction from Henrik, who is undeterred. He will not give up his quest.

Gottfried leans back on the small wooden chair and stares at us both, sitting on the bed.

"It is very dangerous what you are about to do," he says suddenly. "You are good. I don't like seeing good people go."

"We will be safe," I say. "We will make ourselves invisible."

Gottfried laughs, but it is a slow, sad laugh, as if he has heard this before.

He pulls open drawers and takes out clothing: dark trousers, black high-necked jumpers, and caps. He gives us black paint for our faces and tells us that if we are caught in a beam of light, to put our heads down so our eyes do not shine. We must blend in with the spindly trees. There is not much cover behind the winter birches and there is still more snow to come. It will be cold. He gives us each a pack filled with water and bread, cakes and apples.

Henrik is more excited about this quest than he is scared. His spirits are lifted whenever he is busy, even if what he is doing is dangerous; it's the waiting that drives him to despair.

"Gottfried, I can't thank you enough . . . ," says Henrik.

"You can thank me by coming back here safely. But I must ask that if you make your own way back somehow, and you think you are being followed, you do not come to the café straight away. It is important that there are no trails here so I can continue my work."

"You have my word."

I stand up and he wraps me in his large bear hug. "And, my dear Beka," he says, using the pet name he has given me, "make sure you stay alive. I do not want to see your brains and beauty go to waste."

While I am trying to sleep, Henrik pulls out his drawing book. It has travelled far with him, and the corners curl from unintentional misuse. It tells its own story.

He draws a picture by the light of a small lamp. I listen to the scratching of charcoal for over an hour. When there is no more sound, I ask if I can see the drawing.

"You should be asleep."

"So should you," I say.

It is a caricature this time. The man has a wide smile, a large forehead, and large fleshy cheeks. Henrik has captured Gottfried's character in this picture: bold, a jester, and a gentle soul. I think that I would like to see a gallery full of Henrik's pictures at the end of the war.

CHAPTER 29

For much of the night Henrik has been pacing. He has hope, and I want to have hope.

We wriggle through the holes in the crates as planned and Gottfried drives for over an hour. The roads are bumpier than I thought they would be. I can just see Henrik's clothing through the tiny gaps in the crates beside me, though anyone else would not know there was a person there.

Gottfried stops at the outskirts of a village northwest of the camp. If we are not in this same place in four days' time, he will have to drive back without us. From the drop-off point, we are to walk through woodland. On the other side, we will find the camp. Gottfried reminds us that we must lie low and blend into the surroundings, and the dirty patches of snow. We have to make ourselves into trees.

We crunch carefully through woodland but our steps are impossible to silence in snow. It is not long before we see the tall fences, barbed wire, and brick buildings standing in neat formations.

There is a lingering smell in the air, like burning fur or hair. It is putrid and I try to rub away the smell with the back of my hand.

"What are they burning?" Henrik echoes my thoughts.

"I don't know," I say. "Perhaps it is whole carcasses of meat."

"The smell is awful."

"There is the house that Gottfried spoke of," Henrik says, pointing.

I feel exposed amongst the winter birch. We are too close this time: too close to badness. We sit and wait behind the trees.

"What is that?"

It is late afternoon. I must have dozed. It takes me a moment to hear it too.

There is music being played somewhere inside the camp. It is sweet music, played by a small orchestra.

"Why the music?"

I have no idea. I wonder what games these Germans are playing. Soon the music stops, followed by shouts and orders.

We wait till night and then run to hide behind the windowless house that Gottfried described, avoiding the lights from the guard towers. The door is locked, and, strangely, all the windows have been bricked in, except for a section with a small wooden flap that can be unbolted and lifted from the outside. We raise the flap and shine a flashlight inside. The rooms are empty and there is sawdust on the floor. Outside, stacked up against the wall, are empty canisters. There seems to be nothing significant about the house, other than it is too close to the camp, and too close to possible capture the longer we take to investigate.

We return to the forest and, wrapped in our blankets, lie down next to one another to keep warm. Henrik enfolds me in his arms and we listen to the quiet of the camp, unable to sleep.

• • •

We hear commands. It is early, the day not yet bright enough to start.

Henrik climbs a tree; the binoculars hang around his neck. He is nimble, climbing like a monkey, using his knees and the frail-looking branches as leverage.

"Be careful," I whisper, though I am not afraid of him falling. I am scared that the guards in the towers will see the movement.

When he is high enough to see into the camp, he squints through the binoculars, focusing the lens. "I don't see anything yet but it sounds like the prisoners are being counted."

Several minutes pass before he sees anything happen.

"Some men have been led to the rear of the camp. They are standing in a line."

Henrik mutters something to himself that I cannot understand.

"What else do you see?"

"They are wearing pajamas."

"Pajamas?" I repeat with disbelief.

"Yes, or long shirts, I think. They do not look well. They look thin and scrawny . . . sort of starved . . ." He pauses in concentration.

"The guards are pulling some men out of the line and marching them. They are shoving them roughly in the back with their guns."

"Do you see any children?"

"No. But there are some women, I think, on the other side of the men. I can't be sure. They are marching some men away now . . . Wait . . . one has stopped. He is begging the officer . . ." There is a long pause. "Bastard!"

"What is it?"

"The guard has hit him on the head with the back of his gun. I can't see where they are being taken."

Henrik stays fixed in place. A few minutes later we hear a gunshot and faint wails for mercy. Then more shots. I feel coldness travel up my spine and realize suddenly that being here is madness.

Henrik comes down. He doesn't say it but we look at each other to confirm what might have happened.

"I do not know why they were chosen, but I believe it was for execution."

"Why? What have they done?"

"For the same reason your parents died," says Henrik angrily. "Nothing. But I thought I heard children's voices."

I haven't heard any such sounds. I wonder if perhaps it is Henrik's hope again.

It is day three. We have slept two nights and have seen much the same as the days before. I am chilled and wish to be back in Gottfried's warm café, listening to the sounds in the kitchen and his low musical instructions.

"Is that a train?"

An engine purrs in the distance, growing gradually louder, before coming to the end of its tracks on the other side of the camp. There is more commotion this morning. The guards seem restless. There are more coming out to discuss things, their guns poised.

Many voices travel on the wind to make one large buzzing sound. When Henrik checks from the top of the tree, he says there are many people walking across the snow towards the camp. He does not know what nationality they are. Henrik reports that they are being marched through the center.

They arrive at the side of the buildings most visible to us. I am amazed by the number. There are hundreds. The group is split, and the men, some of the women, and older children are being sent back into the camp behind the buildings. It is mayhem as people struggle with their bags, passing loved ones their belongings. The ones who are not sent behind the camp walls are the elderly and women with small children, some of whom are shoved along so brutally that they drop their bags. They are not allowed to pick these up.

We watch all this without fear of being seen because the guards have turned their attention to the newcomers. Henrik is scanning the faces of the children, looking for the ones the same height as Greta. We are far away, but I know that Henrik would find her in this crowd if she were there.

I can hear the crying of the babies held by their mothers. The group is led to an area beside the white house, herded like animals, and made to stand while several guards circle them like wolves.

"What are they going to do?"

We wait while there are more commands issued in German.

"What are they saying?"

Henrik climbs down from his usual position and silently passes me the binoculars. He says he does not want to look anymore, that Greta is not there. I can see the prisoners' faces. They talk amongst themselves with heavy frowns, beseech the guards for answers, and hold one another for comfort. The little ones clutch at their mamas' coats and skirts, their faces stretched with shock and confusion and cold. Without their walking canes, the old men and women lean on women who are more able.

I feel a lump in my throat. I want so badly to run to the group, to tell them that it will be all right. That this is only a formality within this camp, that they will soon be led to the brick buildings where they will find warmth. Though I have no idea what the conditions are really like. I want to tell them that someone plays music in the camp, that they will get through this, even though my words would be the kind of false promises commonly made in desperate, unjust times such as these.

We can hear the sounds of machinery and rail trolleys and the digging of shovels from behind the buildings in the camp.

And then things are happening again. The officers are shouting. The people are herded into a barn. With angry, menacing growls, the dogs force the group to move quickly. One of the guards shoots into the air, also for this purpose.

When the prisoners come out several minutes later, most are not wearing clothes, and those still half-dressed are forced at gunpoint to remove everything else. Many of the women are crying; others wear only sad looks of resignation. I ask Henrik why they look this way. He says he can't hear what they are saying because the crying and wailing is too loud.

Then the people are standing naked, all of them, waiting. I put the binoculars down. I cannot bear to see the indignity as they try to conceal their nakedness with their hands. Henrik and I both watch from a distance as they are then shepherded in groups into the white house.

"What the hell is going on?" says Henrik.

I think that this building might be the washrooms but I do not remember seeing any showers inside. From inside the building come their moans, then their whimpers, and then screams. Agony squeezes through the gaps in the building. They are in there for half an hour while the others stand outside freezing, clutching one another. And then the doors are opened and bodies spill out into a heap.

"They have killed them with poison," says Henrik, and I hear a break in his voice. Several of the men in pajamas from the camp put the dead women and children and elderly in trolleys to wheel them away towards other buildings. The ones who are still alive are shrieking now, knowing what will befall them. I put my hand over my mouth to stop myself from screaming. I turn away. I cannot look upon this evil a second longer. I run deeper into the woods, not caring where I am heading as long as it is far away from here. Henrik runs after me to catch me and we fall in the snow and hold each other—for how long I don't know, but until the sounds of people screaming and moaning and Germans shouting have finished.

I am afraid to move, afraid that should I stand, the images will be clearer, that life will become real again.

That night we do not talk at first. Henrik is silent. He stares at his hands.

"Henrik," I say. "I do not think your sister is here. I do not think she is part of this group. I did not see any who resembled your sister."

"But she could be here," he says. "She could be farther inside."

I shake my head. I do not want to give him any more hope. I am tired of hope.

"Even if she is in there somewhere, you will never get past the guards. There are too many. We must go tomorrow to the checkpoint to meet Gottfried."

"You can go," he says. "I will not leave until I am sure."

"She is not here, Henrik," I say, impassioned. "And if she were, she is not here anymore." It is perhaps hurtful what I say, but I cannot bear to think of losing Henrik.

"How can you say that?"

"Because this is not a camp, not like the one in Cracow. This one is different. This one is for the purpose of extermination; it is here to end the Jewish race."

"Well, as I said, you go. I will stay."

I am saddened. I shiver and he sees this, and I can see that he is torn and carries guilt for everyone—for Greta, for me. But I will not leave without him. I wonder if I might freeze to death tonight. Perhaps it would be better if I did.

I slip into sleep only to be shaken roughly awake. It is still night.

"Quickly," he says. "We have to hide." I do not look to see what has frightened him but follow, crawling insect-like along the ground. We stop when Henrik thinks we are far enough from whatever it is that he has seen.

"There are Germans out walking their dogs. Be silent now, be still."

"They will smell us."

The Germans are coming our way with heavy steps. The dogs are whining. I wonder if we were spotted while we slept.

"You will have to climb."

"I can't."

"You have no choice."

Henrik pushes me up the tree and tells me to press hard against the trunk with my knees and climb fast. He says that unless the Germans shine their flashlights upwards, they won't see us. Henrik tells me to take my gloves off so that I can grip better. I put them in my mouth. I scale the branches gingerly, expecting them to snap. The bark scratches at my hands, and the effort of climbing requires muscles and skill that I have not used before. But fear can sometimes make you do things that you did not see as possible, and I am suddenly at the top.

When I look down, it is far to the ground and I can see lights through the trees. There are two Germans with dogs. The Germans bark their commands. The dogs are excited about something just a short distance away. They are whining, their tails up, their heads high and eager. I wonder if the guards have seen our footprints.

I do not know which tree Henrik has climbed. I am too afraid to turn my head in case the movement attracts the searchers' attention. I know that he is somewhere behind me.

As they reach the base of my tree, one of the dogs sniffs the ground and barks wildly. I see that another soldier is coming with another dog. There is no escape now. The three men gather below me. I close my eyes.

Suddenly, there is a shout. I find the nerve to look down and learn that the shout was not directed upwards, towards me, but farther into the woods. They have seen something and run several yards in its direction. I am praying that it isn't Henrik. Two other

Germans have come in from the far side of the forest. I think how close we would have come to being caught if we hadn't climbed.

The guards drag a man: a man in pajamas. They throw him on the ground and hold back the dogs, which wag their tails, their job done. They bark proudly. I can't stand their noisy boasting.

The guards shout at the man and he is forced onto his knees. I can just see him below me. The flashlight shines into his face, blinding him. He puts the back of his hand against his eyes to shield them from the light. I can almost smell his fear, which matches my own, and my legs and arms tremble so badly I think I might accidentally release my hold.

The shot happens quickly, the snow sprayed with droplets of dark.

I stay fixed to my spot as they drag the man away by the legs, like hunters, towards the camp. The dogs have calmed and I am relieved that they are too fixated on the scent of the man to have picked up my smell. I climb down from the tree once their sounds have dissipated in the whipping wind. I see that Henrik stands only yards away. He rushes towards me and hugs me tightly.

"Yes, we must go," he says. "There is nothing here. Greta is not here." And I wonder if this is what he truly believes, whether he has convinced himself for my sake.

We walk northward towards the checkpoint and wait like criminals in the shadows of buildings. We have no food or water left. Our lips are cracked, our spirits chipped and split.

We see Gottfried's truck around midday. The sound of his engine is the kindest sound of all.

Gottfried opens the door and covers our weary, cold bones with rugs, and hands us water and sweet doughy rolls filled with jellied apricot. His hands are large and gentle as he rubs our shoulders and backs, and then he closes the door. We crawl into our mouse holes once again while he closes the door. The darkness brings up the images of the faces I saw through the binoculars.

Outside the café, we stay inside the truck until night, both of us sleeping. Later, Gottfried comes to collect us and I lean on him as we are taken to our room.

Henrik does not want to talk. He has gone to bed, but I seek out Gottfried.

"You knew about the camp, didn't you?" I say. "You knew what they did."

He nods. "It is best not to see some things. It is best not to think too hard about it or else you can lose hope. Henrik had to see for himself. He is that type of person; he has to know before he can believe. Let's hope that he still has hope."

We are quiet for a moment. I make myself busy helping him in the kitchen.

Gottfried says that it is a joke amongst the Germans that they kill those who can't work, but he wasn't so sure what happened to the children.

"But what about all the clothes?" I say. "The ones you take from the Jews. Do you not feel sad?"

"Of course," he says. "I do what I can. It is the only way I can survive. But I can tell you that whenever I see a small coat of a child, I think of my son, fight back tears, and joke along with the Germans. At the end, the clothes mean nothing to those who are dead. Instead, they become a commodity, and a weapon to use against the Germans. This is the only way to look at it, so I can do what I do."

"Why don't all the Jews revolt in the camp? There are hundreds."

"I think it is the hope that someone will come and save them, or that the war will end. All those I have rescued from the ghetto have said they held on to hope, and it came in the shape of me, and others."

Henrik doesn't talk about what we saw and Gottfried doesn't ask. Gottfried understands; he shows this by his silence. He cooks in his kitchen for much of the evening and I can tell that this is where he is happiest.

For the next two days, Henrik still doesn't speak much, nor does he eat. Sometimes, in his nightmares, he whimpers and calls out to his mama. But when he wakes, there is no expression or emotion. It is as if someone reached into his soul and pulled it out by the roots.

I rise early to help Gottfried with the bread. I talk to him about Henrik, about how I am worried.

"It is grief, Beka," he says. "You have to let him deal with it. He might never see his sister and he is feeling that he has let his mother down. And he has seen much. You have perhaps already gone through your grief and you are stronger for it. Henrik has not had a chance yet to think of his loss. He has been strong for both of you, and for his family also."

Gottfried is right, of course. Henrik has nurtured and caressed my soul. Perhaps it is time he looked after his own.

Hiding in the back of this café feels good. It has been a long time since I have known that feeling. But Henrik continues to worry me. He has buried his thoughts deeply. He does not talk about Greta, and he does not meet my eyes.

I am afraid to ask him about our next plan. I know we can't stay here forever, even though Gottfried has made no hint about us leaving.

In the time we have been here, several refugees have come and gone. One night we share the room with three Frenchmen and Gottfried asks that we do not talk to them, to let them rest. They do not talk to us either, but lie quietly on the floor. They are gone before morning. Gottfried says they are on a mission. He cannot give any details. I have guessed that some of these refugees will die in the course of their endeavors, that some are purposely heading towards danger rather than from it.

It is late. Gottfried has gone to bed and Henrik and I are in our little room behind the wall. Henrik sits perched on the edge of his bed, thinking.

I sit on my bed across from Henrik's, writing in a diary that I have acquired from Gottfried. Suddenly there is a sound like the whining of an injured animal. I look up to see that Henrik has turned to face the wall, his body curled into a ball, his knees against his chin.

I sit beside him on the bed and touch his back.

"Rik?"

He turns. His face is awash with grief. Tears stream down his cheeks. I have never seen him distraught. It is a shock to see him this way.

"I am sorry, Rebekah," he says. "I should not have dragged you through all this. It was for nothing. My sister is probably far away from here or dead, and perhaps I will never know where she is buried."

"Hush," I say. "You must not think about that, Henrik. You have fought hard to find her."

"And you," he says. "You have lost everyone. Perhaps even your brother. This has been a selfish quest."

"No," I say soothingly. "There is nothing selfish about it. Many have lost people they love, but you have tried to save one, and in the process you have made my life better. You have never given up on me. You could have left me in the forest, and again in the barn. I have been like lead around your neck. I am the one who is sorry, Henrik."

The sobbing subsides, though his grief is only partway through. I know this from experience. I too have suffered grief so black that I couldn't see a way out. If it wasn't for Henrik, I would still be in the darkness.

"Rebekah," he says more calmly. "You have been a wonderful friend. I will repay you any way I can."

"Don't be silly," I say. "I have done nothing."

Henrik puts his head in my lap and I stroke his fine hair, imagining that his mother once did the same.

I feel his hand on my leg and touch his strong, firm shoulders. When he looks up at me next, I see a man, not a boy: a man who possesses me. My body trembles at this realization, at our physical closeness. My feelings towards him are so strong and I bend to kiss him.

And then he is sitting upright and his lips are firmly on mine, as if we are fused. I feel my body relax and soften against him. I feel his hand touching my skin, which he says is like silk. He lifts my dress above my head and gently pulls me down to lie with him on top of the blankets. With my ear against his chest I listen to his heart beating rapidly, like my own. The air is cool but our bodies are warm.

"I love you, Rebekah," he says. "I love every little bit of you. I have since the first day I saw you."

I cradle his face and cover it with more kisses. I am crying and he touches my face to wipe the tears away.

"It is nothing to be sad about."

"It is not sadness."

What I feel is overwhelming joy and relief. Henrik's skin is all that I want surrounding me.

• • •

Eventually we grow cold and, cocooned together in blankets, we discuss our plan to return to Zamosc. Henrik talks about how he will fix things around the home, and build an extension room for me to hide in until it is safe. He says that one day he will manage the farm.

We talk about how the Germans will be defeated. How we will laugh about them, at their folly. We talk about how we will name our firstborn girl "Greta," and our firstborn boy after my papa.

He talks about how he is looking forward to seeing his mother, and even his aunt, who sounds quite fierce from his descriptions.

We lie in the darkened, windowless room beneath one light blanket and talk until we are glad to be back in the present because that is the safest place to be; that is what we know.

I hear Henrik's breathing start to slow. I know that he will soon be asleep. He is good at sleeping.

"Henrik," I say.

"Yes," he says croakily.

"I love you too."

We sleep. It is the best sleep I have had in months. I dream again of Henrik, and ships that sail to faraway destinations.

CHAPTER 30

Gottfried says that we can stay as long as we like, especially if we help out.

"I have received further word from my contacts in Lodz. It is good news. There is a place where many of the stolen children are sent. It is called the Litzmannstadt ghetto.

"I am told that this is where they take some of the pastel orphans, where they weed out the ones they don't want to keep."

"What do you mean: *pastel orphans*?"

"Unfortunately, my dear Henrik, the pastel orphans are the ones like your sister: blonde, blue-eyed. Hitler wants to build an empire of Aryans."

"Are you certain the children are adopted by German families?"

"Yes, and others are sent to orphanages. They are forced to forget their real families and their birth records are erased. When they are old enough, they will likely be sent to join the Hitler Youth, or be married off, or used for any other service.

"My contacts in Lodz are kidnapping many children from the ghetto—Aryan, Jew, any race—and delivering them to a safe house in the east."

"To the Soviet Union?" Henrik says incredulously.

"Do you have a better plan?" Gottfried thinks for a moment. "Perhaps you can help with this too. You might get an opportunity to ask someone in Lodz about your sister."

"When do I start?" asks Henrik.

"Not so quickly. It may take a couple of weeks to advise my contacts, and set up a new line of delivery. In the meantime, you can do a little networking from Cracow."

By *networking*, he means helping people escape.

"How do you get them out?"

"Some by the sewers; some through the forests. They are brought here first if there is no direct line to where they want to go. Some are too young to travel alone and need someone to guide them. You already know part of the route."

Gottfried brings out his map and points to the towns Henrik will be passing through. "You take them here, then to the next contact in the east. That contact takes them from you and passes them along the line."

"Maybe after this Cracow job I can go to Lodz myself."

Gottfried has renewed Henrik's hope, but my hopes have fallen. I do not like it that Henrik will take new risks. Henrik suddenly thinks of me.

"You can stay here. You will be safe."

I pull Henrik aside to our room. "I thought you said that we would return to Zamosc."

"We will. I promise. But this could be the place where I find Greta. I have come this far . . ." His words trail away. I know that there is nothing I can say to change his mind. And since he needs to move quickly, there is no question that I will go this time. We both know that I will only slow him down.

I know also that I will wait for him. The only place for me is with Henrik now.

• • •

Henrik successfully completes his Cracow mission, delivering two
children to the café in the middle of the night and then, the following night, taking them safely to another location. It is then that
he begins his missions in the north. He delivers messages to other
locations to advise on safe routes, names, and dates. Sometimes
he has to collect people and take them directly to another base in
Lublin, where they are smuggled by rail.

Sometimes, he brings the refugees back here and they stay in
our room. At one time there are as many as six. But it is usually
only one night before Henrik delivers them safely to the next point
of contact in Gottfried's web.

When the refugees are here, it is my job to attend to their
clothes, food, and bedding. The rest of the time I help Gottfried
bake cakes and even help make up new ones for his shop. He says
they are a success and I try different kinds, with new ingredients.
There seems to be no end to Gottfried's resources. He is a large
man with a hard expression, stubble on his chin, and buttoned
shirts that strain across his belly. First impressions might be that
he is gruff. But he is not. He has a heart as soft as beaten egg whites,
and the temperament of a cherished child.

Henrik is taking longer to return. Sometimes he is gone for days.
In between missions he tells me stories of sabotage. Once he killed
a German who had arrived at their secret location unexpectedly. Henrik says it was fortunate he was there, hiding behind a
door; once the man had entered, he shot him with the pistol that
Gottfried has given him. The entire operation had to be moved.

Another time, he is gone for five days. He had to lead a group
across the river and to the east, to guide them to their safe house in
one of the villages. He says he had to take them all the way because
they were women and children, and they were frightened and crying and sick.

But sometimes he does not tell me things, only Gottfried. I catch whispers of what Henrik says. Once he arrived at a house to collect some Jewish escapees from the north, only to find they'd been caught unaware and slaughtered. Perhaps the Germans had been tipped off by others who had been caught and interrogated, or perhaps the escapees' house had been under suspicion for a while, or they were tracked. I start to worry. What if Gottfried is being spied upon?

When I ask him if he is worried, he laughs. He says that he is invincible because he is cautious. "Your friend might not be, though."

"What do you mean?"

"He does not seem afraid of danger. He seems to gravitate towards it."

I think about this later and wonder if Henrik is trying to make up for the loss of Greta. That nothing will fill the hole, even partly—not even me.

Gottfried takes us out in his little delivery truck. Many from the Gestapo know Gottfried. They do not check his vehicle. We lie in the back between the crates once more.

It seems wild and dangerous but Gottfried is not worried. He trusts his instincts. He takes us to a private place near the river. He says I have been cooped up in the back with the damp for too long, and someone as small and frail as I am needs more daylight.

Gottfried has given me a pale peach-colored dress, which I wear today. Though, in the last couple of weeks, it has been getting tight on me after all the food I've eaten at Gottfried's. I notice that there is the shadow of a beard along Henrik's jawline and chin, and a faint line above his nose.

The three of us share some wine and cheese and chicken beside the river. The sun is shining and out in the open we feel strangely safe. There are small trees lining either side of the river. At the end of the day, Henrik tells me that with my cheeks brushed by sunlight, I have never looked more beautiful.

Since Henrik began his missions, he has not mentioned the house in Zamosc or the future he was planning with me. It is yet another condition of war to sometimes not look forward, simply to live each day as if it is your last.

One day Henrik is gone again, performing his part in yet another operation. He has heard that more children have been taken to Lodz for assessment. This time he will travel all the way to the end of the line, and spend more time with his investigations there. I am starting to have reservations about his work and worry that Gottfried might be recruiting Henrik to do more than he is able.

When I say this to Gottfried, he looks at me with eyes that have heavy bags beneath them—evidence of the worrisome and dangerous work he carries out to save others.

"You are right," he says. "He should be back home with his mother. You should tell him that it is probably time to finish."

I feel suddenly bad for Gottfried and throw my arms around him.

"I didn't mean to sound so forceful. It is just that I am worried."

"You should return to the village, get married, have a life. I mean it! It is time for you both to go."

My face flushes with embarrassment. It has never been formally stated that Henrik and I are together. I thought that we had kept our feelings hidden.

"Don't blush, Beka," says Gottfried. "No matter how careful you think you are, there are some things, like love, that can't be hidden. Don't think I don't see the way the two of you look at each other. It is a beautiful thing."

He says this with sadness, which is uncharacteristic of Gottfried. I sense that something is wrong and he reveals the awful truth: the ghetto in Cracow has been liquidated; all the remaining Jews have been sent to the camps.

Henrik's final mission is to help lead a family of children from Lodz to Lublin. But he has not returned from the mission, and twelve nights have gone, and I am beside myself with worry.

On the thirteenth night, Gottfried gets word to his contact in Lublin. They reply to say that Henrik never arrived.

Gottfried does not know what to do, and for the next two nights I cannot sleep. Gottfried is concerned about us both. He tells me to have faith, not in God but in Henrik.

Several days later, in the middle of the night, I leave my bed to investigate the commotion coming from the front of the building. It is very dark inside the café. Gottfried has covered the front glass door and windows with blackout curtains to stop anyone from seeing in. The room bursts into light as I enter.

Standing in the café is Henrik. He carries one small child in his arms, and the two standing beside him are barely six years old. Their faces are smeared with dirt and their clothes are ragged and torn.

I rush to hug Henrik, who is weak and exhausted. While Henrik reports the incident to Gottfried, I take the weary, hungry children into the back room and hand them each a glass of milk, some bread, and a bowl of leek soup. They are so famished they do nothing but concentrate on their food until every cup, plate, and bowl is empty.

Then I bathe them until they are clean. I raid Gottfried's trunk of clothes until I find some to fit them.

With their bellies full they are now so tired they can barely move. I tuck the children into my bed—the two boys at one end, and the little girl at the other. I hug each of them good night and tell them that they are safe. The younger boy, who is two, and the girl fall asleep instantly but the older boy begins to weep for his parents. I sing a tune that my mother used to sing to me, until his eyes close.

In the café, Henrik and Gottfried sit quietly. When I enter, they do not say anything; they do not even look up. They have run out of talk. I leave them to contemplate in silence. It is late when Henrik comes to bed, and I pretend to sleep so that he does not feel the need to speak, to relive the events a second time that evening. I am just grateful that he is here, and alive.

The next day, the children and Henrik sleep late and I hear the story from Gottfried. Henrik had collected the children without issue but found German roadblocks along the route to the next point of contact. He could not go to any villages because of the strong anti-Semitism that hovers above Poland even towards children. So they hid in the forest. But the Germans had heard there were partisans there, and the military stormed directly into the areas where Henrik and the children were hiding. Sometimes they had to hide under brush, with the Germans very close, and there was much gunfire. Henrik had to keep the terrified children from crying.

These children had escaped the Lodz ghetto and had been housed and hidden by sympathizers since. The purpose of Henrik's mission was to get the children to a contact in Lublin. Someone else would take them southeast from there.

Gottfried admits that some of these attempts have been unsuccessful, some of the recruited and the escapees never heard of again. He thought something terrible might have happened to Henrik, but says that he also believes in him: "There is something about that boy. It is the need to save many for not saving one. It is a need to survive despite the odds. It is neither desperation nor madness, but something more powerful."

Henrik, knowing that his access east was temporarily blocked, had no option but to bring the children to Cracow, since the place he had collected them from could no longer be reached.

When Henrik wakes, he fills in the gaps. He tells me that several times the children cried and he thought their sounds would give them away. He says that he thought of my face and held Greta's locket, and this had made it bearable.

While they were hiding in trees, Henrik played a game to distract the children, to stop them from crying. The officers were so close, the fugitives could see their faces. Henrik told them that the game was "who can spot the ugliest German." When they saw the ugliest one, the children had to pinch the inside of Henrik's arm. He says that from the moment they started the game, he was pinched continuously. He shows me some tiny fingernail marks on his arm as evidence, surrounded by scratches where he has crawled through barbed wire fences. I smile despite the seriousness.

Then the journey back to Gottfried's and reentering the city was just as bad. He says they have doubled the manpower at some entry points. Twice he had to carry the children, who were so weary they could barely walk. He carried two at once: one on his back and the other in front. And they took turns so that each could sleep while Henrik carried them. He says that his arms and shoulders ache but there is no regret or bitterness.

I am so proud of what he has done and astonished by his endurance.

"And Greta? Is there any word?"

He shakes his head.

"She is not there. Many were shipped to camps. She may have been sent elsewhere." It sounds like the hardness has set in for him also.

I take his hand and squeeze it tightly.

"What about the children here now? What will happen to them?"

"We have to try again to get them to Lublin."

"You?"

"Yes," he says. "Gottfried is studying the maps to see if there is another route that will not be so heavily manned."

I am angry inside. Gottfried promised that this was Henrik's last mission. I confront him when Henrik is not in earshot.

"I have told him not to go, that he must return to his mother. That he must concentrate on looking after you—but he can be stubborn."

"Henrik, if you go, then I am going too."

"No," he says firmly.

"Why? Because I am frail? Because of my weak lungs?"

He brushes some strands of hair away from my eyes.

"No, because I don't want to lose you too."

He looks worn and vulnerable, younger suddenly, and I throw my arms around him protectively. He smells like Henrik: of industrial soap and earthy, warm skin. I do not want to let him go.

"I don't want to lose you either."

He sits down on the bed. The three children are in the kitchen eating. I can hear Gottfried singing a humorous tune to them. His waitress is out front.

"I have been thinking of something. Something that worries me," says Henrik. "How can I return to Mama without Greta?"

"How can you *not* return to your mother? She wants you just as much as she wants Greta. You can't do this to her. You have helped enough. You have done more than most. Perhaps Gottfried can go this time."

"It is a long journey. He is too well known and if he gets caught, then the whole operation would close. He is the most valuable person within the network. Besides, he needs to show up at Gestapo quarters several times a week with deliveries. If he doesn't show, they might become suspicious, and they might turn up here to search the premises.

"These children have lost their parents. They watched their father hang, and the youngest was in his mother's arms when she was gunned down. I can't just walk away from that."

I know that he speaks the truth. The children are depending on him. Gottfried's safe house is only a temporary solution. I am just saying anything to put off the inevitable.

"Tell me, Rebekah," he says. "Are you well enough to make the journey to Zamosc?"

"Yes," I say. I am feeling stronger from the warm bed and food, but my voice cracks when I say this. I do not sound convincing, even to myself. I do not tell him that sometimes it is still a struggle to breathe, that sometimes my chest aches for more air.

"I know what you are thinking: that I will never give up on Greta. I asked Gottfried's contacts, and all those I smuggled, if they had seen her. I gave everyone her description. She is not there, she is not here. Many were sent away to camps months ago. She may even be in Germany. I have failed Greta and Mama, but I cannot fail you as well. If you are well enough to travel, we will leave as soon as I return."

I suddenly feel selfish and remember it was my choice to follow him.

"I am sorry, Henrik," I say. "Do what you must do. If that means we have to travel to Germany to find her, then I will do that too."

He sighs and reaches out to pull me down beside him.

"No. We won't do that. It is pointless, if not impossible. I see that now. After I have delivered these children to safety, we will return to Zamosc."

The children play in the secret room. Gottfried tells them jokes and they laugh. I think that after all the destruction, these tiny moments in the children's lives are the ones that will build their strength and determination, and these are some of the good things they will remember.

Henrik makes the journey again a few nights later. Before they leave, the children kiss me good-bye. The older boy cries. Like me, he has got used to Gottfried's cakes, the smell of baking bread, the warmth and sounds of the kitchen, and sharing a safe room that has a bed. He does not want to leave me either. Gottfried and I kiss them and they disappear into the night.

Henrik is gone for over a week, but this time the mission is successful. He returns weary.

We will never know the fates of the children after Henrik left them at the next contact point, but I pray for them daily.

CHAPTER 31

On a warm spring morning, after Gottfried arrives home from his deliveries, we announce our departure. He hides his disappointment well, disguising it with jokes and discussion about our futures.

"You have done well, my little friends, and you have been good company. The café won't be the same without you. I'm so sorry I could not find your Herr General DW."

Since Henrik and I arrived, Gottfried has been making discreet inquiries about the SS in the area, to see whether there is a man who has these initials. At one time he is given a list of names but there is no one with these initials in the area.

"It may have been a temporary assignment only, if he was ever stationed here," Gottfried says. It might also be that this officer was in Poland solely to deliver children to camps before returning to Germany. He is likely not based here, or his mission is so secret that even other officers do not know what he is doing. "Some of these officers are so secretive, with orders direct from the Führer himself. They come and go like the night.

"But, I have to tell you something I heard this morning. There is a man . . . a member of the Nazis . . . known as 'The Wolf.' The soldiers were talking about him when I arrived with their bread. Apparently he has been away for quite some time, but has just come back. They say he was here when the first shipment of Polish children arrived, that he was the first to inspect them. I asked if they knew his name, but they could not tell me, and I did not want to sound too interested with any further questions. They did volunteer, however, that he has a large river house east of the city, where he stays sometimes. You will be heading that way. Perhaps you can look in . . . or perhaps it is nothing."

"You are probably right . . . It is likely to be nothing," says Henrik.

Gottfried gives us a map of the forests and roads, and another compass. He says Henrik can keep the pistol. Gottfried seems to have unlimited resources, all thanks to his "friends" in the Führer's army. They are in as deeply as he is, and this is what Gottfried relies on to keep their alliance.

That evening we leave, promising that we will return when the war is over, when it is safe enough to come. He does not say anything to this. Perhaps he does not want to talk anymore of the future. Perhaps he cannot see as far as I can now. I understand. I have had those moments many times.

We say good-bye tearfully, and then we are gone. I will miss Gottfried. I will miss the café.

Gottfried has told us to exit the city a different way from where we came in, since there are fewer soldiers in the eastern farm areas and—other than the information he gleaned earlier—it is not known to house any German officers.

We walk past residences, hand in hand, looking for the large Nazi house that Gottfried spoke of earlier that morning. Though there are none that stand out, there are many that are large.

We are several miles from the city when we pass a well-lit house with sounds of celebration coming from inside, and two stately black vehicles parked in front. The house is bordered by others just as large. Someone is playing the piano and there is singing.

"This might be the one."

I don't like that we are not rushing to leave this city and tell Henrik this. I worry that we may in fact find this man, "The Wolf," and that we may not care to learn what he is capable of.

"Don't worry. It will probably be nothing. I will just have a look inside and then we can go."

He leans over to kiss me, to reassure me. We are like any other lovers, except for the fact that we are fugitives also.

"I will be back in a moment. Stay here."

I lose sight of him briefly as he crouches to blend into the shadows beneath a side window. Henrik stands cautiously to peer inside and then a moment later appears again at my side.

"Wealthy Germans, Nazis . . . nothing else. Let's get out of here."

As we are walking away, a child cries excitedly from behind the house. This time I follow Henrik to investigate. A yard at the back stretches towards the river. It appears that the adults are in the house while children play on swings at the back. There is a nurse or guardian nearby, watching them. She is young herself.

We stand with our backs to the wall at the side of the house to make ourselves unseen, and Henrik turns his head around the corner to sneak a look into the yard. He pulls back suddenly, his breathing labored, his chest heaving as if he has seen a ghost.

"She's here."

At first I don't know who he is talking about. In my mind, Greta had almost been buried.

"You don't mean . . ."

"Greta's here in the yard!"

Henrik leads me to hide behind a shed on the property adjacent to the yard.

"Are you sure?"

He nods. "I am. It has been many months and she has grown, but it is her. They have cut her hair shorter."

I am not yet convinced. "Are you sure it isn't the poor lighting, that it isn't someone who looks similar?"

"I would know my own sister," he says.

There is silence.

"What do we do?"

"I am thinking."

"How many were there?"

"Children? About five. She looked like the oldest."

"What were they doing?"

"They were playing a game. They were running around chasing each other. We must go back. I must try and get her attention. You stay here."

I watch him go. I see him crawl across the grass and disappear into the shadow of the wall. I can see the children from a distance, and hear their laughter. They are all fair. The yard is lit up with tiny yellow lights that hang between the trees. The older girl I took to be a nurse is sitting near the steps at the back. She is watching them play. A short time later Henrik returns.

"I can't get her attention. Every time I peer around the side, there is a child looking my way."

"Maybe we should go back to the café."

"No," says Henrik. "We stay here beside the house until morning."

"But they might be able to see us in the morning. We will also be exposed to the other houses."

He thinks about this. "Maybe it is best if you return to the café. I will come and collect you after I get Greta." There is excitement and desperation in his voice, as if he will do something reckless.

"No," I say firmly. "I am not leaving you, ever."

He squeezes my hand.

"I don't want anything to happen to you."

"I'm not leaving," I say. "But it is dangerous. I think we should break into the shed." We try the doors but they are bolted with iron. There are no windows to break this time.

"What about the coop?" says Henrik.

The house where Greta is staying has a small chicken coop at the back.

"They will screech if we enter."

"If they make a noise, we break their necks."

The children are called inside. One of the cars drives away. The lights go off at the back of the house, and we scurry like mice towards our destination. Only a couple of chickens cluck softly as we enter their netted pen. The coop is quite visible to anyone looking from the windows at the back of the house, except for the inside of a small wooden hutch where several hens are nesting.

We crawl inside and these occupants become noisy and indignant when we chase them out. We do not sleep or talk but lie there waiting.

It is early morning and through the gaps in the hutch we watch another car leave, steam trailing behind as the smoke from the exhaust pipe meets the cold morning air.

There are sounds from within the house, of tin pans and commands. It has been a cramped night and I long to step out to stretch my legs. I think that we might have to stay here all day as well.

My head rests on chicken straw and droppings. We do not see or hear the girl enter. She leans into the hutch, her head above me, holding a basket.

I pinch Henrik on the arm and he sits up quickly.

The girl is frozen. She studies us both before resting her eyes on Henrik.

"Greta," says Henrik. I see that he fights the urge to step out and greet her, knowing that he will risk being seen.

"Henrik?"

He puts a finger to his mouth to tell her to be quiet.

My heart is beating fast from fear and joy. I cannot quite believe that we have found Henrik's pearl in such a large sea. It is a miracle.

"What are you doing here?" she says.

"Come into the hutch. Are you collecting eggs?"

"Yes."

"Come in and pretend you are looking, so it doesn't look like you are talking to anyone."

She puts her head in only. There is no room for a third person in the hutch; it barely disguises us.

Henrik reaches his hand out but she recoils slightly to avoid his touch. I think she is perhaps still in shock.

"Why have you come?"

"To take you home."

She looks down into her basket. She is a pretty girl with healthy pink cheeks. She wears a light blue skirt and shirt, and a dark blue vest over the top that has pink flowers embroidered on the front. Her eyes are round and blue and I can see why she was taken. She is the perfect Aryan.

"Henrik . . ." She struggles to find the words. "You have to go. You can't stay. If they catch you . . ."

"What are you talking about?"

"I am quite safe here," she says haltingly. "You don't have to worry about me."

"Are you crazy?" He reaches for her hand but she draws back again, more forcefully this time. I can see the concern in Henrik's eyes. "I have spent months looking for you."

She looks up towards the house and then back at Henrik, and then to me.

"Hello," I say putting out my hand. "My name is Rebekah." She touches my hand gently and studies my face.

"I don't think it is safe for you here," she says to me. I can see that she knows something about race, and I wonder how much she has been told.

Henrik has read my mind. "What have they been filling your head with?"

"I am German, like you, Henrik—though, they only want ones like me."

"Blonde, you mean?"

"Yes."

"Did they tell you why?"

"They say that there are others . . . darker ones . . . who want to kill us all and replace our kind with their own. They have taken me so that it doesn't happen, so that I am not replaced. Perhaps, Henrik, you can find someone to take you in also. You are German."

Henrik shakes his head. "Gretel, do you not see?" Upon hearing Henrik's pet name for her, her nervous, darting eyes suddenly focus on her brother. The name has triggered a memory. "They have brainwashed you into believing their nonsense. They lie to you so that they can take over the world. It is they who want to replace everyone else. It is they who are cruel. If you could see what I have seen . . ."

"Stop it!" Greta drops the basket to cover her ears. When she sees that Henrik is no longer talking, she picks it up again. Henrik is shocked by her reaction, his mouth open. He cannot find any more words.

"You must go," she says, and she rushes from the coop without the eggs—the eggs we crushed during the night, in the dark.

We creep towards the shed behind the house next door and lie in the long grass. It is the only place where we can hide from the road, but it is visible from houses across the river and from where Greta is living. If anyone were to gaze too long from one of the back windows, they would see us.

"We must convince her that she has been wronged. They have spoiled her with food and clothes and singing, and games with the other children."

I agree, though I can't see how it will be done.

The children come out during the day but Greta is not amongst them. Henrik is getting worried that she will not come out at all.

"If I have to, I will break in and carry her, kicking and screaming, from this place."

Nighttime and we hear a car, its headlights shining onto the field and water behind us, and then there are voices. We watch an officer ascend the stairs to the front door.

"I think it is him," says Henrik.

"Who? The one who took Greta?"

"Yes. The same one who hit my mother."

"Are you sure it is him?"

"Almost sure."

"I don't think Greta realizes this. She must not have seen him strike her."

"Who knows what lies they have said about that."

There are sounds of greetings and laughter, of fondness. I hear footsteps going up and down stairs, and the aromas of cooking infuse the air, and then the house slowly grows silent, and then dark. We eat some of the food in our packs and wait.

From behind the shed, Henrik is assessing the windows and considering where he will enter when a light-colored shape emerges from the house. It is Greta in her nightgown. She is like a beacon in the night. She rushes to us, crouching low as if in some way this might help her avoid detection.

This time the brother and sister hug, but still Greta is holding back.

"I pretended to be sick so that I would not be disturbed today. I have come to say good-bye. You must go back, Henrik. Tell Mama that I am well."

"I am not leaving without you. That man you live with is a killer."

"We call him Papa and he is not a killer. He has been kind to us."

"You are too young to see."

"See what?"

"What they are doing. You must trust me, Greta. You must come back with us."

"With both of you?"

"Yes. Rebekah has helped me find you. Do you remember being taken?" Henrik asks.

Her little mouth twists as she looks at me curiously, then to Henrik as she tries to remember.

"Sort of. I was put in the back of the car and they threw a blanket over my head. I fought with them to pull it off. I remember seeing you run behind the car. I was frightened at first but then they apologized and took me to a house where a lady gave me an injection, and then I slept."

"You know the man you call Papa nearly killed your mother. He hit her so hard she fell back and hit her head."

"Henrik, you are making that up. Papa would not do something like that."

Henrik squeezes his hand into a fist. I touch his arm to calm him.

"You have to believe me. I have not come all this way to make this up. That man has taken many children."

"He said Mama tried to stab him after she had sold me."

"He lied. Mama didn't sell you. She is a broken woman, not just her body but her heart."

I can sense that she struggles with the truths just learned, that her loyalties are still divided.

"Are you saying that he lied . . . Are you sure?"

"I am telling you that he lied. They are stealing children from the arms of their mothers."

"The others aren't stolen. Their parents died."

"Probably killed by Germans so they could be taken. They are trying to create a blonde-haired, blue-eyed race. You are just part of their breeding program to produce more. Don't you see? They might get rid of you tomorrow. Maybe give you to some German that you don't like so that down the road you will give them more babies just like you."

"You are lying," she says, her voice breaking. She is scared.

"Henrik, enough," I say. "She is frightened and she is young. What you are telling her does not make sense to someone her age. She would not understand."

I hold both her hands, hoping that she does not run away again. "It's all right, Greta. Your brother is just worried. The Germans have been mean and cruel and they have hurt a lot of people for no reason other than greed. Unfortunately, the man here is not a good man. He only pretends to be. Your brother has not come all this way to lie to you. And I can promise you, even though I have never met your mama, that she did not sell you."

I can sense that some of the tension has left her.

"My name isn't Greta. It is Johanna now."

Henrik rifles through his bag and pulls out a drawing of his mother. He pulls out his small flashlight and shines it on the page.

"Henrik, the light!" I protest. "Someone will see us." But he doesn't hear me. He is too busy, too desperate to win his sister back.

"See, here is your mama. The mother who raised you and gave you everything, who tried to protect you and who nearly died trying. And this is how you repay her!"

Greta touches the page. "Mama," she says, and she is remembering. Her eyes are filling with tears.

"What is the name of the man who lives here?"

"Dieter Wolff."

Finally, we have found the owner of the lighter.

This makes Henrik angrier and he paces and curses, and when Greta starts to move away again nervously, Henrik rushes at her and grabs her, pinning her arms by her side with one arm and placing a hand over her mouth.

"It can't be done this way," I say.

"It has to be like this. Can't you see?"

Greta is squirming and struggling.

All of a sudden we are in a beam of bright light, and we are facing the man who started it all. Dieter Wolff has a gun in one hand and a flashlight in the other.

"Release her or I will shoot you."

Henrik does so but Greta doesn't run away as I expected her to. Instead, she stands between the two men, wondering who she will trust. The menacing one with the gun or her brother who has just tried to kidnap her back.

"What are you doing here?" says Wolff. "Who are you?"

"I've come to take my sister home."

Dieter is silent while he examines Henrik.

"That sounds very endearing," says Dieter in a condescending tone. "The boy from the farm here to rescue his sister from a terrible predicament. Is that right, Johanna, it is terrible for you here?"

Greta is too frightened to speak. I can't tell yet if she is afraid more for Henrik or for herself.

"As you can see, she is well taken care of—she does not need rescuing . . . Johanna! Come here!"

Wolff does not look at Greta. He has the gun trained squarely on Henrik, whose face is tilted slightly downward, filled with something greater than hate.

Greta does not move. Tears stream down her cheeks and she is trembling, but not from the cold.

"Johanna, go back to the house!" Wolff's command is more forceful this time.

"Don't hurt him, Papa," says Greta.

"Go," he barks, and she jumps at the sound. Greta edges away reluctantly as Dieter steps forward, only feet from where I stand. Henrik stands several yards away from us both.

"What do you want with my sister?"

"Isn't it obvious? She is my daughter now . . . a gift for my childless wife. You can at least die knowing that she has a better life with me. That she will never know poverty."

I breathe in suddenly at these words, which slice apart our hopes, and are trailed by silence to allow us briefly to contemplate our end. I think of all that we have been through, of what Henrik has done to find her. I think of all those he has rescued and tell God that he does not deserve to die. I cannot let Henrik die.

"Your wife will never be her true mother," I say.

"You couldn't be more wrong. There are now records that say otherwise."

I can see that Dieter's knuckles are white as he tightly grips the weapon.

"I will find you in hell then," says Henrik, in that confident tone I love best, and the way he can rise above disaster to appear the victor, even in defeat, fills me with wonder.

I wrap my hand around a cool metal handle in my pocket, a gift from Gottfried.

I hear the click of The Wolf's gun.

My hand trembles slightly as the sharp knife is drawn, and in one sweep I lunge and slash at the outstretched arm. The gun drops to the ground as Dieter grabs at the deep wound inflicted. There is blood on my sleeve. I am shocked at my capacity to do this.

Henrik quickly picks up the gun, and Dieter stumbles back towards the house.

"Hey, Hitler dog!" says Henrik calmly. "Did you know that Greta's father was a Jew?"

Dieter has only moved yards when the shot erupts and breaks the night into sound and color. The bullet pierces the space between Dieter's shoulder blades and he falls forward onto the grass.

Greta rushes back to Dieter and covers her mouth in horror.

"Come," I say. "Quickly!" And she does. Greta hitches up her nightgown and we run through the fields fast, and we don't look back.

We run into the darkness until the wailing of sirens is far behind us. We run until there is no sound of the city, only the sound of birds and creatures scurrying in the forest.

Then we stop. Henrik unclasps Greta's locket, which hangs around his neck, and puts it on his sister. She clings to Henrik, her tears flowing.

"I want Mama," says the girl in a small voice, and at first I wonder which one she means.

But she is no longer Dieter's perfect German. She is someone's daughter and sister once more.

CHAPTER 32

I hear the sound of insects and there is newness to the air, as if it has been filtered by the snow and sent out fresh again. There is new growth sprouting from the earth.

We have found our buried packs and rifle. I have cut down Greta's nightgown to make her a shirt, and given her a pair of my trousers, shortened and tied around her tiny waist with string. When she looks down at herself for the first time, I wonder if she is thinking about her nice clothes and soft bed and the adopted brothers and sisters she has left behind. I wonder how kind her new mama was, but I am afraid to ask. Afraid to hear anything positive, in case this is something Henrik does not want to hear.

We walk in the forest through the night and over the next day, and then, finally, we rest. That night I hear Greta crying and I put my arm around her. We lie on the earth, which grows cool during the night. Henrik lies with his back to us. He is not yet over his anger. Greta falls asleep in my arms. She still has a smell of roses in her hair. She has been well cared for. We should be grateful, at least, that we found her that way.

Greta is staggering, her legs close to giving up, and I touch Henrik's arm. He looks at me and then Greta and his shoulders slacken with frustration. We wash by the river while the air is still warm. Greta's feet are blistered from hiking in her soft leather slippers, which are not for walking across the uneven forest floor.

I put dampened rags on her feet to soothe them. She does not cry out. She is afraid to upset Henrik.

Greta stays close to me and sneaks glances at Henrik to check his mood. She has not once complained.

Down at the river I give her a small cloth to wash herself with. Away from Henrik I ask her: "What was it like . . . at the house?"

"It was nice," she says, her lips pinched to stop herself from saying too much.

"It's all right. I won't tell Henrik."

She thinks on this and eyes me to see if I am being truthful. Her guardedness and measured speech are perhaps things she has acquired at the Wolff house.

"It was very pleasant but strict. They had so much food, and we would celebrate lots of things. Not like at my old home."

"Was your . . . was Mr. Wolff kind?"

"He wasn't there much but he would sometimes come back with gifts. He gave me this watch." She displays the gold at her wrist.

I think of Emelie's clothes and necklace brought home by her father, and wonder if this also has been stolen from a Jew. There is a pause while she studies me. She looks down, her hands clenched together as if she is in a classroom, as if she is awaiting her next instruction.

"Where did you meet Henrik?"

"My brother and I found him in the forest. He had only been travelling from Zamosc a few days, to search for you, when he became lost and sick."

"Where is your brother now?"

"Fighting the Germans."

She looks away.

"Is he a Jew too?"

"Yes. But it is not just a war against the Jews. The Germans have taken French, Polish, Norwegian, and Yugoslavian lands, and now they want Russian lands too. And, who knows, they will take the world if they can."

"But it is because they want to help nations. With the Führer in control those countries will prosper."

I am glad that Henrik is not listening. This talk would not be tolerated.

I am careful with my words: too harsh, and she may find what I say difficult to take in. She might become resentful.

"Greta, it is what the Germans tell their own. If you are in England or America or you are in the prison camps you wouldn't be saying that. You would know the truth. They only tell you what they think you want to hear. Unfortunately, the German leader and his armies have hurt so many, and nothing, dear Greta, is worth so many lives, especially of innocent men, women, and children."

"Children?"

"Yes. Children have been imprisoned and killed for no reason other than who they are. It matters not to the leader of Germany how good or kind these innocents are. They are faceless to him. The Nazis only want the pastel children—the pale ones—the ones they believe are pure and deserving."

Greta frowns at this and I think it is enough for her young mind to take in, but she asks, "Is it true that my father was a Jew?"

I nod.

"And my mother . . . are you sure she didn't sell me?"

"As I said, it was a lie so that you would forget your mama, so that you would no longer care for her. They told you this so that you would be theirs to control. Your mama loves you so much, Greta." My throat tightens when I think of my own mother and the way she died. How cruel it is to be separated from those you love.

She has seen my face. "Do you miss your brother and your family?"

"Yes, very much."

When we return to our small camp, Henrik is skinning a rabbit. Greta watches him carefully. Her wide-eyed gaze suggests that, like me, she admires his fast hands and skill. She perhaps sees what I do, even in the short time I have known him: that he has grown. He is a man, tall and strong, square-shouldered, his face browned, his hair fair at the tips. He has gained much confidence since we first met. He would make a good partisan because he is not afraid of anything. He wears a rifle across his bare back, the strap across his torso. He has taken up smoking too. Gottfried has given him cigarettes and one now hangs from the corner of his mouth.

When he catches me staring, he winks.

I place roasting sticks crossed at angles on either side of the fire, in preparation for the rabbit.

When it is ready for cooking, Henrik turns the skinned rabbit with practiced skill so that it is cooked evenly. The smell is wonderful and I see that Greta's lips are wet in anticipation.

Henrik cuts off a piece of meat with his knife and passes it to her. She takes it in her small hand. There is a look between them when their hands touch, a connection from blood, and a link that Dieter Wolff can never break.

"It is good, huh?" he says to Greta.

She nods, and the corners of her mouth flicker.

Later, when Greta is sleeping, I move away from her to talk to Henrik. He turns and kisses me gently and I kiss him harder, afraid to let him go.

"You have to give her time. You can't be angry at her. She has suffered in her own way. The separation from you and your mother would have been traumatic and then she finally conceded that you were not coming, that you were no longer a part of her family, believing that your mother had given her up. She accepted her new family and believed their propaganda because there was no one and nothing else to tell her otherwise."

"I know. But it is not just her; it is that man and what happened. It is that he made all this happen. It is that he died too quickly, that he did not account for any of it . . . not in the way I wanted."

"We had to act quickly. There was no time for slow revenge. He would have killed us."

"You did well with the knife. I did not know you were such a fighter," he says, giving me his Henrik smile, wide and narrow lipped.

It is silent then and we can hear Greta's heavy breathing. We snuggle together for a while, and then later I roll next to Greta to keep her loved.

Finally—tired and scratched from our long journey through the wilderness—we reach the house where we last saw Kaleb. It is abandoned, the doors open. Flies buzz around the kitchen over food that has thawed since the frozen winter, and dishes lie unwashed. The lights do not work; there is no diesel left in the generator.

We decide to stay the night there and I clean the kitchen. Henrik finds wood to light a fire in the oven and I find flour to make some bread. I pluck out the weevils and crush them between my fingertips. Some supplies have been preserved by the cold of winter.

It looks like no one has been here for many weeks. Kaleb has not returned. There is no trace of him in any of the rooms, yet I can still feel him there. I can still see him lying on his back on the bed, his arms folded behind his head, daydreaming.

There are clothes still in the cupboard. I wonder how it is that no one else has found this place to hide.

We will spend one night here. Henrik has studied the maps and it is possibly only two more days before we will arrive at my new home. He has come to the conclusion that when he first left Zamosc he was going around in circles in the forest. He assures me that with a compass for him to use, there will be no mistakes this time.

The bread is tasteless without salt, but it is warm and soft in the center. There are also potatoes, which I have fried in the teaspoon of fat we kept from the rabbit.

Henrik is talkative. I can sense his excitement. He is looking forward to the look in his mama's eyes when she sees Greta. I am so happy to see him happy.

Greta talks about the other children. How at night they would cry sometimes and she would do what Henrik did for her and try to make them laugh, but it did not always work. She tells us how she would have writing and arithmetic lessons in the morning, help with baking in the afternoon, and then play games in the evening with the other children.

Henrik reminds her of the fields behind Femke's house. He tells her about the many cows that they will buy and milk when they return. Greta's eyes are bright. She is becoming excited to see her mother, to see their farm, to ride Henrik's bicycle.

I feel that in time we will need to talk about the death of her adopted father. But something tells me that once she sees her mother, everything will fall into place, that things will be clearer to Greta. She will know her true home.

CHAPTER 33

I will soon meet Henrik's mother and his aunt Femke, and suddenly I fear they will not like me.

Henrik sketches in his art book. It is a scene of the three of us near the fire, on a clear, starry night. He has drawn himself like a giant beside us, his muscled frame bursting through his shirt.

Greta and I share a room. When she is asleep, I creep into bed with Henrik.

Henrik talks about Zamosc and about how much he loves me. I kiss him to stop him from talking. At that moment I am just happy to lie together in the present; the outside world is suddenly too big. I put my head on his chest.

"What's the matter?" he asks.

"I am frightened of losing you."

"You will not lose me."

"What if your mother doesn't approve of me?"

Henrik laughs at this. "She will love you like I do."

I do not fall asleep straight away but lie in the crook of Henrik's arm and feel his chest rise and fall. I listen to the crickets outside the window and the night birds. It is as if they know we are inside, as if they are singing to us. I fall asleep and dream of rivers and blue skies.

We load our packs with the remaining food and fill our water bottles. I change into the dress that Henrik said he liked months earlier. I find a dress for Greta. It is too big but I think that a dress will make her feel good.

Henrik says that Tobin had a secret place to hide medicines but that they are gone. Perhaps taken by the partisans, knowing it was unlikely they would return. I have nothing with which to treat the scratches and sores on our feet, so I tear up strips of fabric and make them into bandages.

It is early when we set out. Henrik is keen to get home. In the back of my mind I am still worrying about Zamosc, still worrying about what we might find and whether there are Germans there and what they are doing. I hope that the partisans are safe wherever they are, and say a prayer for my brother that he is alive, and that we will find each other in Zamosc at the end of the war.

As we walk, the forest becomes brighter, as if we have come out of the darkness. Through the trees we can see a village but there are no signs of life. Henrik creeps to the edge of it and returns to say there is no one there. There is no smoke from kitchen fires.

We walk into the village, eager to find more food. I walk between two small houses and Henrik and Greta walk the other way, to the other side of the village. As I walk around a corner, I see that several people have congregated in the center. Several Germans with guns have surrounded them. I see the Nazi symbol on the front of the car and shrink back against the wall.

I turn to go the way that Henrik and Greta were headed, towards the back of the huts closest to the forest, but the tip of a gun is now pointed at my face.

"Halt," says a man with a hard, craggy face. "Are you alone?"

I say nothing, overcome with disbelief. He asks me again. Once I nod, he shoves me towards the center to join the others.

There are several women, old and young—and children. One woman holds in her arms a baby who suddenly starts to cry, the sound bouncing loudly off the forest walls. My legs are trembling and I look around cautiously to see if Henrik and Greta are watching. I hope the sound of the baby has alerted them.

We are steered towards a large truck. One German grabs my arm roughly and tells me to climb up into the vehicle. The back is filled with people. Some are lying down, others are crying, and some look like they have been there for a long time, all traces of hope gone from their faces. A couple with one small suitcase clutch tightly to one another, and I am forced to climb over them to make room for more people climbing behind me. It is hot in here.

At first I feel nothing, like this was always to be my destination. But then I feel regretful that I have let Henrik down, and Kaleb, that I have been so foolish as to be caught. I think of Greta and wonder if she is worrying about me. And then in the back of my mind I wonder if I have only held on to life temporarily, if I was meant to go with Mama and Papa.

The doors close and I am in darkness. There is a smell of urine, feces, and sickness. I feel nauseous and lean my head against the wall as the vehicle starts to move.

And suddenly there is more commotion outside.

"I'm a Jew! Take me too," a voice says.

The truck stops, the doors open again, and the light shines in brilliantly. I hadn't noticed before, but it is a perfect sunny day, without a cloud in the sky. A dark silhouette fills the space of the doorway but I already know who it is. I have already recognized the voice.

He looks around at the mass of bodies that fill up every space in the compartment. I do not put up my hand. I do not have to. It is Henrik and he can find a needle in a haystack. He found Greta in Poland. His eyes lock onto mine, and he scrambles over people to get to me, moving assuredly as always.

"You must let me through," he says, and no one argues, for Henrik has an urgency that can never be ignored.

He squeezes between me and an old man who does not look up. The man's coat is wrapped around him like it is a cold day.

Once I feel Henrik's body, I know that I can breathe again.

I listen to his voice. It is low and gravelly. It reminds me of the men who used to stay late after dinner and talk with my father in soft, gentle voices, which always put me to sleep.

PART THREE

GRETA

CHAPTER 34

1956

Mama looks small and frail behind the piano. She has suffered much. She did not want to leave Zamosc before the end of the war. But now she never wants to return, because they are Jew haters, she says.

When I returned after my kidnapping, Mama had mostly recovered from her stroke, though she did not move as fast as before. I did not see her when she was first struck down but Femke told me that she nearly died. When Henrik did not return with me, there was too much pain. Mama would sit for hours at the window. She would look at the pictures he had drawn. She would talk about him throughout the day. She would say, "Remember when . . ." and then remind us of the things he had said and done. Her memories were so vivid that sometimes I could picture him standing there in the living room, telling the stories himself.

Femke seemed a different person also when I returned. The person I left was hard and bitter, but Henrik's departure softened her. She stayed strong during that time for all of us.

"We must never give up on him, Greta," she said. "Henrik will return one day. He will find us. Henrik can do anything he puts his mind to."

We had no choice but to leave Zamosc shortly after I returned. We had no food. There was nothing to farm and the Germans took over the land. Femke was ill—she had been sick for a long time but had kept this hidden. We went to Warsaw and just after we arrived, we heard of fights in Zamosc between the partisans and the Germans. We were thinking of returning, but Femke died and then Mama met a German officer.

I kept her secret: that she was kept by a German officer. Many would not have forgiven Mama if they knew her secret. But I was there. I know what it is to have no food in your stomach, to have nothing—not even a roof over your head or medicine to cure illnesses. Mama did what she did so that we could both survive.

Her German soldier said that he was powerless to help her find Henrik. It was like sorting ants; there were too many and they were now just numbers.

Mama suffered many nightmares towards the end of the war, worried that Henrik would return to Zamosc and she would not be there for him. She wrote letters to people she used to know there, letters that went unanswered and finally were returned by the postmaster.

Then it was 1945 and the Russians were coming, and the German soldier returned to his country and his wife when the Nazis began losing the war. Mama and I were left alone again in Warsaw. When the war was over, carrying nothing but suitcases containing our clothes, we returned to our village in Zamosc and found that our house was no longer there. It had been destroyed and another had been built in its place. Our land had been divided up and we had no proof that it was ours, no claim to anything. There was no one left there that we knew, and the ones we didn't

know weren't welcoming. The atmosphere in the town and villages was hostile. We stayed for a day and left quickly to return to
Warsaw.

My Polish had never been good, perhaps because I refused to
try too hard to learn it, and Mama and I had always spoken to each
other in German. The Allies were shipping all German-speaking
people back to Germany and we didn't feel safe in Poland. At the
end of 1945 we returned to Berlin. The conditions were awful but
we suffered because we had to. Because we were German too.

Our Berlin apartment had been seized and part of the street
was bombed, so we moved into a small, empty apartment on the
other side of the city. Mama destroyed our fake identity documents so that we were no longer Klaus. We took back Papa's name
of Solomon. Many Jews did not return to Germany, emigrating to
America, Australia, Palestine, and other places where they believed
peace was assured. We helped the community repair itself slowly
while we tried to heal inside.

Mama tells people her name now. She is no longer afraid but there
is still an air of caution as if, to some, our Jewish name is somehow
to blame for everything that happened.

Mama still has nightmares. She lives in hope that Henrik will
return to Berlin.

Today, I kiss Mama good-bye and tell her that I will return
soon with any news. I shut the door behind me and walk across the
pavement, past the street vendors, towards the bus.

I get off the connecting train from Warsaw but there is no one to
meet me. I have to walk several miles to reach the rural villages of
Zamosc. I pass farms that are plentiful and walk along the streets.

Much has changed, even the air. Here the air now smells free. There is no one to fear, no one who will take me away.

I pass the old school that Henrik and I attended before we were told that schooling was only for those who the Germans thought worthy. I remember the time I was taken. I remember how lonely I was, and how I was taken to live with a family who did not seem to welcome me at first. Over time, I was accepted, and the food there was good and the people were nice to me. But the things I learned later about the suffering my mother went through do not make the memory a good one.

I take the path to the forest and find our secret burial place beneath the memory tree—Henrik's and mine—near the edge of a clearing. A new warehouse has been built not far away, and I wonder if someone is watching me, if they will come to ask what I am doing.

With a rock I dig away until the rock hits the top of the tin. Inside, there is no message to me from Henrik, but there is a torn patch: a Jewish star. I sit and ponder this. I feel a moment of excitement but then the questions surface: Did he put this here before the war or afterwards? Was this perhaps a star from someone he knew or could it be his?

Then I pull out the yellowing notes, each with our distinctive writing from when we were children, many years ago.

Henrik's reads: *I hope that Greta will not be mad at me when she discovers that I tricked her into leaving wishes beneath the tree.*

Mine reads: *I hope that my family will be together, and Papa will come, and Henrik will make him laugh.*

I pass a decommissioned tank, now used for other pastimes. A child stands atop and gives me a salute as I pass. I wave back, then come to a little cemetery by a chapel to read the headstones and the memorial wall bearing the names of the dead.

I see the two-story house that stands in place of our own, with its gabled roof and bright paint. I knock at the door but there's no answer. I turn then to walk across the fields I used to run in as a child, always following Henrik. There is a man nearby. He is pulling lettuces and other vegetables from his crop, planted in the field of rich, black soil. I approach him.

He has aged. His hair and beard are gray, and he is holding his lower back as he stands. He is no longer as big as I remember.

"Hello, Mr. Lubieniecki," I say.

"Hello," he says. "And who might you be?"

"Greta Solomon . . . Greta Klaus, I mean."

He looks a little confused and then his face brightens.

"Little Greta?" He holds out his hand to show the height of me the last time he saw me. "I remember. Karolin's daughter."

"Yes," I say.

"For a minute I thought you were Karolin. The resemblance is remarkable, though you perhaps are a little bit taller, no?"

"Yes," I say.

"Well, this is a surprise."

"When did you come back?" I ask. "You weren't here after the war."

"No. It was 1947 before we had the courage to return. And then we managed to secure our home again. How is your mother . . . and your aunt?"

"Mama suffers from aching joints and she never fully recovered from the stroke, but she is teaching piano again. It makes her happy to be with children."

I tell him about Femke's passing, and he says that she was a fine woman and good worker. He talks about the farm and about his daughter and grandchildren, who have moved away. I ask about the doctor and his wife who hid beneath their stairs. My aunt often spoke of the doctor, of how brave he was to come out of hiding to help Mama and others.

The farmer shakes his head sadly. "I do not know. They left one night to try and make their way to England but I never heard from them again."

He tilts his head back suddenly.

"Oh, I have something for you. You must come to the farm."

I help with his baskets of vegetables and we carry them to his house with its small front porch. His wife is there and she greets me warmly. She is smaller and rounder now. She asks about my life and I tell them that I am a secondary school teacher, of mathematics, German, and English.

"You always were a bright one . . ." He pauses before remembering. "Oh yes, the letters." He turns to his wife. "The letters for Greta. Where are they?"

Mrs. Lubieniecki puts on her glasses and disappears into the next room. She reappears with two letters. One is addressed to Greta Klaus, the other to Mama.

"The people in the new house, where you once lived, brought these to me a couple of years ago and asked if I knew you. I did try to make inquiries as to where you might be, but we could not find any trace of your mother or you. We feared the worst. But I kept them anyway, hoping that one day someone from your family would come back."

The envelope has an Australian stamp.

"Most of the mail to unknown recipients is returned to the sender and if there is no return address, it is returned to the post office or ends up as waste. It is a miracle that these did not meet a similar fate."

I touch the front of the letter, tenderly looking at the uneven, tall letters written in black ink. A flood of memories rushes at me: Henrik marching me up and down the hallway, with me dressed up as a soldier's assistant; Henrik carrying me on his shoulders as he crosses a creek; Henrik's face in the chicken coop, the shock of seeing him there, and my desire to hug him hard until he broke. It is the memory of a brother who stole me back. Tears threaten to escape from the corners of my eyes.

"Are you all right?" asks Mrs. Lubieniecki. "This must be quite a shock. War separated so many."

"Yes," I say.

"I will make some tea, if you like, and you can go and read the letter on the porch."

"Thank you."

I walk outside and look up and down at the uncurbed streets. I can see the remnants of a broken stable, the top half of its walls missing; grasses grow over unused, unworkable machinery, and opportunistic trees sprout where nature was once torn up by its roots.

Apart from the broken building, there is little evidence of the atrocities committed along this street, of people taken. The lands are green and there is a familiar smell of fertilizer and smoke coming from recovering factories, and there are sounds of cars and bicycles, and of people making their way in a free society. I do not belong here. The memories that we made here, Henrik and I, have been replaced.

I open the envelope carefully, so as not to tear the precious paper sent from the other side of the world.

There are several pages, folded. Some are cartoons taken from newspapers. The first cartoon shows Adolf Hitler dressed as the Pied Piper. It depicts him losing control of his army. His face is flushed and puffed with anger and there is steam coming out of his ears. In his hands he holds a broken pipe, in two pieces. There are many rats in little coats with swastikas, all scurrying to the corners of the room where there are mouse holes, but these are too small to squeeze through. They are all trapped. The words underneath are supposedly Hitler's: *Who broke my pipe?* The type is in English and a German translation is handwritten underneath.

The next cartoon is a picture of SS officer Karl Höcker, the man responsible for sending so many Jews to their deaths, his name in the center of a star tattooed on the top of his arm. The former SS officer is lying on an operating table. There are dots on his forehead to show where the operation will take place. He is tied down and his lips are stretched in terror. Above him stands a doctor who wears a Jewish skullcap and a sinister smile. The caption below says *I hear you have had trouble remembering.* It makes fun of the Nazi who denied he played any part in the atrocities inflicted upon the Jews.

At the bottom of both cartoons is the artist's name in italics: *Rik Solomon.*

I read the first sentence of the letter:

Dear Gretel,

If you have this letter, it means you are alive and as you can see I have found an employment that suits me.

I start to cry and have to put the letter down for a moment to clear my eyes. My funny, silly brother, who never gave up, and never gives up still.

I returned to Zamosc after we were freed from the camp but I found no trace of you and people said that if you weren't there, you were most likely dead. Jews and Germans were no longer welcome and since I fell into both those categories, I had no choice but to leave. I took the opportunity to return to Germany but not to stay. I went to Munich, where I recovered from the camp.

I think how close we came to finding each other. It may have been that we were in Zamosc at the same time. I think how unlucky it was that we did not meet.

I chose Munich as it was something I had been planning to do before I found you in Cracow. I had memorised Otto's address. You may not remember what I told you of Otto because we had so little time together but he was a good German who died for no good reason. Though that story is probably best told in much more detail when we meet.

Otto's house was half-destroyed by bombs and I found his mother and two sisters living there. They were most keen to hear Otto's story, and I told them of his unfortunate end. I assured them that he was very brave. They told me that many of their friends had died during the Allied bombings at the end of the war. Otto's brother had also been killed. At just fifteen, near the end of the war, he was sent to Berlin and told to fight like a man. He died in his first battle—a street battle that included only young and old Germans against the force of the Russians.

I stayed with the Petersens and helped them rebuild for a while, then moved on. I did not know whether you were in Germany, someplace else, or dead. I sent a letter to the apartment in Berlin and did not receive a reply. I wrote another letter to the Berlin Registry but they had no record of you, and no one had been there to list me as missing. They also advised me that our apartment building was badly damaged and there were no occupants. I thought there was no point in going back. Perhaps it was the trauma of being in the camps, perhaps I was scared of what I would find. Some memories are too painful to relive. Berlin was a place I had decided I would never see again. But then never is perhaps too long, isn't it, dear little Gretel?

I imagine that he must have gone to Munich immediately after the war. It was many months before we returned to Germany, his letter eventually discarded like so much else, human and other.

The family was appreciative and I stayed with them for a while before I left Germany. After several months, Otto's sister Gretchen and I became good friends.

A long story later: Gretchen is in Australia with me now and we have two children, Rebekah and Otto. Gretchen said that we should name our daughter Greta but there has been something telling me that you are out there somewhere, that to give someone else your name is somehow wrong while you are alive.

And now you must realise from the previous paragraph that Rebekah didn't make it. She was chosen to be killed in the buildings we called the killing chambers. She was dying, her chest failing her, and I remember her face on the last day as she walked past our camp quarters. She had given up. She was resigned. Her face haunts me still, though now at least my little Rebekah's face appears alongside hers in my mind—justification to continue with life.

I will not recall the details of the camp. I will only say that the pain was so enduring it became normal, and for many months just prior to our salvation I thought that I did not have the strength to go on. But thinking of you and Mama and even cranky Femke gave me the strength. And then during a death march from the camp, the British came and I walked free, first to Zamosc and then in the direction of Germany, until I was picked up by Australian journalists. They took me to Germany and friendships were forged, and it was their description of their home that got me to thinking.

Then I arrived in Germany and saw the destruction there. I went on to Otto's to recover, to rebuild, and to begin to believe again.

I tried to contact an old friend of mine, Gottfried, who had helped me look for you after you were kidnapped. I sent letters to the café until I received a letter to say there was no one by that name or description there, only that the café had been empty since the end of 1943.

I put the letter down because the tears are blinding me. The joy of discovering that Henrik is alive; the sadness of discovering Rebekah is gone. I only spent several nights and days with her, but the heartfelt kindness I felt from her touch had a profound effect on me over the years—the portraits of her that I kept, always a reminder. When my eyes are clearer, I continue reading:

You must write to me at the newspaper and you and Mama and Femke can come and live with us.

I see you there, your head bent over this letter, for you always were the one to study things—you were always the patient one and I am sure that hasn't changed. Little Rebekah is wild and crazy like me but Otto is studious. He has your calm.

You must come here. You must! You can raise your own children here if you have any. Mama would be sailing on the Sydney Harbour if she had half the chance, for she always said she wanted to live beside water.

People ask me why was it that you were chosen by the Germans that day, why you were stolen. I tell them, "If you knew her, if you could see her, you would understand. Everyone wanted her."

Dearest Greta. Now it is a time for children.

Riki.

I stand up and take a look at Zamosc for the last time. If I run, I will make the last train to Warsaw.

EPILOGUE

GRETA, SPRING 1943

Henrik and I are behind one of the houses when we hear a baby cry.

We crouch low and Henrik is listening. We hear an order given in German and some shots in the air and the sound of a large truck pulling up. He pulls me into the forest and we crawl alongside the first row of trees till we stop at another side of the small village. There we hide behind brush to spy.

"Where is Rebekah?" I ask, suddenly fearful.

But he throws his hand over my mouth to prevent me from talking any further.

Then he releases me and puts a finger to his lips. I remember the times we would hide together in "hide-and-seek." I trusted him then and I trust him now.

We peer between the breaks in the trees. I can see that there are soldiers in high black boots, like Dieter in their smart uniforms, though these soldiers wear round helmets, not smart hats.

A number of people stand in a group, their hands on their heads. The women look frightened and the children are crying. The men say nothing. I wonder what it is that they have done and remember what Rebekah told me previously, how cruel and mean some people can be.

The soldiers point guns at these people and wave them towards a truck that is coming their way. Several more soldiers appear from around corners. They hold guns to other villagers, rounded up from elsewhere, perhaps discovered in their homes. One woman has fallen on the ground beside a man and she is told to get up or she will be shot.

I cannot look anymore and put my face into Henrik's shoulder.

Then I hear Henrik whisper Rebekah's name, which makes me look up. One of the soldiers has a rifle against her shoulder blade and pushes her into the group where the others are huddled and fearful.

I want to yell that they have made a mistake, that she is not part of this group, and I bite my lip so hard that I taste blood.

Henrik watches the soldiers march the people to the back of the truck, which looks large enough to hold cattle. I notice there are many people already in there and that it is crammed. I do not think that they can fit any more people in.

Some of the soldiers get into cars now, while others continue to shove more people into the back of the truck. These people are poor. I can tell from their clothes. I do not understand why they can be treated this way, and suddenly I am hating Dieter Wolff and my adopted mama and her housekeeper, the mean Mrs. Fromm. I am hating all those people who take people away from their homes and families they love.

Henrik turns from the spectacle and sits a moment. He appears to be in pain at first, rubbing his temples, but then he hits at his head with his fist.

"No, no, no!" he says.

I am suddenly frightened for him. There are tears in his eyes and he keeps turning back to look at the truck, willing Rebekah to come back out. I touch his arm. He stands then and paces. This makes me start to cry because I think he will be seen.

He stares at me with large eyes, and then looks at the truck, and then grabs my hand and takes me farther into the forest.

"Greta, do you remember when we played hide-and-seek?"

I nod.

"Well, I want you to play that game now and go deep into the forest where no one will find you." He puts his compass in the palm of my hand, and holds my hand in his own to steady it. He explains which way the arrow points, and the way I must go.

"Are you going to follow me?"

"No."

I cry some more.

He leans down to me, because he has grown very tall, and he holds my arms.

"Greta, if you follow the direction I have pointed to on the compass, it will take you through the forests to Mama's house. If you walk fast, you will get there before nightfall. But you must follow the compass and if you can't hear the river, then you are going the wrong way. Do you understand me?"

I nod.

"Once you are at the edge of the forest, you wait until it gets dark, then you run across the fields to the roads that will take you home. Do you remember them? Do you remember the stables and the factory? Do you remember our house just up the road from there?"

I do. Henrik cycled those every day with me as his passenger.

He pulls out his notebook of drawings. Some of the pages are loose.

"I want you to keep this safe and give it to Mama. She will understand much from this."

"But I want you to come too, and Rebekah."

"I have to get Rebekah first, do you understand?"

"What do I tell Mama?"

"Tell her that I will come back."

The truck has started its engine and Henrik looks in that direction anxiously. I see that there are no more tears in his eyes, and that he is calmer—much calmer than I remember him to be.

I am trying to fight back more tears but it isn't working. They rush out in rivers.

"Greta, tell Mama and Aunt Femke that I love them and that I have one more thing to do, and then I will come home. And when you get back to Mama you can have all my books."

"Even *Hansel and Gretel*?" I ask curiously. This book was kept in a drawer. He had let me borrow it sometimes, but I always had to return it, and he would check the cover to see if I had left any smudges.

"Yes."

"But . . ."

"Yes?"

"But I don't want your book." And tears keep spilling.

"Greta, I love you. Look after Mama. She needs you more than you need her."

The truck has started to leave.

He kisses me and then he is gone.

I stay hidden in the bushes and watch Henrik run towards the truck, waving his arms.

I hear one of the soldiers shout in German to stop.

I watch Henrik climb into the back of the truck and I stay there until there is no one left, until there are just the sounds of the forest.

I wipe my tears away and walk home.

THE END

ABOUT THE AUTHOR

Gemma Liviero holds an advanced diploma of arts in professional writing, and she has worked as a copywriter, a corporate writer, and a magazine feature writer and editor. Liviero is the author of two gothic fantasies, *Lilah* and *Marek*. *Pastel Orphans* is her first historical novel. She now lives in Brisbane, Australia, with her husband and two children.